AMONG THIEVES

Also by David Hosp

Dark Harbor
The Betrayed
Innocence

AMONG THIEVES

David Hosp

GRAND CENTRAL
PUBLISHING

NEW YORK   BOSTON

The events and characters in this book are fictitious. Certain real locations and public figures are mentioned, but all other characters and events described in the book are totally imaginary.

Grand Central Publishing
Hachette Book Group
237 Park Avenue
New York, NY 10017

Visit our website at www.HachetteBookGroup.com.

Printed in the United States of America

First Edition: January 2010
10 9 8 7 6 5 4 3 2 1

Grand Central Publishing is a division of Hachette Book Group, Inc.
The Grand Central Publishing name and logo is a trademark of Hachette Book Group, Inc.

Library of Congress Cataloging-in-Publication Data
Hosp, David.
    Among thieves / David Hosp. — 1st ed.
        p. cm.
    Summary: "Attorney Scott Finn is drawn into the deadly search for missing art"—Provided by the publisher.
    ISBN 978-0-446-58015-1
    1. Art thefts—Investigation—Fiction. 2. Boston (Mass.)—Fiction. I. Title.
    PS3608.O79A8 2010
    813'.6—dc22

2008049188

For Joanie, with my love

FACT

The largest art theft in history took place in the early morning hours following the 1990 St. Patrick's Day celebrations in Boston. Two men dressed as police officers entered the Isabella Stewart Gardner Museum off the Fenway, tied up the guards, and made off with thirteen works of art. Several of the stolen masterpieces were priceless, including two oil paintings and an etching by Rembrandt, a rare work by Vermeer, a Flinck, and a Manet. The thieves also took works of lesser value, including five unfinished Degas sketches, a Chinese beaker from the Shang dynasty, and a finial that adorned a flag from Napoleon's army.

The works have never been recovered. Today, their value is estimated at half a billion dollars.

AMONG THIEVES

Prologue

Liam Kilbranish looked down at the lump of flesh curled in front of him on the cement floor. His heart rate was steady; his movements economical. His eyes were nearly as black as his hair.

"Still no answer?" he asked.

The lump gave a moan. Liam knew it was useless. It would continue.

He could remember how it had started for him. Or ended. It was all a matter of perspective, he supposed. Whichever view he took, the memory was etched in his mind, as solid and real to him as the gun in his hand. He would have said he remembered it as if it were only yesterday, but no yesterday he'd known in the three and a half decades since had ever lived and breathed for him like that night. It was what drove him; what made him who he was, for good or for bad.

He'd been reading when they arrived, tucked away in the tiny closet of the ten-by-twelve room he shared with his brothers in the row house south of Belfast. A worn woolen blanket was bundled about his spindly, pale, nine-year-old legs; the beam of his flashlight was trained on the pages cradled in his lap. He'd always been a solitary boy, and the closet had been his refuge—a place where he spent hours on end, reaching into other worlds as his brothers slept undisturbed.

1

He was devouring *Winnie the Pooh* yet again. It had been a favorite of his since the times, years before, when his father would read to the family in front of the fireplace in the living room. Gavin Kilbranish, his father, was a hard man; a dangerous man when crossed or disobeyed; a man who saw the world in bold strokes of black and white. And yet when he read to his children there was a richness to his voice that hinted at another side, banished and almost forgotten. It was that side of his father Liam sought through the words on the page as he nestled on the closet floor.

Pooh had just gorged himself on Rabbit's honey, swelling his belly until he could no longer escape from Rabbit's hole, when Liam heard the front door shatter. He switched off the flashlight and brought the blanket up around his chin. The smell of the plain, soapy detergent that reminded him of his mother still lingered in his mind, haunting him.

There were four of them. Dressed in black, with ski masks and assault weapons that gave off a dull gleam when they caught the shafts of moonlight carving through the saltbox house's narrow windows, the men moved through the dwelling with military efficiency. Liam listened as they rounded up the others in his family from the front of the house—Mother and Father and Meghan and Kate—and pushed them into the back bedroom he shared with his brothers.

He watched the scene unfold through the crack in the closet door as his parents and siblings were lined up in front of the bed along the far wall. He could read the confusion in their faces—expressions of fear and shock, mixing with the disorientation of being ripped so abruptly from deep slumber. Only his father's face reflected comprehension. Gavin glanced briefly at the closet door and gave a nearly imperceptible shake. Liam fought the urge to emerge from hiding to join his family.

The tallest of the intruders stepped forward and addressed Liam's father. "Gavin Kilbranish," he said. It sounded as though he was pronouncing a verdict. "You know who I am?"

Liam's father nodded slowly. His expression didn't change.

"Then you know why we're here."

Gavin nodded again.

The man stepped back and turned to one of the others. "He's yours
if you want him, lad."

The second man walked over to Liam's father, unslung his gun
and drove the butt into Gavin's stomach, doubling him over. Then he
swung it upward, connecting with his jaw, and Liam's father crumpled to his knees. He was on all fours, spitting blood into the cracks
between the scarred floorboards. It was the first time Liam had ever
seen his father at the mercy of another human being.

The second man knelt before him and produced a small weathered
book of snapshots. Opening it, he held up a picture of a hard-bitten,
middle-aged man. "My da," he said.

He drove a fist into Gavin's nose. The sound of cartilage snapping
was loud, and Liam was afraid he might be sick. The man flipped a
page and held up a new picture, this one of a younger man. A shadow
of the previous face remained. "My brother, William," the man said.

The words still hung in the air as he cracked the butt of his gun
down over Gavin's head. His scalp split and blood flooded forward
over Liam's father's face.

A new page was flipped, revealing the image of a young woman.
"My wife, Anna." The man stood and kicked Gavin hard in the ribs,
drawing a wheeze and a grunt. Gavin's spit was now a frightening
mixture of blood and mucus.

The man stepped back and turned to a final picture that showed
the angelic face of a young girl. She couldn't have been more than
five, and her gap-toothed smile seemed at once joyous and mournful.
The man pulled a black pistol from underneath his coat and pointed

it into Gavin's face. Gavin rose up on his knees and looked back at the man. He showed neither panic nor fear; only hatred and defiance.

The man in front of him had both hands out now, one pointing the gun at Gavin's head, the other clutching knuckle-white to the picture of the girl. "My daughter, Katherine," he said. His voice cracked with unredeemed rage as he said her name.

He pulled the trigger.

The screaming lasted for only a moment, and it was drowned out by the thunder of gunfire. Liam's mother and four siblings jumped and danced as the bullets shredded their bodies. They fell over each other in their attempt to twist free, toppling onto the bed behind them, settling and then sliding onto the floor, leaving the sheets stained red.

At last there was silence. Two of the men dressed in black moved forward, nudging the bodies with their toes to make sure the family was dead. After a moment Liam heard a choked sob from the man with the pistol who had killed his father.

The tallest of the group—the leader, Liam assumed—slapped him. "We'll have none of that shite," he said. "Bastard had it coming. He knew it."

"And his wife? His children?"

"It's war. Did he show pity to your family? Besides, do you think this would have ended it for them? It won't be ended until they're all dead—or we are. Which would you have?"

One of the other men stepped back from the bodies. "It's ended for these now," he said indifferently. "All done for. Good enough."

"Good enough," the leader acknowledged.

Then they were gone.

Liam stayed in the closet until the military came. The police wouldn't enter the Catholic neighborhoods anymore; it was too dangerous. The armored vehicles rolled in and squads of soldiers in riot gear cordoned off the area, enduring the taunts and jeers from the crowds that had gathered outside the Kilbranish home. Liam was questioned, but said nothing. Not a word. Not for six months. Everyone thought that the trauma had destroyed him. In a sense it had, though not in the way they supposed.

Now, thirty-five years later, he knew the leader of the death squad had been right. It hadn't ended, even now that the politicians had signed their unholy alliances and smiled their oily smiles at each other across mahogany conference tables. It would never end; not as long as he lived.

He took a deep breath and brought his pistol up, leveling it at the man on the ground in front of him. Blood had soaked through what was left of the man's shirt and there were places on the man's face where the skin had been ripped so thoroughly that bone flashed through.

"Mr. Murphy, I'll give you one last chance," he said. "Tell me what I want to know."

The man sobbed. "Please . . . I don't know." He had his hands up in supplication, the blood dripping down from the holes in his palms and running off his elbows.

"That's too bad," Liam said.

He pulled the trigger and the man's head snapped backward, one last spray of blood coating the wall behind him. Liam walked over and fired another round into the pulp that remained above the man's shoulders. It was unnecessary, but he was well trained. He reached down and dipped a gloved finger into the pool of blood by the body. He took a step away, and wrote two words in blood on the floor. Then he stood and nodded to Sean Broadark, who remained by the doorway. Few words had been exchanged between the two of them. They weren't friends, they were professionals.

"Why?" Broadark asked, looking at the bloody scrawl.

"I want to send a message to the others."

Broadark holstered his pistol. "There's more, then?"

Liam nodded. "There's more."

Broadark asked no more questions. He watched Liam as he took one last look around the garage. Then Liam walked past him, to the door, and the two of them walked out into the cool South Boston evening.

Chapter One

Scott Finn trudged up the front steps of the Nashua Street Jail. A thin streak of sunshine poked through the clouds, drying the cement in uneven lines. It was the fourth week of spring, but a few isolated piles of brown snow could still be found dying slowly in the cervices of Boston's streets and alleys, and the city smelled of dog shit and winter rot—an oddly satisfying sign that warmer weather was on the way.

Tucked behind North Station and the Garden, the jail was not a place stumbled on accidentally. You had to be looking for it, and even then it wasn't an easy find. To make the effort less inviting, there was no public parking. None. Not that it was a problem for Finn, of course. Every month he slipped the parking attendant at the rehab hospital across the street fifty dollars to let him park his battered MG there when he needed to. It made his life easier. He was a lawyer; he made life easier when he could.

He walked into the lobby of the jail, a tall, narrow, yellowy space occupied only by two uncomfortable metal benches, and headed to the front desk. It was a holiday morning; the place was empty. Finn was dressed casually in a polo shirt, khakis, and a spring overcoat. He was heading out to the Sox game later that morning, and he'd vowed that the trip to the jail wouldn't interfere with his day.

"Officer Hollings," he said to the uniformed woman standing at the front desk. Her face was down, and she was churning through paperwork.

She looked up and smiled. "Attorney Finn," she said. She had a pretty smile that made it easy to overlook the acne scars on her cheeks. Her polyester uniform tugged at her tight curves, and she had an admirable sense of humor for a corrections officer.

"You here for Malley?" She chuckled as she asked the question.

"Yeah," he admitted, throwing his bar card and driver's license on the counter. "How'd you guess?"

"You're a sucker for the hard-luck cases. His is as hard as they come." She laughed again as she picked up his identification and handed him a locker token and a yellow laminated lawyer's pass to hang around his neck.

Finn slipped the pass over his head and took the token over to the wall lined with dented steel lockers, sliding it into the key slot of one and opening it. He knew the drill by heart: he took everything out of his pockets—wallet, keys, phone, BlackBerry—and tossed them into the locker. Then he took a legal pad out of his briefcase and slid the case into the locker. Only the pad was permitted into the jail.

He put his overcoat on top of the pile before he closed the door and turned the key, hearing the token drop into the lock. He tugged once on the door to make sure it was secured, and walked over to the metal detector. Carol was waiting there for him.

He stepped through the archway and the metal detector buzzed once. She beckoned him forward, and he moved toward her, keeping his feet shoulder-width apart and putting his arms out to his sides, palms up. She picked up a handheld security wand and began running it over his torso. She was still chuckling softly to herself.

"It's not nice to laugh, you know that, Hollings?" he said.

"How can you not laugh?"

"He's my client. At least, he may be."

"That doesn't mean it's not funny." She passed the wand over his belt buckle and it gave a chirp. She looked down at his crotch and passed the wand over the front of his pants a few times. The wand whined rhythmically in time with the motion of her arm. "You got anything in your pockets, or is that just the buckle?" she asked.

"You're welcome to check."

"Tempting, but I'm engaged."

"Really? Tragic. Still, it's your job to make sure this facility is safe. For the inmates, for the city"—he winked—"for me."

She raised her eyebrows. "My fiancé's a Statie. SWAT team. If you're worried about your safety, the last thing you want is me digging around in your pants." She put the wand down and waved to another guard behind four inches of bulletproof glass that separated the lobby from the rest of the jail. "He's good," she called.

The guard pressed a button, releasing a hydraulic lock on the steel door that led into the jail. Finn walked through.

"Good luck up there," Hollings said.

"You're all heart." Finn looked back, admiring her uniform again. *Well, maybe not* all *heart.*

He stepped up to the small window that separated him from the interior guard. The door behind him closed again, and Finn was now trapped in a tiny vestibule between two three-ton steel doors. One led back out to freedom. The other didn't. It felt like a decompression chamber. He put his arm through the small window where the interior guard was sitting and the guard stamped the back of his hand with fluorescent ink, marking him as a visitor.

"Don't wash that off 'til you're out," the guard said. Finn had seen him before, but didn't know his name. He made a mental note to find out what it was. In his line of work it was always good to be on terms that were at least cordial with the corrections guards.

"Thanks. Good advice."

"You know where you're going." It wasn't a question. The guard recognized Finn.

Another buzzer sounded and the bolt slid free on the interior door. Finn walked through it and into a small elevator lobby. He pushed the button and the elevator door opened. He stepped in and pressed the button for the second floor.

When the door reopened, he exited and walked down a long empty linoleum corridor. At the end was another thick metal door. Behind that, two guards sat on a raised platform looking out through more heavy glass into the cell block. From where Finn stood, he couldn't see the cell block itself, but he didn't need to; he'd seen it before—from both sides. It was a crescent-shaped area with two levels of cells opening into a large, high-ceilinged common area. The guard station was at the center of the crescent, allowing the corrections officers a good view of every area on the block.

Finn flashed his lawyer's pass at one of the guards through the window, and the guard pressed a button, opening the door and waving him through.

"Attorney Finn," the guard said. His voice wasn't quite friendly, but it wasn't hostile either. Some of the corrections officers understood that Finn was just doing his job. Others . . .

"Officer DiNoffrio," Finn replied.

He noted Finn's casual attire. "You going to the Sox game today?"

"Yeah."

"Lucky bastard."

"Yeah. I'd offer you one of my other tickets, but . . ." Finn shrugged.

"Bullshit."

"Yeah. It's the thought that counts, though, right?"

DiNoffrio shook his head. "Not even close. Who are you here to see?"

"Devon Malley."

"Shit. You serious?"

"I guess."

"You might as well give me your ticket. By the time he finishes trying to explain this, it'll be the bottom of the ninth."

"I charge by the hour."

"Still . . ." DiNoffrio swiveled in his chair, facing back out toward the cell block. He grabbed the microphone that extended up from the control board at the center of the guard station, flicked the power switch on. "*Devon Malley. Visitor.*" His amplified, mechanized voice echoed off the smooth cement surfaces of the cell block. It didn't sound like him; it sounded like God. For those living on the block, it might as well have been. He looked back at Finn and nodded toward another steel door off to the side of the guard station. He pressed a button and the door unlocked. "He'll be in in a minute."

"Thanks." Finn walked over and stood in front of the door. He looked up at a clock in the guard station. Nine forty-five a.m. The first pitch was at eleven oh-five. *Devon better talk quickly.* He took a deep breath and walked through the door.

———◆———

The room was small—smaller even than the single cells in which the inmates were kept for most of the day. Two plastic chairs were the only furnishings. No table. The lock on the door behind him buzzed shut, and Finn took quick, shallow breaths, trying to keep the stink of inmate sweat and vinegar-based disinfectant from reaching too deeply into his lungs. It was useless, he knew from experience. The odor would stay with him for the rest of the day.

The buzzer on the door that led directly into the jail's common area sounded, the door swung open, and Devon Malley stepped into the room. He was dressed in the standard-issue faded blue smock and drawstring pants. The two men looked at each other without saying anything.

11

Devon looked more or less the same as he had the last time Finn had seen him a few years before. He was around five years older than Finn—late forties—and just over six feet tall. He had dark hair, cut short and streaked with gray, and a round face with well-defined features. His eyes had a guileless look to them incongruous with his chosen profession.

Finn had known Devon since the old days, when Finn was still running with his gang in the Charlestown projects. He wasn't part of Finn's crew—he was from Southie—but they hung around some of the same people. Devon was the sort of guy people usually took little notice of. He wasn't bright enough to be a leader, but he was pliable, and he could round out a decent crew. He wasn't a complete psychopath, which was refreshing. Many of the people Finn knew from back then would kill without thought or provocation. That was never a worry with Devon. Finn didn't think he had killing in him. Finn liked him for that.

Neither of them said anything for a moment, and the silence was awkward in so small a room. Devon finally stepped forward, extending his hand. Finn shook it.

"It's good to see ya, Finn," Devon said. His heavy South Boston accent brought Finn back to his youth. "R"s came out as "aah"s and the gerund form "-ing" had been lost forever. Curses replaced all punctuation. Finn had worked hard to lose that dialect.

"You too," Finn replied.

"It's good of ya to do this. Showin' up on a fuckin' holiday and all." Devon let Finn's hand go and stepped back, pulling one of the chairs over and sitting down.

"Anything for an old friend."

"Anything for an old friend who'll pay your fuckin' fees, you mean," Devon corrected him.

"That, too." Finn pulled over the other chair and sat in front of his client. "You can pay my fees, right?"

Devon smiled, but avoided eye contact. "We never change, do we?"

"Not in any way that matters," Finn agreed.

"Jesus, what's it been, five years? Ten? How you been?"

"Okay."

"From what I hear, you been better than okay," Devon said. "You're gettin' a fuckin' reputation for yourself. 'Miracle worker,' that's what I heard you called." He rocked back and forth as he spoke.

"Really? That's a good one. I'll have to put it on my business cards."

"No fuckin' need. You do right by the right people and you don't need to advertise no more." He sounded like he was trying to convince himself of something. "You must be making a pretty fuckin' penny, too, huh?"

"Right. That brings me back to my fees."

He nodded, still not looking directly at Finn. "I'll pay 'em. I need a miracle worker."

"Apparently. You want to tell me what happened?"

Devon shrugged. "I don't fuckin' know. My night didn't go like I planned it."

Finn looked around the tiny room. "So it would seem." He went silent for a moment. "You want to tell me about the lingerie?"

Devon put his head down. "That's all anyone's gonna fuckin' talk about, isn't it. Fuck."

"You've got to admit that when a guy gets caught with an armful of women's underwear it paints a picture that's hard to forget."

"It wasn't just underwear," Devon said. "It was dresses, too."

"Right," Finn said. "Dresses, too. Does that make it sound better?" He watched his client get up and pace in the tiny room like a tiger at the zoo. "The cops are calling you the G-String Bandit."

"Fuck 'em. They ain't got nothin' better to do with their lives but fuck with me? I got enough to worry about, right?"

"It was apparently a toss-up between that and the Panty Raider. Personally, I like the Panty Raider, but that's probably because I went to college at night, so I feel like I missed out."

Devon stopped pacing and looked at Finn. "This is fuckin' funny?"

"Maybe a little," Finn replied. Then he turned serious. "Tell me what happened."

Devon sat down, leaned back in the little chair, and took a deep breath. "It shoulda been the easiest night of my fuckin' life. You know Gilberacci's on Newberry Street? High-end fashion place?" Finn nodded. "They just got in the new shipments for summer. The place was stocked."

"A little smash-and-grab?" Finn asked. "The notion of you getting pinched fondling a bunch of silk bras is a little hard to swallow."

"You're not listening," Devon said. "This wasn't no fuckin' smash-and-grab. I had over fifty designer dresses, up to six thousand retail for each one. Plus some jewelry and—yeah—very expensive panties and bras and shit like that. All in all, close to half a million dollars in the store, low six figures on the street."

Finn whistled. "That's expensive underwear."

"That's what I'm sayin'. Plus, it shoulda been easy. Johnny Gilberacci's one of the owners, and he's got a serious fuckin' gambling problem."

"Johnny Gilberacci? He's the guy who's always in the society pages with his little dog with the pink collar, right?"

"That's the guy."

"A little weak in the wrists, isn't he?"

"He's queer as a fuckin' ballerina, but he's still got a gambling problem."

"Really? What does he bet on?"

"How the fuck should I know? Whatever it is, he's no fuckin' good at it. He loses a fortune, and he's been paying off Vinny by stealing the shit outta the stuff in his store. This was gonna even everyone up. He's got insurance on the place for twice the inventory that's actually there. I had the keys and access to the loading dock in back. No risk, and no one could get hurt."

"And yet here you are."

Devon nodded. "Yeah, here I am." He looked around the small room. "There was no fuckin' warning. Everything was goin' fine. I had most of the shit loaded up already, and I'd just gone back in to grab a few more things. All of a sudden I look up and there are these two fuckin' cops looking back at me, these big, wide, shit-eating grins on their faces."

"So, what do you think happened?" Finn asked.

"Only one possibility."

"Someone dropped dime?"

"I don't see how else this happens. There was no alarm, I didn't make any fuckin' noise, and there was no one else around. The cops had to be tipped."

Finn thought about this for a moment. "Who else knew?"

"I got the job from Vinny. You know Vinny Murphy, right? He's moved up, and I've done a bunch of work for him. He's always been a stand-up guy, though, and I don't see his angle on me gettin' busted, so I don't think it was him. I don't know who else coulda known, but someone did. If I was out on the street, I'd find out quick enough. In here I'm fucked, though."

Finn nodded in understanding. "I could help with that, at least. I could probably have you out of here pretty quick," he said.

"Really?"

"Bail hearing shouldn't be too bad. I took a look at your sheet, and it's been a while since you've picked up any convictions. The DA will be looking for high bail, but I'm guessing the judge would be reasonable about it if it's handled right."

"I been arrested a couple times in the past few years," Devon said. He sounded skeptical. "And the shit I was caught with ain't cheap."

Finn shook his head. "Bail isn't what I'd be worried about. The problem is what happens after bail. Your case sucks."

"No shit. That's why I need a fuckin' miracle worker."

"Even miracle workers hate to lose cases, Devon. Unless you've got something to give to the DA to get him to make a decent plea offer, you're screwed. You really think you can get some sort of helpful information once you're out after the arraignment? Something we might be able to trade?"

"Maybe. When's the arraignment?"

Finn scratched his chin. He hadn't shaved that morning and a dark patch of stubble covered his face. "Don't know yet, it hasn't been scheduled. You were picked up on Sunday, and today is Patriots' Day, so the courts are closed. They'll put you on a schedule when they get in tomorrow, but given the three-day weekend and the inevitable backlog, I wouldn't expect you to be seen anytime before Wednesday."

Devon shook his head. "No good. The longer I stay in here, the colder the fuckin' rat's trail gets. You want me to get you something to use with the DA, you gotta spring me sooner."

"You may be putting too much stock in the 'miracle worker' reputation I have. There's no way I can change the court's schedule."

"No, I guess not," Devon said. He looked down at the floor as he tapped his feet anxiously. Then he looked up at Finn. "How 'bout if you was to move things on the outside?" he asked. "You know, poke around, see what you can find out?"

"I don't do windows," Finn replied.

"C'mon," Devon pleaded. "I'm not askin' for much. Just ask a few fuckin' questions. Otherwise, we may never find out who tipped off the cops."

Finn thought about it. He hated the idea of getting his hands dirty;

he'd given up that kind of work. "I charge by the hour," he said. "You're not going to want to pay as much as it would cost."

"I may not want to pay it, but I will," Devon said. "I'm desperate, and payin' you beats the shit out of going to jail. Besides, don't you have some sort of private investigator you could use?"

"Sort of," Finn admitted. "But he's an ex-cop. He's not the kind of guy someone like Vinny Murphy is gonna want to talk to."

"Take him anyway. You want someone ridin' shotgun. Guys like Vinny don't fuckin' play. They're serious people."

Finn considered the suggestion some more. "It's gonna cost you a boatload of money, y'know? Not a little—a lot."

"I know. I'll pay it," Devon replied simply. "I need this."

Finn shot Devon a look. "And you really can pay my fees?"

"I swear to fuckin' God, Finn. The second you get me out, I'll pay you cash for what you done so far. Plus a fat fuckin' retainer for the rest. I swear it, on my mother's fuckin' grave."

"Your mother passed?"

"Not yet, but she's got the cancer. Any day. Shit, Finn, I just need your help."

Finn rubbed his hand over his stubble again. "I've got to talk to the others in the firm. If you're really willing to pay, we'll think about doing some poking around. Don't get your hopes up too high, though. I don't know whether my people are gonna want to take this on, and even if we do end up taking the case, I can't imagine we're gonna get too far."

"You're a good shit, Finn," Devon said thoughtfully. "A really good shit."

Finn sat up straight in his chair. He caught a calculating tone in Devon's voice. "What is it?" he asked.

"What do you mean?"

"Don't bullshit a bullshitter, Devon. There's something else."

"Don't know what the fuck you're talking about."

"Yeah, you do."

Devon was silent for a moment. "Okay. I got one other favor to ask," he began.

"Of course you do."

"There's a woman in my apartment. It's a little fucked up with her."

"You never change, do you Devon."

"Like you said, not in any way that's important. I didn't call her when I got pinched, so she's probably a little twitchy. She's gotta go down to her ma's place in Providence today."

"You want me to get her a message?" Finn asked.

"It's not that simple."

Finn frowned. "Why isn't it that simple, Devon?"

Devon looked hard at Finn. "I trust you," he said.

"You'd better," Finn replied. "I may end up being your lawyer."

"You don't understand; there's no one else I trust. I'm not in the right business for trust—not when it comes to shit that really matters. You know that better than anyone, right?"

Finn didn't like the turn the conversation was taking. "Crap," he muttered. "What's this about, Devon?"

Devon sighed. "It's about my daughter."

Chapter Two

Detective Paul Stone drove. He and Elorea Sanchez had been partners for two weeks. Though he'd been a cop for five years, he was a rookie on the homicide squad, and she had every right to take the wheel, but never did. They walked out of the station house that first day to the dented, unmarked Lincoln and Sanchez had tossed the keys onto the driver's seat. She'd never said a word about it, and Stone had driven ever since. He'd joked once that she must like having a younger man chauffeuring her around the city, but it hadn't gone over well. She just stared at him with a hard look that was effective at cutting off conversation.

She wasn't easy to figure out. They'd spent nearly ten hours a day together for two weeks, but they seldom spoke more than a few words to each other at a time. Her idea of conversation was to tell him where to turn. Most of what he knew about her he'd gotten from her personnel file and station gossip. She was fifty years old, female, Hispanic of unspecified geographic origin, five-seven, one hundred and thirty-five pounds. She had joined the police force later in life than most cops—after the army, college, and a master's degree in criminal justice. She'd even done two years of law school, but hadn't finished. No one knew why she'd dropped out. What people did know was that she had shot up through the BPD ranks with incredible speed. The jealous credited affirmative action, ignoring the fact that she had the best clear rate in the homicide unit. In her fifteen years on the detective squad, she'd cleared over seventy-five percent of her cases. That meant that if a case was assigned to her, three out of four times someone was convicted of the crime. The national average was sixty-five percent. In Boston, the average had sunk in recent years as low as thirty-three percent. That meant that only a third of all murders were being solved. It was one of the worst records in the country. Given that grim reality, affirmative action or not, seventy-five percent made Sanchez a star.

Word was, though, that she was difficult to work with. Since joining the detective squad, she'd churned through five partners. Those inclined to give her the benefit of the doubt claimed that her intensity burned partners out. Those less charitable said it was because she couldn't be trusted, and without trust there could be no real partnership. Whatever the reason, she was working alone when Stone was bumped up to homicide. He'd been told the arrangement was on a trial basis, but had been given no indication when the trial would end or by what criteria he would be judged. He was a team player, so he kept his mouth shut. At the very least, he figured, he could learn something riding with someone who had a seventy-five percent clear rate, no matter for how short a time.

"You got the address?" she asked.

"Yeah."

He didn't need the address; he'd grown up in Southie. Never left there, in fact. When he was growing up, the Body Shop had been a landmark. The sign that hung from the grimy, low-slung stucco building read "Murphy's Car Body and Engine Repair," but it was known to everyone in the neighborhood simply as the Body Shop. It was located on an oversized lot fringed with knee-high weeds, set back from the street, in an area that drew little traffic. That hardly mattered, though—no one ever took their cars there anyway. A mechanic was on the premises during the daytime to keep appearances up, but anyone looking to have a car repaired was invariably told that all of the appointments were booked. The only auto-body work performed there took place at night, and few of the cars that found their way into the garage emerged again in one piece.

Notwithstanding the lack of legitimate automotive services offered, the place usually buzzed during the day. Murphy, a leader in what remained of the loosely affiliated Irish-American gangs, kept his office in the back, running his crews and brokering a tenuous peace among those in the neighborhood who operated on the wrong side of the law.

The place was humming with activity as Stone guided the car into the driveway, though not with its normal daily business. The driveway was crammed with BPD squad cars and crime scene units. Yellow tape was strewn loosely around the entire complex, and a patrolman had to lift one of the banners strung across the entryway to allow the detectives' car in.

"You think this is the start of another war?" Stone asked as he eased the Lincoln around to the back of the lot.

"Don't know," Sanchez replied. "Been a long time since the last one, and things have been outta whack since Whitey took off. If it is another war, it's gonna get ugly."

"Yeah," he agreed. He remembered the times when he was a boy and he'd heard whispers about the wars that went on between the rival gangs back in the sixties and seventies. They had seemed at the time like mythic, almost heroic battles. Later he came to understand that they were more like scraps between vicious animals.

"You grew up here, right?" Sanchez asked.

"Yeah."

"Did you know him?"

"Murphy?" Stone thought about his answer. "Everyone knew him.

He was one of Whitey's guys back in the day. He had a rep as being nicer than most, but still dangerous. You ever deal with him?"

Sanchez shook her head. "Not really. I watched him get grilled after a bust back in the nineties, but that's it."

"What did you think?"

"I thought he was smart. One of the smartest I've seen." She opened the door and slid out of the car; Stone did the same. She looked around the front of the building. A young man from the coroner's office was leaning against his van, a gurney at his side. Piled loosely on top of the rolling stretcher were two empty black vinyl body bags. "Not smart enough, I guess."

She started walking toward the doorway and Stone fell in just behind her. As he walked, it dawned on him that the exchange was the longest conversation they'd had since they'd become partners.

⚬

The stench in the Body Shop was overpowering. It was a warm day for April in Boston, and the aluminum-lined building seemed to trap the heat. Sanchez could feel the sting of oil and gasoline in her nostrils, but the odors were swallowed up in the sickly sweet aroma of death and decay. It smelled like rotten meat boiled in sour milk and honey. She clenched her jaw so as not to betray her nausea. She'd been on the force long enough to understand the double standard—men could show their disgust at a crime scene, but for women it was viewed as a sign of weakness.

"Any word on the time of death?" she asked Stone as they walked through the front-counter section, past a couple of uniformed officers acting as bored sentries, and back around into the garage bays.

"Doc thinks Saturday. No time yet, and even the day's an estimate until they get the bodies back to the lab to run some tests."

"Smells like Saturday," she said.

"Smells like shit," he said. He coughed and put a hand to his face.

"Found this morning?"

Stone nodded. "Place was closed yesterday, and no one was around. They were supposed to be closed today, too, for Patriots' Day, but one of the mechanics stopped by to do some work on his own car and found them."

She threw a quick look at her partner. He was young and good-looking in an overmuscled, athletic sort of way—the kind of a man whose neck strained against his collar, and who developed a five o'clock shadow as he pulled away from the sink after shaving. His hair was thick and dark and his brow jutted forth just a little more than necessary. His accent chopped his hard consonants and slid through his "r"s in a manner characteristic of lifelong Bostonians from working-class neighborhoods. She'd worked with men like him before. The jury was still out on him, as far as she was concerned. She'd be disappointed in the end, she was sure—she always was. It had become such a predictable pattern that she now thought of a "partner" merely as an obstacle to be negotiated as she focused on getting the job done.

As they approached the back of the building, toward the bays where the cars were dismantled, a uniformed sergeant in his early fifties broke free from a group of officers and strode to meet them. She reached into her pocket and fished out her badge, holding it up for the sergeant.

He nodded to her. "Detective," he said. He looked at Stone and said nothing.

"Sergeant . . ." Sanchez scanned her memory and the tag on the front of the man's shirt for a name, "McAfee." She squinted at him. "We've worked together before."

"Yes, ma'am," he replied. "Two years ago."

"Right. The Darvos case."

"That's correct, ma'am."

She said nothing more about it. "What have we got?"

"Nothing good. You just missed the doc, but he said he'll be in the office writing up some notes later if you want to talk. He's gonna do the autopsies once we get the bodies to him this afternoon. He got a good first look, but we put the bodies back the way we found them. I figured you'd want to see them the way they were found."

She nodded. "Good." She looked around the room and noticed a tall black man in the corner talking on a cell phone. He was dressed in a dark blue suit, white shirt, and a dark tie. He was wearing sunglasses. "Feds got a line on this?" she asked.

McAfee looked over his shoulder and grunted in distaste. "Yeah. He showed up about ten minutes after we got here. Don't know how he found out about it."

"What's he been doing?"

"Just looking. We haven't let him touch anything, but I didn't know whether we could kick him out. He's got a badge."

She nodded and walked toward the man. He saw her coming and closed his phone. As she got nearer, he took off his glasses. "Detective?" he said.

She nodded. "Sanchez. And you are?"

"Special Agent Hewitt."

"Special Agent Hewitt, what are you doing at my crime scene?"

He stared at her. "Looking," he said after a moment.

"For anything in particular?"

"I'm on a task force that deals with organized crime. I heard there was a murder down here at the Body Shop."

"Do you have any specific reason to believe that this case is federal in nature?"

The agent sucked slowly at his teeth. "Murphy was a well-known gang leader. He was involved in everything from guns to drugs to prostitution to extortion. I don't have any reason to believe that this wasn't related to his racketeering activities."

Sanchez folded her arms. "Let me ask the question a different way, Special Agent Hewitt: are you asserting federal jurisdiction here? Because if you are, I'll have our people out of here in about five minutes and you can take over. Then if something goes wrong, it's your ass in a sling, not mine."

It took him a moment to answer. "No, I'm not asserting jurisdiction," he said.

"Good," Sanchez said. "In that case, I'd appreciate it if you'd clear out until my people are done. I'll get you a report as soon as one is ready, but until then, I have control over the crime scene, and I can't have my people working with someone looking over their shoulders."

"Detective Sanchez, I'm a special agent with the FBI," Hewitt began in protest. She cut him off.

"So was John Connolly, and he's still got three years left in supermax out at Allenwood for tipping off Whitey Bulger and his mob, right? For years, your federal boys ran interference for these guys whenever we tried to put them away, so you'll pardon me if the 'Special Agent' mystique doesn't cut a whole lot of shit with me. I'll keep you informed as appropriate, but I need you out so we can do our job. Either that or you take the lead yourself. Which is it gonna be?"

Hewitt put his glasses back on. "I'll expect a full report, complete with pictures, by the end of the day," he said.

"You can expect whatever you want," Sanchez replied. "No skin off my nose."

Hewitt stood there for a moment, then walked past them, out toward the front door to the garage.

"Cocksucker," McAfee said under his breath as he watched Hewitt walk out of the Body Shop.

"Maybe he's just doing his job," Stone offered.

"Maybe," Sanchez said. "I'm not taking any chances, though. We have a job to do, too. And I don't want the feds fucking up one of my cases." She looked at McAfee. "Let's get to it. What are we looking at?"

"You want to look at Bags first?" he asked.

"Should we?"

McAfee gave a gesture falling somewhere between a nod and a shrug. "He's a good warm-up. He's in better shape than Vinny." He pointed over into a corner behind a tool rack. Sanchez moved in that direction and Stone followed.

John Smith was known to most as "Johnny Bags." The nickname came from his early career ferrying loads of cash to local political bosses. His body was crumpled in a corner of the garage, tucked behind a rack of utility drawers. In life he'd been a fearsome man, six-five with an angry face and a disposition devoid of humanity's finer traits. In death he looked almost peaceful, curled into a fetal position, his head resting on his left hand. Only the angle at which his right arm was twisted—straight out from the shoulder, its palm turned upward in an impossible feat of contortion—suggested that the man was anything other than resting. A closer look revealed the two holes in his forehead, and stepping over the body, Sanchez could see flies buzzing around a dark pool of congealed blood spread out from his black hair.

"Not much left of the back of his skull," McAfee commented. "Looks like they used shredders. Pretty much blew off the back half of his head."

"Nasty," Stone said with a frown.

"Effective," Sanchez replied. "Any other points of entry?"

McAfee shook his head. "Just the head, from what we can tell. Doc'll confirm it with the autopsy."

"Anything else? Cuts? Contusions? Anything?"

"Just the arm," McAfee said. "Looks like it was pulled out of the socket. Could've happened when he fell after he got popped."

Sanchez lingered over Smith's body for another minute or two, drinking in the scene. Other than the body and the stagnant, well-defined mat of blood underneath the head, the area was neat and tidy, with tools stacked in an orderly fashion on top of the utility cabinets. She pulled back the jacket and patted it down. There was nothing in the pockets. A shoulder holster was strapped to his torso, and a gun was tucked into it.

"Okay," Sanchez said at last. "Let's see Murphy."

McAfee nodded. "The main attraction. If either of you have a weak stomach . . ."

"Just show us the body, Sergeant," Sanchez said.

McAfee said nothing, but led them to a mechanics' bay at the very rear of the building. It shot off from the main space, and was concealed from view. They rounded the corner, and Sanchez heard Stone suck in his breath.

Murphy's body was there. At least, she assumed it was Murphy's body. It was difficult to tell given the amount of damage. It looked more to her like two hundred pounds of ground beef covered in torn clothing than what she remembered of Vinny Murphy. It didn't appear that any spot on the body had escaped violence.

"Holy shit," Stone whispered softly.

"Nothing holy about it," Sanchez said. "An impressive piece of work, though." She moved slowly toward the body, being careful not to disturb the scene. "Are the pictures done?" she asked.

"All done," McAfee replied. "The whole lovely scene has been recorded for posterity."

"Crime scene?"

"They've done all they can do until the body is moved out. Prints, scrapings, the works. They'll do it all again once we've cleared out, but they think the place is pretty clean." He tossed her a box of latex gloves. "He's all yours."

She took two gloves out of the box and passed it to Stone, who did the same. They both pulled the gloves on and advanced toward the body.

"Jesus," Stone said as he looked at the area that had once been Vince Murphy's face. "What did they use?" Sanchez said nothing.

"Not sure," McAfee said after a moment. "Could have been chains. There were a bunch of them hanging over in the corner, and it looked like there could've been blood on them. The crime scene boys bagged 'em and we'll know soon enough. Doc should also be able to get us a read on any patterns to the abrasion, which may tell us something."

Stone moved slowly around the corpse. Sanchez watched him out of the corner of her eye. She was annoyed at the distraction of having him there, but said nothing. He was her partner, after all, at least for the moment, and there was no way to prevent his participation. As long as he was careful to stay out of her way, she could live with it. "Shit, they even got the bottoms of his feet," Stone said.

"Yup," McAfee said, using a fingernail to pick some of his breakfast free from his teeth. He pointed to a hook hanging from a hydraulic lift used to get engine blocks into and out of cars. "Looks like they had him strapped to that for at least part of the time. They found a couple of torn pieces from his shirt on the hook."

"Why?" Stone said to no one in particular.

"I guess that's the sixty-four-thousand-dollar question, isn't it?" McAfee said. "My guess is that he pissed off one of the goombahs in the North End, or maybe one of the Salvadoran gangbangers over in Eastie. Who knows, could have even been one of his own boys looking to move up in the world."

"Doc give any thoughts on the extent of the injuries?" Sanchez asked.

"Just that the gunshots to the head were pretty clearly the cause of death. And the external injuries are mainly superficial. There may be some broken bones, and he won't know about any internal injuries until he splits him open to look inside. The only other thing that sticks out is the hands."

"The hands?" Stone said.

"See for yourself," McAfee said.

Sanchez looked at the body. It was turned to the side, and both hands were underneath the torso. "Help me turn him," she said to Stone.

The two of them reached down. She placed her palms flat underneath the shoulder, and he lifted from underneath the hip. Rigor had set in, so the body rolled easily, like a mannequin, and the arms shot upward once released from under the body.

Sanchez frowned. The skin on the hands had a ghostly white, fleshless tone to it below the wrists. Dark holes marred the palms, and looking closely, Sanchez could see that the injuries went all the way through the hands.

"Doc picked up some ligature marks on the wrists," McAfee said. "Looks like they tied his hands together and shot him clean through the palms."

"Why?" Stone asked.

"Who knows," McAfee said. "Maybe just for kicks."

"*Padre Pio*," Sanchez said quietly.

"*Padre Pio*?" Stone replied.

"*Padre Pio*," she repeated.

Stone looked at McAfee. "You know what *Padre Pio* means?" he asked.

McAfee shook his head. "Sorry, I'm not Mexican."

Stone looked back at Sanchez. "What does *Padre Pio* mean?" he asked.

"It means you need to pay attention." She moved to the other side of the body. "The message?"

McAfee pointed to the left of the head. "It's up there. No one has any idea about it. It's not gang-related as far as we know, and no one has seen anything like it before."

She bent down. It was there, though it had faded as the blood had dried. "The Storm." She looked at Stone. "You're the local, you know what that means?"

Stone shook his head. "Doesn't ring any bells."

"Anyone go by that nickname?"

"Not that I've ever heard."

"Great."

"Maybe it's just some sort of psycho with a flair for drama."

She stood up. "Maybe. It's definitely a psycho. I don't think it's got anything to do with drama, though."

"What, then?"

She took off her gloves and they snapped as she rolled them into a ball. She tossed them to McAfee. "That's what I expect you to find out."

Chapter Three

Back behind the wheel, Stone pulled out of the driveway to the Body Shop. "Where to, boss?" he asked Sanchez.

"Back to the station house," she replied.

"What for?"

"I need to check something on a computer." She looked out the passenger window as the Convention Center in South Boston drifted by, its huge front canopy hanging over the entranceway like some great homage to the 1960s television show *The Flying Nun.*

"Right. Check something out. Good idea. Me, too, I need to check something out, too. Maybe it's the same thing."

She turned to look at him. "I doubt it," she said after a moment.

"Maybe not. Of course, there's only one way to know, right?" He drove on, his frustration building through the silence. "So, are you gonna talk to me about that shit back there? We are partners, after all, right?"

She said nothing.

"Look, I know I'm the new guy, but how are you gonna know if I can contribute if you won't even talk to me?"

"Fine," she said, her tone challenging. "Why don't you tell me about the scene back there?"

"Is this some sort of a test?"

"Yeah, it's a test."

"That's fucked up. I don't have to prove shit to you."

"Suit yourself." She lapsed back into silence.

He drove on, going over the scene in his head. He was determined not to give her the satisfaction of rising to her bait. *Seventy-five percent clear rate or not, who the fuck was she?* "McAfee was wrong about one thing," he said after a while, trying to sound conversational.

She looked at him but said nothing.

"Whoever did that wasn't just settling a score. It wasn't some simple beef with the North End boys, or even with the Salvadorans in MS-13."

"What makes you so sure?" she asked.

He shook his head. "Too messy. Too involved. If the wops or a rival mick gang felt disrespected or was settling a score it would've been cleaner. They would've taken him out quickly and gotten the hell away. Double tap to the head—like they did to Bags—or maybe even a drive-by when he was out in the open. No way they'd spend the kind of time they needed to do the damage we saw back there. And if MS-13 wanted to make a point, they would have used machetes on him. It's their thing."

She shrugged, as though the observations were beneath acknowledgment.

"And Murphy knew the people who did it."

"People? How do you know it was more than one?"

"Johnny Bags. It had to be more than one, and they had to know Murphy because of Bags." He felt her lean toward him, and he continued. "Bags was Murphy's bodyguard. That was his job for the past ten years. His only purpose in life. From what I hear he was no rocket scientist, but he was good at his job, and loyal to a fault. There's no way someone gets that close to Murphy if they didn't know him without Bags putting up one hell of a fight. Plus, whoever did this managed to get Johnny back into that corner of the garage voluntarily. The body wasn't dragged—the blood pooled under his head where he fell, and there was no messy trail—so he died where he fell. He didn't even get his gun out before he was shot. I can't imagine Bags leaving Murphy alone and going back into that corner with someone he didn't know. And once he was there, Murphy would have had time to run when he heard the gunshots, unless there was more than one guy there—so we know it wasn't a single perp."

"What's that tell you about who did this?" Sanchez asked.

"Nothing for sure," Stone admitted. "But I'd start by looking within Murphy's own organization. Could either be someone above him who felt threatened for some reason—"

"Which could only mean Ballick," she pointed out.

"Right, if the order came from above. But it could also be someone underneath him. Or maybe even someone on his level trying to move up. The organization's been all fucked up for years. Ever since Bulger took off."

"Why torture him, then?" she asked.

He shrugged. "Not sure. Maybe there was a personal aspect to it. Or maybe they were trying to make it look like something it wasn't. I'm just guessin', though."

"And the message? 'The Storm'? What's your thought on that?"

"I got no idea. Maybe it's just adolescent bullshit. Some of these guys never get past the comic book stage. But it's taking a risk to leave something that distinctive behind. Seems like there should be a better reason. Guys who do shit like what we saw back there usually aren't holding on to reason too tightly, though."

She turned and looked out her window again. They had pulled past the Federal Courthouse down by the water and were crossing the Evelyn Moakley Bridge back into Boston, heading toward the Rose Kennedy Greenway, which wound through the city above the Big Dig. The bridge was named after the wife of Joe Moakley, a powerful congressman. The Greenway was named for Rose Kennedy, the mother of John, Bobby, and Teddy Kennedy. Only in Boston were public works named for the relatives of politicians. It said so much about the place.

"So, what do you think?" he asked.

"I think you're right," she said. "I think you're just guessing."

He shook his head bitterly. "That's it? That's all I get?"

"Like you said, it was a test."

"So, what'd I get, like a C?"

"It was pass/fail."

"And?"

She hesitated before she answered. "I'll get back to you."

Special Agent Robert Hewitt sat in his car, watching the activity at the Body Shop from across the street. Things had quieted down, and now those who remained were loitering, mainly. They stood around, smoking cigarettes or leaning against their cars, cracking jokes as they waited for the bodies to be rolled out. He'd watched as the detectives pulled away, and he was tempted to go back in to get another good look. He was sure that no one who remained would have the balls to force him out without Sanchez there, but his presence would draw too much attention, and too many people on the force would start to ask questions. That would make his life more difficult.

He took out his cell phone and dialed the number.

"Yes," the man answering the line said.

"It's me."

"And?"

"Murphy's dead."

"How?"

"How do you think?"

"Are you sure?"

"I'm sure. He was beaten. Badly."

"Tortured?"

"That's a reasonable conclusion based on what I saw. And there was a message written next to the body."

"What was it?"

"'The Storm.'"

"That's our boy. Have there been any others yet?"

"Not that I know of. Murphy's bodyguard was killed, but he's not involved, and he wasn't tortured. Maybe there won't be any others at all." As Hewitt spoke, the coroner's assistants wheeled two gurneys out of the Body Shop. They were laughing as they slid the body bags into the van.

"There will be others. Otherwise, why send the message?"

"If so, then we don't know who they are yet. I haven't heard about anything else that matches what was done here, and I would have heard about it."

There was silence on the other end of the line. "Stay on top of it. This is the break we've been looking for."

"What are you going to do?"

"I think it's time for me to be more involved. I'm coming to Boston."

Chapter Four

It took Finn nearly an hour to make the two-and-a-half-mile journey from Nashua Street to Fenway Park. Normally the drive would have taken fifteen minutes, but it was Patriots' Day and the streets were packed.

Patriots' Day, which marks the battles of Lexington and Concord in 1775, is celebrated only in Boston. It's one of three smug local holidays intended to remind an indifferent world of Boston's place in American history. For all the city's parochial pride, however, few Americans would have heard of Lexington and Concord were it not for *Schoolhouse Rock*. Even worse, few Bostonians have any idea what Patriots' Day is intended to celebrate. They do know, though, that it means an extra day off, and it's the day on which the Boston Marathon is run every year. It's also a day the Boston Red Sox play a special morning game at Fenway Park. The holiday causes mayhem in the city, as people line the streets early, and the bars are packed by midmorning.

Finn parked at the edge of the Fens, close to the Back Bay, in a lot owned by a client. He'd called ahead to reserve a space, knowing that otherwise there was little chance of finding anyplace to leave his car. By the time he'd pushed his way through the carnival atmosphere around Fenway Park it was nearing noon. When he found his seat next to Tom Kozlowski and Lissa Krantz two rows behind the Red Sox dugout, Boston was leading six–nothing in the fourth inning.

"Sorry I'm late," he said, squeezing into his seat.

"Your loss," Kozlowski replied. He was a butcher's block of a man in his early fifties, with a bold, carved face marred by a long scar that ran from the corner of his right eye to the bottom of his ear. He was dressed in cheap polyester slacks and a sport coat Goodwill would have turned down. Blue collar through and through, he'd spent a quarter of a century in the Boston Police Department, most of it in homicide, before he was pushed out and became a private detective. The cop inside him wouldn't let go, though. He worked out of a small office in the brownstone in Charlestown where Finn had his law practice, and did enough work for Finn that they loosely considered themselves partners. "You missed a few good innings," Kozlowski said.

"I said I was sorry."

"I heard you."

"What's the problem?"

"Problem is, you're late. We been coming to this game ever since you started the firm. It's a tradition."

"I only started the firm a couple of years ago," Finn pointed out.

"Even worse. New traditions are fragile."

"Quit your bitching and watch the game," Lissa said. She was a small, attractive, razor-tongued woman in her mid-thirties, with thick dark hair and a strong jaw. She'd worked as a paralegal for Finn while attending law school at night, and since graduating and passing the bar the previous year had been taken on by Finn as an associate. She was wearing capri pants and a cashmere sweater that had probably cost more than Finn paid her in a month; she came from that kind of money. She and Kozlowski had been dating for over a year, and Finn couldn't imagine a stranger couple. The thickness of their skins and their physical attraction to each other seemed the only things they had in common. Apparently that was enough.

"You're the one who's been bitching about him for the past hour," Kozlowski said to her. "Don't play all innocent."

"I've never played innocent."

Kozlowski grunted. "True enough." To Finn he asked, "Where were you, anyway?"

"Nashua Street."

"New client?"

"Maybe. Old acquaintance; we need to talk about whether he's gonna be a client."

"Anyone I would know?"

"You remember Devon Malley?" Finn asked.

"From Southie? The thief?"

"That's the guy. You know much about him?"

Kozlowski shook his head. "Not really. He had a rep for a while, but it died. He was basically a minor player."

A beer vendor passed in front of them in the aisle. Lissa put her fingers in her mouth and gave a deafening whistle. It was loud enough to startle the young man, and he nearly dropped his tray. "Yo! Three over here!" she yelled.

Finn put a finger in his ear and gave a pained shake. "Is that really necessary?"

"Jesus, you're a pansy," she replied. She pulled out her purse and found a twenty.

"You sure you don't want me to get these?" Finn asked. "It's a work function."

"Keep your wallet in your pants, boss. I've got more money than you."

"True. But still . . ."

She looked at him. "You really want to pay?"

"Not really, no."

"Fine. Then shut up."

Finn smiled at Kozlowski, who just shrugged. "So, what did Devon get pinched for?" the ex-cop asked.

"Robbery," Finn answered.

"No shit, that's what he does. You wanna be a little more specific?"

"Not really." Finn took a sip of his beer. "He was robbing a clothing store," he said after a moment.

"Allegedly," Lissa tossed in.

"Good girl," Finn said. "Allegedly."

"How allegedly?" Kozlowski asked.

Finn shrugged. "The police walked in on him in the store at midnight holding a bunch of women's lingerie," he admitted.

Kozlowski shook his head. "That's not very allegedly. It's gonna be hard for him to live that down."

"It was high-end stuff," Finn said.

"I'd hope so." Kozlowski took a huge bite out of a bratwurst that had been sitting on a cardboard tray on his lap. A chunk of sauerkraut and mustard toppled off the end and splattered onto the front of his shirt. Finn thought it was an improvement. "So, does he have any kind of a case we can work with, or would we just be looking to plead it out?"

"Don't know yet. All I've got is his side of the story. I don't know where the cops are with this. Maybe we can come up with something. Devon seems to think that when he gets out he might be able to throw someone else to the DA. Maybe get probation." Finn thought about it for a moment. "Probably not, though."

"So it sounds like a shitty case," Kozlowski said. "Why would we want it?"

Finn sighed. "I knew the guy back in the day. Back when I was mixed up in all that. I feel sorry for him. How can I say no?"

"Easy," Kozlowski said. "Tongue on the top of your mouth, exhale and round your lips. *N-n-n-o-o-o*. See?" Finn didn't smile, and the ex-cop's face darkened quickly. "You didn't tell him yes, did you?"

"No, I told him maybe. But I'm thinking yes."

"I thought you said we were gonna discuss new cases. All three of us."

"So, I'm discussing. Like I said, I feel bad for the guy. I'd like to help him out."

"How old is he?" Lissa asked.

"Somewhere in between Koz and me," Finn said.

"That old?"

Kozlowski stared out at the field. "Thanks."

"I didn't mean it that way," Lissa said. "I was just thinking being a criminal must suck as you get older."

"Everything sucks as you get older," Koz pointed out.

"It's different," she said. "If you guys screw up at least you don't end up in jail."

"No, if we screw up someone else ends up in jail," Finn replied. "Besides, it's not clear that he screwed up. It was an inside job, and it looks like the cops were tipped. It may be that someone wanted him taken out."

"Any idea who?" Kozlowski asked.

"A few possibilities. I told Devon we might be willing to check them out."

"Great. Is he going to pay us to do this?"

"He said he would."

"Will he give us a retainer?" Lissa asked.

Finn shook his head. "He said his money's in cash and he's got to get out before he can get it to us."

"You're kidding me, right?" Kozlowski said. "Please tell me you're not actually stupid enough to believe that."

"He could be telling the truth," Finn said.

"No, he couldn't. And you know it. So what the hell is going on?"

"He's got a daughter."

"And?" Kozlowski asked. "If we've got a policy of doing charity work for anyone with a kid, I missed that in our marketing materials."

"She's fourteen. Devon didn't even know about her until last year. Her mother's a fuckup; she dropped the girl off with Devon and ditched. Now he's taking care of her. If he goes in, she gets put into the system. I'd like to prevent that if I can."

"Jesus, Finn," Lissa said. "You don't even know this girl, do you?"

"No, but I know the system. I lived in it for fifteen years. It's not a good place to be. If I can do something about it, I'd like to."

Kozlowski shook his head in disbelief. "So much so that you want to do this without getting paid?"

Finn looked at him. "Yeah, if necessary. What's the problem? You feeling poor? You're making twice what you were when you left the department. You afraid you won't be able to afford the summer clothing sale at Wal-Mart?" He glanced over at Lissa. "And I know you're not worried about the money."

"No, I'm not," she admitted. "As long as we don't make a habit out of it."

"Good," Finn said. "So we're all on board? We'll get him out on bail and do what we can do. We'll treat it as a pro bono matter, and if by some miracle he actually pays us—"

"Not gonna happen," Kozlowski said.

"Fine, but if it does, then it's like a windfall. You could even take your share and buy yourself a new suit. Maybe something made of natural fibers. It won't repel the rain the way rayon does, but you might like it anyways. So? Agreed?"

"Agreed," Lissa said.

"Fine, but I don't like it," Kozlowski mumbled.

"I don't know what you're bitching about. This is gonna be a lot harder on me than anyone else," Finn said.

"How so?"

Finn took a sip of his beer. "I told him I'd keep an eye on his daughter."

Lissa shouted loud enough to draw stares from those around her in the stands. "You told him what?"

"You heard me. I'm taking his daughter for a few days."

"Oh, this gets better and better," Koz grunted.

"What did you want me to do?" Finn asked.

Lissa rolled her eyes. "It's all making sense now. This is some kind of a fucked-up crusade for you, isn't it? That's why you want to take on the case. You think if you can keep her out of the system, it'll make up for how messed up you were when you were her age? When are you gonna learn? You're Devon's lawyer, not his family. It's not your responsibility."

"Of course it's not my responsibility, but it's a couple of days, tops. What's the big deal?"

"Have you ever dealt with a fourteen-year-old girl?" Lissa asked.

"Not since I was fifteen. Millie Donnolly. God she was cute."

"I was fourteen once," Lissa said. "I'm telling you that this is a big fuckin' mistake. Where is she now?"

"She's at Devon's apartment. Devon's girlfriend is there, but she's headed back to Providence today. I told Devon I'd pick her up after the game. He said he didn't have anyone else—he just got arrested last night."

"It's still a mistake to get involved with a client like this, Finn. You can represent them, but you can't fix their lives."

"I like to think of us as a full-service firm," Finn replied.

"You like to think of yourself as a savior."

"Right. Me and Jesus. Practically separated at birth. He had longer hair and a beard, of course, but—"

"And more patience. Trust me, you'll find that out after a few days with a fourteen-year-old girl." She took a long swig of her beer.

"After a few days or so, it'll be over. We'll get Devon out on bail, and we'll see where the case goes. If we can't cut a deal that keeps him out of jail long-term, he'll find someone else to take the girl."

"How do you know?"

"He gave me his word."

Kozlowski sighed. "*Great*. Who could worry once you have the word of a man in prison?"

———

Boston had taken an eight-to-one lead by the seventh inning, and the game was turning ugly. The sun broke through the cloud cover in the eighth, and jackets and sweatshirts came off around Fenway Park. In the bleachers, a group of beefy twentysomethings stripped to the waist, revealing their bloated bellies, painted bright red and blue, each with a letter to spell out "RED SOX." At one point the fourth young man in the chain was overcome by a morning of drinking and passed out in his seat, leaving his friends to advertise themselves as "RED OX." In fairness, Finn thought, they did more resemble bulls than ballplayers.

Finn, Kozlowski, and Lissa stayed through the last pitch, as did nearly every other fan in the stadium. Then they all filed out of the park together, spilling into the melee surrounding Fenway. The entire area reeked of stale beer and fried meat. The front windows of the bars and cafés were open, and young men and women, fully inebriated at two-thirty in the afternoon, leaned out from the jambs, laughing and screaming.

Finn frowned as he dodged a young man on Rollerblades be-bopping down the sidewalk, the paper bag ineffectively disguising the forty-ounce bottle of beer in his hand.

"I'm so fucking old," Finn said.

"Yes," Lissa agreed. "You are."

"What's that make me?" Kozlowski asked.

She laughed. "Sensitive, apparently. I try not to think about what it makes you."

"Seriously," Finn said. "When did this happen? When did I become the guy who thinks kids play their music too loud and don't respect their elders?"

"It happens to all of us eventually," Kozlowski said.

"Really? When did it happen to you?"

"When I was nine."

"Right."

"We could stop inside Sonsie for a drink," Lissa suggested. "It's a little bit of an older crowd in there. Very cosmopolitan and chic. Maybe it'll make you feel better."

Finn shook his head. "I don't think so. I have to go pick up Devon's daughter. Besides, I'm not wearing enough black to get into a place like Sonsie."

"Suit yourself." She looked at Kozlowski. "How about you, old man? You want to take me to Sonsie for a drink?"

"I don't own any black."

"Fake it. If you're nice to me, you might even get lucky later."

"It's not luck."

"Trust me, old man, sometimes it's luck."

Finn cleared his throat. "On that note . . ." Finn gave them an abbreviated wave and peeled off onto Commonwealth Avenue, following the marathon course, heading back to his car.

He hadn't enjoyed the game. He was nervous about the prospect of taking Devon's daughter in, even for a short time. Lissa was right, he had no experience with children at all, much less with fourteen-year-old girls. He'd been raised as an orphan, though, shuttled from foster family to Catholic orphanage to state-run facility back to foster family, so he knew what that kind of life was like. He'd grown up quickly and hit the streets by the time he was fifteen. Crazy as it seemed, he felt he had a responsibility to at least try to help Devon to keep his daughter out of that life.

He opened the door to his car, slid into the front seat, and pulled out the address Devon had given him. How bad could it be? After all, it was only for a couple of days.

———————

Liam Kilbranish sat at the kitchen table in the weather-beaten cape-house two blocks from the water in Quincy. An RPB MAC 11 .380 submachine gun with a detachable suppressor was disassembled and lay in pieces on the table in front of him, each component individually cleaned and oiled. A .223-caliber AR-15 semiautomatic rifle leaned against the kitchen wall, and the nine-millimeter SP-21 Barak semi-automatic pistol was breached and two full clips were lying next to it. An eight-inch knife lay next to its ankle sheath, gleaming under the flickering bare bulb of the overhead light.

Sean Broadark was on the sofa in the living area, which was sep-arated from the tiny house's kitchen only by a countertop. He was flipping channels disinterestedly on the tiny twelve-inch television. He was an unattractive specimen. His face was cragged with pits and moles, and he was balding in an unusual pattern that left an island of graying red at the crown. He had a paunch that evidenced the kind of personal neglect Liam deplored. In all other respects, though, he was a model soldier: more dedicated to the cause and to the command structure than he was to his own life. A patchy beard was beginning to take root on the man's pockmarked face, like weeds growing through the cracks in a dilapidated sidewalk. He looked to Liam like one of God's unfinished works—the sketch of a monster the Almighty had never come back to.

"He didn't know anything," Sean said from his perch. It was the first time he'd spoken in nearly a day.

"So it would seem," Liam replied.

"He'd have talked if he knew anything. No one could take what he took without talking if he had anything to say."

Liam said nothing.

"You said he would know. You said he would have the answer."

"Aye. I did," Liam conceded.

"You were wrong."

Liam picked up the Barak and slid one of the magazines into the pistol grip, pulling back on the release to chamber a round. He held the gun loosely. "Aye, I was."

Broadark seemed unfazed. He'd seen enough violence in his lifetime that attempts to intimidate him were useless, and Liam knew it. "So, what now?" was all he said.

"There are two more," Liam replied. "We find them and make them talk."

"How do you know they'll have something to say?"

It was a question that had gnawed at Liam since they had set out from Belfast a week before. It was a question his superiors—those few who had approved of his mission—had asked him as well. *How do you know?* And to that, there was only one answer: *Someone has to know.* It was the only answer that would keep alive everything for which he had fought a lifetime; the only answer that would allow him to live up to a promise he had made silently to his father more than three decades earlier.

"They'll have something to say," Liam replied.

Broadark never turned. His eyes remained on the television as the stations flashed aimlessly by, one after another. "That's what you said about Murphy," he said simply.

Chapter Five

Devon's apartment was in a section of Southie that had as yet escaped the onslaught of gentrification eating away at the area year after year. It was the first floor of a clapboard double-decker in desperate need of a paint job. Finn felt like he was getting lead poisoning just looking at the chunks of paint chips collecting in the corners of the front landing. As he looked around the place, any thought that Devon would make good on his promise of payment slipped away.

The woman who opened the door was probably in her early thirties, but extra mileage was evident in the lines in her face. She regarded Finn with an expression equal parts suspicion and annoyance.

"What the fuck do you want?" she demanded.

"I'm Finn," he replied stupidly.

"Congratulations," she sneered. "That don't answer the fuckin' question."

He blinked back at her, and for the first time it occurred to him that Devon might not have called ahead to let her know that he'd asked Finn to take care of his daughter.

"I'm Devon's lawyer," he began again. "He asked me to stop by."

The woman raised an angry hand to her brow and wiped a wisp of dyed-blonde hair from her eyes. "What's he done now?" Her posture hadn't softened and her tone carried no greater civility.

"He's in jail."

She put a hand on her jutting hip. "Motherfucker," she said. "That figures. *Come on up and we can have a few laughs*, he said. Only he doesn't mention that his daughter's staying with him, or that he's gonna take off and I was gonna spend a couple days taking care of the goddamned little brat."

A small girl with ragged-cut straight black hair topping a furrowed brow appeared in the narrow space between the woman's arm and the doorjamb. She wore a sweatshirt two sizes too big, with the words "What are you lookin' at?" emblazoned across the chest.

"Who is it?" the girl asked.

The woman turned sharply. "I thought I told you to watch TV."

The girl ignored the woman and evaluated Finn with clear, intelligent eyes sharp enough to drill through bedrock.

"You must be Devon's daughter," Finn said. He recognized that his voice was patronizing, as if he were talking to a three-year-old. He winced.

The girl nodded. "The little brat," she said.

"Get back inside," the woman ordered.

The girl looked at the woman with contempt. Then she backed away and disappeared.

"You shouldn't eavesdrop, you little shit!" the woman called after her. She looked back at Finn. "Kids today . . . no fuckin' manners." She let out an exasperated sigh. "Look, I'm not even *with* Devon," she said. "Not really. Not like that. And he knows I've got a sick ma down in Providence I gotta take care of. I don't need this shit. You tell him he'd better find someone else to take care of Little Miss Sunshine, and damned fuckin' quick. Otherwise, she's gonna be out on the fuckin' street."

Finn nodded. "That's why I'm here. He asked me to look after her for a couple of days."

She looked at him as though seeing him for the first time, then let out a bitter laugh. "You?"

"Me." He tried to put some conviction in his voice, but he was pretty sure he'd failed.

She shook her head angrily. "Fine. Don't that just take the fuckin' cake? I come all the way up here for a little time with him, and the cocksucker don't even trust me with his kid."

"I thought you said—"

"Fine." She wasn't listening. "That's fine. You takin' her with you now?"

"I don't know," Finn said. "I guess."

"You guess? Great. Just fuckin' great." She stamped her foot and turned, slamming the door behind her. "I'll send her out in a couple minutes!" she yelled through the glass.

Finn was tempted to leave. It was difficult to believe that anything good could come from this, but he'd given his word. Besides, he worried about what might become of Devon's daughter if left with someone as unstable as the woman Devon had apparently conned up from Providence to watch her while he was off committing grand theft. He had no choice, he knew, so he waited on the front stoop, shifting his feet back and forth.

It would be all right, he told himself. Devon would be out in a few days, and then this was no longer his problem.

"I'm Finn," he said to her at last.

The girl looked over at him. She hadn't spoken since she'd walked out of Devon's apartment, an oversized military duffel slung over her back and a look of defiance on her face. She'd marched past Finn straight to his little MG, thrown her bag in the back, climbed in, and slammed the car door, staring forward without asking any questions.

Finn had turned on the stoop and started to follow, then paused and looked back at the woman standing in the doorway.

"Don't worry," the woman said, reading his mind. "I'm on a six o'clock train, and there ain't a goddamned thing in the fuckin' place worth stealing."

Finn thought about it for a moment and then continued on, sliding into the driver's seat beside the young girl.

The woman cracked the screen door a little and leaned out over the stoop. "You give that bastard a message for me!" she yelled. "Tell him not to call me again. Ever! Tell him he can go to hell. Tell him that from Shelly!"

Finn put his hand up and gave her a grim wave, then threw the car into gear and pulled out.

The traffic was heavy as he guided the car through Southie and into downtown Boston, headed back to his apartment in Charlestown. It had taken ten minutes for him to muster the courage to say anything to the girl in the passenger seat next to him, and then all he could think to do was introduce himself. He could feel her staring at him, saying nothing in reply, and it made him shift uncomfortably in his seat. His agony was made whole by the fact that he couldn't remember whether Devon had told him the girl's name. If he had, Finn couldn't remember what it was.

She continued to stare at him in silence.

"And you are . . . ?" he prodded at last, striving unsuccessfully to infuse his voice with some small amount of humor.

After a moment she looked forward through the windshield again. "Fucked, by the look of things," she answered.

Finn winced at her language and the venom in her voice. "No, I meant your name," he said.

"I know what you meant." She lapsed into silence again.

"I know this is hard," Finn said. "It's only for a few days, though. Until your father gets . . ." He wasn't sure how to continue. "Until he gets back. Did she explain it to you?"

"Shelly? Yeah. Devon's in jail. You're his lawyer. I'm fucked."

He took his eyes off the road for long enough to look at her. Devon had said she was fourteen, but she was small and slight for her age. Her bangs were cropped across her forehead and she wore a stack of cheap metal bracelets around her wrist that jangled as the car crawled over bumps in the road. She looked like a normal kid, but she had the speech patterns and attitude of someone much older.

"Yeah, that's right," he said. "Basically. Except for the fucked part. Like I said, it's only for a few days."

"What's he in for?"

Finn glanced at her. "Robbery."

"No shit, Sherlock, that's what he does. What'd he steal?"

"Clothes." He didn't mention the panties. He considered telling her not to swear, but figured it wasn't his responsibility.

"Clothes?" she asked. "What, is he down to shoplifting? Is that even a felony?"

"They were really expensive clothes," Finn replied.

"So definitely in felony territory," she deduced. It occurred to Finn that no fourteen-year-old should be so well schooled in the specifics of criminal practice. "Well then, you must be a pretty good lawyer if you think you're going to get him out of it. He's been in before, so it's not like a judge is gonna feel sorry for him. If you're doing anything other than collecting a fee, you must be a real genius." It was also remarkable how well she had mastered the subtleties of sarcasm at such a young age.

"Why don't you let me worry about that," Finn said. "That's my job." Candidly, he agreed with her legal assessment, but he didn't mention that to her. "In any case, he'll be out on bail by Wednesday, Thursday latest, and the time will go faster if I know your name."

She twirled a finger angrily in her hair. "Sally," she said.

"Sally," he repeated. "Really? Sally Malley?"

"What can I say? My mom has a quirky sense of humor."

"That's a good thing, I guess."

"And a wicked bad crack habit."

He let that sink in for a moment, and once it had he realized there was nowhere to go with it. "It's a good name," he said instead. "*Sally Malley.*" He tried saying it with some amount of reverence, but the damage was done. She stayed silent. "Say, I know a good ice cream place," he said after a moment. "You want to grab some ice cream on the way back to my apartment?"

"So, I'm guessing you don't have any kids of your own, Finn?"

He could feel his teeth grinding. "It shows?"

"Only when you talk."

"I'm still young," he said. "Maybe someday."

"I wouldn't bother. Kids are nothing but a hassle. I remember the day my mother dropped me with Devon. The look on his face was priceless. He didn't even know I existed before that moment."

"That must have been strange."

"Let's just say that 'surprised' doesn't begin to describe it. That was a year ago, and we haven't seen my mother since. Devon does the best he can, but he's not exactly cut out for the father scene."

"Seriously, it's really good ice cream," Finn said after a moment. He threw a look at her and thought he could detect a smile tug for just a moment at the corner of her mouth. Then it was gone.

"Okay," she said. "Ice cream would be okay. But it better be good goddamned ice cream."

"Trust me."

She turned her head to look out the passenger window, away from Finn. "Right. Trust you," she said quietly. Finn could tell she'd heard those words before.

It was a nice house, at least. Sally tossed her duffel onto the bed in the guest room. Much better than the dives and flophouses where she'd often found herself in the past when her mother was bingeing. Still, no matter how nice the surroundings, she was fending for herself again, and that meant she had to keep her guard up. If life had taught her anything it was that you had to look after yourself, because no one else would.

She reached out and put her hand on the bottom of the duffel bag, feeling around for the familiar lump. She hadn't taken the stuffed bear out of the bag in over a year; she was too old for stuffed animals. It was a gift from her mother on her fifth birthday, though—one of the few birthdays her mother had remembered—and she couldn't bring herself to throw it out. She kept it buried at the bottom of her bag, rubbing it through the canvas only when she really needed to, but never taking it out to be seen. It seemed a reasonable compromise. She lived her life based on suspicion and compromise.

"You okay in there?"

The voice belonged to Devon's lawyer—her benefactor, for the moment. He seemed like a decent sort, at least on first impression. But she knew that first impressions could be misleading. She'd been around men enough to know to be careful. She was small for her age; that played to her advantage. She dressed in loose T-shirts and baggy pants. Better not to draw attention; attention could be dangerous. In a just and reasonable world, her youth alone would have been sufficient protection from unwanted advances, but she had learned that the world was neither just nor reasonable.

She'd been ten the first time one of her mother's "boyfriends" tried something. He and her mother had been out for most of the night and her mother had passed out cold upon their return to the apartment. Frustrated, angry, and high, he had come into Sally's room and stood over her bed. She'd been petrified as she lay there, pretending to be asleep, praying that he would go away. He hadn't, though. She heard him pulling his clothes off. Shirt first; then pants; finally his underwear. He stood there a few moments longer, staring at her, before he pulled up the blanket and climbed into bed with her. She could smell the booze on his breath and oozing from his pores as he inched toward her. When he put out his hand and pulled her toward him, she hadn't fought. She rolled over toward him and opened her eyes. His pupils were wide and glassy, and a serpentine smile crept across his face as he looked at her. Then he reached for her again and she closed her eyes and kicked out with all the force she could muster, her shin driving home between his legs.

He screamed and she ran into the bathroom where her mother lay unconscious with her head against the sweating base of the porcelain toilet. She locked the door and curled up beside her mother as the boyfriend, wounded both in body and in ego, beat on the door and screamed curses at them both. The next morning, after Sally told her mother what had happened, the boyfriend was sent away. Her mother cried for days and begged forgiveness from Sally, promising that she'd gotten high for the last time. She was convincing enough that Sally even believed her, giving in to a flicker of hope.

A week later her mother came home, stoned again, with another man. That was when Sally realized fully for the first time that no one would ever really protect her. After that, she learned how to protect herself at all costs, and few people messed with her more than once.

The knock on the door came again. "Everything okay in there?" the lawyer called once more, an edge of concern in the voice.

"Fine," she responded. She was wearing a T-shirt and sweatpants that doubled as pajamas.

"Can I open the door?" he asked.

"It's your door."

The door slid open slowly and every muscle in her body went tight, the fight-or-flight response well conditioned. He looked nervous as he stuck his head in the room, keeping his feet in the hallway. He stood there for a moment, leaning awkwardly. "I have a TV," he finally offered.

"Cutting-edge," she replied.

"I don't watch it much, but you're welcome to watch whatever you want."

She shook her head. "I'm tired. I'm going to bed."

He nodded. "Do you have everything you need? You want a glass of water or something?"

She shook her head again.

"Okay. If you need anything, give a shout." He looked at her again for another moment, as if waiting for a response. Then, clearly realizing that the conversation was over, he pulled his head back and closed the door.

She waited a couple of seconds before she got up and walked quietly over to the door, pushing in the small round button on the knob until she heard the lock engage. It wouldn't keep him out if he was determined to get in, but it might buy her a little time if necessary.

She walked back over to the bed, shaking the blanket out of its folds and pulling it over her. She didn't sleep under covers—they made her feel trapped.

She turned off the light and lay back, staring up at the ceiling, running through all her options in her head. It didn't take long for her to conclude that she didn't have any.

Chapter Six

Devon Malley lay on the cot in his cell. It had been two decades since he'd spent real time in jail, but the rhythms came back to him quickly. In some ways, they'd never left him. There was a certain comfort to it all. There were few decisions to make in jail. They told you when to get up, when to eat, when to shower, when to shit. If you knew how to protect yourself, it was a simple existence. The trick was keeping your sanity.

Prison was the safest place for him now. He wasn't one of those saps who couldn't survive on the outside—he valued his freedom. But the streets held dangers over which he had no control. In jail, he could keep his back to the wall and his mouth shut. That would be enough to keep him alive. In the meantime, he had Finn on the outside, looking into things for him. It would only be a few days, and then he'd know for sure what he was facing. He could handle the jail time until then.

The only thing he missed from the outside was Sally. When her mother had brought her to his apartment over a year ago, Devon nearly panicked. He couldn't imagine living his lifestyle with a kid hanging around. He'd hated the idea. But after a while, he came to see that she was smart and tough—everything he would have hoped for her to be. He took pride in that; pride in her. Were it not for the fact that he missed her now, jail would be a breeze. Still, he knew he had no choice. It was better for her, too.

As he lay there, the sounds of the jail filled his ears. Those around him rustled in their cages. Some slept soundly, snoring or talking through their dreams. Others were grunting openly as they relieved their sexual frustrations. There was no etiquette about that in jail— men did what they had to do. He didn't mind. The only sound that haunted him was the crying. There was always one, a first-timer usually, new to the system. Sometimes it was on their first night; other times they managed to hold themselves together until after there was a trial and a verdict—or a plea bargain that sealed the fate just as tightly—and all hope was destroyed. Then the fear and the pain seeped out in low sobs. It made Devon's skin crawl. The criers would be taught a lesson the next day; the other prisoners would see to that. For now, though, the dismal sound had to be endured.

Devon did everything he could to block it out. He hummed softly to himself, he focused on the ceiling, he thought about the women he'd slept with in the past. Nothing worked. The sobbing cut through everything else. It wasn't until he lost himself in memory that it disappeared.

Devon got the call in February, in the dead of winter, years before. It was Murphy. "We've got a job for you, Devon," he said.

"What sort of a job?" Devon asked.

"Your sort. Meet me at the Body Shop tomorrow morning at ten." Devon asked no more questions. Murphy wasn't the type to be questioned. Devon showed up the next morning fifteen minutes early.

There were four of them in the room, not including himself. Devon had worked for Murphy and Ballick before. They were sitting on chairs against the wall. The third he'd never seen before: a thin man with jet-black hair and dark, angry eyes sitting in front of Murphy's desk. At the desk on that day was a fit man in his early sixties with silver-

white hair pulled back from the crown. He was leaning back in the chair, but had an aggressive energy about him, as if he was coiled and ready to attack.

"Devon, this is Jimmy Bulger," Murphy said.

It was an unnecessary introduction; everyone knew Bulger. Many knew him better as "Whitey," though he hated the nickname. It had been given to him as a boy with bright blond hair. Those who valued their lives at all called him Jimmy. Those who valued their lives more called him Mr. Bulger.

Devon nodded. "Mr. Bulger," he said.

"Vinny tells me you been doin' good work for him. That right?"

"Vinny doesn't lie." It was a stupid thing to say and he was smiling when he said it, which was a mistake. Bulger didn't like people smiling unless he told them to.

Bulger's eyes went dead. He looked as if he was going to put a knife in Devon's heart. "Wipe that fuckin' smile off your face or I'll cut your fuckin' lips off and stick 'em up your ass," he said. "I didn't ask you if Vinny lies; I already know Vinny fuckin' lies. I know he lies, because I tell him to lie. I asked you if you do good fuckin' work."

"Yeah," Devon said. He tried to sound as if he weren't scared, but he wasn't smiling anymore. "Yeah, I do."

Bulger looked at him for a little while. Then he turned to the man Devon didn't recognize. "This is a friend from Belfast. The two of you are gonna do a job together. You piss him off, and I'm gonna fuckin' hear about it. Okay?"

"Yeah," Devon said. "Okay."

Bulger looked at the Irish guy. "Okay?"

The man stood up and walked over to Devon, stood right in his face, so their noses were almost touching. Devon was taller, but the man had a crazy look to him—not the manic, uncontrolled crazy that so many in the game had, but a quiet crazy; a dangerous crazy. He was wiry in the way Devon didn't mess with. "Is he Irish?" the man asked Bulger in a thick accent.

"Born and raised in Southie," Bulger said. "Makes him more of a fuckin' mick than you." Murphy and Ballick laughed at that. Everyone laughed at Bulger's jokes.

The Irish guy didn't laugh. He just looked at Devon. Finally he said, "Okay."

"I expect you to do good work for me," Bulger said to Devon. "You think you can do that? Keep doin' good work? 'Cause if not . . ." Bulger's voice trailed off.

"I can do good work, Mr. Bulger," Devon said. "What place we talkin' about?"

"We'll come to that, don't worry," Bulger said.

"Okay." Devon looked at the Irish guy, his new partner. "You got a name?"

"No names," the man replied.

Devon looked at Murphy. "What am I supposed to call him, he doesn't got a name?"

"Who the fuck cares," Bulger said. "Call him 'Irish' for all it fuckin' matters."

Devon looked at the guy. "That work for you?"

The man said nothing.

"Good," Bulger said. "Irish it is." Everyone just sat there, saying nothing. "Understand your role in this," Bulger said after a moment. "Your job is to get Irish here into the place. That's it, got it?"

"What place?"

"Don't you get fuckin' smart with me!" Bulger screamed. For a moment, Devon thought he was dead. Then Bulger cleared his throat and calmed down. "You get this done, and I'll take care of you. You fuck this up, and I'll only see you once again. You understand?"

"Yeah, Mr. Bulger, I understand."

Bulger looked at Devon as if he were something to be scraped off his shoe. Then he gave a carnivorous smile; the kind of a smile that shows more teeth than necessary. "Call me Jimmy," he said.

Chapter Seven

"Don't mess with me."

Those were the first words Lissa Krantz spoke to Sally Malley. Finn brought Sally into the office at seven-thirty the next morning. He, Koz, and Lissa were all early risers, and the office was usually busy for a couple of hours before most lawyers at other firms got to their desks. Lissa was already sitting at her computer when Finn ushered the bleary-eyed girl through the front door.

"I have to drive her to school over in Southie," Finn said by way of greeting. "I figured Koz and I could head over and talk to Vinny Murphy, as long as I was going in that direction anyway." He looked down at the girl as though he'd forgotten for a moment that she was still with him. "This is Sally," he said. "Sally, this is Lissa."

Lissa nodded.

Sally said nothing, plopped down in one of the uncomfortable chairs against the wall. The tiny firm was thriving financially, but Finn hadn't yet plowed any of his profits back into the office décor. An architect had drawn up ambitious plans, but Finn hadn't had time to follow through. The office still consisted of one large open space where both Finn and Lissa had desks. Kozlowski's office was in the back.

"Koz in?" Finn asked.

"His office," Lissa responded.

"I'll be right back."

Lissa wasn't sure whether Finn was speaking to her or the girl. In either case, he disappeared into the back without another word. Lissa looked over at Sally. She wore thick black work boots, a black skirt over leggings and an oversized sweatshirt. Nothing about her demeanor or her wardrobe invited interaction. She was looking back at Lissa, scowling slightly. Neither of them said anything for a few moments; they just stared at each other, seeing who would crack first. In the end, it was the girl.

"You're pretty," she said to Lissa. "Is that how you got the job, or can you type, too?"

"Don't mess with me," Lissa replied.

"You're tough, then?" Sally asked.

"Only compared to some. And only when pushed."

The girl said nothing.

"I'm sorry about your father," Lissa said.

"Why? He's not dead."

"I know."

"So, why are you sorry?"

Lissa considered the girl and the question in equal measure. She liked both, she decided. They both seemed brutally honest—a quality, in Lissa's experience, that was hard to come by. "I don't know," Lissa said. "I guess I was just assuming his arrest might be hard on you. I was trying to offer some sympathy. You can take it if you want. Or not. Up to you."

"You gonna tell me it's all gonna be all right now?"

"No."

"Good. I hate it when people say shit like that."

"So do I."

They lapsed into silence again, the girl slouching down deep into the chair, her brow furrowed, looking stymied by Lissa's refusal to play the traditional establishment role of coddling adult.

"So, what do you do around here?" Sally asked after a moment.

"I'm a lawyer," Lissa replied. "I work with Finn."

"Really?" The girl seemed both impressed and skeptical.

"Yeah, really."

Finn and Kozlowski came in from the back room. Lissa was amused by Sally's reaction to seeing Kozlowski for the first time. His size was imposing, and while his features hinted at a time when he might have been handsome, the long, deep scar on the side of his face gave him a distinctly menacing appearance.

"Sally, this is Tom Kozlowski," Finn said.

She sat up a little straighter but didn't respond, trying to dispel any impression that she was intimidated. Lissa could tell it was an act, though. Kozlowski said nothing.

"Right," Finn said. "We have to drop you off at school, and then Mr. Kozlowski and I have some business we have to deal with together. My car's a little small for the three of us, so I figure we can take Koz's car."

Lissa could see the girl go a shade paler at the thought of riding with Kozlowski. She stood. "You two have a lot to deal with today. I have a doctor's appointment later, but other than that I'm not that busy, so why don't I take Sally to school?" She wasn't sure who looked more relieved, the men or the girl.

"Really?" Finn said. "That'd be great. I want to get over to the Body Shop as early as possible."

"No problem," Lissa said. "You ready?" she asked Sally.

The girl got up and picked up her bag. She walked over to the door and looked back at Lissa. Lissa started toward the door, then turned and walked back to Kozlowski, lifting herself up on her toes and giving him a kiss that lasted longer than necessary. Kozlowski was taken by surprise, but she didn't care. She turned and walked past Sally, whose mouth was open wide enough to count teeth. "C'mon," she said. "Let's go." With that, Lissa opened the door and walked out, a broad, amused smile breaking over her face as Sally followed her out to the car.

Detective Stone crouched near the spot where Vinny Murphy's body had been found. He stared down at the rough outline traced around what had been left of the man before they poured it into a body bag, rolled it on a stretcher, loaded it into a van, and drove it to the morgue to be deposited in a refrigerated drawer. The autopsy had revealed little that wasn't apparent from a visual inspection. The injuries that preceded the fatal shot to the head had been inflicted carefully, to maximize pain while keeping Murphy alive and conscious.

It was still an hour before Stone's shift started at nine o'clock, and he'd already been at the Body Shop for half an hour, considering the entire scene in the glint of the morning. He wasn't entirely sure why he was there. It was unlikely that the teams of forensic specialists that had been there the day before had missed anything. And yet there he was, squatting by the dark stain that was the last impression Murphy would leave on the world.

It was because he wanted to gain Sanchez's approval, he recognized. There was no getting around it. He hoped to gain some additional insight he might share with Sanchez at the start of their shift to earn her respect. It was foolish, probably. He was a damned good cop, and if she couldn't see that already, she would likely not be convinced. They had gone back to the station house the previous day and she had gotten on her computer and tapped away at the keyboard for more than an hour. He'd asked twice what she was researching, but she hadn't responded. He could see why she lost partners.

He stood up, taking one last look around the garage before walking back out to the parking lot. As he approached his car, a tiny, battered convertible pulled into the driveway, rolling over the line of yellow police tape Stone had left on the ground.

Stone waved his arms and yelled, "You can't come in here! This is a police investigation scene!" Ultimately it mattered little—the forensics team had swept the entire property for anything that might be helpful to them. They had taken plaster molds of tire tracks and sifted through the dirt of the driveway for anything they could find, like archeologists on a dig, bagging and tagging every cigarette butt and every piece of trash. Nevertheless, Stone had no intention of letting civilians into the crime scene area while the investigation was continued. It would open the door for a defense lawyer to argue that the evidence was tainted if they ever caught the bastards. He waved his arms again as he pulled out his badge and held it up for the driver to see.

The car pulled to a stop, but didn't turn around. Instead, both doors opened and two men got out. Stone squared his shoulders, drawing on the authority of indignation. He slowed, though, as the bigger of the two men pulled himself from the low-slung passenger seat and looked at him. Stone recognized the man instantly.

"Jesus," Stone said. "Kozlowski. You'll get yourself shot, pulling into a crime scene like that, y'know? You're not a cop anymore, in case you'd forgotten."

"Maybe if they'd put a real cop in charge here it wouldn't be such a problem," Kozlowski replied. "Maybe someone who wasn't a rookie, and who'd know to put the tape back up in front of the driveway."

"Been a while since I was a rookie. Been a while since I saw you."

"No shit? I'm old; time moves faster for me," Kozlowski said. He looked Stone up and down. "I'd heard they put you in civies full time," he acknowledged. "Vice?"

Stone shook his head. "Homicide."

"No shit, again. A real job? I guess they'll take anyone these days, then, huh?"

"They have to. We used to have a bunch of old guys who fucked things up pretty bad."

"I never fucked up a case in my life," Kozlowski growled.

"No, you never did," Stone admitted. "You just pissed off the wrong people in the department." He moved forward and put out his hand. "How you been?"

Kozlowski shook the hand. "Getting by."

"Good to hear."

"You remember Scott Finn, right?"

Stone regarded the second man. "From the Caldwell case, right? Hard to forget." Neither of them offered his hand. "I heard Koz was working with you now. Hard to believe. If I remember right, he had you pegged as a murderer a few years ago."

"I was wrong," Kozlowski said.

"He also had you pegged as an asshole," Stone said.

"So, he was partially wrong," Finn replied.

Stone turned back to Kozlowski. "What are you doing out here?"

"We need to talk to Vinny Murphy," Kozlowski replied. "I take it he's not around?"

"That's an understatement."

Kozlowski exchanged a look with Finn. "How so?" he asked.

"I mean he's gone. Really gone."

"Arrested?" Finn asked.

Stone shook his head. "That'd be an upgrade. He was murdered. You read the papers?"

Finn shook his head. "I had a busy morning. I haven't had the chance." He looked at Kozlowski, who just shrugged. "What happened?" he asked Stone.

"Pretty nasty. We're not sure exactly yet."

"When?"

"Saturday night. Maybe early Sunday morning."

"Any leads?" Kozlowski asked. He still sounded like a cop.

"Not that I can talk about," Stone said.

"Anything you can tell us?" Finn asked.

Stone hesitated. Kozlowski had been one of the best detectives in the department; his insight might be useful. Stone wasn't going to give up any information without getting something in return, though. "Why don't you tell me why you're here first."

The two men looked at each other. "We can't," Finn replied.

"No?"

Finn shook his head.

"Well then, it looks like we're not going to be able to help each other."

Finn sighed. "We're here for a client. For information. That's all I can say."

"I could ask you to come down to the station to talk," Stone said. "This is a murder investigation."

"Wouldn't do you any good," Finn replied.

"No, probably not. But without more, this conversation isn't gonna go anyplace."

Finn put his hands in his pockets, but Kozlowski spoke up. "Devon Malley was picked up Sunday night for a robbery." Finn's head spun toward the private detective, but Kozlowski waved him off. "Rumor had it that Murphy might know something about the crime. We were just out looking to see what we could find out."

"Koz—" Finn protested, but Stone cut him off.

"Don't worry," Stone said. "I know Devon. He's got nothing to do with this."

"What makes you say that?" Finn asked.

"Devon's a thief, not a murderer. Right circumstances, he might be able to push a button on a guy—maybe even pull the trigger himself if he was scared enough. But that's as far as he'd go. He wouldn't be a part of what went down here. He's not the brutal type, and this was brutal."

66

"How so?" Kozlowski asked.

"Vinny was worked over before he was killed. Whoever did it knew what they were doing. Lots of pain, but nothing that would kill until the final shot. Very fucked up. They used chains, they broke bones. They did stuff to him you only read about."

Finn frowned. "Why?"

"That's the question." Stone looked at Kozlowski. "You got any thoughts?"

Kozlowski shrugged. "I don't know enough about the man's business to tell. He chose a livelihood that makes this sort of thing a risk."

"True," Stone said. "But this doesn't seem like just a turf war. There's something more. Something I can't figure out. They didn't do anything to conceal the body or make it difficult to identify him. They left him in a heap in his place of business. There's only one reason to do that."

"They wanted to send a message," Kozlowski said.

"That's the only thing I can come up with," Stone agreed. "But to who?" He thought about the message written in blood, but decided it would be disclosing too much.

"That's your problem, not mine," Kozlowski said. "I don't get paid by the city anymore."

"We should go," Finn said. There was an edge in his voice.

Kozlowski put his hand out first this time. "If I hear anything on the street, I'll pass it on if I can," he said.

Stone shook his hand. "I'd appreciate anything I can get."

Finn was already heading back toward his car, and Kozlowski followed him. He walked around to the passenger side and opened the door. As he started to lean down to get in, he looked over the soft top and spoke again. "Stone," he said.

"Yeah?"

"The civies look good on you, but it's not the clothes that make the cop."

"You taught me that one already."

"Doesn't mean it's not still true."

———⬦———

Finn started the car, whipped it around in a mangled three-point turn, and pulled out into the street. He didn't say anything until Stone had faded from the rearview mirror. "What do you think?" he asked then.

"Bad luck for Murphy," Kozlowski replied. "Bad luck for Devon, too."

"Anything else?"

Kozlowski sighed. "You mean, do I think this has anything to do with Devon?" It took him a moment to answer. "I don't see how. Even if Murphy set Devon up and dropped a dime on him for some reason, Devon hadn't been picked up by the cops yet when Murphy's ticket got punched, so he wouldn't have known to be pissed yet. Where's the motive? Plus, the level of violence doesn't fit. Stone's right about that, it wouldn't be Devon's style, even if he wanted to kill the man. He's not a psychopath."

"I don't disagree," Finn said. "We're still shit outta luck with no place to go."

"Murphy definitely isn't going to be of any help at this point."

"Clearly not." Finn blew out a long breath as the lines of Southie's row houses flashed by, each corner dividing one block from the next with identical pizza parlors, pubs, and liquor stores. "Sounds like he went out in a bad way."

"Unlike all those good ways to go out? He played the game. He had it coming."

"Maybe. I knew him. He wasn't all bad."

"Right. Hitler liked dogs and kids. I'm still not gonna shed any tears for him."

The scenes kept rolling by, and as they passed a bodega on West

Broadway, Finn spotted three young Irish-looking men tumbling loudly out the door, slapping each other on the back, laughing. They wore jeans and sweatshirts, and they pulled out cigarettes in unison. Construction workers, Finn thought, on their way to the work site, a little late for the job but without any real care in the world. Or boyos, back from a night of mischief, stopping off for a quick bacon-and-egg sandwich before heading back to their apartments to sleep for the first time in days. There was no way to tell the difference from the driver's seat of Finn's car.

"Coulda been me," Finn said. "I was in the game."

"You were a kid," Kozlowski said, waving his hand. "Besides, you got out."

"I got lucky."

"That's not luck. Not in this world."

"A lot of it's luck. I think about the people I ran with; the stuff we did. Then I think about what I do now. I'm not sure there's a difference in the end."

"There's a world of difference."

"Is there?"

Kozlowski looked at him and shook his head. "Goddamned Irish. Angst-ridden to the core, every last one of you. Why the hell is that?"

"The Irish are cursed with brains. You're Polish, you wouldn't understand."

"Maybe not. So, what now?"

Finn shrugged. "I guess I'll drop you off at the office and head over to Nashua Street to see Devon. Maybe there's someone else who can give us some information."

"Sounds good."

Neither of them spoke for a while. Then Kozlowski said, "You're gonna pay for the Polish crack. You know that, right?"

Finn smiled. "I figured. I couldn't resist."

Chapter Eight

"So, are you, like, dating that guy?"

Sally's elbows were on the dented metal table, a fried-egg-and-bacon sandwich hanging from her fingers. As Lissa suspected, Finn hadn't fed the girl any breakfast. There was a diner near the office, and still almost an hour before Sally had to be at school.

"Which guy?" Lissa asked, sipping her coffee, feigning ignorance.

"The guy you kissed. The guy with the fucked-up face."

"You shouldn't swear."

"Why not?"

"Because I'm buying you breakfast."

"Everybody swears."

"Not at breakfast."

Sally took a huge bite of her sandwich and yolk dripped down her chin, splattering on the table. She didn't seem to notice. "So, are you dating him?" Her mouth was full and more yolk trickled down her face.

Lissa pulled a napkin from the dispenser on the table next to the ketchup bottle and put it on the table in front of Sally. The girl picked up the napkin and moved it over next to her plate, careful to keep it as far away as possible from both the egg on the table and the egg on her face. "That's a personal question," Lissa said.

"Not really," Sally argued. "If I asked you when was the last time you guys had sex, or what he was like in bed, that would be a personal question. All I asked was whether or not you were dating."

Lissa took another napkin from the dispenser and reached over toward Sally, moving the girl's plate so that she could mop up the egg on the table. She was tempted to go after the girl's face, but thought better of it. "Are you sure you're only fourteen?"

"Half the girls in school are pregnant," Sally said. "It's not like I don't know about sex. You want to ask me anything?" She looked up at Lissa through her uneven, razor-cut bangs, a challenge in her eyes.

"Yeah," Lissa said. "I'm dating him."

The girl kept looking at her, as if deciding whether to believe her. Finally she lowered her eyes to her sandwich and took another bite. "Cool."

"So, how long have you lived with your father?" Lissa changed the subject.

"A year," Sally replied. "Maybe a little less. My mom split. Couldn't handle the pressure anymore."

"That must have been hard."

Sally shrugged. "I don't know why she waited so long. I mean, why bother putting up with the first thirteen years if she wasn't going to stick it out, you know? It's like she waited around for long enough to see what I turned out like, and then took off when she didn't like what she saw. Pretty fucked up, huh?"

Lissa nodded. "It's not as unusual as you think, though. And you seem smart enough to know that it had nothing to do with you."

"Did your parents take off, too?" The look in the girl's eyes resembled hope.

"Not officially. They didn't need to. They ignored me instead."

"That's like Devon—my father. He lets me stay with him, but

that's about it. He can't seem to really figure out the whole *dad* thing, y'know?"

"Do you have any aunts or uncles—grandparents, maybe?" Lissa asked.

"Nope. It's just the nuclear family for me. As in meltdown."

Lissa stared at her coffee. "So," she began carefully, "if your dad ends up going away for some amount of time, do you know where you'll stay?"

The girl attacked what was left of her sandwich. "Not really. I'll figure out something, though. I've been getting by more or less on my own for a while now."

She shoveled the last of the yellow-stained English muffin into her mouth. Lissa tried to think of something to say, but nothing came to her. She opened her mouth and took a breath, but no sound came out. She went to try again and Sally looked up at her. For a moment the air between them was charged with expectation, and then the moment was over. Sally picked up the napkin and wiped her chin. "It's getting late," she said. "I gotta get to school."

"Murphy's dead."

Finn delivered the news to Devon as soon as he was alone with him inside the tiny visiting room at the Nashua Street Jail.

"Dead?" Devon seemed shocked, and Finn could read nothing from his reaction. "How? When?"

"Murdered. At the Body Shop, looks like on Saturday night. Ugly stuff, too. He was beaten beyond recognition from what they say. Then shot in the head."

Devon hadn't even had time to sit. Now he slid slowly into the tiny chair in front of Finn. "Jesus," he said. He rubbed a hand across his face. "Do they know who did it?"

Finn shook his head. "If they do, the cops aren't sharing. Not yet, at least."

"No, I guess they wouldn't, would they."

"Devon, I need to know if this has anything to do with your case."

"Are you asking if I killed him?"

"Not really. I just don't like surprises."

Finn would have expected Devon to be offended or defensive. He wasn't, though. He just sat there, impassive, his eyes focused on some imaginary point in the distance. "How could I have anything to do with it?" he asked at last. "He'd just given me a job to do. Why would I?"

"He'd just given you a job that landed you in here."

Devon shook his head. "That wasn't his fault."

"So you've told me," Finn said. "It all seems a little coincidental, though—you get busted and send me out to talk to Murphy, and now Murphy's dead."

Devon lost the thousand-yard stare and looked at Finn. "I had nothing to do with Murphy's murder, Finn," he said.

Finn kept looking at him for another few seconds. "Good enough." He sat down in the other chair in the room.

"What now?" Devon asked.

"I guess that's up to you. Murphy was the only lead you gave me. Is there anybody else?"

"Maybe," Devon said. "You're not gonna like it, though."

Finn frowned. "Who?"

"Eddie Ballick."

"The Fisherman? You're kidding, right?"

"Ballick was Murphy's boss. If anyone would know anything, it would be him."

"Maybe, but so what? What's Ballick gonna say to me that's gonna be useful? He's not gonna incriminate himself just to get you out."

Devon shook his head. "No. But maybe he'd give up someone else.

I been tryin' to figure out something to give the DA. I give them someone good enough, maybe I can cut a good deal. Maybe even stay outta the joint?"

"I guess that depends on who you could give them. I'm not sure they're gonna be interested in Ballick tossing them Murphy at this point. They'll probably feel like justice has already been served as far as he goes."

"What if we could give them someone more interesting?"

"It'd have to be someone pretty interesting. Who did you have in mind?"

"How about Johnny Gilberacci?"

Finn thought about it. "Play it out for me."

"I told you," Devon said, "it was an inside job. Johnny'd been boostin' shit from his own store—stealing from his partners—for almost a year, just to keep his legs in one piece. Even that was only enough to keep up with the vig. This job was gonna get him off the whole fuckin' nut. Murphy and his people were gonna take the merchandise to sell on the street, and the insurance was gonna be split down the middle."

"So what happens now?" Finn asked. "Given that the whole thing blew up?"

"With Murphy dead, who knows? There's gonna be a fight over his business, but a lotta shit falls through the cracks. Johnny might come out of this pretty good. In some ways, it's a pretty good motive for Johnny to kill Murphy, don't you think?"

Finn laughed. "Murphy wasn't killed with pinking shears, Devon. You really think Johnny Gilberacci did the kind of damage we're talking about to Vinny?"

Devon shook his head. "No, probably not. But we can still give him up on the burglary and insurance fraud, right? The murder angle is just a bonus that the cops might want to play with a little."

Finn let the notion percolate for a moment. "It's the kind of a case that DAs love," he admitted. "It's high-profile, and Johnny hasn't made many friends in the press, so it's not likely that he'll be seen as a sympathetic defendant. It could actually be the kind of a case that some ambitious prosecutor would jump at."

"That's what I figured. It could actually get me out of this in the long run."

Finn shook his head. "Don't get too far ahead of yourself. The DA's office would still want you to do some time, but it could reduce the stretch—if you can actually deliver. Did you ever deal with Gilberacci directly?"

Devon shook his head. "I only talked to Murphy. That's why we gotta get Eddie Ballick on board. The whole thing swings on him."

Finn shook his head. "There's got to be someone else."

"Not that I can think of."

"Think harder."

Devon sighed. "You know how shit works, Finn. Eddie keeps everything under his control. He only deals with his boys—like Murphy—and they only deal with the people who need to know about a particular job. The fewer loose ends, the less chance that the cops can get a clear shot at anybody."

"They got a clear shot at you."

"I'm tellin' you, the only person who might be able to connect the dots straight back to Giberacci would be Ballick. There's nobody else."

Finn rubbed his temples. "The Fisherman," he said. "I'm not really that anxious to have this conversation."

"You ever meet him?" Devon asked.

Finn nodded. "I did work on a few jobs for him back when I was hustling. Grunt stuff. He probably wouldn't even remember. Not exactly a warm, fuzzy guy."

Devon agreed. "No, he's not. But he'll remember. He remembers everything."

"He still down near Quincy?"

"Yeah. At the shack on the water. You couldn't pry his ass away from there."

Finn looked at his watch. "Okay," he said. "Fuck it, why not? We have your arraignment tomorrow, and I need to know what kind of cards we're holding."

"Do me a favor," Devon said.

"You're about out of favors, Devon."

"Give me a call when you're done with him, okay? I wanna hear what he says."

Finn got up and walked over to the steel door, pressing the button by the side of it to let the guards know that he was ready to leave. The buzzer sounded on the electronic lock on the other door, to let Devon back into the cell block.

"Wait, Finn," he said before he left the room.

"What?"

"How's Sally? She okay?"

"Yeah," Finn replied. "She's okay. She's a piece of work. I like her."

Devon smiled. "She's a fuckin' pistol. Hell of a lot smarter than either of her parents. Her mom's a real fuckup. No one ever gave Sally a chance. Shit, I didn't even know she existed until a year ago."

"She seems to be getting by," Finn said.

"Yeah, getting by," Devon said. "She's a survivor, that's for shit-sure. I should be doin' better by her than this. With all the crap she's been through she deserves better than just getting by."

"We all deserve better than just getting by," Finn said. "Sometimes, that's the best we can hope for."

"Yeah," Devon said. He was back into the thousand-yard stare. "Sometimes that's right."

Chapter Nine

It was lunchtime at Nashua Street just after Finn left. Devon moved through the chow line like a zombie. Food was ladled out onto his tray without his notice; he walked alone over to a table in the corner. He sat with his back to the wall, and kept his head down. He felt as if he were underwater as he pushed the mush around on his tray with his fork. He couldn't have eaten if he'd wanted to.

Devon felt bad for Murphy. Not nearly as bad as he felt for himself, but bad all the same. Murphy had tried for him. Even after the others had given up on him, Murphy had kept him afloat, even if just. Had things been different, maybe the Gilberacci's job would have been enough—the beginning of a comeback. A comeback clearly wasn't in the cards now, though. He'd made his choice and there was no going back.

He turned his thoughts back to Murphy's murder. It was hard not to leap to the obvious conclusion. It fit with the rumors he'd heard. It would make sense. But he still wasn't certain. Murphy'd led a dangerous life. He'd pissed off lots of people, and he'd run with a vicious crowd. His murder could be a coincidence. It wasn't likely, but it was possible, and Devon clung to that possibility.

There was only one way to be sure. Ballick was the key. They'd made their mistakes, but they'd made them together. Until he knew for sure, Devon was safer in jail.

He thought back over the past decades and wondered whether he'd have done anything differently. Probably not. He was who he was, and nothing would have changed that. Even if he'd known.

———⋆———

The Irishman didn't trust Devon. It didn't take a lot of brains for Devon to recognize it. In some ways, Devon could understand. Devon was undisciplined. He talked too much. The Irishman had a singular purpose, and from what Devon knew of him, he had dedicated his life—everything he was or would become—to waging a war that required the kind of commitment Devon would never understand.

It had been more than four weeks since they'd met at the Body Shop, and Devon still hadn't delivered. They'd made one try, and it had been a farce. Two weeks earlier they had acted out a pathetic pantomime in front of the museum off Fenway. The Irishman and Devon pretended to assault another one of Murphy's crew out on the street late at night, well within the range of the outdoor security cameras. The third man then ran to the museum's side entrance and started banging on the door and ringing the bell, calling out for help. The guards, though, had been more cautious than Devon had expected, and had simply called the police, staying locked up in the museum themselves. The three of them had just barely cleared the area before the cops arrived.

"Don't worry, Irish," Devon had said. "I got another plan." It was a lie at the time, and for three days Devon hadn't slept or eaten. He knew his life was on the line. It took some time, but eventually he hit on another idea.

In some ways, the new plan seemed as foolish as the first. They were parked on the street in a beat-up red Toyota on a Saturday night, just a hundred yards or so from the museum's main entrance. It was St. Patrick's Day, and Boston was consumed in a spastic, celebratory madness. Even Dublin didn't debase itself the way Boston did in recognition of Ireland's savior.

It was just the two of them, Devon and the Irishman, and they were dressed in police uniforms, complete with caps, badges, and fake mustaches. Devon felt as if he were in a cheap Laurel and Hardy remake, and he had to stifle a laugh at the thought. He'd been around the Irishman enough to understand that he was not a fan of levity.

They had planned to make the move just after midnight, but there was a delay. A party was in full swing in an apartment building near the museum and there were too many people out on the street. They decided to wait until the party broke up, and they just sat there in the car, for all the world to see. If they got caught, Malley knew that the Irishman would kill him as soon as he had the chance. Even if that didn't happen, one of Bulger's guys would push a button on him in jail, just to cut the line to the boss. Any way he looked at it, failure at this point would be fatal.

At one o'clock in the morning, the party in the nearby apartment building was just starting to break up. People were stumbling out of the building and moving on. A group of revelers broke away and started heading toward the car.

"Fuck," the Irishman cursed. Devon's heart stopped in his chest.

"Just wait," he said. He pulled the brim of the police cap lower on his forehead.

There were four of them, all male, headed straight toward the car. They looked young and drunk. The Irishman reached into his pocket for his gun. "Not yet," Devon said.

They sat there for what seemed like an eternity as the boys approached. Out of the corner of his eye, Devon saw two of them look into the car, and he considered getting out. They moved quickly past the car, though, and picked up their pace.

"Kids," Devon said. "They're underage, and they're more scared of us than we are of them."

The Irishman reached up and swiveled the rearview mirror so that he could get a look at them. They were nearly a block away and still moving quickly. "Maybe," he said. "That doesn't mean they didn't see us."

"All they saw was the uniforms. They're drunk. They won't be able to tell the cops shit. Don't worry." Devon turned to look at the Irishman and smiled reassuringly. He could tell that the other man wanted to kill him.

"We move now," the Irishman said. "We're not sitting here anymore."

"The party's almost over," Devon said.

"I don't give a fuck. We're not waiting anymore." The Irishman opened the door and stepped out onto the street.

Chapter Ten

Stone stood before Sanchez's front door in Brookline, just to the west of Boston. She'd called in sick. Word at the station was that she would likely be in later in the day, but he had no idea when. He checked the address listed in her personnel file and headed out. She didn't know he was coming, and he figured she'd be pissed, so he was holding a container of chicken soup he'd picked up at a local deli, hoping it would allay her annoyance. Probably not, but he figured it couldn't hurt. Ultimately, he didn't care; he wasn't going to spend his life with a partner who wouldn't discuss cases with him. He'd decided to push the issue.

When he'd visualized Sanchez's home, he'd pictured a small, dark apartment somewhere in one of the city's worst neighborhoods. Two, maybe three rooms, sparsely decorated, with few pictures and no personal items. A place befitting this woman who was so focused on her work, and so distant from those around her willing to help. It was a dark, lonely, angry life he'd envisioned for her.

The dwelling that matched her address from the personnel files met none of his expectations. It was a medium-sized house in a nice neighborhood right off the Green Line. Two blocks from Commonwealth Avenue, it had a large well-tended yard, and flowers flanking the covered entryway. The driveway had been swept, the flower beds had been edged, and there wasn't a hint of peeling or cracking in the bright yellow paint on the home's exterior. The place exuded contentment.

He rang the bell and waited. It took a moment, but the door opened, and a young boy stood in front of him, wearing pajamas. "Hello," he said. He had dark hair and dark skin—far darker than Sanchez's. His eyes were bright and trusting. He couldn't have been more than six years old.

"Hello," Stone replied. "I may be in the wrong place. I'm looking for Detective Sanchez."

"Mom!" the boy shouted. "She's here," he said. "I'm Carlos. I have the flu."

"Carlos, get back in bed!" Sanchez's voice was unmistakable, though the tone was softer than Stone was used to.

A moment later, Sanchez was standing in front of Stone. She was dressed in chinos and a loose blouse, and he barely recognized her. The difference wasn't so much in the way she was dressed, it was in her face. She normally wore her hair pulled back from the temples, giving her face a severe, angry look accentuated by the scowl she wore as a permanent expression of contempt for the world. Now her hair was down and her features were relaxed. She resembled less a bitter cop, more an attractive middle-aged woman.

She recognized Stone, and her expression changed. She morphed before his eyes into the angry woman he knew from their time together. "What the hell are you doing here, Stone?" she demanded.

"I heard you were sick," he said. "I brought chicken soup."

The boy, who had disappeared for a moment, was standing behind Sanchez now. "I don't like chicken soup," he said.

"I asked you to get back in bed," she said to him.

"Aw, Mom," he replied sullenly. He headed back into the house.

She looked back at Stone. "This is my personal, private space," she said. "I don't want you here."

Stone stood his ground. "We need to talk."

"He's adopted."

Carlos was in the family room, watching television, and Stone was alone with Sanchez in the kitchen. He was sitting at the table; she was cleaning the breakfast dishes. The question had been unspoken. He was glad she'd answered it without his having to ask it, though; he wasn't sure he'd have had the guts. It was clearly a question she had to address fairly often. She was a single cop in her fifties. A six-year-old calling her *Mom* didn't fit.

"He's normally in school, but he woke up this morning with a fever, and the woman who takes him in the afternoon isn't available this morning."

"Seems like a cute kid," Stone said.

"He was two when he came to this country. Now you'd never know he lived anyplace else. Funny how the world works that way, isn't it?" she said. "Time moves on; kids forget the bad."

"Is he your only child?" Stone asked.

"I had a daughter," she replied. "She was murdered. So was my husband."

He had no idea what to say. "That's why you became a cop." It was the only thing that came to mind.

She glared at him. "Yeah. That's why I became a cop. And that ends our discussion of my personal life. You wanna talk work, fine, but talk quickly. Then I want you out of here. You shouldn't be here in the first place."

"Fair enough," Stone said. "Let's talk work. Why would the IRA kill a Boston mob boss?"

She sat down across from him at the kitchen table and stared at him warily. "What are you talking about?"

"I'm not stupid," he replied. "I know how to use the Internet. *Padre Pio.* It's a form of torture used by IRA enforcers. Named after some

Spanish monk from the 1960s who had the stigmata—bleeding from the palms and feet where Jesus was nailed to the cross. IRA enforcers tie their victims' hands together and shoot clean through, so it looks like they've been nailed to the cross. They say they save it for people who've betrayed the cause. So why was it used on Murphy?"

She tilted her head. "Not bad," she said grudgingly. "But I gave you that one."

"Fine, you gave me that one. I thought that was what partners did—they gave shit to each other."

"Keep your voice down," she ordered him. "If my son hears you swear, it'll be the shortest partnership in departmental history."

"It already has been," he said. "It's never been a partnership at all."

She took a deep breath. "Look, you seem like a decent kid—"

"No," he interrupted her. "I'm not a decent kid. I'm a good cop."

"You may be," she said.

"No, not *I may be*. I am. You'd know that if you gave me a chance. So I'll ask you again, what is the IRA doing knocking off a Boston mob boss?"

"I think it's about art," she replied after a moment.

"Art who?"

"Not art *who*; *art*, as in paintings."

"Okay, I'll bite. What does this have to do with *art*?"

"Maybe nothing. Maybe everything. How old were you in 1990?"

He thought for a moment. "Ten," he replied.

"Jesus," she said. She rubbed her forehead wearily. "I'm too goddamned old."

"What happened in 1990?"

"You remember the theft at the Isabella Stewart Gardner Museum?"

He sat back in the kitchen chair. "Not from back then, but I know about it now. Two guys got away with a couple of paintings, right?"

"That's one way of putting it. Another way would be to say that it was the greatest art theft in modern history. They say the stuff that was stolen would be worth close to half a billion dollars today."

"Billion? With a 'b'?"

"Yeah, billion." She stood up and walked over to the kitchen counter. "Coffee?"

"Sure. Black."

She pulled out a coffee brewer. It had tubes coming out of it and looked as if it would take a degree from MIT to operate. He wondered where her money came from.

"It was the easiest robbery imaginable, too," she said, her back to him as she continued to brew the coffee. "There were just two of them, and they faked their way into the museum. The guards were amateurs; not real security guards at all. They weren't properly trained; they didn't follow proper procedures. The robbers tied the guards in the basement and spent an hour and a half pulling artwork off the walls, then left. The paintings have never been found." She brought two mugs over to the table.

"Interesting," he said. "What's this got to do with Murphy's murder?"

"People have searched for these paintings for twenty years," she said. "The police, the FBI, Interpol, private detectives, insurance detectives, art historians, treasure hunters. People have spent an enormous amount of energy trying to find these things, but no one has done it yet. There have been lots of theories about who was responsible. The most popular is that the IRA teamed up with the Boston mob to do the job, then split the take between the two groups."

Stone considered this. "It's an interesting idea. But it seems like a pretty big stretch to assume that this is what Murphy's murder was about, isn't it?"

"Maybe," Sanchez said. "But one of the works stolen was a painting by Rembrandt. It was one of the most valuable pieces the thieves got away with. The title of it was *Storm on the Sea of Galilee*."

It took a moment for the connection to register with Stone. "'The Storm.' You think that was the message that was being sent? That whoever did this was coming for the paintings?"

She shrugged. "I don't have anything better to go on at this point," she said. "Do you?"

He shook his head. "No. It just seems a little thin."

"It does," she agreed. "But it would also fit with the *Padre Pio* they pulled on Murphy. Back in 1990, nothing happened in this town without Whitey Bulger's say-so, and Murphy was working closely with him at the time. Maybe this has nothing to do with the art theft. Maybe it's just a beef between the IRA and the boys in Southie over drugs or guns. But then why paint 'The Storm' in blood?"

"Okay," Stone said. "It's a possibility. I'm not sold yet, but it's some-place to start." He took a sip of his coffee. "Thanks for sharing. It's almost like we're partners."

She was looking at him across the table. "Don't let it go to your head. In my book, I still don't know whether this 'partnership' is gonna work. I like to work alone, and I don't trust people easily. We'll see where this goes; that's the best I can do."

He nodded. "Fair enough. I'm just looking for a chance. You may even find it's easier to do the job if you have someone you can rely on." He took a final sip of the coffee and put down his mug. "One ques-tion," he said.

"What is it?"

"How do you know so much about the robbery?"

She frowned at him. "I may be old, but I can use the Internet, too."

———

Special Agent Hewitt paid the barista for his coffee at the Starbucks in Government Center. It was overpriced, but he'd gotten to the point where he could no longer drink the swill that dribbled from the 1950s coffeemaker at the office. There were some sacrifices he wasn't willing to make, even in the name of justice.

He walked out of the Starbucks and across the brick tundra that surrounded City Hall. He looked up at the building and grimaced. Boston's City Hall had been built in the 1960s, and was the most renowned example of the Brutalist school of design popular at the time. A monumental nine-level cement inverted pyramid set on eight acres of brick and stone, it won praise from the architectural community as a notable achievement in the creation and control of modern urban space. In a poll of historians and architects, it was voted the sixth greatest building in American history. To Bostonians, though, it was an eyesore. With all the warmth of a mausoleum, it loomed over the classic architectural beauty of Faneuil Hall and Quincy Market across the street.

The Boston field office of the FBI was housed in the John F. Kennedy Federal Building next to City Hall. It was a nondescript concrete structure in the heart of Government Center, close to the backside of Beacon Hill.

Hewitt flashed his badge at the guard standing next to the metal detectors and walked around the line. He took the elevator up to the eighth floor, walked through the gray industrial-carpeted hallways, past a warren of cubicles inhabited by dull-eyed functionaries trying to make it through another day on the government payroll, and into his office. It was small by the standards of those he had gone to law school with years ago who now made millions representing huge corporations in the great glass towers of private practice. The furniture was faux-wood laminate over particleboard, and the cabinetry was gray-steel government issue. Nonetheless, he was comfortable there. It was where he belonged.

As he hung up his coat on the hook behind the door he heard a voice coming from behind his desk. "Robert," it said.

Surprised, Hewitt spun, his hand involuntarily going to his hip, where his gun was encased in a holster.

"No need to shoot, Robert. I'm one of the good guys." The voice belonged to Angus Porter, special agent in charge of the FBI's Art Theft Program.

"Porter," Hewitt said with a heavy sigh. "What the fuck are you doing here?" Hewitt wondered how he'd managed to enter the office and hang up the coat without noticing the man sitting in his chair. On the other hand, it was Porter. He couldn't have been taller than five-seven, and if he weighed more than one hundred and twenty-five pounds with his shoes on, Hewitt would have been surprised. He had wispy blond hair growing out of a pale scalp that looked too small for his skull. It was pulled impossibly tight and gave off a dull shine. He had the spoiled air of someone who'd grown up without having to worry about money.

"I told you on the phone I was coming to Boston," Porter said with a smile. His teeth had been whitened, and were brighter than the starched collar of his tailored shirt.

"I don't mean here in Boston, I mean here in my office."

"You're the only person here I came to see. Where else should I be?"

"I'm sure we have an office or a cubicle here we can get for you. You can work out of that."

Porter shook his head. "No need. I'm not here officially, and I'll be working out of my hotel."

"Why?"

"You know why, Robert. On this investigation it's just you and me, and that's it."

"I'm still not sure why," Hewitt said. "We could have all the players blanketed with the right amount of manpower. You give the word and we could mobilize twenty agents. We could control the whole thing."

"It wouldn't serve our purpose. It would be like sending an army of fishermen into a shallow river. We would scare away the fish. But one or two men with the right bait—that's how this must work."

Hewitt walked around his desk and stood in front of Porter. "You're in my seat."

Porter looked up at him for a moment. Then he stood up and walked around to the far side of the desk. He pulled a chair over from a small table in the corner and sat in front of Hewitt's desk. Hewitt sat down in the chair Porter had just vacated. "Have there been any further developments?" Porter asked.

"No," Hewitt replied. "At least, none that have been discovered so far. How about on your end?"

"The offer seems genuine," Porter said. "We intercepted physical evidence—paint chips. They match. Between that and the photographs, I have a high level of confidence that this time it's for real."

"Shit," Hewitt said. "You sure we don't want to bring in some additional help?"

"Absolutely. You and I were both here in the eighties and nineties. We know the players better than anyone. I have all the contacts we need in the art world to guide what's going on from Washington. Bringing in others from the Bureau would only complicate matters."

"What about the locals?"

Porter gave a grunt. "The local police? You must be kidding. They'd only create problems. You know the kind of jurisdictional tug-of-war that gets into."

Hewitt picked up a souvenir baseball that was sitting on his desk. If it had been someone else sitting across the desk from him, he might have tossed the ball to him—physical activity helped him think. Porter didn't seem like the kind of guy who liked to throw baseballs around, though. Hewitt tossed it in the air instead and caught it himself. "If Murphy was involved, chances are that Ballick's involved as well. He was Whitey's right hand back then. He was higher up than Murphy, too. Should we tail him?"

Porter shook his head. "Keep tabs on him, but don't get too close. He may be involved, but maybe not. Whitey could have used someone else, and I don't want to put all our money down on one bet."

"Whoever was involved is in some serious danger. I haven't seen anything like what was done to Murphy in all my time at the Bureau."

"Murphy got what he deserved," Porter said. "I don't care how many of their own these people kill, as long as we find the paintings."

"You really think the art is more important than lives."

Porter seemed to consider the question. "Not all of the art, only some of it. The Vermeer and the Rembrandts, certainly. Maybe even the Flinck and the Manet. The rest of it, though, is irrelevant. The five unfinished sketches by Degas? Certainly not worthless, but trivial compared to the other works. I can't even begin to fathom why the bronze beaker from the Shang Dynasty was taken, and the notion that they took the finial from the top of Napoleon's battle flag is just flat-out insane. That's one of the great mysteries of the theft. In so many ways it was perfectly executed, but why waste time on trivial pieces like that? Not to mention what wasn't taken. These men were only steps away from Titian's *Rape of Europa*. Arguably the greatest and most valuable Renaissance piece in the United States. If they had the knowledge necessary to identify the Vermeer and the Rembrandts as worthwhile, surely they would have known about the Titian."

"Maybe they just got lucky."

Porter laughed. "It wasn't luck. Not with how smoothly the job went off. Not with how successful they have been in keeping the paintings hidden all this time. There are just some things about it that don't seem to fit."

Hewitt folded his hands on his lap. He wished Porter would leave; he didn't enjoy being around him. There was something bloodless about the little man that set him off. "If we do this right, maybe you'll be able to ask these guys about all that. We just need to keep them alive."

"That's hardly a priority of mine at this point," Porter said. His expression darkened, and his eyes glassed over in anger. Even when Porter had been an agent in the Boston office, he had always seemed off to Hewitt, particularly when it came to art. It was an obsession of his, and it had led him to push for the establishment of the special unit in the FBI to focus solely on art theft. It was a small group, but they were dedicated, and they were the best in the world at locating stolen art.

"What these men did wasn't just a crime," Porter said. "It was a sin. They deprived the world of some of the greatest works of art ever produced. I have no sympathy for them, and I wouldn't let a little thing like their safety jeopardize a chance to give these works back to the public."

Chapter Eleven

Eddie Ballick loved the sea as much as he was capable of loving any-thing. There was something about the unforgiving nature of the deep gray waters off the northern shores of the Atlantic that made him feel as though he had a place in the world. As a young man in the 1970s, he'd worked as a hand on the swordfish boats out of Gloucester. On his tenth run his boat ran into a squall and foundered. Three of the six-man crew had gone down with the ship. He, the first mate, and one other had survived for three days in a tiny raft, riding through some of the roughest seas of the season, before they were rescued. Since that time, Eddie Ballick feared nothing.

He'd never planned to enter a life of crime. But fishing jobs could be hard to come by, particularly for a hand who had already been on one doomed ship. There was never a suggestion that he was at fault, but it didn't really matter; sailors are a superstitious lot, and in the minds of many, Ballick was a jinx.

Jobless, and without any friends or family to speak of, Ballick drifted through his early twenties. He was a big man—not tall, but solid, with bones as thick and strong as petrified branches, held to-gether with thick slabs of muscle. He found work as a bouncer at one of the roughest bars, where some of the city's connected hung out. It wasn't long before some of them recognized the potential in a strong young man without fear.

Ballick was a perfect fit for Boston's criminal underworld. He had a disdain for other human beings that allowed him to cross lines of cruelty even some of his colleagues found troubling. He lived to live, without any care given to how long or how well. As a result, his rise through the ranks of Boston's organized crime in the eighties and nineties had less to do with any active ambition, and more to do with an oddly indifferent efficiency. Within five years, he owned the bar where he'd first been hired to run the door. It was rumored that his former boss was buried under the parking lot out back.

The bar was only one of Ballick's quasi-legitimate businesses. For him, the crown jewel in his mini-empire was a run-down fishing shack at the edge of the water at the southern tip of Boston, just north of Quincy. It was the only place he cared about, and it was where he spent most of his time. It wasn't much to look at: a small, rickety two-story building ready to slide into the edge of Quincy Harbor.

Ballick was sitting in a cheap aluminum folding chair at the corner of the building, watching the activity on the pier closely, when Finn and Kozlowski arrived. He looked as if he fit in there, and as if he would have a hard time fitting in anyplace else. He was in his late fifties, with a large round head fringed with matted white hair. A fisherman's beard traced a smooth oval from ear to ear under his chin, and the only parts of him that seemed to move at all were his eyes. Boats were pulled up along a nearby pier, some of them already unloading their catches in the mid-afternoon sun. A few of Ballick's buyers from the shack moved along the pier, watching over the unloading process, calculating their needs and the respective purchase prices in their heads.

"Eddie Ballick," Finn said as he approached. He'd called earlier to tell Ballick he was coming; Ballick was known to be a man who abhorred surprises.

Ballick turned his head; the rest of his body remained still. He said nothing.

"I'm Scott Finn. Devon Malley's lawyer. We spoke earlier."

Ballick looked past Finn toward Kozlowski. "You didn't say you were bringing someone with you."

"Sorry," Finn said. "This is Tom Kozlowski. He and I—"

"I know who he is," Ballick said. "He's a cop."

"He's no longer with the department," Finn said. "He's a private detective now."

"He's still a cop," Ballick said. "Now he's just a cop without a badge."

Ballick's head turned back toward the pier. "I only got a few minutes. I'm busy." He shifted in his seat and brought his hands together on his lap. Finn had never seen thicker fingers. "Scott Finn," he said. "I remember you."

"I didn't know whether you would," Finn said.

"Looks like the other side is working out for you."

"I suppose."

"Fuckin' shame."

Finn was noncommittal. "In some ways, maybe."

"And now you want to talk to me about Devon Malley."

"It would be helpful."

Ballick frowned. Then he got to his feet slowly. "We'll talk inside," he said. "Cop stays out here."

Finn followed him around the corner of the building and through an undersized door that looked as though the hinges might fail soon. One room took up the entire first floor. It was concrete from wall to wall, and along the back there was a long sink where men in blood-stained sweatshirts and aprons worked steadily with long, thin gutting knives, slicing into the bellies of fish carcasses stacked in holding bins. With each casual flick of their wrists, innards spilled into the sinks and were washed down through an open drain that emptied into a trough in the cement along the wall, and were carried out through a chute in the corner of the building that led into the harbor. The sights and smells brought a rush of bile into Finn's throat, but he managed to suppress the gag reflex.

"Upstairs," Ballick said, nodding toward a rickety plywood staircase in the corner. "Mikey," he called to one of the men bent over the bloody sink. The man stood and looked over his shoulder. Finn could see the muscles rippling under a thin T-shirt. "Keep an eye on the guy outside." Ballick walked to the stairs and the entire building seemed to list to one side as the heavy man headed up.

The upstairs was only marginally less retch-inducing. The walls were open to the studs, and Finn could see patches of mold along the walls and on the ceiling. The stench from below seemed just as powerful. There was a small desk in the center of the room—painfully small for a man of Ballick's girth—and a few rusted folding chairs placed haphazardly around. Stacks of newspapers and filing cabinets stood along one wall.

"Nice office," Finn commented.

"Not what you're used to, Counselor?"

"Actually, my office isn't much bigger. Better ventilated, maybe."

"With all the money you must be making these days?"

"I make a lot less than you do. Appearances notwithstanding."

Ballick sat down behind the desk and slid open one of the bottom drawers, pulling out a thermos. He took the cup-shaped top off and turned it upside down on the desktop, then unscrewed the cap and poured out some of the contents. A thin wisp of steam wafted up. "I've never given much of a fuck about appearances," Ballick said as he lifted the cup to his lips.

Finn nodded and pulled a chair over, sitting in front of the desk. "Me neither."

"So?" Ballick said. "You said you wanted to talk. Talk."

Kozlowski was leaning against the side of the building, close to the doorway so that he might hear it if things got loud upstairs. He'd have felt much better if he could have seen Finn and heard exactly what was going on. It was unlikely that Ballick would do anything. There were too many people around, and it wouldn't be worth his effort. Still, Kozlowski felt uneasy.

The door opened and a man stepped outside. He was in his late twenties, a little taller than Kozlowski, with a shaved head and a goatee. An apron hung from his shoulders, covered in blood and fish guts, and his T-shirt, presumably once white, was splotched with yellow and gray. The arms that protruded from the sleeves were covered in green-black prison tattoos; cables of muscle and treads of veins shifted as he moved.

He paused as he adjusted to the light, his hand to his eyes, looking for something. Then he turned in Kozlowski's direction. It took a moment for the recognition to flash in the man's eyes, but once it did, it morphed instantly to hatred.

"Muthafucka," he said. He was only a few feet from Kozlowski.

"Mikey Sullivan," Kozlowski said. He nodded to the man. "How you been?"

"Fuck you care, Kozlowski?" the man said.

"C'mon, Mikey. I care. It makes me feel good when I know that the people I put away have been rehabilitated. Nice to see you got yourself a real job. Can't say too much for your employer, but hell, I guess you gotta take what you can get. You just gut fish for Ballick, or you gut other things, too?"

The man took a half-step back, his hand going to the pocket at the front of his apron. "You ain't on the job no more, from what I hear."

"True."

"So, what the fuck are you doin' here, Kozlowski?"

"Maybe I'm just checking up on you. Maybe this is how I like to spend my days."

"Maybe you made a mistake. Maybe you ain't so fuckin' tough without a badge."

"Maybe," Kozlowski said. He took his weight off the side of the building and secured his footing. He had a good idea what was coming.

"Maybe we'll see," the man said. He drew his hand out of the apron pocket, and Kozlowski could see the knife. It was long and thin and covered with blood. Then Sullivan lunged.

"Devon's in a difficult spot," Finn said.

"Yeah, so?" Ballick replied. "Fuck's it got to do with me? Fuck's it got to do with you, for that matter?"

"He's my client," Finn said. "I was wondering if there would be anything anyone could tell me that might help him out. Hypothetically speaking."

"Hypothetically speaking?"

"Yeah." Finn decided to tread lightly. "I'm not looking for you to say anything that might implicate yourself in any criminal activity. On the other hand, you may be able to give me some information that I could trade on his behalf."

"What kind of information?"

"Information about who was involved in setting up the robbery at Gilberacci's. Devon says there was inside involvement—that Johnny Gilberacci helped plan the whole thing."

"Don't know shit about it."

"I understand," Finn said. "But let's just say for a minute—again, hypothetically—that Johnny Gilberacci was involved."

"Okay, let's say that."

"If I had some way of confirming it, I'd have something to trade to the DA to cut a deal for Devon. You see what I'm saying?"

"No."

Finn took a deep breath and regretted it immediately as the stink of fish swarmed his sinuses. "Well, as it stands now, I've got nothing to bargain with. If we had some concrete information it would change things."

Ballick took another sip from the plastic cup. "And you want me to give you something that would help you prove this thing with Johnny Gilberacci?"

"It wouldn't have to come directly from you. If there's some way to do it so that I can get something—anything—to give to the DA, or even just to get him curious, there might be something I could do for Devon." Ballick leaned back in his chair. "I wouldn't be here at all, but Devon only talked to Murphy about the job, and he's dead now."

"Hypothetically." Ballick's stare was cold.

"No," Finn said slowly. "That's not a hypothetical. On the other hand, his death could give us an opportunity. Let's say that you weren't involved in the robbery, but you were aware that Murphy and Gilberacci were. If you had anything that would tie the two together—without implicating yourself—that would go a long way toward helping Devon." Ballick didn't respond. Finn suddenly felt out of his depth. He cleared his throat. "Maybe there's nothing you can do," he said. There was still no response. "I just figured that Devon's one of yours. He's made a lot of money for people over the years. I thought, maybe, you'd want to help him if you could."

"You thought wrong. Devon hasn't been one of mine for years. Plus, a rat's a rat, no matter whose cheese he's eatin'. I ain't no rat." In the moment of silence that followed, Finn thought the stench of fish might overwhelm him. "You know why I agreed to talk to you?"

"Because I'm Devon's lawyer?"

Ballick shook his head. "I don't give a fuck about Devon. Devon's done. He's a loser. He's a punk. Always has been. I don't owe him shit. Murphy should never have hired him on this Gilberacci's thing."

"No?"

"No."

"Then why did you agree to meet with me?"

Ballick coughed, and Finn could hear the rumble deep down in his chest. "I remember you from twenty years ago. You were a punk back then, too. But you were always straight. Word was you're still straight today. I wanted to see for myself."

"I appreciate that."

"You shouldn't. You fuckin' disappoint."

"Sorry."

"You want me to roll on a guy you think I'm doing business with. You come in here with your 'hypotheticals' and expect me to play rat so you can get a deal for your boy. I don't live in the hypothetical world; I live in the real fuckin' world. In my world, a man says what he means and gets shivved if he don't. Devon got himself where he is today, and there ain't shit I can do to help him. He's your problem, not mine."

The lunge would have been effective had Kozlowski not anticipated it. It was aimed straight at his abdomen, which in most circumstances would have maximized the likelihood of catching him. He'd set his feet, though, and he stepped back and swiveled his torso effectively, twisting just out of the knife's reach.

Once he was sure he hadn't been cut, Kozlowski knew the fight was over. The lunge had put Sullivan off balance, weight forward, head down. He was an easy target.

Kozlowski grabbed his wrist with his left hand, just below the knife, and pulled it forward, throwing the man even farther off balance. Then he swung his knee up hard into the outstretched arm,

hyperextending the elbow. He was hoping to hear the pop of liga-
ments and cartilage, but he wasn't that lucky. It was enough, though,
that Sullivan gave out a pained scream and dropped the knife.

Kozlowski raised his right fist and brought it down on the back of
Sullivan's neck. So much of the man's weight was forward that he fell
to the ground on his stomach at Kozlowski's feet. "Didn't they teach
you to fight any better than this in Walpole?" he asked. "You must've
gotten your ass kicked up there every day, huh?"

"Fuck you!" Sullivan screamed. He scrabbled toward the knife,
which had fallen just a few feet away. Kozlowski cut him off, though,
and brought his foot down on the man's wrist with all his weight just
as he was reaching for the weapon. Sullivan screamed out in pain. He
recovered quickly, though, and rolled onto his side, swinging his free
hand at Kozlowski's crotch.

The blow glanced off Kozlowski's thigh, missing its mark. It was
close enough, though, that Kozlowski decided it was time to end the
matter. Still standing on the man's arm, he reached into his coat and
pulled out his gun. As Sullivan struggled on the ground to free himself, Kozlowski leaned down and put the muzzle against his cheek.
Sullivan went still instantly.

"Looks like six years went by too fast for you to learn anything,
Mikey," Kozlowski said. "Shame. All that taxpayer money wasted."

"Just do it, piece of shit!" the man yelled. "You ain't even a cop
piece of shit no more, so do it! Put a bullet in my fuckin' head an' you
go off to the fuckin' MCI! Let's see how you like it on the inside, I'm
sure they'll love your ass in there! You ain't shit anymore!"

Kozlowski raised the butt of his gun and drove it into the man's
forehead. The man let out a cackle. "Do it! Muthafucka do it!"

Kozlowski put the barrel of the gun back to the man's cheek and
pulled the hammer back.

"What's your angle on this?"

Ballick had finished drinking from his thermos, and he lit a cigarette. Finn looked around at the ancient newspapers on the floor and the half-rotted wood in the studs on the walls. He wondered how the place hadn't burned down. "What do you mean?"

"You know what I mean. You're a hot-shit lawyer. You can pick and choose your clients. Devon's got no fuckin' money, so what the fuck you care what happens to him?"

"He's a friend," Finn said.

"Bullshit. You two weren't even friends back in the day. I'd bet ten large you haven't talked to him in a fuckin' decade. Besides, Devon's got no friends. So what's your interest?"

"He's got a daughter. I'm trying to help him out."

"You fuckin' his daughter?"

"She's fourteen."

"Makes me more curious about your answer."

Finn shook his head in disgust. "It's not like that. Her mother split. If Devon goes in, she's got no one to take care of her."

"So what? How's that your fuckin' problem?" Finn didn't answer. "Well, fuck," Ballick continued, "if it's the daughter you're worried about, give her my phone number. I'm sure I could find work for her."

"Doing what?"

Ballick shrugged. "She'd make more if she was a little younger. The hard-core perverts think of thirteen as some sort of a fuckin' cutoff. Still, if she's cute and she looks young enough, she could lie. Girl like that under the right circumstances can make a shitload of money." He smiled and his eyes grew smaller.

"Don't talk about her like that."

"Like what? I didn't make this fucked-up world, I just work here." Ballick shook his head in mock pity. "Girl like that, that kind of background and fucked-up parents, she don't end up with me she'll end up with someone worse. Why not me?" He chuckled.

Finn leaned in toward the table. "Maybe I need to be clearer. Stay away from the girl. If I find out you've been anywhere near her, I swear to God . . ."

"You swear to God what?" Ballick asked. He'd lost his sense of humor. "You threatening me, Counselor?" He opened the desk's top drawer and pulled out a revolver, put it down on the desk. "Let me explain something to you: I got a lotta shit to worry about in my life. You ain't any part of it. You got that? You wanna come in here and tell me what to do? You wanna threaten me? Maybe *I* should be clearer. I ever see you again and you won't have to worry about Devon's kid anymore, 'cause I'll put a bullet in your fuckin' brain. That clear enough? You ain't a part of this world anymore; don't go playin' like you are."

"Stay away from her. I'm serious."

Ballick stood. "No, I'm fuckin' serious." He picked up the gun and pointed it at Finn. "This conversation's over."

———◦———

Kozlowski's finger trembled, tightening on the trigger. "Get the fuck up."

Sullivan got to his feet. Kozlowski twisted his arm and faced him toward the side of the building. "Hands on the wall," Kozlowski said. "You've done this before, spread 'em."

Sullivan assumed the familiar pose, leaning forward on the building. "What the fuck you gonna do? Arrest me?"

Kozlowski kicked at the man's feet. "Farther apart, asshole." He stuck the barrel of the gun into the man's back and bent over as he used his free hand to frisk him. His hand slid over the blood and fish guts that covered the apron.

"You can't arrest me," the man taunted. "You're not a fuckin' cop no more."

Kozlowski straightened up and put the gun at the base of the man's skull. "Who said anything about arresting you, Mikey? You been in twice already. Consider this my own version of the three-strikes rule." He pushed the gun harder into the man's head, until his face was rubbing against the building's raw wood siding.

"You can't fuckin' kill me!" the man yelled.

"No? Why not?"

The door banged open and Finn stepped out. Ballick followed him, holding a gun. He looked at Kozlowski. "You see what I mean?" he said to Finn. "Once a cop, always a fuckin' cop." He raised his gun and pointed it toward the back of Finn's head. "Okay, if you're the cowboy, I guess that makes me the fuckin' Indian. You wanna play?"

"It's not my fault," Mikey pleaded with Ballick.

"Shut up, you worthless piece of shit. What do you think, cop? Should we waste 'em both?"

Kozlowski uncocked his gun and lowered it. Ballick did the same.

"Too bad," Ballick said. "For a second we both had a chance to do some fuckin' good here today."

Kozlowski grabbed Mikey by the back of his shirt and pulled him off the building, then shoved him toward Ballick. "Maybe next time."

Ballick looked at Mikey. "Thanks for keepin' an eye on this guy."

"I'm sorry, Eddie." Mikey barely got the words out before Ballick whipped the gun around, catching him in the face with the butt. He went down instantly.

"I said shut the fuck up."

"Let's go," Kozlowski said to Finn.

Finn nodded and the two of them started walking toward their car. "Hey lawyer-man!" Ballick called out. Finn turned. "You should get to know your fuckin' client a little better. He's playin' you. Swear to God, he's playin' you better than I'm gonna play his little girl when she shows up on my doorstep lookin' for food."

Kozlowski looked back and forth between the two men.

"You're not part of the game no more!" Ballick yelled. "You remember that!"

Finn and Kozlowski got into Finn's car and Finn pulled out. Kozlowski looked at him. "So, how'd it go?"

Chapter Twelve

The guard's voice echoed off the walls of the central area at the jail. "Devon Malley! Phone call!"

Devon knew it had to be Finn. Phone calls only came in to inmates if there was an emergency, or if it was a lawyer. Other than that, calls had to be placed by the inmates themselves during specified times. He headed to the long, narrow corridor off one side of the cell block. A guard was there to open the door for him. "Number three," he said. Along the wall of the corridor were several phones spaced evenly apart. Devon went to the third one in the line and picked up the handset. "Finn?" he said.

"Yeah," Finn replied.

"Did you see him?" Devon held his breath waiting for the answer.

"I got nothing," Finn replied.

"What do you mean?"

"I mean it was a waste of time. There's nothing we're gonna get from Ballick."

"Why not? Did you see him?"

"Yeah, I saw him," Finn said. "He wouldn't give us anything even if he had something to give."

"But you saw him? You spoke to him?"

"Yeah."

"In person?"

"Yeah. What the fuck does it matter? Weren't you listening? He's not gonna help us. He wouldn't give up Gilberacci even if he could. What the fuck is going on?"

"Nothing," Devon said, smiling to himself. "He say anything else?"

"Yeah, he said that you don't do any work for him anymore. He told me you're playing me. You wanna tell me what that's all about?"

"That's nothing. Eddie's always been a hard case, you know that."

"Yeah, I know," Finn said. "That wasn't it, though. There was something else. I need you to be straight with me, Devon, if you want me to keep representing you."

"You worry too much, Finn. You've got to trust me a little more; everything's gonna be okay. The arraignment's tomorrow, right?"

"Yeah."

"Good. You get me out, and I'll get you the money I owe you."

"I'm not worried about the money," Finn said.

"Yeah, right. A lawyer not worried about money. Who the fuck you think you're dealing with, Finn?"

"I saw your apartment when I picked Sally up," Finn said. "I know you can't pay me. Not if that's the shithole you've been living in."

"Don't ever judge a book by its fuckin' cover, Finn. I just need you to get me out on bail. I'll take care of everything else."

Devon heard Finn sigh on the other end of the line. "We're in pretty good shape as far as the hearing goes. I'll get there a little early and we can talk through any questions you have. The most important thing will be for you to keep your mouth shut and let me do the talking."

Devon laughed again. "Right. You're the boss."

"I'm serious about that, Devon. Judges don't like to hear from smart-ass defendants. Nothing pisses them off faster," Finn said.

"Don't worry, I'll be good," Devon replied. "And I swear to God, I'll get you your money when all this is done."

"Whatever."

"How's Sally?"

"She's fine. She's fourteen."

"Yeah, I know. Fucked up as it sounds, though, she's the best thing that ever happened to me. Will you give her a message?"

"Sure."

"Tell her I'm getting out tomorrow. Tell her everything's gonna be fine. Tell her to trust me."

"I'm pretty sure she's heard that before," Finn said.

"She has," Devon admitted. "This time it's true, though." He hung up.

As he walked back to his cell, he took his first deep breath of the day. Ever since he'd heard about Murphy's murder, his chest had felt constricted. Now he had real hope. Perhaps the past would remain in the past after all.

Devon would have waited a little longer. The St. Patrick's Day fete in the building next door was winding down, and in a matter of a half hour the risk of being seen would have gone down dramatically. Being seen wasn't necessarily fatal to the job—undoubtedly the four young men who had passed by them on the street had seen them—but it increased the risk of something going wrong. The Irishman was not going to be restrained anymore, though, so Devon got out of the car.

It was unseasonably warm. It had been down in the thirties the night before, but by midday it was well into the sixties, and by the time the sun went down the temperature had passed seventy degrees. Devon had spent some of the day walking the city, trying to clear his head before the job. Drunk girls were walking around in loose T-shirts, and the bars opened their windows to let the people breathe. The city was so packed you could hardly move on the streets, and the heat brought out the best and the worst in everyone. St. Patrick's Day was like that in Southie. It was like Christmas and New Year's all rolled into one with a keg of green beer to top it off. Devon never liked it. It was amateur hour out at the bars, with every rich prick from the colleges or the suburbs with an Irish grandmother or maid walking around screaming "Kiss me, I'm Irish," like they had any real fucking idea what it meant to be Irish.

Devon met up with the Irishman at around ten, and they went over the plan again. That took about twenty minutes. Then they sat in the Irishman's apartment, saying nothing. Devon turned on the television and started watching some of the NCAA tournament, but Irish turned it off. He didn't seem to be much of a hoops fan.

At eleven-thirty, they put on the police uniforms Vinny had gotten for them—real ones, not some costume-shop fakes, complete with guns and utility belts—and pasted on cheesy fake mustaches. Then they headed out.

The drive over to the Fens took a little time. Devon was careful to stop at the lights and keep to the speed limit; the last thing he wanted at that point was to get pulled over. Not that anyone was likely to pay them any attention; there were still so many people out on the street drunk off their asses. That was good in the sense that the real police would already be overwhelmed responding to reports of drunk and disorderly behavior, bar fights, and traffic accidents. Devon had tried to keep Irish as relaxed as possible, but had only been successful for a time. Now he was at a half-jog, trying to keep up with the man as they made their way the short distance from the car to the museum.

The warm weather made their overcoats seem more out of place. It was the one part of their uniforms that wasn't authentic, and Devon hoped that the security guards wouldn't notice. There was little they could do about it; the coats were necessary to conceal some of the tools they would need to do the job.

They walked up to the back door and rang the bell. It was one o'clock, and it took a minute or two for someone to answer. The voice on the intercom sounded as if it belonged to a kid. "Hello?" he said.

Chapter Thirteen

Lissa Krantz sat on the enormous sofa facing the fireplace in the living room of her top-floor apartment in the Back Bay. Her legs were pulled up underneath her and a cashmere blanket was pulled up to her waist. Looking out through the bay windows, she took in the Esplanade that wound along the banks of the Charles, and looked out toward Cambridge on the other side of the river. She'd always enjoyed the apartment, but it had only felt like home for a year or so—since Tom Kozlowski had all but moved in.

"You want a glass of wine?" he called from the kitchen. The apartment was large enough that he had to yell.

"No thanks," she called back.

"Beer?"

"Nope."

They were a mismatched couple. She'd grown used to the quizzical stares that greeted them wherever they went. He was nearly twenty years her senior, and despite having been off the force for a few years he would always look like a cop. Not the Hollywood variety, with their silk suits and their styled hair, but an old-school cop—the kind of wash-and-wear, just-the-facts-ma'am kind of cop who still viewed the world through a two-toned lens. She would never change him. Fortunately, that had never been her goal.

It was ironic. She recognized that when people looked at the two of them out on the street, they wondered how on earth he had managed to catch her. And yet she had chased him. Everything about him had captured her from the beginning. Her psychiatrist no doubt still tied the attraction to a troubled past and unresolved parental issues. Maybe he was right. On the other hand, she seemed to have less need for her psychiatrist these days.

In her heart, she knew that the attraction was more than just repressed childhood insecurity. Deep down he was smart and decent and kind, and something about his rough features, scarred and uneven, stirred a base passion in her. The past year with him had been the best of her life.

Now, in all likelihood, it was about to end.

He walked into the room, beer in hand, and sat down into an overstuffed chair cornering the sofa. "Long day?" he asked.

She shrugged. "You were there for most of it."

"How'd it go at the doctor's?"

"Fine." She opened her mouth to say more, but nothing came out. "How did the meeting go with Ballick?"

He shook his head. "Not very well. Safe to say that he won't be helping us out. On the other hand, we didn't get shot, which is always a plus."

"That's good. I mean the not getting shot part."

He looked at her and she turned away. "You sure everything's okay?" he asked.

"Yeah. Why?"

"I don't know. You seem weird."

"How so?"

Kozlowski's face twisted. He was still a novice at deciphering her moods, and he approached conversations like this the way an apprentice animal trainer approaches a tiger for the first time—carefully, and with a healthy amount of fear. "Don't know," he said finally. "I can't put it into words." It was a catchphrase he'd picked up somewhere in the past year, and he used it as a fallback defense. It was usually effective.

"Well, I'm fine," she replied.

"Good."

She said nothing for a while, and the two of them just sat there as he sipped his beer. "There is one thing we need to talk about," she said finally.

"Sure," he said. "What is it?"

"I'm pregnant."

She had planned to say the words gently, so they would land with the weight of a feather. Instead she blurted them out, the consonants exploding in her own ears. Kozlowski looked as though he had been slammed over the head with a toaster. He sat there, his beer dangling midway between his mouth and the side table.

"I found out today," she continued. "I was expecting the doctor to tell me that I had the flu, but, nope, turns out I'm pregnant."

Kozlowski still said nothing.

"Well?" she said, looking at him. "You wanna join the conversation?"

"I think we should get married," he said at last.

"Fuck you," she replied, getting off the sofa and storming out toward the kitchen.

"Is that a yes or a no?"

"You really don't get it, do you. You don't understand that this isn't the 1950s, and you and I aren't Ozzie and Harriet. I'm not some fucking damsel in distress you have an obligation to. You don't even know whether or not I want to keep the baby."

"Do you?"

"Of course I do, asshole."

"So, what's the problem?"

"The problem is that I don't know whether I want to be married. I've never seen myself in that role. And I sure as hell don't want to be married to someone who's only asking because he knocked me up and he thinks he owes it to me."

"Who said anything about owing?" Kozlowski's voice was raised, though it wasn't quite at her decibel level. "I love you, and you love me—at least it seems like you do when you're not acting like a crazy person. You're pregnant with my kid. I'm sorry if it seems to me like these are all good reasons why we should get married." He got up and walked over to the window.

"I don't care about *should*."

"It's *not* about *should*! Not in that way. But I am who I am." He turned and looked at her. "I'm fine with what we're doing now—this thing between the two of us—when it's just us. But you start adding a kid into it, then, yeah, I want to be married. I want my kid to have real married parents."

"Parents are real whether they're married or not."

"That's great—for other people. But not for me. Not for us. I love you, and I'd want to be married with or without a kid, but if we're going to have a child together I *need* to be married."

"So are you saying you want to be married, or you need to be married, or you should be married? Which is it?"

"Jesus Christ! I don't know!" he yelled. His face was turning red now. "I don't parse every goddamned thought I have out like that! Tell me which is the right answer, for the love of God, and that's the answer I'll give you!"

They stared at each other for a few moments. "You want to get married."

"Fine," he said, "I want to get married."

"Fine." She walked back and sat on the sofa.

"Good," he replied, walking over and sitting next to her. They sat

there, next to each other, both staring straight ahead, not saying anything for several minutes. Then he picked up his beer and took a sip.
"So, we're gonna have a baby," he said, still not looking at her.

"And we're gonna get married," she added.

"I'll be in my seventies when this kid graduates college," he said,
his voice flat.

"If you're expecting me to wear some big frilly white dress and walk
down an aisle somewhere, you can forget it," she replied.

"My seventies," he repeated. He took another sip of his beer.

She looked over at him, studying his face. Then she reached over
and slid her arm under his, grasping his hand. "You'll be a better father
in your seventies than any other man I've ever known at any age."

He squeezed her hand, then turned to look at her. "You'll look
beautiful no matter what you wear," he said.

They sat there for a long time, both of them struggling to adjust to
the sudden, tectonic shift in their worlds. Neither of them was particularly comfortable with change, and Lissa knew that this was a bigger change in Kozlowski's life than he could ever have anticipated. But
she also knew that he would handle it. As much as he hated change, he
was the most reliable man she had ever met.

As she considered the changes to her own life, a strange feeling
came over her. It was a feeling with which she had little experience,
and it overwhelmed her as she tried to put her finger on what it was. It
took several moments, but at last she figured it out: for the first time
in her life she felt totally, utterly happy.

Sally wasn't used to the quiet. She'd spent her life in neighborhoods
where the noise never died. There was a constant stream of yelling and
slamming doors and sirens. There was always a bar nearby that vio-
lated last call, and her mother was always one of the last to leave, often

just coherent enough to find her way home. Sally couldn't remember a night when her sleep wasn't interrupted.

In Finn's apartment near the top of Bunker Hill at night, though, there was no noise. Every once in a while a car would drive by, but the cars on the hill had decent mufflers and never backfired, so she had to strain to hear them. There was no screaming, and people kept their televisions low enough that their neighbors didn't have to listen to the show on next door. She found the silence disconcerting. Left alone with her thoughts she felt physical discomfort, as if she were lying in a pool of insects crawling over her skin, around her eyes and ears, into her skull.

She sat up in bed. Finn was downstairs, and she was alone in the guest room. She stood up and walked over to her duffel, reached inside, and pulled out a pack of cigarettes. There was a fire escape landing outside her window; she opened the screen and stepped out onto it. Sitting down, she pulled out a cigarette and struck a match. She took a drag as she thought about her predicament. Notwithstanding the kindness her father's lawyer had shown her, she was still pretty sure she was fucked.

She'd had a glimmer of hope a year before, when her mother left her with Devon. She'd felt deserted, but she was old enough to recognize that her mother had sunk so low that she wasn't able to function. Sally had been taking care of herself for a couple of years by then, and had already come to terms with the fact that her mother loved her drugs more than she loved her daughter.

When her mother announced that Sally was going to go to live with her father, Sally was shocked. Her mother had never mentioned her father before. Sally had grown up under the impression that her mother wasn't entirely sure who her father was. That wouldn't have surprised Sally; monogamy didn't seem to be an instinct her mother possessed. Not even on a weekly basis. Sometimes, Sally feared, not on a nightly basis.

And so, when her mother announced that she was taking Sally to live with her father, Sally allowed herself to hope. For just a split second, she indulged in the fairy tale all unhappy children hold in their hearts. She let herself believe that she was a part of something greater. She let herself envision her father as a lost prince who would deliver her from her life of squalor and fear.

Devon hadn't quite fulfilled her dreams.

It wasn't his fault, she knew. Sally's mother had never told Devon about her. They showed up that morning on Devon's stoop, and Devon had come to the door warily. Sally wondered what had transpired between the two of them for her not to tell him he had a daughter, and for him to approach the door that day with such trepidation. They never told her, though.

The introductions were short. "She's yours," her mother said. "Her name's Sally."

Devon had just stood there, his mouth open, a cigarette hanging from the corner of his lips. He was wearing a dirty T-shirt and he hadn't shaved in days. Neither one of them knew what to say. For a moment, Sally thought he was going to slam the door in their faces. She wouldn't have blamed him, either. He didn't, though. After a healthy pause, he said, "I'm Devon."

To his credit, he never complained about taking her in. Most guys would have, Sally knew. Most guys would have at least asked for a paternity test. That was never an issue with Devon, though. He seemed to accept instinctively the fact that Sally was his daughter. In some ways, he even seemed excited about the prospect. He treated her with a sort of fearful awe. She supposed it was something approaching love, but she had little with which to compare it to verify her suspicion.

All the love in the world, though, couldn't improve their living conditions. It was a step up from her mother's situation, but then a step up from crack houses wasn't exactly the Ritz. She gathered quickly from his schedule that Devon didn't have any legal employment, and she deduced that he was a thief. She asked him about it once, and he didn't even try to lie. That didn't bother her; in her experience, theft seemed a minor sin. She just wished he was a better thief; he was barely making enough to feed them and pay the rent. Every once in a while she would catch him looking at her with what she could only describe as shame in his eyes. As if he was failing her. Maybe he was, a little, but she was safe and dry. She'd learned not to hope for more.

Recently, that look had begun to recede from his eyes. He'd seemed more confident; optimistic, even. Once again, she had allowed herself to believe that maybe—just maybe—better things were on the way. Now he was in jail. She vowed never to feel hope again. It was a promise she'd made before, but seemed unable to keep. Hope was crack to her; she couldn't seem to give it up no matter how hard she tried.

She took another drag off her cigarette just as the silhouette of a head appeared in the window to her room, making her flinch. "You scared me," she said.

Finn poked his head out the window. "I scared you? I came up to see if you needed anything and found the room empty; talk about scared. What are you doing?"

She considered lying, but decided against it. She held her cigarette up in view.

"You shouldn't smoke," Finn said.

"You're not my father," she replied. It came out with a harsher edge than she intended. "Devon lets me smoke," she explained. "My mother was too fucked up to care one way or another."

Finn climbed out onto the fire escape. It was an awkward fit out the window for a grown man. Once outside, he stood up and looked around. "I've never been out here," he said. She looked around. The window was located on the back side of the building, and the fire escape looked sideways on the hill. Down below she could see the street and the upscale brownstones across the way.

"It's not bad," she said.

"There's a roof deck upstairs. It's got a better view. You can see both the water and the monument."

"This is better than any view I've ever had."

He looked down at her. "Fair enough." He stood there for a moment, then took two steps down the fire escape and sat next to her. It was cramped, and she shimmied toward the building to give some room; she didn't want their legs touching. He sat there for a minute. Then he turned and looked again at her cigarette.

"I swear, my father lets me smoke," she said. She'd picked up smoking from her mother a couple of years before. She figured it beat suicide.

"I didn't say anything," Finn said. He was still looking at the butt. "It's just . . ."

"What?"

"You got an extra?"

She reached into her pocket, pulled out the pack and tossed it to him. "You shouldn't smoke," she said.

"So I've heard."

He lit the cigarette and took an ex-smoker's drag. He held the poison in his lungs for a long time, milking its full effect, like a man lost in the desert drinking at an oasis. Finally he let the smoke out in a loud, long, satisfying exhale. Looking at the glowing ember of the cigarette, he asked her, "So, you doing okay with all of this?"

She shrugged. "Which part? My mom ditching? My dad being in jail? Having no place to live?"

"Your father being in jail and you having to stay here with me."

"Par for the course in my life," she said.

He took another long drag off the cigarette and held it for a shorter time. "It's not always gonna be like this," he said as he exhaled.

"No? What's it gonna be like?"

"That's up to you."

"Is this the part where you share an inspirational story about how hard life was when you were growing up, and how you beat the odds?"

"No," Finn said. "Not anymore."

"Good. I've heard it before. It's like every guidance counselor's been given the same script. *I'm in control of my own life; I can do whatever I want; if I just apply myself, all the doors in the world are open to me.* Except it's a load of shit. Worse, they know it's a load of shit. They say the words, but they know what really happens."

"So, what is it you want?"

She shook her head. "I don't know. A view as good as this, maybe." There was a part of her that wanted to cry, but she wouldn't let herself. What would be the point?

Finn sat smoking his cigarette for a while. He wasn't looking at her anymore, he was back to looking out at the street. "You're right," he said at last. "I'm not your father. And I can't tell you what to do. All I can do is try to get your father out of jail, and try to help you out in the meantime."

"Thanks."

"It's not much."

"I know."

"I really do want to help. So does Lissa. So does Kozlowski."

She looked at him with a puzzled expression.

"Okay, I don't know about Koz. He's tough to read. I'm sure he'd want to help if he gave it any thought, though."

Sally thought about it. "Why?"

"Why what?"

"Why do you want to help? Why does Lissa want to help? What do you care?"

Finn stubbed out the butt on the fire escape and threw it over the side. "You're the daughter of a client."

"That it? My father's a client, that's why you're helping me out?"

He nodded. "That's why I agreed to take you in. I didn't know you then."

"And now?"

He shrugged. "I'd help you out even if you weren't Devon's kid."

"I guess that's something," she said.

"It's a start," he said. He reached out and tousled her hair. It was an awkward gesture, and her first instinct was to slap his hand away. In a strange way, though, she liked it. She couldn't remember anyone ever doing that to her before. Most of the physical contact she'd had in the past had been either violent or inappropriate. Even her father, who clearly cared about her, seemed afraid to hug her.

She reached up and tousled his hair back. "It's a start," she agreed. Then she moved toward the window.

"One last thing," he said.

"What?"

"You still shouldn't smoke."

She looked back over her shoulder at him. "Neither should you."

Chapter Fourteen

Eddie Ballick stood at the edge of the water. There was no moon out that night, and a heavy layer of clouds blacked out the stars. The harbor was as dark as he'd ever seen it. He wondered briefly whether he was doing the right thing, but the thought was fleeting. He wasn't someone who dwelled on such matters.

"Do you think he's coming?"

The question came from Jimmy Kent. Jimmy had been with him for more than a decade. If Ballick had allowed himself to have friends, Kent might be one. Ballick viewed him as competent and trustworthy. Other considerations never entered his mind.

"I don't know. There were only four of us, and he thinks one of us crossed him. Bulger's gone; that leaves three. Rumor is he's coming after us." It was more than a rumor. Vince Murphy's murder confirmed it as far as Ballick was concerned. Many people might have wanted Murphy dead, but Ballick could think of only one man who would carry out the job in the way it had been done. "Are we ready?"

Kent nodded. "Our three best guys. Positioned just the way you told me."

"Good."

"I wish we had more," Kent said. "There's still time to get some of the others."

Ballick shook his head. "He's too smart for that. If he thinks he's outmatched, he'll wait. I can't surround myself forever. If he thinks I'm an easy target, he'll come quickly, and we'll be able to deal with him. Or not. Either way, it needs to happen now, and this is the best place for us."

"What if they send others after him?"

"There are no others. It's him, and that's it. If he fucks it up, it's over."

———

Ballick had chosen a good spot; Liam had to give him credit for that. The shack was located on a narrow strip of land jutting out into the water, sandwiched in between a deserted boatyard and an open marsh that pushed up against the high metal fences of a gas station and two car dealerships. There was only one way in—a long narrow driveway with trees running down both sides. A steel swinging-arm gate was locked across the entrance to the driveway. It wouldn't keep a man on foot out, but it would present an obstacle to a full assault by vehicle. The driveway set up a bottleneck that would make anyone approaching an easy target.

Liam had been watching the place for more than a day. He kept tallies in his head of everyone coming or going, and watched the patterns of activity. He knew Ballick wasn't alone. If his count was accurate, there were four others on the property. His count was always accurate.

Five men presented a challenge, but not an insurmountable one. Even the best that Boston's underworld had to offer had never been to war. They were little more than bullies, and they wouldn't understand the principles of ambush and counterattack.

The key was determining where they were positioned. He could be pretty sure that Ballick would keep his most trusted man with him as a last line of defense. It was likely that two others would be hidden in the trees along the driveway—one on either side to catch him in a cross fire if possible. That left one more. Where he would be hidden was the main mystery. The driveway ended at a spot where the land broadened, and beyond was a parking lot and scrub that eased into the marsh. The property was littered with derelict boats up on cradles, stacks of docks and floats and lobster pots ready to be put into the water once the weather warmed, as well as piles of netting and un-identifiable junk. The place presented a thousand places for a sniper to sit and wait, fully concealed. If he guessed where among the mess the fourth man was hidden, he would make quick work of all of them. If he guessed wrong, he'd be dead before he was aware of his mistake.

Liam was concealed at the edge of an outcropping of small trees and bushes around twenty yards from the gate. From his position, he had a perfect view down the driveway, and could see the corner of the fishing shack in the distance. He was armed with his nine-millimeter, four clips, and his knife. Sean Broadark was in a car parked across the street, his head down. Liam's instructions had been explicit, and he knew they would be obeyed. Broadark was a soldier.

As he lay there, a beat-up Honda with a square plastic sign advertising Domino's Pizza pulled up to the gate. The driver hesitated, then got out of the car to examine the lock. When it became clear that he could not swing open the arm, he got back into his car and leaned on his horn, giving off two long blasts.

Liam reached into his coat, pulled out a pair of night-vision binoculars and focused them on the driveway; it was all about to begin.

———

Kent looked at Ballick when he heard the car horn. "Go check it out," he said after a moment.

Kent put the hand that held his pistol into the outer pocket of his coat and walked around the corner of the building. As he headed toward the driveway, he glanced at the stack of lobster pots behind which Tom Shavers, the best shot among all his men, was concealed. It was a perfect sniper position, with a clear view of any approach to the shack. The tarps over the pots gave complete cover. They had ripped a seam in the tarps so that Shavers could see out. In the darkness, there was no chance of him being spotted.

Kent walked quickly up the driveway, his head on a swivel, looking for anything out of the ordinary. He knew that two others were in the trees along the driveway, but he couldn't tell exactly where. He hated being out in the open.

As he got to the end of the driveway, the driver of the Honda got out of his car and opened the rear door. Kent's grip on his gun tightened in his pocket. "What the fuck are you doing?" he called out.

"Pizza," the driver said, pulling a box out of the back.

"We didn't order any pizza," Kent replied. "You got the wrong address."

The driver looked at the sign just next to the gate. "This is eleven-oh-eight?"

"Yeah, but we didn't order any fuckin' pizza."

The driver was a young man with long hair and a fuzzy chin. He looked stoned as he bent down to look again at the sales slip in the car's interior light. Then his head popped up above the car roof again. "That's the address they gave me," he said.

"I don't give a fuck what address they gave you," Kent said. "I'm telling you, we didn't order any fuckin' pizza. Get the fuck out of here."

The driver ran his greasy fingers through greasier hair. "Fuck," he muttered. "I hate this job." He tossed the pizza box into the backseat. Then he slid into the driver's seat and pulled away.

"Fuckin' moron," Kent said. He stood there, his eyes searching the street. He'd never seen Ballick so concerned, and he didn't understand why. Kent had his best men in place, and they were ready for anything. After a moment he turned and started back to the little shack by the water.

He took two steps before the shot tore through the center of his back. It felt as though he'd been hit with a baseball bat, and he pitched forward onto the pavement. In his mind he was moving, his gun out as he whirled around to shoot back, shouting directions to the men in the trees. In reality, he lay still. The bullet had blown through his spinal column just between his shoulder blades, and the instructions from his brain had nowhere to go. His mouth was moving, but no sound came out. Blood fought its way up his esophagus and trickled out of the corner of his mouth onto the driveway. He was dead within seconds.

Liam was moving as soon as he pulled the trigger, silently shifting his position ten feet to the left. The bushes where he'd been standing exploded from the rounds fired from the trees along the driveway. He watched the flashes and took careful aim at the spot from where the shots came on the left, firing six quick rounds into the trees.

Then he was moving again, running toward the driveway.

More shots rang out from the right-hand side of the driveway, and Liam could hear the shots whistle by him. Then he heard a number of gunshots coming from behind him, and he knew that Broadark was returning fire, just as instructed. The gunshots from the trees stopped, and Liam kept moving, hurtling the metal fence and diving toward the far edge of the row of trees.

The trees were now his allies, providing him with cover as he moved quickly down the row toward the shack. Halfway down the driveway, he came across the body of one of Ballick's men. He was slumped against a tree trunk, his neck tipped back at an awkward angle, his eyes wide open, staring at the overhanging branches. Liam bent down to feel his neck for a pulse, though he knew there would be none. He could see the hole that had been ripped in the man's chest.

Now he had a decision to make. He'd seen the man who came out to chase away the pizza delivery boy take a long look at the canvas mass to the left of the shack, and it gave him a good indication that the fourth man was hidden there. The approach would be better from the other line of trees. At the same time, that line would require that he cut across the narrow drive, leaving him exposed. He decided it was necessary—not only to give him a better angle at the fourth man, but also to make sure that the shooter in the opposite row of trees was dead. There had been no shooting from there since Broadark ripped off his rounds toward the rifle flashes. It was possible that the shooter was merely playing possum, waiting for Liam to get overconfident and show himself in the open. It was unlikely—these men weren't that well trained. Liam was that well trained, though, and he knew better than to leave any loose ends.

He crouched down low, in a runner's stance, slowing his breathing and filling his lungs. Then he fired out with his legs, driving forward across the driveway.

He kept his head moving, looking out for shots both from in front of him—from the man in the trees—and to his left—from the canvas-covered stack. He was almost hoping that the man under the tarp would take a shot; the chances of a hit at that range on a moving target were slim, and it would confirm the man's location. He was fairly certain that the fourth man was there, but confirmation would have been nice.

No shots came.

Liam slid under the branches of the trees on the far side, and almost toppled into the other shooter. He was lying there, a few feet from the tree trunk, breathing heavily. A rifle lay a few feet away. Liam moved forward, kicking the gun even farther away from the man and kneeling on his chest. There were at least two wounds he could see; one in the belly and one in the throat. Neither had been fatal as yet, though the throat injury looked severe. It appeared as though the front half of the man's windpipe had been blown out. As he sucked for breath, Liam could see the hole in the man's neck whistle and contract; any air he was getting was coming from there, not from his mouth or nose. He looked down at the man, and could see his lips forming the words, *Help me, please!*

Liam nodded to the man. Then he pulled out his knife and slipped it into the wound, slicing deeply in one motion, severing the carotid artery that had somehow been spared when the man was shot. The man's eyes went wide with terror, but darkened in a matter of seconds as a flood of dark red flowed from the wound, around his neck and into the soft ground beneath him.

Setting his gun on the ground, Liam pulled the body into a sitting position and slipped the sweater off it. He removed the man's shoes and wrapped them in the sweater, tying the bundle tight. Then he picked up his gun and moved down toward the last tree in the line, which sat no farther than thirty yards from the shack.

He crouched under that last tree for a few moments, watching the area in front of him. Whoever the fourth man was, he was the best trained of them all, and he hadn't given up his position. He also, un-doubtedly, had seen Liam move across the road, and had a rough idea of the direction from which Liam would be coming.

After a while, it became clear that the fourth man had no intention of betraying himself, and Liam decided to take the fight to him.

He picked up the bundle he'd made of the dead man's sweater and shoes and moved to the side of the tree closest to the driveway. Hold-ing his gun in his left hand, he threw the bundle as hard as he could with his right hand out from under the tree branches, then dove to the other side of the tree's coverage.

As the shirt and shoes skidded across the driveway, tumbling in the dark night toward the shack, several gunshots rang out from under the canvas, and Liam could see quick flashes illuminating the slit opening in the center. The man was a decent shot, at least, as the bundle jumped and hopped, hit twice by the bullets.

It was the confirmation he needed.

He slid to the edge of the branches and aimed carefully at the opening. Then he unloaded the rest of the clip at the spot from where the shots had come.

He waited a moment, listening carefully for any signs of life. There were none. The nature of his mission—and the betrayal that had inspired it—ran through his mind. Then he slid a fresh clip into his gun, took aim at the opening in the canvas that was now flapping slightly in the breeze, and fired another fifteen rounds.

Chapter Fifteen

"Hello?" the guard said.

Devon held up his badge so it could be seen on the security screen. "BPD," he replied. "We've had a report of a disturbance on the grounds. They sent us out to make sure everything's okay."

"We haven't seen anything," the guard said. "Who reported the disturbance?"

"One of the neighbors," Devon lied. "If you'll let us in, we can do a quick search of the place and get out of your hair."

"I don't know." There was a slight quiver in the guard's voice. "I'm not supposed to let anyone in after hours." Devon could sense that the guard was deliberating; it was taking too long. He nodded to the Irishman to assure him that this wasn't a problem. It was to be expected. It would have been nice if the guard had buzzed them in without any resistance, but that wasn't realistic. Devon was prepared to apply whatever pressure necessary.

There were risks involved. If the guard called the real cops to confirm the report, they were screwed; once it was clear that two men impersonating the police had tried to get into the museum, the job was over for good. Security in the place would triple overnight. Bulger's words echoed in his ears as he stood there—"If you fuck this up,

128

I'll only see you once more." The meaning was clear. And yet Devon knew this was their best chance.

According to the information Bulger had given them, the guards were not really guards at all; they were music students. It was a perfect job for someone in that position. The shift started at midnight and ran until eight a.m., and a struggling musician could play in a band, then head over to work. It was a low-stress gig; there were two of them on duty at night, and their main responsibility was to watch for fire and make sure the plumbing didn't explode. The museum housed literally tens of billions of dollars' worth of art, and the greatest threat to the collection was from water and smoke. Theft was a theoretical risk, but a remote one at most. The place was shut up tight every night, and a button underneath the security desk could easily be tripped, which would immediately notify the police of any trouble. On the other hand, it wasn't clear that a kid in that position would have the balls to keep out the police if they showed up unannounced.

Devon got himself into character quickly. He looked straight into the camera. "Look, you fuckin' rent-a-cop," he said, "we have a report of an alarm at the museum. My partner and I can't leave here until we check it out. This is our last call of the night, and we've been on duty for more than twelve hours dealing with nothing but punks and drunks. You don't wanna open the door? Fine. I'm gonna call in the fuckin' SWAT team to surround the place. Then I'm gonna call the captain, and I'm gonna have him wake up every one of this museum's fuckin' directors and get their asses down here to explain why one of their employees is interfering with officers responding to a report of a disturbance. I'm sure that's gonna make your whole fuckin' week. Either that, or we can come in for two minutes and verify that it's a false alarm. It's your choice."

Devon wondered if he'd overplayed the hand. He'd been around cops enough to know that their power and authority was most often projected through aggression. Cops liked nothing less than being questioned, and any time their authority was challenged by a civilian, the response was predictable.

He looked over at the Irishman, who was standing there, glowering at him. From the man's expression, Devon wouldn't have been surprised if he slit Devon's throat then and there if the ruse didn't play out. Devon had seen the knife the man carried.

Finally, after an eternal moment, the guard came over the intercom again. "I'm not allowed to leave the security desk," he said. "Do you know where it is?"

Devon winked at Liam and turned to face the camera. "Up on the main floor?"

"Yeah, that's right. Take a left and then follow the signs for the men's room. You'll see it."

"Okay," Devon said. The buzzer on the door rang, and Devon reached forward to pull it open for Liam. He didn't thank the guard; cops rarely thank the person they've just browbeaten. Besides, they needed the guard to remain nervous if they were going to pull this off. A lot still could go wrong. Bulger had given them a complete layout of the security system. Devon had never asked where it came from, but it made clear that the only point of contact with the outside world was at the security desk. If the guards managed to set off that switch, they were done. If they could get the guards out from behind the desk, though, the danger would be over. There were no other external alarms that would alert anyone to what was going on inside the place. Now it was all a mental game, and if Devon could out-duel the security guards, they would be fine.

He looked up at the security camera once more and shook his head, as though in utter contempt for the man at the controls. He hoped the guard was watching.

———◆———

Ballick knew he was alone. He could have run; maybe he should have, but that wasn't who he was. He accepted his fate with the same ambivalence he'd shown toward life. The precautions he'd taken had not been sufficient. It was enough, and he sat down in the chair out back of the shack to look out at the water and wait.

It didn't take long. It was only a matter of minutes before he heard a footstep on the gravel to his right. "I figured you were coming," he said simply.

"So it seems." Ballick could hear the streets of Belfast thick in Kilbranish's accent. "Only four? I feel insulted."

"Who says there ain't more," Ballick replied. "Maybe inside."

"No," Liam replied. "We've been watching. Only four."

"We? I thought you worked alone."

"Aye. Except when necessary."

"Like twenty years ago?"

"Like twenty years ago. Only it didn't work out so well for me then, did it?"

Ballick heard shuffling off to the left of the building and glanced over to see a shadowy figure blocking any escape in that direction. "Maybe it'll work out better for you this time."

"That depends on you," Liam said. He stepped forward and the thin beam of light cast by low-wattage spotlights hanging precariously from the corners of the roof bisected his face, showing his eyes but concealing his mouth and nose. It made him look like some sort of masked bandit. "Talk," he said.

Ballick looked at Liam. The determination in his eyes seemed balanced on the edge of madness, and Ballick knew he'd seen his last sunrise over the water. He looked out at the bay, his sight drawn naturally to the horizon, where the dark steel of the water faded into the charcoal sky. "You're not going to like what I have to say."

"Try me."

"We don't know where they are."

Liam was standing only a few feet from him now, and he raised his arm, pointing his pistol at Ballick's head. Ballick hoped he would pull the trigger then and there, but knew it would be too easy. "You're going to have to do better than that."

"I'm telling you, we don't know where they are," he said again. "No one does."

"Someone does," Liam replied. He motioned toward the door to the shack with the barrel of his gun.

"It's gonna be like that?" Ballick said.

"It's up to you."

Ballick stood. "Nothing I can tell you is gonna be of any use," he said. Liam didn't respond, but motioned to the door again. To Ballick's left, the other man emerged from the shadows. He seemed large and shapeless, and he had a face from a child's nightmare. He had a gun, too, and he moved with economy and confidence.

Ballick turned toward the water to take one last look. A stiff breeze kicked off the harbor and swept in, working over his face like a farewell. He inhaled deeply, letting the frigid air fill him to the core, closing his eyes in memory, feeling comforted.

Then he took two steps toward the door, and flanked by Liam and the other man, he stepped into the shack.

———◆———

Devon led the way through the museum hallways and around to the security guard's desk. He and the Irishman had discussed the fact that Devon was the only one who would talk. He had the thick Boston accent shared by the vast majority of the police on the streets. It wasn't as though there were no cops in Boston with Irish accents, but it would stick out, and possibly give the guards cause for alarm. They couldn't afford to take the risk. The Irishman had reluctantly agreed to allow Devon to do the talking.

Devon came around the corner first and saw the guard standing behind the security desk. That was bad. He was hoping the man might have come around from the back, and they simply would have tackled him to prevent him from setting off the alarm. Now it looked like Devon was going to have to lure the man away from his post.

"You the guy givin' us such a hassle out there?" he yelled at the guard. The kid couldn't have been older than twenty-two.

"Sorry, Officer," the guard said. "I wasn't sure whether I was supposed to let the police in. I was told no one gets in after closing."

"That's the dumbest fuckin' thing I ever heard," Devon pressed. He looked at the Irishman. "You ever heard anything so fuckin' stupid? It don't even make any sense." He turned back to the guard. "You wanna try again?"

The guard was nervous now, Devon could tell. That was the goal—make him nervous. Some ratty little pot-smoking musician-slash-security-guard would be naturally scared of the cops, and fear would make him compliant. "I don't understand," he said. "That's what I was told."

"Bullshit," Devon shot back. He stepped in close and examined the kid. He was so close that the guard involuntarily pulled back from the security desk. "Don't I know you?" Devon asked him.

"I don't think so."

"Yeah, I do. I busted you three months ago down on Mass Ave, right? Possession, or some shit like that. You never showed for your court hearing. Bad mistake; you probably would've gotten probation, but judges don't like when you skip. We got a warrant out for your arrest."

The guard shook his head so hard, Devon thought he might break a vertebra. "You've got me confused with someone else, Officer. I swear it."

Devon made his eyes go dark and he moved toward the desk. "You little shit! You callin' me a fuckin' liar? I swear to God, if you are, I'll make you fuckin' pay. I know a bunch of guys down at Corrections;

I make one phone call, and you'll be fucked so hard in jail, you'll shit spunk for weeks. You got that!"

"Yes, Officer, but I swear you never arrested me." The guard was in a panic now, and Devon could literally smell the fear on him. For a moment he wondered whether the kid had pissed his pants.

"You got someone else here, a partner?"

"Yeah," the guard stammered. "He's just finishing his rounds. I called him, and he'll be right down."

"He better be, because you're in a shitload of trouble, and we're gonna have to deal with it. Is there anyone else here?"

"No, sir, just the two of us. I don't understand why I'm in trouble."

"Get your ass out from behind that desk," Devon ordered. The guard hesitated. "Move, you little shit! Or I will make you wish you'd never been born, I swear it!"

The guard relented and walked around the desk. "What? What do you want from me?" he asked.

"I want you to shut your fuckin' mouth, and I want you to move over toward the wall." As the kid moved toward him, Devon knew it was all just about over. It was unlikely that, even if the guard realized there was a problem now, he could get back to the desk to set off the alarm. Still, Devon wanted to play the role out so that it would make the rest of the evening as simple as possible.

"This is ridiculous," the guard said. "I haven't done anything!"

Devon spun him by the shoulder and pushed him in the center of his back toward the wall. "Keep talkin'," he said. "It only gets worse." He shoved the guard against the wall and kicked his feet. "Spread 'em," he said. The guard spread his feet. His hands were already up against the wall. "Now put your hands behind your back," Devon said.

"You're making a serious mistake," the guard pleaded.

"We'll know soon enough," Devon said. "I'm gonna call this in and run you through the system. But right now, I want you to put your hands behind your fuckin' back!" The guard put his right hand behind his back, and Devon closed the handcuff around his wrist. Almost there. "Now the left one."

The guard put his left hand behind his back, and as the second cuff closed, Devon realized he hadn't frisked the kid. Not that it really mattered—he knew the guards weren't armed. But no cop puts someone in cuffs without frisking him first. He turned the guard around and smiled.

"You're not the police, are you?" the guard said.

Devon could feel his smile broaden.

Just then the other guard walked around the corner from finishing his rounds. He saw the first guard with his hands cuffed behind his back, and the two police officers standing there. "What's going on, Officer?" he said.

Devon nodded to the Irishman, and passed the first guard over to him. Then he moved toward the second guard. "This asshole's under arrest," he said. "You're next if you don't watch it. I want you up against the wall, now." He was manhandling the guard, who was so taken by surprise he wasn't even resisting.

It took less than five seconds for Devon to cuff the second man, and by the time it was over, the last chance the guards had to avoid disaster had slipped fully away. All he said as Devon put the cuffs on him was, "I don't understand why you're arresting me!"

Devon spun the man around. "You're not being arrested," he said evenly. "This is a robbery. If you don't give us any trouble, you won't get hurt."

"They don't pay me enough to get hurt," the guard said.

Devon smiled. "Good. You boys keep your mouths shut and don't tell the police anything for a year, and we'll send you a reward." Neither of them replied to this. "Which way is the basement?"

"Down the hallway," the second guard said, motioning with his chin.

Devon nodded again to Liam. "Downstairs," he said. They walked the two guards down the hall to a doorway that led down to the basement. As they walked, Devon questioned the two captives briefly. "No more guards, right?" he said. That was the information they had—that there were only two guards on duty at night, but that sort of intelligence can be wrong, so he figured he'd confirm it.

"Just the two of us," the first guard said. He seemed to be the senior of the two, though he was only in his early twenties.

"No other external alarms, right? Other than the one behind the desk?"

"No other alarms."

Devon stopped them on the stairs. "If you're lying and the cops show up, the first thing I'm going to do is run down here and put a bullet in your head, okay?"

"I understand."

Devon looked at the man, but saw no evidence of deception on his face.

They led the two men down to the basement and found two posts about a hundred feet apart. They had the men turn around and bound their hands and feet tightly with duct tape. Then they tore strips and put them over the guards' mouths and eyes. They pushed them down on the ground and taped them to the posts. "Nighty-night, boys," Devon said. "We hear any noise and we're coming down shooting. Remember what we said." He looked at Liam and nodded.

They were in, and they hadn't even needed to pull out their guns. His job was done.

Chapter Sixteen

Detective Stone arrived at the waterfront at dawn. The buildings were silhouettes against a gray sky to the east, and a light mist hung in the air, reflecting what seemed like a thousand blue-and-red flashing lights. Police tape blocked the driveway, and a bleary-eyed patrolman directed him to park on the street. "There's a lot of ground to cover in there," he said to Stone. "It's gonna take the crime scene boys a while to finish."

As Stone got out of his car and started walking toward the driveway, another car pulled up and flashed its brights at him. As it pulled alongside him, Sanchez rolled down the window. "You just getting here?" she asked.

"I just got the call," he replied.

"Me too." She looked toward the driveway. "Ballick?"

"Sounds like it. Some of his men, too. We don't have confirmation yet."

Sanchez rolled up the window and pulled forward, parking her sedan in front of the unmarked car she and Stone shared when on duty.

The view down the long driveway, flanked by the trees on both sides, seemed surreal to Stone. As the crime scene technicians did their work, flashlights sparked the fog in the growing light, like the warning signals of a dozen tiny lighthouses.

It only took a few yards before they were upon the first signs of the massacre. A body lay facedown in the middle of the driveway, covered with a light sheet. Stone bent down and lifted a corner. "Jimmy Kent," he said to Sanchez.

"That's about all the confirmation we need on Ballick," Sanchez said. "We'll find him here somewhere."

"Looks like he was shot in the back. Clean kill would be my guess. Nothing out of the ordinary."

They could see three other areas of activity outside, one set of lights on both sides of the drive, and a couple of lights on what looked like a pile of lobster pots at the end of the entryway. The little shack out toward the pier, however, seemed to be the center of attention. There were half a dozen cops and technicians milling about in and around the doorway. Even from a distance, some of them looked shaken.

Stone and Sanchez took a brief look at each of the three other bodies outside the shack. They didn't recognize any of them, but they all had the same look of thug soldiers. "Whoever did this is good," Sanchez said.

"I'm not sure 'good' is the first word that comes to mind," Stone replied.

"Skilled, then. Whatever you want to call it, we're dealing with someone who knows what he's doing."

They headed over toward the shack and cut through those loitering outside. No one seemed to want to look them in the eyes. As they approached the door, Sergeant McAfee stepped outside. "Detectives," he said. "You're not gonna believe this. You may wanna take a minute and get prepared."

"Like Murphy?" Stone asked.

"Sort of," McAfee replied. "Only way worse. There are lots of different knives and hooks in there used for gutting, scaling, and cleaning fish. Motherfucker got creative with his work. We assume it's Ballick, but it's gonna take dental records to be sure. There ain't much left that's recognizable. There's a huge sink in there. That's where he is. What's left of him. Makes it a little cleaner, I guess."

Stone peered around McAfee inside the shack. He couldn't see much; there were too many people. He recognized one of them. He was difficult to miss. He was around six-four and black. "Feds are here," Stone said to Sanchez.

McAfee nodded. "He got here around the same time we did."

"How'd he find out about it?" Stone asked.

McAfee shrugged. "Don't know. Maybe the feds have some sort of newfangled crime detectors they aren't sharing with us. Could've heard it on the radio, but he would have had to have been listening for it."

Sanchez stepped into the shack. "Hewitt!" She didn't quite shout it, but it was close. "Out here!"

Hewitt was standing against the far wall of the shack, staying out of the way, observing the crime scene people as they went about their business. He stepped around one of them who was on the ground, pulling up some debris and tagging it. "Detective Sanchez," he said. He put his hand out.

She ignored the hand. Instead she pushed him toward the door.

"Take it easy, Detective," he said. His voice was deep and there was a hint of a threat in it. "We're on the same team."

"Bullshit," Sanchez said. "This is my team. I'm in charge here. If you were on my team, I'd know what the hell you're doing here. I don't."

"I told you last time, at the Body Shop," Hewitt said. "I'm involved in an organized crime task force. We have to investigate when connected guys get killed."

"Bullshit again. Connected guys get killed in this city every day. I've never seen you at a crime scene before."

Hewitt looked uncomfortable. "It's a recent investigation," he said. "This may be relevant to it."

Sanchez put her hands on her hips. "Oh, well, why didn't you tell me that? What's the nature of the investigation? If we know that, then maybe we can help."

Hewitt's look went from uncomfortable to pained. "I'd like to, but it's classified," he said. "If there was any way . . ." His voice trailed off.

"Right," Sanchez said. "*If there was any way.* . . . I'll tell you what, Special Agent Hewitt. You have three choices at this moment. You can tell me what you're investigating, and we can work together. You can assert jurisdiction right now, in which case I'll pull all my people off this. Or you can file an official request for cooperation through channels. Barring any one of those three, however, I want you to get the fuck out of my crime scene. I swear to God, if I see you within a hundred yards of any of my investigations, I will arrest you for obstruction of justice."

"You wouldn't," he scoffed.

"I would. I'm sure the FBI's Boston office would love another investigation into its operating procedures right now. The last one went so well." She stood there with her arms crossed. Stone decided at that moment to try to avoid ever crossing her.

"I'll file a request for cooperation," Hewitt said after a moment. He walked past the officers who had gathered around the scene to watch the show.

"You do that!" Sanchez called after him. "I'll make sure it gets exactly the consideration it deserves." Hewitt didn't turn around. "I don't trust them," she said in a quieter voice.

"The FBI?" Stone asked. "You don't trust the entire organization?"

She looked at him. "You weren't here back in the nineties. We had Bulger and his crew nailed a dozen different times, but the feds tipped him off every time. We'd have the bastard nailed, and then he'd skate. We thought he was clairvoyant. But no, it turned out that the FBI was crooked. So, no, I don't trust the entire FBI."

"That was one agent, though, wasn't it? John Connolly, and he went to prison for it. You can't blame the entire organization for that."

"John Connolly was the only one caught. He was the only one prosecuted. He was the only one who went to jail. You think he was the only one involved? How likely is that? He was involved, but no one else in the entire office could figure it out in more than a decade? C'mon."

"You really think Hewitt's mobbed up?" Stone whistled doubtfully. "I ran a check on him; he's got a solid rep, even with our people. He doesn't seem like the type."

Sanchez looked back up the driveway. Hewitt was nearly to the end of it now. The flashlights had been turned off as the sun came up, and the property had lost the otherworldly feeling to it. Now the dead men outside had the full edge of reality to them. "I don't know. I'm just saying there's something bad going on here, and I don't trust them." She looked up at Stone. "Now, are you ready to deal with the mess inside?"

Stone nodded.

"Good. Let's get this done." She walked back into the building.

As Stone followed her, he took one last look down the driveway. Hewitt had disappeared now. That was for the best, he thought. Given Sanchez's opinions, they would never be able to be productive as long as he was there. Still, in his heart, Stone couldn't accept the notion that Hewitt and the FBI might be involved.

Chapter Seventeen

The morning of Devon's arraignment, Finn arrived at the office later than usual. He'd dropped Sally off at school, and by the time he got back to Charlestown, it was nearly nine o'clock. Kozlowski was already cloistered away in his back office when Finn pushed open the door to the brownstone. Lissa was working at her desk. She looked up to say a quick hello and then put her nose back into her computer screen.

Finn had a couple of hours before he had to appear with Devon, and he planned to use the time effectively. He had a number of briefs and motions in other cases he had been neglecting, and he knew that if he didn't get to them soon, he'd start missing deadlines. Tardiness was the only true cardinal sin in the judicial system. You could be a terrible lawyer in other respects—you could mis-cite precedent and fudge facts; lack logic and structure in your arguments; have trouble putting together a competent, grammatical English sentence—and you'd still receive a fair and reasonable hearing. But heaven help the lawyer who missed a deadline. For that transgression, the weight of the legal system would land with full force upon the lawyer's client.

Fortunately, Finn liked writing. Since leaving the world of the mega-firm, he no longer had endless amounts of time to spend polishing his written work, but he still had a good feel for telling his clients' stories. His approach was simple: state relevant facts and apply the appropriate legal principles from the case law in as few words as possible. Judges appreciated his brevity.

He was shortening a brief in a civil case for one of the few corporate clients he had when the phone rang. He picked it up. "Finn here," he said.

"Mr. Finn, this is Detective Stone."

"Detective," Finn replied. "What can I do for you?" He tapped away at the keyboard as he spoke, rushing to complete the brief so that he could get it filed on time.

"We'd like you to come down to the station today to have a talk."

"We?" Finn was deleting a redundant paragraph and only half paying attention.

"Me and my partner. Any chance you could make it this morning?"

"Today's a little busy for me," Finn said honestly. "What's this about?"

"It's about Eddie Ballick. We understand you talked to him yesterday."

"I did."

"We'd like to know what about."

Finn was wrapping up the conclusion in his brief, typing out the last few words. "I can't really talk about that, Detective. I was doing work for a client."

"We'd still like you to come down."

Finn finished the last sentence. He scrolled to the top of the document and started reading it through to make sure it made sense. "I'm very busy today," he said. "Why are you interested in my conversation with Ballick?"

"Because he was murdered last night."

Finn stopped reading the brief. He blinked hard and looked at the phone in his hand. A million questions ran through his head. He didn't ask any of them; all he managed to get out of his mouth was a feeble, "What?"

"He was murdered, Mr. Finn," Stone replied. "What time can we expect you at the station house?"

Finn hung up the phone and leaned back in his chair. He looked over at Lissa, who had overheard his half of the conversation. "What was that all about?" she asked.

"That was about Eddie Ballick. He was murdered last night. Apparently he b—"

Lissa raised her hand to stop Finn. "Hold on," she said. "No point in going through this twice." She stood up and walked to the door at the back of the office, which led out to both a back door and to Kozlowski's office. "Koz!" she yelled. "You need to get in here." She walked back and sat down at her desk again.

A moment later, Kozlowski emerged. "What's going on?" he asked.

"That was Detective Stone on the phone."

"Stone? What did he want?"

"Ballick was murdered last night."

Kozlowski stopped. He turned and looked at Finn. "That can't be good."

"No, I wouldn't think. They found him early this morning. Four of his boys, too. Stone didn't give me all the details, but from the sound of it, it wasn't pretty."

Kozlowski sat on the chair in front of Finn's desk. "What are you going to do?"

"I put them off; told them I was too busy today, and that I'd get back to them as soon as I could. Devon's being arraigned this morning."

"You think he's caught up in all this?"

"If not, it seems like one hell of a coincidence. Either way, I want to have a long talk with Devon before I deal with the police. And that talk will be a lot easier to have once he's out on bail."

***

The courthouse was a twenty-story slab of gray concrete in Center Square, downtown. It was cut in an unadorned, utilitarian style that seemed calculated to betray the mechanical nature of the judicial system.

Finn parked in a nearby underground garage and entered the building, flashing his bar card at the door to bypass the line of civilians waiting to pass through the metal detectors. He went straight to the courtroom and inquired about Devon's whereabouts from the clerk. She told him his client was in transit, and that he wouldn't have time to meet before the hearing. That was frustrating; he had much to discuss with Devon.

Finn took a seat at the back and watched the courtroom. It was packed with lawyers milling around, hustling in and out, shuffling stacks of court files. Clients dragged their feet and looked about with angry, distrustful eyes. Police officers strutted in and out through the swinging doors at the back. Justice was a messy process.

Arraignments are short affairs. They're designed to advise defendants of all the charges against them, ensure that they have legal assistance, obtain initial pleas, and set bail if appropriate. In a few misdemeanor cases, plea agreements will have been worked out even before the arraignment, but in most serious matters an initial plea of not guilty is entered, and plea arrangements are reached through negotiations afterward.

On that day, the Honorable Myron Platt was presiding over the arraignments. Platt was in his mid-fifties, with a slight paunch and a receding hairline. He had been appointed a few years before in the final days of an outgoing gubernatorial administration as a reward to a loyal political hack. The bench was not the dream job he'd hoped for, and he let his boredom show. In most other respects, however, he was reasonable—even if that reason was primarily a by-product of disinterest.

Two assistant district attorneys sat at the prosecutors' table, alternating on cases as they were brought up for preliminary dispositions. One was a young man Finn didn't recognize who was probably less than two years out of law school. The other was a woman in her forties whose name was Kristin Kelley, against whom Finn had tried a number of cases in the past.

It was a virtually automated process; the prosecutors had only a few minutes with any given file, and they treated each according to established guidelines. Finn had to sit through six arraignments before Devon's case was called. The court clerk read out the case caption, "Case number 08-CR-2677, Commonwealth versus Devon Malley! Come forward and be heard!"

Finn stood up. "Scott Finn for the defense," he announced as he moved forward to defense counsel's table.

Kristin Kelley stood up. "Attorney Kelley for the Commonwealth," she said. She looked over at Finn as he put his briefcase down on the table. It was not a friendly look. Finn had beaten her every time they'd gone head to head, and nothing annoyed prosecutors more than being beaten. It probably would have been better for Devon if she hadn't pulled the case, but there was no helping that now.

Devon was led in from the front of the courtroom, still in his jailhouse fatigues. He was shackled at both his wrists and ankles, but otherwise he seemed relaxed. "Your Honor, if I may confer with my client for a minute?" Finn said.

"Thirty seconds, counsel." Judge Platt yawned. "All we need right now is an initial plea—guilty or not. Anything more complicated than that you can deal with once we're done. I don't want to hold the others here up."

Devon duckwalked in his shackles behind the desk. He put his fingers to his lips and made a zipping motion. "I'm keeping quiet," he said, winking. "This is your show."

"Good," Finn said. "But we need to talk seriously once you're out."

"I know," Devon said. "I swear, though, you're gonna get your money. I'm not gonna leave you hangin' out to dry on this."

"It's not about the money, Devon," Finn said. "Ballick was killed last night. That makes you two for two—Ballick and Murphy. The cops want to talk to me, and I don't know what to tell them. All I know is that I don't like being connected to murders through one client. It means you're either really bad luck, or you're not telling me everything I need to know. Either way, it pisses me off."

Finn watched as the blood drained from Devon's face. "Ballick?" he said. His voice had gone hoarse. "Murdered?"

"Yeah," Finn said. "Murdered."

Judge Platt shifted in his chair on the bench. "Time's up, counsel," he said. "Do you waive reading?"

"Yes, Your Honor," Finn said, turning to look at the judge.

Any sense of confidence that Devon had exuded when he walked into the courtroom was gone. His eyes were wheeling. "Wait, Finn, I need to think," he whispered.

"How does your client wish to plead?" the judge asked.

"Not guilty," Finn said.

"Finn!" Devon was hissing now, and even Judge Platt was forced to take notice.

"Counsel, please instruct your client that I will not tolerate outbursts."

"Yes, Your Honor." Finn turned to Devon and put his hand up, making clear that it was time for him to be quiet.

"I assume you're looking for bail, Mr. Finn?" Judge Platt continued.

"Your Honor, we would ask that the defendant be released on his own recognizance."

"Mr. Finn has an excellent sense of humor, Your Honor," Kelley interrupted.

"That's true, Judge," Finn replied, "but I don't happen to be exercising it at the moment. My client has been a resident of this community for his entire life. He has a daughter who resides with him. This is the kind of case where no bail is required."

"We've got to talk!" Devon said, louder this time, drawing another look from the judge.

Kelley used Finn's distraction with his client to butt in and try to control the argument on bail. "Your Honor, the defendant was caught with over a hundred thousand dollars' worth of stolen merchandise that he was loading onto a truck. To release him on O.R. would virtually guarantee that he would never be seen again. He is well known to the law enforcement community as an accomplished thief—"

"Mr. Malley has not been convicted of theft in more than twenty years," Finn interjected.

"It's true, it's been a while since he was convicted of a crime," Kelley conceded. "He has been arrested seven times in the past decade, though."

"He was not convicted in any of those cases, Your Honor. You can't really punish him for the overzealousness of the police department and the DA's office, can you?"

"Your Honor, this is outrageous!" Kelley nearly shouted. "To suggest that this man is somehow a victim of the system is over the top, even for Mr. Finn."

"Settle down, both of you," Platt said. He waved his hand in a dismissive way, but Finn could tell he was interested in the argument. There was no way Finn was going to get Malley out on his own recognizance, but he might get bail set lower than normal. "He has a daughter?" Platt asked.

"He does, Your Honor," Finn said. "She's fourteen and she's living with him."

"Where is she staying at the moment?"

"For the past two nights she has stayed with me, Your Honor." He laced his fingers in front of him and looked down, adopting the posture of an altar boy. "She has no relatives, and with Mr. Malley in jail there have been few options." He was selling now, and he was hoping Platt was in a buying mood. "Mr. Malley's primary concern at the moment is to make sure that he is there for his little girl."

"Oh, please," Kelley objected, rolling her eyes. "If Mr. Malley is such a model parent, why did he spend last Sunday night out in the Back Bay ripping off a boutique? This man is a real flight risk, Your Honor."

"You really think he's going to abandon his daughter?" Finn asked.

"Mr. Finn makes some good points," Platt said to Kelley. "I'm not sure I should penalize him for arrests where no convictions were ultimately obtained. He also does have strong roots in the community, including a daughter who resides with him." He paused, then turned to the clerk. "Can I see Mr. Malley's file?"

Finn turned to Devon and nodded reassuringly. He'd done his job well and he knew it. He was expecting a grateful acknowledgment in Devon's eyes in return. To his surprise, however, his client's face betrayed a mixture of fear and frustration. Devon turned toward him, dipping his shoulder down and leaning his head down. Assuming Devon wanted to whisper to him, Finn leaned in as well.

Devon punched him in the face. Hard.

It was an excellent shot, made more effective by the fact that Finn had stuck out his chin in order to listen to his client. He was off balance, and the blow was completely unexpected. As Finn started to fall, he tripped over the chair behind him, overturning it. That sent him sprawling to the floor, nearly smashing his head on the banister that separated the front of the courtroom from the gallery.

There was a moment of silence in the courtroom, followed by pandemonium. The bailiffs were running at Devon, their nightsticks drawn, and Devon was ducking down, trying to shield his head. It wasn't easy with the chains and cuffs around his body. It took only a moment before two other bailiffs were on top of him, pummeling Devon.

"Okay! Okay! Okay!" Devon screamed as he fought to fend off the blows. It was useless, though, and Finn saw several solid shots land on his arms and back. Then they had him on his feet, and they scurried him out of the courtroom, his feet dangling off the ground as four bailiffs carried him.

The din died almost as quickly as it had started once he was gone. Finn got to his feet, rubbing his chin. He looked at the judge, unsure what to say. Kelley recovered more quickly than he did.

"Your Honor, the Commonwealth opposes bail in any amount," she said simply. Finn could see the smirk on her face.

"Judge," Finn began. He wasn't sure where to go from there. "I would like to point out—"

"Save it, Mr. Finn," Platt said. "Bail is denied."

"But Your Honor," Finn protested.

"Enough, Mr. Finn!" Platt thundered. It was the first time Finn could remember Platt ever raising his voice. "If Mr. Malley would like to make bail, he will have to come in here and apologize and show me that he can behave like a civilized person. Even then, I will have to consider whether or not to grant bail in any amount. Until then, he stays locked up!"

Finn rubbed his jaw. He could feel the swelling. The judge just looked at him, daring him to say anything. Finn was the one who had been assaulted, yet the judge was just as angry at him as he was at Devon. Finn wasn't surprised. The feeling among judges, prosecutors, police, and much of the public was that defense lawyers deserve whatever clients they take on. In fairness, Finn wasn't sure they were wrong.

He looked up at Platt and swallowed hard. "Yes, Your Honor," he said. "Thank you, Your Honor."

Chapter Eighteen

Gavin Middle School in South Boston looked like every other school in Boston built in the first half of the twentieth century. It was a two-story brick-and-cement structure next to the Church of St. Mary on Dorchester Street, on the edge of Dorchester Heights. It had fallen into squalor in the latter half of the century, and sections of it were now roped off with bright orange safety netting. It was bordered on three sides by dilapidated residential housing the color of dirt and depression. The pointing between the bricks on the school's exterior was chipping, causing the corners to sag wearily.

It had been designed to accommodate three hundred students in the sixth, seventh, and eighth grades. More than twice that number now trudged up the walkway every morning hoping to be educated. One-third of those who attended were enrolled in special educational programs. Two-thirds were classified as either failing or performing below acceptable standards. Not a single student was classified as "advanced." The school itself had been designated as "restructuring"—the lowest classification for public schools, entitling parents to opt out of the place and send their children to another school within the district. Many did. The students left were those whose parents lacked the wherewithal or the motivation to find their children a better alternative.

It was the fourth school Sally Malley had attended in three years. She'd left two schools as a result of the wanderlust of her two parents; she'd been forced out of another because of disciplinary problems.

It was lunchtime, and most of the students were in the cafeteria. Sally could hear the screaming from the basement lunchroom even at the side of the building, down the alley that separated the school from St. Mary's. She hated the screaming. It seemed as though it was almost involuntary, the way all of the students screamed whenever they had the chance. The lunchroom was the worst, and she avoided it at all costs.

As soon as the bell rang for lunch, she sneaked out and ducked down the alleyway into a step-down covered doorway that led to the church's basement. As far as she knew, the door was never used; she'd never seen anyone come in or go out. It was her sanctuary.

She put her bag down and reached into her jacket pocket, pulling out her Marlboros and a book of matches. She tugged a cigarette out with her teeth, struck the match and held it up in front of her face. For a moment she was tempted to skip the cigarette and light her hair on fire. Or maybe her face or her hand; a good burn would get her out of classes for a while. She sighed and lit the cigarette instead. She hadn't quite lost her instinct for self-preservation.

She inhaled the cigarette smoke deeply, letting it fill her lungs, wondering how quickly she might be able to develop a tumor. Probably not quickly enough to get her out of math class, she guessed.

She was running through scenarios in her mind by which she might be able to avoid school altogether that afternoon when she heard them coming from the back of the school. They were loud. They were laughing in that vicious, brutal way that immediately identified them as adolescent boys who'd given up on life too early. They spoke in the heavy dialect of the projects, and their banter was punctuated with a curse every other word.

Sally shrunk back from the mouth of the overhang, tucking herself into the shadows as far as possible. She wasn't scared; not really. Not the way others might be. This was a part of the life to which she had become accustomed. Threats were everywhere; she accepted them as inevitable, and treated them as an inconvenience. If she could avoid dealing with this particular threat, terrific. If not, she was ready. Always would be.

There were four of them, and they were even with the doorway before any of them noticed her. For a moment, she thought she was going to get lucky and avoid the hassle. It wasn't to be, though. One of them stooped to pick up a rock, probably to throw it through one of the already-broken windows in the school, and as his head came up it was turned toward her, and he caught sight of her.

"Yo," the boy said, smacking one of the others in the arm. "Check this shit out."

All four boys stopped walking and turned toward her. She stared at them and took a strong drag on her cigarette.

One of them looked older than the others; probably seventeen. He had a bad case of acne and a mass of reddish-brown hair. He was tall, and his mouth turned up at one corner and down at the other, giving him the appearance of a perpetual sneer. The others were closer to her age—maybe fifteen—and they were followers. The leader nodded to them, and they took a few steps over toward her.

She moved quickly to step out of the doorway, so she wouldn't be trapped, but she was too slow. They cut her off and formed a semicircle around the alcove, blocking her escape. That was bad, she knew. She'd have been all right as long as she could run, but that was no longer an option.

"You got a smoke?" the older boy asked. The others laughed.

She reached into her pocket and pulled out her pack, shook a cigarette free and held it out. Her mind calculated her odds. She thought about lashing out, taking preemptive action in the hopes that it might catch them off guard. She didn't think it was likely to yield the desired result, though, and she was still hoping that they were merely going to hassle her and then leave her alone.

Acne-boy took the cigarette from her and held it up. "You got a light?" he asked. There were more titters from the others, though they seemed more tense now.

She reached into her pocket again and pulled out her matches. She tossed them to him, and he caught them. He licked his lips and put the cigarette in his mouth. Then he lit a match and held it to the tip, never taking his eyes off her. She could feel all of their eyes moving up and down her young, developing figure. He took a drag, and the tip of the cigarette glowed angry red, the tobacco crackling ever so softly. The smoke drifted out of his nostrils for a moment, and then he exhaled a cloud into her face. He held up the cigarette in front of her at eye level, then dropped it onto the cement in front of her and stepped on it. "You got anything else?" he asked.

She moved quickly, darting to his left, in between the older boy and the smallest of the others, ducking as she tried to bolt past them. It was a good effort, but they were faster than she was, and they both held out their arms, catching her by the neck and shoulder, throwing her back toward the door to the church basement.

Acne-boy shook his head. "Fuck you doin'?" he asked. "We're bein' all polite and shit, and you fuckin' disrespect us like that?" He cleared his throat and spat the haul onto the ground in front of her. The orange wad just missed her foot. "Looks like someone needs a lesson she won't fuckin' learn in school, huh?"

None of the other boys said anything; but they didn't step aside, either. "You like that?" the older boy asked. "You wanna learn something today?" He reached out toward her, his hand brushing her collarbone, then tracing a diagonal line toward the center of her chest.

He looked at his friends and laughed. It was one of the ugliest sounds Sally had ever heard. Then his hand stopped and moved up again, back toward her neck and beyond.

He caressed her cheek with his fingertips, and she could smell dirt and grit and sweat. He put his finger to her lips. "Open your mouth," he said.

She wondered when the last time was that he washed the hand, and shuddered. Still, she had little choice. She let her lips part and unclenched her jaw. He pushed his finger into her mouth slowly. She gagged at the thought of what he was doing, and a dribble of saliva ran down her chin. She thought her revulsion might make him reconsider, but if anything it only seemed to excite him more. He licked his lips as he watched her. "Suck it," he said.

She forced herself to relax as he pushed his finger farther into her mouth. She watched him closely, swallowing it up past the middle joint. It was almost over, she told herself. He closed his eyes, and tipped his head back ever so slightly, enjoying himself. She looked around briefly; his posse was transfixed by the scene.

Then she bit down on the finger as hard as she could.

He screamed and tried to pull his hand away, but she had hooked her teeth on the far side of his knuckle, and by fighting he drove her teeth deeper through the skin and muscle. His friends stood shocked, faces slack, unsure what to do.

"Get the fuckin' bitch off me!" the boy screamed, thrashing his hand about, but it did no good. She could taste the blood as it filled her mouth, and she was afraid for a moment that she might gag again, but she held on to his wrist and kept her jaw locked. She was pretty sure that she was down to the bone, and she wondered, if she twisted slightly, whether the finger would break and come off in her mouth. It would serve him right, she figured.

He was screaming so loudly now that she almost couldn't hear the man's voice over the screeches. "What the devil is going on out there?"

Out of the corner of her eye, she could see a figure in black standing on the landing of the stairs that led up to the sacristy of the church. She unclenched her teeth and the boy stumbled backward, still howling. "You fuckin' bitch!" he yelled.

The priest was coming down the stairs now. "You there!" he yelled at the boys. "What are you doing?" He was in his fifties, with a flame of thick, bright white hair rising up from his head. "Stay there!" he yelled.

The boys were moving away, gathering themselves into a run. Blood was running down Acne-boy's hand and onto his arm. "I'll fuckin' kill you, you little cunt!" he yelled.

The priest hit the ground and took a few strides toward the boys, looking for a moment as though he would go after them. She knew he wouldn't really, though. He understood the dangers of the neighborhood as well as she did; the collar only provided so much protection, and he broke off any pursuit before it really started.

She was breathing hard, and the flood of adrenaline was making her shake. She reached into her pocket and pulled out another cigarette, reached down and picked up the pack of matches the boy had dropped. She lit the cigarette and took a drag.

The priest turned and headed back to her, regarding her as if she were an alien life-form. "Are you all right?" he asked.

She nodded. "Yeah."

"You belong in school," he said.

She wiped her mouth with the back of her hand that wasn't holding the cigarette. Looking down, she could see a smear of blood on her skin. "I'm going," she said.

He reached into his pocket and pulled out a handkerchief, held it out to her. His arm extended its fullest from his body to make the gesture, as though he didn't want to come too close to her. She took it and wiped off the back of her hand. Then she wiped her mouth, and the red stain on the white fabric grew significantly. She spat, and a mouthful of blood hit the ground. She was pretty sure it was the boy's blood, and it disgusted her. She spat again, and then took another drag from the cigarette.

The priest was just standing there, and she could feel his disgust and judgment. She didn't blame him, really; she felt disgusted with herself. "You shouldn't smoke cigarettes," he said after a moment. His tone carried the implication that she had brought the attack on herself. It was more than Sally could take.

"You shouldn't blow altar boys," she replied.

His face contorted. "Get away from this church!" he hissed.

She dropped her cigarette on the cement and wiped her mouth once more. She tossed the handkerchief back at him, and he dodged it, letting it fall to the ground. "I'm going," she said. "I'm late for math."

She picked up her bag and walked past the priest, turned right, and headed up the alley to the main entrance of the school. She could feel him watching her the entire way. She didn't care, though. What more could God do to her, she figured.

Chapter Nineteen

Finn headed upstairs to the holding cells. Devon was still in shackles as he awaited transfer back to Nashua Street. Finn rubbed his jaw, shaking his head back and forth. "You want to explain what the hell this is all about?"

"Sorry," was all Devon said. He looked sorry, but not about the incident in the courtroom. Instead his sorrow seemed deeper. He hadn't gotten his color back, and he sat hunched over, his shoulders drawn around him like a protective shawl.

"Sorry doesn't really help me, Devon. I need to know what's going on."

Devon shook his head. "You don't wanna know what's going on, Finn."

"Yes, I do," Finn replied. "It's been a while since I took a shot like that. I want to know why. I'm busting my ass trying to help you—trying to help your daughter. If you don't tell me what's going on right now, I'm walking."

Devon looked up at him. "I can't leave the jail. Not now."

"Why?" Finn said. "What are you talking about?"

"You were gonna get me released, and the judge was buying it. I couldn't let that happen. I can't be on the street. Not now."

"Jesus Christ, Devon," Finn said. "You didn't have to hit me; the judge wasn't going to release you on your own recognizance. I was just arguing O.R. so he'd set a reasonable bail. If you didn't want to get out, you could have refused to post the bond."

"I couldn't take the chance," Devon said. "You were arguing too fuckin' good, and I couldn't risk the judge cuttin' me loose."

"Why not? Whatever this is about, isn't it easier to deal with on the outside?"

Devon shook his head. "I wouldn't last a fuckin' night on the outside. I'd be dead before the sun came up."

Finn sat back in his chair. "Murphy and Ballick," he said. "This all ties in to them. Did you have something to do with their murders?" Devon just stared back at him. "No, of course not," Finn thought out loud. "If you had them killed, what would you be afraid of, right?" He rubbed his jaw again. "You're afraid of the people who killed them. You think whoever killed them would kill you if they get the chance."

"I don't think it, I know it," Devon said.

"Who is it? Someone in the organization? Someone trying to move up?"

"No. There are rules in the organization, and you don't break the rules like this without someone's say-so."

"So, someone from outside. Another gang?"

Devon shook his head again.

"Who, then? And why would they be trying to kill you?"

"Because they think I know where they are."

"Where who is?"

"Not who, *what*. They think I know where the paintings are."

"The paintings?" Finn was confused, but somewhere in the back of his mind an alarm went off, and he had a sense that both he and his client were in much more serious trouble than he had ever suspected.

Devon nodded at him, his shackles clattering as he brought his hands up to his face. "*The* paintings," he said.

Devon had never been in the Gardner Museum before. He'd grown up in Southie and never finished high school. He'd been stealing since he was a teenager, but he'd always been a blue-collar thief, and he'd never delved into thefts involving priceless art. As he walked through the great cavernous space, he could feel the ghosts on the canvases looking down on him, powerless to intervene as the corridors echoed with the footsteps of the two thieves.

The place was huge. He'd heard it had once been a private residence, but he found it hard to believe. The floors alternated between hardwood and mosaic, and there was artwork on every wall, in every nook and cranny. The main staircase, roped off, was a great marble affair, sweeping up to the second floor. At the foot of the side staircase, the Irishman took out a diagram of the museum's layout and a list. Devon had no idea where he had gotten them; presumably from the same source who had given the information about the museum's security provisions. It didn't really matter to Devon. He was responsible for getting them into the place; what they stole once they were in wasn't his decision.

The Irishman frowned as he oriented himself. "Upstairs," he said.

"You need any help?" Devon asked.

He looked at Devon with contempt. "I work alone."

Devon put his hands up. "Fine with me," he said. He was put off by the Irishman's manner. Who the hell was he to look down his nose at Devon? Devon had gotten them into the place, hadn't he? Still, his annoyance was eclipsed by his relief. Bulger would be pleased, and pleasing Jimmy Bulger was a good thing to do. He'd get better jobs now. More lucrative jobs. Jobs that would help make his reputation and give him the cash he needed to be the player he'd always wanted to be. Let the Irishman be a prick; Devon's future was made.

He loitered in the lobby for a few moments, but got bored quickly and decided to see what the second floor looked like.

He strolled up the stairs; he was in no hurry. At the top, he looked around. The Irishman was grunting in a room off to the right; it sounded as though he was struggling with whatever prize he was after. Devon considered offering his help again, but decided against it. Fuck him; if the bastard was too good to accept assistance the first time around, then he could handle whatever heavy lifting there was by himself.

He headed left instead, walking down the hallway that ran along the stairs to the galleries beyond. He walked quietly, though he knew there was little reason to worry. The guards were bound tight, and there was no chance that their activities would be heard outside the wall of the museum.

The first gallery he came to bored him. It was a medium-sized room at the corner of the floor, the walls painted a pale color he couldn't quite make out in the wan light. The artwork was religious in nature; three representations of the Virgin Mary with the baby Jesus. The lines in the paintings were clean and well defined, giving the subjects a cartoonish character to his untrained eye. They reminded him of the stained-glass windows that had adorned the church his parents attended when he was little, and the thought depressed him enough that he moved through the place quickly.

The next room was different in subtle respects. The subject matter of the paintings was religious, to be sure, but the individuals within the works took on more of a lifelike, three-dimensional quality, almost as though the human form had evolved and taken on substance in the few feet from one room to the next. The walls were covered in an embroidered maroon fabric, and uncomfortable-looking chairs upholstered in a hideous pink lined the walls. One painting—a monk in scarlet robes—caught his eye. There was something in the face, a hint of a smile that drew him, as though the man was mocking the very nature of his beliefs.

The third room impressed Devon. Moved him, even. Gone for the most part were the religious images and holier-than-thou sentiment. This room, much smaller than the first two, felt solid and real, as though it might have once belonged to an individual—a wealthy one to be sure, but flesh and blood nonetheless. One luminous piece dominated the space and drew him in.

It was a woman. She was dressed in white, and she was standing against a darkened background looking through an arched doorway that receded to a darkened landscape. There was something bewitching about the image. There were no clear lines defining her. Her arms were held out in a sensual invitation, and the boundaries of her gown, indeed of her very flesh, seemed to blur into her surroundings. The lines of the painting, despite their lack of definition, felt more honest to Devon, as though the truth in her beauty could not be contained. She floated on the wall like a spirit, looking down at him with inscrutable eyes, and Devon felt both exhilarated and shamed by her image. He stood there looking up at her for a few moments before he pulled himself away.

Once he did, he found himself examining each image on the walls with more interest. There was a portrait of an older man in profile. He looked to Devon as if he was sitting on a park bench, watching with an amused heart as those he loved played in pastimes for which he was too old. He seemed more reserved than the woman, but no less real.

Against the far wall from the entryway on a series of hinged wooden panels were a series of sketches, most of which were so unfinished that Devon wondered why they would be included in a museum at all. And yet they seemed to fit with the rest of the room, each of the works implying some undefined and incomplete aspect of humanity.

Devon was drawn to two of the sketches in particular. They were framed together, and both portrayed horses. Devon loved racing; whenever he finished a job he spent the days afterward flush with cash out at the track. There was majesty to racing, with the horses brushed and sparkling, and the riders in their bright, colorful costumes. For all the polish, though, it was a brutal contest, with thousand-pound beasts unleashed, their jockeys muscling each other for their livelihood and their lives.

The two sketches captured the dichotomy for Devon. One was a sketch of a horse and rider being led into a stadium for a race. It was colorful, with splashes of pink and aqua on the rider and in the procession. Spectators milled about, heading into the stadium themselves, admiring the horse and rider, adorned in tall top hats and formal dresses. It captured the grandeur of the races—in every way an upper-class affair.

The second was very different. It was a study of three riders in black and white. The central figure sat unfinished on a portion of a horse's torso, leaning back in the saddle. His face was a mask of death, with oversized ears and sunken eyes and an expression that suggested a looming ride through Hades. Beneath him, strapped upside-down to the belly of the same horse's torso, were two smaller jockeys. They were unfinished and impersonal, and hung there, as if idly waiting for the weight of the horse and rider above to fall on them.

Devon was fascinated, and he reached out to touch the works. They were sketches on paper, and they were framed in thin pieces of wood and glass. He picked them off the panel and held them up, surprised by how little they weighed. At that moment, the thief in him took over; he turned the frame over and punched through the back of it along one of the sides with his gloved hand. The wood in the frame was thin enough that it gave little resistance, and the glass popped out. He threw the broken wood on the floor and lifted the glass off the backing and slid the two paper sketches out. He looked at them, incredulous. Could it be that easy?

He took another frame off the wall, this one holding three sketches, each unfinished. None of them held the power over him the first two had, but it mattered little. It took only a moment for him to pop them out of their frames. The realization hit him, and he looked around and laughed. He had been so focused on the limits of his responsibilities for the evening that he hadn't even considered the breadth of his opportunities. All he needed to do was choose what to take next.

He saw it instantly.

The flag was mounted on the wall. The words "Garde Imperiale L'Empereur Napoleon Au Ier Regiment Des Grenadiers A Pied" were embroidered on it. He couldn't read French, but he understood well enough that it was a flag from the armies of Napoleon, and he recognized it was a perfect tribute. Jimmy Bulger was a history buff, and he often spoke of the mistakes that the great leaders of the world had made in their time. Mistakes of arrogance; mistakes of ignorance. Napoleon was a passion of his. Few things in the world would advance Devon faster than such a gift for Bulger.

He pulled a chair over to the flag and stood on it. The cloth was encased in glass, and he hoped it would be as willing a trophy as the sketches. He was wrong. The glass was screwed into brass anchors every few inches. There were dozens of them.

Still, Devon figured he had time and he got to work. Concealed under his coat was a tool belt that had a number of screwdrivers. He pulled one out and sized it correctly, then attacked the first of the screws.

They were old. They had not quite fused to their anchors, but it was close. He was breathing heavily, throwing his shoulder into the work, and he was through three screws before he admitted to himself it was worthless. He pounded on the glass with the butt of his screwdriver to see whether the glass would break, allowing him an easy shortcut, but it just gave sharp cracking sounds echoing throughout the building. He raised his hand to his head and wiped the sweat away from his brow in defeat.

A moment later the Irishman poked his head into the room. He looked around the place and saw the broken frames on the ground. He looked at Devon up on the chair, screwdriver in hand. "What the fuck are you doing?" he demanded.

"What does it look like I'm doing?" Devon replied. "I'm helping myself."

"The fuck you are."

"What's your problem? I'm not messin' with you, am I? You didn't want my help, fine. But I'm not gonna just stand around waiting." He turned and looked at the flag again; it wasn't going to be a willing trophy. Still, there might be some consolation. On the top left corner was a bronze eagle capping the exposed flagpole. That, at least, should be easy enough. He reached up and wiggled it, and to his relief it budged without much effort. He began unscrewing it.

"Get down from there!" the Irishman hissed.

"Fuck off." He kept at his work.

The man spoke again. "I said get down." The command was punctuated with the sound of a hammer being drawn back on a revolver. Devon didn't turn around.

"What are you going to do? Shoot me? That'd turn this into a whole other fuckin' scene, wouldn't it? Even if the cops don't find you, what are you going to tell my people? Besides, I got the car keys, and you don't know how to get back to Southie." It was a risk, but a calculated one. The man was an asshole, but he was also a professional. Leaping from robbery to murder wasn't worth the risk. Devon kept turning the eagle faster and faster, the sweat pouring off his brow.

"I'm warning you," the Irishman said.

"Fuck off." As he said the words, fear sliced through his heart. Was he pushing this too far?

He heard a loud crack and he stumbled forward slightly on the chair, almost falling off. His hand flew to his chest, feeling for an exit wound. It took a moment for him to realize he hadn't been shot. In his exuberance, the eagle had separated from its screw and had fallen through his fingers to the ground. The noise he had heard was that of it hitting the floor.

Devon straightened himself and stepped down off the chair. He picked up the eagle and held it up, showing off his prize. He was smiling.

The Irishman was still pointing his gun at him. He took two steps forward and swung the butt of the gun down on the space where Devon's neck met his shoulder. It was a well-placed blow. Devon nearly lost consciousness as he tumbled to the ground, and his arm went numb. By taking the soft flesh, the Irishman had inflicted the pain without spilling any blood that might be used to track them down. As Devon opened his eyes, he was staring into the barrel of the gun.

"Get this straight, lad," the Irishman said. "This is my job. You're hired help. Do as I say, or I will kill you." He pushed the barrel of the gun into Devon's eye.

"Your job?" Devon said through the pain. "You're in Boston, asshole; this is Jimmy Bulger's job. I work for him."

"He works for me on this," the man replied. "Remember that." He put his gun back in its shoulder holster and turned and left the room.

Devon didn't take anything else from the room. It took a moment before he felt able to drag himself onto his feet. He gathered up the sketches he'd already pulled from the wall and rolled them up. Then he picked up the eagle, put it in his coat pocket, and stumbled back through the galleries toward the staircase. He could hear the Irishman, still hard at work in the room to the right of the stairs, and he walked in that direction.

The room was immense, much larger than any of the galleries Devon had seen on the far side of the building. The ceiling was carved wood and the walls were covered in large, heavy oils that appeared far more substantial than the religious scenes Devon had seen, or even the portraits he'd found fascinating in the room he'd pillaged.

The Irishman was working efficiently: the floor was littered with the waste of several heavy gilded frames. Canvases were rolled in a pile near the door. "How many more?" Devon asked. The Irishman didn't reply. "How many more?" Devon asked again.

"Just one here. There's one more on the list, but it's downstairs." The Irishman moved over to a heavy, dramatic oil of a seascape. The water in the painting roiled, and a large ship was being tossed about, completely at the whim of fate. Devon could relate.

The Irishman grabbed the heavy painting by its sides and struggled to lift it off its perch. As he did, an alarm sounded. It pierced the silence and both men jumped. The Irishman nearly dropped the painting.

Devon ran toward the stairway. There was nothing in the information they had been given about such alarms, and none of their activity had triggered anything similar. Nonetheless, there was every possibility that the police were already on their way. They had to get out. "Come on!" he shouted. "Hurry the fuck up!"

He was at the staircase when he realized that the Irishman wasn't following. He was tempted to leave anyway, but he knew it wasn't an option. If the Irishman was caught, Devon was screwed; if not with the cops, then with Bulger. He turned back and looked at the door to the gallery. As he did, he noticed that the sound from the alarm was weaker where he was.

He headed back to the gallery. "What are you doing?" he demanded.

The Irishman was standing over a small electronic device on the floor. He kicked it hard, and the alarm skipped a beat. He kicked it a second time, harder, and the plastic casing smashed, the alarm dying instantly. "It's internal," the Irishman said. "To keep the museum visitors from knocking the painting. It's not hooked into the system."

"You know that for sure?"

"Aye. I'm sure."

"How sure?"

The two men looked at each other, and Devon could see the shadow of doubt in the Irishman's eyes. "I'm sure," he said again.

"We got to get out of here," Devon said.

"We're finishing the job."

"Fine. Then finish it fuckin' quickly."

The Irishman's eyes narrowed in anger, but it wasn't directed at Devon. He nodded. "Quickly. Give me a hand."

The two of them lifted that seascape off its hanger and set it down on the floor. The Irishman pulled out a straight blade; he clearly wasn't going to waste time dismantling the frame. He stuck the point of the blade into the canvas at the edge of the frame. With four quick, brutal cuts he freed it, leaving behind a small frame of canvas that had once been a part of the masterpiece. He rolled it up and placed it with the pile of the other works. He pulled two cloth bags out of his jacket. He opened one and slipped the paintings into it. He tossed the second to Devon. "Put those into this," he said, nodding to the drawings Devon had taken from the gallery on the other side of the museum.

"These are mine," Devon said.

"I'll deal with that with your boss," the Irishman said. "Put them in."

Devon took the bag and did as he was told. No point in arguing; Bulger would make the final call. He took the eagle out of his pocket and slipped that in as well.

"One more, downstairs," the Irishman said. "Let's go."

Devon followed him. As he headed out of the room, he grabbed a small Oriental-looking vase from a display and slipped it into the bag. The Irishman gave him a lethal look, but said nothing. Devon didn't care anymore.

They headed downstairs. "I'll get the last one," the Irishman said, consulting his list and the hand-drawn map of the museum's layout. "You go to the security office and make sure the alarm hasn't been tripped."

"I thought you said you were sure about the alarm?"

"I am. Check it out anyway."

Devon frowned, but headed back to the security office. It made no sense; if an external alarm had been tripped, then they were doomed either way. Checking on it wasn't going to do any good. He was in the office before it occurred to him that the Irishman might have sent him off to prevent him from lifting any more artwork.

The Irishman was only gone for a few minutes. Devon had just finished looking over the electronics on the security desk when he walked in carrying a painting of an effete man in a top hat. It was still framed. "Any problems?" he asked.

"None that I can see," Devon replied. "How the fuck should I know?"

The Irishman nodded and went to work on the frame. It took only a few moments before he had effectively dismantled the thing and was pulling the canvas off the remnants. He rolled the work up and slipped it into his bag.

"That's it?" Devon asked.

"That's it."

"Okay, let's get out of here."

They headed back to the door where the guard had buzzed them in earlier that evening. "You ready?" Devon asked.

The Irishman frowned. "Shite," he said. "I forgot something."

"What?" Devon said.

"The security tapes," the Irishman replied.

"You kidding?"

The Irishman handed his bag to Devon. "Go. I'll be right there. If you're not in the car when I get there, I'll kill you. Slowly." He was gone before Devon could argue.

Devon shook his head. The next two minutes would be dangerous. A man walking out of a museum at two-thirty in the morning carrying a couple of sacks would draw attention, police hat or not. He opened the door and walked out into the darkness.

There was no one on the street; not that Devon was looking. A key to getting away cleanly was to act as if there were nothing unusual about your behavior. He reached the small, beat-up car still parked on the street and opened the hatchback, putting the two bags in and closing the door. He climbed into the front seat, put the key in the ignition and waited. It felt as if he were lying naked on the pitcher's mound at Fenway Park.

It took only a moment for the Irishman to show up. He got into the car. "Drive," he said. Devon didn't need any encouragement.

"Did you get the tapes?" Devon asked.

The Irishman nodded. "I took care of it." He held up three VHS cassettes.

Something in the way he responded sent fear through Devon. "You didn't go back for the guards, did you?"

"I went back for the tapes," the Irishman said.

"Jesus Christ," Devon said. "If you killed them, we're fucked."

"I went back for the tapes," the Irishman said again. He looked at Devon, and Devon took his eyes off the road for just an instant to look back at him. He was impossible to read. The man's eyes betrayed nothing. Devon turned his attention back to the road and directed the car through the streets of the city, back to Southie. He was eager to be done with the Irishman.

The next day the newspapers reported that the guards had been found alive. They were lucky, Devon knew. To the Irishman, there was little difference between retrieving a security tape and putting a bullet in a man's head. Both were operational issues and nothing more. Devon prayed he would never see the man again.

Chapter Twenty

Finn met Kozlowski and Lissa at the Green Dragon pub. It was tucked back into a maze of tiny streets off Congress, in the ancient part of the city, back behind the Union Oyster House. It had been established in the 1700s, and the Sons of Liberty had once met behind the same door that still swung from the rusted hinges out onto the street corner. The décor could have been handed down through the years, for all the modern style it captured. The stone floors kept the place cool, even as the sun started warming up the city at midday. A new stereo system and the small stage for three-man bands on the weekends were the only nods to the passage of time the place would admit.

Finn took a table at the back of the place and waited. Kozlowski and Lissa arrived five minutes later. They ordered some coffee, and Finn relayed Devon's story. The other two sat listening, sipping their coffee, without interruption, for over fifteen minutes. It was a record.

When Finn finished, he looked at them. They looked back. "Well?" he said.

"Holy shit," Lissa said.

"That's all you've got?"

"Yeah. You call us here and tell us our client was responsible for the biggest art theft in history? Sorry, 'Holy shit' is all I've got for the moment."

Finn looked at Kozlowski. "What about you?"

"I'm with her," he said. "Holy shit."

"I need a little help here."

"Where are the paintings now?" Kozlowski asked.

"Devon doesn't know. They took them back to Southie and gave them to Bulger. Devon's understanding was that the Irish guy paid Bulger for the paintings, and they were smuggled back to Ireland."

"Why'd the Irish guy come back now?" Lissa asked. "It's been almost twenty years, for Christ's sake."

"Nobody seems to know. Apparently the guy isn't entirely right in the head."

"Nobody who did Vinny Murphy the way he was done is right in the head," Kozlowski said. "What's Devon gonna do now?"

"He doesn't know," Finn answered. "He's still trying to figure all this out. All he knows is that he's safer in jail than out on the street. The way he figures it, if the guy thinks he knows something, he can't just have him killed. He needs a face-to-face to get any information he thinks Devon's got."

"Like what he had with Murphy and Ballick," Kozlowski said.

"Exactly. If he wants to find out anything useful, he actually has to get Devon alone to talk to him—torture him if necessary. As long as Devon's in jail, that can't happen, so for the moment that's where he wants to stay."

"Who cares what Devon's gonna do," Lissa interjected. "What are we gonna do?"

The two men looked at her. Finn said, "Stone and Sanchez want to talk to us about Ballick's death. I'm not lying to the cops, so we've got to stall."

"We can't bring them in on this art theft thing?" Kozlowski asked.

Finn shook his head. "No. Devon won't let us."

"He won't let us?"

"He won't. He's afraid that he'll be prosecuted for the theft."

"Seems like he should be more worried about this Irish guy," Kozlowski said.

"What if we could cut a deal with the cops?" Lissa suggested. "He tells them what they need to know, and there's no prosecution? They might be willing to go for it."

"They might—if he could produce the paintings. Unfortunately he can't, so I doubt there'd be much interest. Besides, it's not just the cops Devon's worried about. Bulger's still on the run."

"Are you serious?" Kozlowski said. "Bulger's been on the run for fifteen years. There's no way he's gonna show up here in Boston. Not for anything."

"Probably not," Finn admitted. "But that's Devon's call. All I know is that he's not gonna let us bring the cops in. And if he won't let us, then we're under a legal obligation to keep the information to ourselves. We can work on him over time to get him to change his mind, but for now we don't have any options."

"So what do we tell Sanchez and Stone?" Kozlowski asked. "We can't tell them anything?"

"Like I said, we stall. Anything we can tell them about this is covered by attorney-client privilege. If Devon's right about the man who killed Ballick, then the whole thing ties back to a crime committed by our client. If we talk about it, we breach the privilege."

"Great," Kozlowski said. "Stalling cops ain't the easiest thing to do in the world. I know; I was one, remember?"

"You got any better ideas?" Neither Kozlowski nor Lissa said anything. "Good. I guess that's everything for now."

"Not everything," Lissa said. "What happens to Sally?"

Finn looked at her. "She stays with me for now."

"Jesus, Finn, this is insane," Kozlowski said.

"What other option is there? There's nowhere else to take her at this point."

"How about the Department of Social Services?" Kozlowski offered.

"No way," Finn responded. "We're not putting the state in charge of her. I've been there; I know what can happen."

"We should never have gotten involved in the first place," Lissa said.

"Maybe not. But now we're involved, and I'm not gonna let you push her off into the system. That's a sure recipe for disaster. Have you seen her? She'd skip out of foster care in a heartbeat, and then we're responsible for putting her on the street."

Kozlowski shook his head. "We're not responsible for anything that happens in her life. We're not her parents."

"Like I said, that was before we were involved."

Kozlowski looked at Lissa. "You believe this?"

She took a deep breath. "I do. And I agree with it."

Kozlowski said nothing for a moment or two. He sat there, sipping his coffee. "Well, I guess I'm overruled, aren't I? Seems to be my goddamned destiny."

———— ✦ ————

Sean Broadark stood on the street corner near the safe house in Quincy. He held his cell phone to his ear. It was strange; the house itself was quaint, if somewhat in need of attention. Inside, it had the feel of a lower-middle-class summer retreat. But when he stepped out the front door, there was nothing but cement as far as he could see. It made the house seem sad and out of place, like a country orphan in a big city.

"There's one more, he says," Broadark said into the phone. "He's in jail." He listened for a few moments as the response came back. "I don't know, right now we're sitting around on our arses." He listened some more. "I give it another couple of days; no more than three. After that, we're wasting time." A bird flew overhead as the conversation continued, searching in vain for a tree or a soft spot on which to land. "He won't." The bird circled; Broadark thought it was looking at him. "I'll take care of it."

He clicked off the phone, put it in his pocket, and turned back toward the house. Looking around him, he could see why so many of his countrymen had come to Boston when they left Ireland: it wasn't so different from their homeland. Like Belfast, it had a subdued urban feel to it, as if it was struggling against the notion that it was a city at all. Only recently had the Emerald Isle begun truly dragging itself into the modern world, allowing itself to flow with the trend it had resisted for so long. It was a good thing in many ways, he supposed. The modernization of the country, particularly in the area of computer software development, had brought more jobs, more money, and more stability to a land that had been without those things for so long. With them, though, came a complacency that many in the movement detested. Creature comforts, many said, robbed the people of their will to fight for those things most important. A man with nothing is willing to risk it all; a man with something to protect is far more likely to shrink from a confrontation.

More than anything else, that was what had led to the peace—a better economy that gave those in the country something to protect. Deep in his heart, Sean Broadark was okay with that. He would follow his orders to the end. But he allowed himself, on occasion, to hope that those orders someday would be to stand down.

———

Liam Kilbranish watched Broadark as he approached the house. He knew where the man had been; Sean hadn't tried to hide it. "I have to check in," he'd said. The fact that he'd left the house made clear that there were things he had to talk to his superiors about that he didn't want Liam to hear.

Liam wasn't surprised. When he had laid out the plan, he'd made it all sound so easy. Perhaps he'd even believed that it would be easy. He'd certainly wanted to believe it. And yet, deep in his heart, he'd always known it wouldn't be.

He blamed himself. Not for his failure in the past few days, but for his failure twenty years before. The plan had been perfect. They had all the intelligence they needed; the target was virtually unprotected; the information regarding the paintings themselves was flawless. If the execution was imperfect, that was the fault of the man assigned to him by the Boston contingent. Even with Devon Malley's lack of professionalism, though, the objectives were achieved—at least Liam thought they had been.

Now, as he looked out the window toward the depressing concrete yards surrounding the safe house, watching Broadark climb the front stairs, he knew he was suffering for his own shortcomings, and he was petrified that the silent promise he'd made to his father years before would go unfulfilled.

It was ironic. If not for him, the movement would have stalled even earlier. Fund-raising was always the difficulty. The fighting came easy, but keeping the supply lines flowing with guns and explosives and ammunition was a challenge that required more ingenuity than most possessed. By the late 1980s, the wells were running dry on both sides of the Atlantic. People were losing heart and losing commitment. Those who had given generously before were tightening up, unwilling to continue giving to a movement that had lost direction. Those who had not given before were turning them down flat, unwilling to cast their lot with a cause that had become unpopular. People seemed weary of the death and destruction.

By then fighting had become a way of life for Liam. He couldn't imagine himself without it. His hatred had burned for so long that it had consumed much of what had been human inside of him. Without the money, though, the fighting would end.

The drug trade served as a band-aid for a while, but it was a dangerous business. Art theft had been Liam's brainchild. There were so many private museums throughout the UK and continental Europe that were ripe for the plucking, and the proceeds kept the money rolling in. American targets were less plentiful—the Americans were, by their nature, less trusting than their European counterparts, and security was generally much more severe. Liam had stumbled onto the idea of the Gardner Museum during one of his visits.

Now, what had been the perfect job and the perfect fix had destroyed the fight. He wouldn't let that be the end.

Broadark opened the door and walked into the tiny house. He didn't even look at Liam. He walked over to the refrigerator and pulled out a beer. The fact that the man had the temerity to drink simmered in Liam's craw. It seemed to him a statement that the mission was lost.

Broadark walked over to the sofa in the living area and sat down. He turned on the television and began ritually flipping though the channels. It was a compulsion. He never stopped long enough to see anything coherent on the screen, and it was clear that there was nothing in particular he was looking for. He just kept flipping as the panoply of mindless, sex-filled American bubblegum pop culture flashed by like some eye-searing experiment in subliminal torture. The man was so attached to the process that he slipped the beer under his arm so he could open it without breaking stride.

Liam walked over and grabbed the remote out of Broadark's hand, pointed it toward the television and pressed the power button. The set blinked once hard, the light exploding in a flash that consumed the screen, then receded from the corners to a pointed horizon in the center of an ancient, darkened picture tube. "No more television," he said.

Broadark looked up at him from the sofa. Liam wondered whether he would make his move. It depended on the orders he'd received on the phone call. Liam figured he'd rather know sooner than later.

He could see the calculations that ran through Broadark's mind. In some respects they both functioned in the same way. Confrontations like this came down to a series of calculations: who could reach his weapon first? What were your adversary's weaknesses? Where was he exposed? Who was more willing to take the chance? How far were you willing to take the fight?

Liam could see all these questions rattling off in sequence in Broadark's eyes, the sums of the equations being added and multiplied and calculated. Then an answer was reached. Broadark shrugged and pulled his beer out from under his arm and took a sip.

Liam reached out and grabbed away the beer. He walked over to the sink and poured it out. "No more booze, either," he said. He knew Broadark was not a threat—yet. If he had the go-ahead to take Liam out, he would have reached for his gun when Liam took the remote. Liam had a little more time. Not much, though.

Broadark rose from the couch. He walked over to the narrow counter in the kitchen. "What, then?" he asked.

"I told you, there's one more."

"Yeah, you told me," Broadark said. "You also told me he's in jail. Not much we can get from him while he's there, is there?"

"There are other ways."

"What are they?"

The truth was, Liam didn't know. He was running out of time, and he had lost all his leverage. "The lawyer," he said. He wasn't even sure what it meant when the words came out of his mouth, but when he heard them, they triggered something in him—a hope that had been slipping away.

"The lawyer," Broadark repeated. There was skepticism in his voice. "What about the lawyer?"

"We follow the lawyer," Liam said. "He's the only contact we have with the last one, but we can use him to make our point."

"How?"

"I don't know yet. All I know is that he's the key."

For a moment, Liam thought Broadark would pull out his gun right then and be done with it all. Instead, though, he nodded without conviction. "All right, then," he said. "Follow the lawyer."

Chapter Twenty-One

Captain Melvin Skykes shared little with other Boston police officers. He didn't swear; he didn't drink; he didn't smoke. He ran to stay in shape, and he ate no meat. He was partial to dark pinstriped suits more appropriate for a Wall Street trading floor than a grimy police station. He was devoid of ethnicity. In appearance he was nothing like most of the officers who served beneath him; and yet he commanded respect. He had built his career by being the best example of the "new cop" Boston had tried to introduce to the force in the wake of scandals in the 1980s. Most of the others brought in had long since sought refuge outside the department. Skykes succeeded because his attention to detail—whether investigative or administrative—was unparalleled. Those who entered his office unprepared to discuss every aspect of any case on which they were working risked their careers. The detectives under his command toed a line straighter and sharper than any other in the department, and the results showed.

Sitting in Skykes's office just after lunch, Stone felt as if he were sitting for an oral exam. He didn't particularly mind; he was prepared.

"Seven dead," Skykes said. He was leaning back in his chair, the tips of his fingers brought together in a steeple. He spoke slowly, and there was no emotion in his voice. You might have thought he was talking idly about a baseball score, except that most people in Boston could never maintain his level of equilibrium discussing the Red Sox.

"Five," Stone offered. It was a stupid response—as though five murders wouldn't be a problem. "There were only five last night."

Skykes gave Stone an impatient, condescending look. "I was counting Murphy and Johnny Bags."

"Yes, sir," Stone said. "With them, that's right. It's seven."

Skykes began again. "Seven dead," he said. He threw Stone a look that dared him to interrupt. Stone didn't. "Any leads?"

Stone kept his mouth shut. He was learning.

"Nothing concrete," Sanchez said. "Not yet."

"Anything at all?" Skykes asked.

"Long shots right now," Sanchez said. "Nothing that would be helpful in keeping the press at bay."

Skykes whirled on her. "Who said anything about the press? My only concern is solving these murders."

"Right," Sanchez said. "Nothing that gets us close to figuring out who actually did it, then."

"So we have seven dead bodies in this city—connected people"—Skykes flicked a piece of lint off his lapel as he spoke—"and we have nothing to go on whatsoever?" The challenge was plain.

"I didn't say nothing to go on. Just nothing definitive enough to call a concrete lead," Sanchez replied.

"Let me be clear, Detective," Skykes said. "I want to know about anything we've got. I don't care if it's concrete. I don't care if it's Play-Doh. If it pertains to this case, I want to hear about it."

Sanchez cleared her throat. "The IRA may be involved," she said. She looked again in Stone's direction.

"I assume you're not talking about someone's retirement account," Skykes said.

"No sir, I'm not. The other IRA," Sanchez said. Skykes focused hard on Sanchez. The stare was penetrating, and Stone wondered how she withstood it in silence.

"The Irish Republican Army," Stone offered. Skykes's attention shifted to Stone, but the intensity of the stare remained. Stone bore the look for a few moments, then cracked. "From Ireland," he said.

"I'm aware of the IRA's origins, Detective Stone," he said. "What I'm not aware of is how they have any connection to a bunch of murders in Southie. Don't you read the papers? The IRA's dead; what in God's name makes you think they're tied up in this?"

"*Padre Pio*," she said after a moment.

"*Padre Pio*," Skykes said. "The torture technique?" Stone was impressed.

"Exactly," Sanchez said. "Both Murphy and Ballick were shot through the hands, so we figure there's a possibility this was an IRA job."

Skykes shook his head. "It still doesn't make sense. There's a truce in Northern Ireland, and a government has been formed from parties on both sides. The IRA disarmed; turned in all their weapons."

"Maybe it's not the IRA itself, then, but someone close to them," Sanchez said. "The boys in the IRA always had close ties to the Irish mob here in Boston. Some of them still have smuggling connections. Maybe one of them is freelancing."

Skykes considered this. "There's something else you're not telling me. This is too thin to count as even a theory from what you've told me; it's hardly a lead."

Sanchez could feel Stone looking at her. She knew what he was thinking, but she was resistant to sharing any more with the captain. Her success had come, in many respects, as a result of her ability to keep secrets.

Skykes could read her hesitation. "If there's more, I want to know about it, Sanchez," he said.

"'The Storm,'" she said.

"'The Storm'?"

"It's what was written at the scene of Murphy's murder," Stone said.

"There's a chance that it's a reference to one of the paintings that was stolen from the Isabella Stewart Gardner Museum back in '90," Sanchez said.

Skykes nodded. "The speculation has always been that the IRA was involved in that theft," he said. "Do we have any point of contact? Any way we can work the theory?"

"Not really. Just the lawyer."

"The lawyer." Skykes closed his eyes and Stone had the impression that his mind was processing information like a computer. "Finn, right?"

"That's right, Captain," Sanchez said.

"What do we know about him?"

"Good reputation for courtroom work. He handles mainly criminal defense cases; he'll take on a civil matter here and there if the payout is good enough. Lives in Charlestown, where he's got his office—grew up there too. When he was younger he got into some trouble. Managed to pull himself out, though."

"So how is it that he came to show up at both Murphy's place and Ballick's shack right around the time they got dead?" Stone couldn't tell whether the captain's question was rhetorical; he let Sanchez deal with it.

"We don't know. When he showed up at the auto body shop, he told Stone that he was there for a client—Devon Malley. Malley's a thief. There's a chance that he was involved in the Gardner job, too. He was busted Monday morning looting Gilberacci's on Newbury. Someone called in a tip it was gonna go down. Don't know who."

"So Malley may be tied in to all this?" the captain asked.

"It's possible," Sanchez said.

"When's the lawyer coming in?"

"He was supposed to be in today, but he called and said he had an emergency. He said tomorrow, maybe."

"Maybe?" Skykes said. "We're the police; since when do we accept 'maybe' in a murder investigation?"

"Finn's a lawyer, and unlike most, he's not dumb. We lean on him too hard, we won't get anything; he'll show up and claim privilege on everything he knows. The conversation will last all of thirty seconds. If he doesn't want to, he won't tell us what he had for breakfast without a subpoena and a couple of trips to the appellate court."

Skykes grunted. "Probably right. Anyone else we can work on?"

"Finn works with Kozlowski. He handles Finn's investigations. It's a good bet that if Finn knows something, Kozlowski knows it too," Sanchez noted.

"Tom Kozlowski? Former cop?"

"That's him. You know him?"

Skykes shook his head. "Not personally. I know of him. He was a good cop, but a pain in the ass. You won't get anything out of him. He's too smart to make a mistake, and anything he found out from Finn is covered under attorney-client privilege too."

"Can we lean on him?" Sanchez suggested.

Skykes laughed. "Sure, but it'd be like leaning on Mount Washington. He'll hold you up, but he won't move. That's not who he is."

"What, then?" Stone asked.

Skykes looked at Sanchez for an answer. "We put a tail on the lawyer," she said. "See where he goes; who he talks to. He's gotta know something."

"That could take weeks," Stone lamented.

"Maybe, but unless they're willing to talk to us voluntarily, it's the best we've got," Sanchez said.

Skykes nodded to them. "However you want to work it is fine with me. Just make sure we get something useful. I don't care that the dead guys were scumbags when they were alive; seven dead bodies is seven dead bodies. I don't like it in my city."

Chapter Twenty-Two

Lissa left the Green Dragon ahead of the others and headed to Southie to pick Sally up from school. Finn and Kozlowski stayed for a little while to talk strategy; then Finn drove Kozlowski back to the office in Charlestown. The brief respite of seasonable weather had ended, and New England was exacting its revenge as the skies turned gray and troubled and the wind spat drizzle at Boston's inhabitants. It was like this every year, and yet people seemed to forget. A few mild days in April tempted Bostonians into believing winter had been banished, but it always regrouped for a final assault. It was usually May before the weather was consistently pleasant.

Finn, a meteorological optimist, had put the top down on his battered MG, and when he and Kozlowski emerged from the bar, he struggled to pull the canvas covering back out. By the time it was back up, the interior was soaked.

Kozlowski stood outside the car, looking angrily from Finn to the passenger seat.

"Wipe it down," Finn said. "There's a towel in the back."

Kozlowski reached into the back and grabbed the towel. "Wiping it down doesn't do a goddamn thing," he said. "The seat's cracked. The water soaks into the cushion so it's like sitting on a wet sponge. Why do you think the car smells like mildew all the time?"

"I thought that was you."

"Asshole."

"You wanna call a cab? I can meet you back at the office," Finn asked.

"No, I don't want to call a goddamned cab. I want to work with someone who drives a real goddamned car. Not some piece of crap clowns should be jumping out of."

"So sit on the towel then. That'll keep you dry."

"I would, but then my head scrapes against the roof of the car."

Finn looked again at Kozlowski. His expression had turned from anger to disgust to plain unhappiness. "You have seriously turned into a major whiner," Finn said. "Are you going soft on me?"

Kozlowski's look was sharp. "I'm not going soft, I just don't want to sit in pants with a wet ass for the rest of the goddamned day." He frowned again, then spread the towel over the seat and slid in gingerly, trying to hold some of his weight off the seat. Finn had to stifle his laughter. They drove like that back to the office with Kozlowski leaning on the door and holding himself up with the windshield. The rain pelted him through the window, drenching his head and shoulders.

It was after four o'clock when they arrived. Lissa and Sally were already there when Finn and Kozlowski walked through the door.

"What happened to you?" Lissa asked Kozlowski, noting his wet head.

"Don't ask," Kozlowski replied. He nodded to the girl and padded down the hall toward the bathroom to dry himself off.

Finn looked at Lissa. "Did you tell her?"

"Yeah," she said. "I told her."

"I'm in the room," Sally said. They looked at her. "You were talking about me, right?"

Finn nodded. "Yeah," he said. "Sorry, didn't mean to ignore you, I just . . ."

"She told me," Sally said. "My dad's not getting out today."

"Not yet," Finn said. "We ran into an issue that we didn't expect."

"Yeah, sounds like Devon pitched a fit," Sally replied. "He's a fuckup; I already know that."

"I might have used different terms," he said. "But yeah, he had a little outburst. I'll get another bail hearing set, though." He glanced at Lissa, wondering how much she had told the girl. She frowned and gave a slight shake of her head that Finn took as a signal that she hadn't gone further. He breathed a sigh of relief; the last thing he wanted was to have to explain anything more than the basics to Sally. He looked back at the girl. "So, I guess you're staying with me for a couple more nights. That okay with you?"

She shrugged. "I don't have any choice, I guess," she said.

"That's all you have to say?" Lissa asked.

Sally looked up at her. "What else do you want me to say?"

"It's okay," Finn began, but Lissa cut him off.

"No, it's not okay," she said. "You wanna spend your time playing savior, that's your call, but I'm not gonna sit here and watch the person who's benefiting from your generosity be rude to you." She looked at Sally. "When someone does something nice for you, you say *thank you.*"

Sally stood up. She was wearing her coat, and her bag dangled from her hand. Finn thought there was a good chance that she was about to walk out the door. That was the last thing he needed; he had no interest in combing the city, looking for Devon's kid. He felt a bolt of annoyance with Lissa. "I could go to the street," Sally said. "I'd survive, y'know."

"I know," Lissa said. "That's why Finn's offer is nice. He doesn't have to give you a better option, but he's doing it anyway. Some appreciation is in order. If not . . ." Lissa swept her hand toward the door as she let her ultimatum trail off.

Finn rubbed his temples. He was about to cut in when Sally turned and looked at him, biting her bottom lip. "Thank you," she said.

Finn just stared at her. Then he looked with incredulity at Lissa. After a moment he turned back to Sally. "You're welcome," he said.

"Good," Lissa said. She looked at Finn. "You've got a dozen messages on your desk, and your voice mail is full. It's gonna take an hour or more to deal with whatever's there. I have some things that I gotta take care of, too. Sally can use the time to do whatever work she has." Sally blinked at her. "You do have homework, I assume?"

"I guess."

"Good. Then, when we're all ready, I'll take us to dinner."

"You don't need to," Finn said. "I can feed her at my place."

"On what? Ketchup? I've seen your refrigerator."

"I've got more than ketchup," Finn said.

"Yeah? What else?"

"Mustard and relish," Sally answered before Finn could respond. He looked at her. "And something in an old Chinese takeout carton that's growing feet. I was hungry last night," she said. "I looked."

"Did you check the cupboard?" he asked.

"I'll make some reservations," Lissa said. "An hour?"

Kozlowski was walking back into the office from the hallway. His hair was tousled but dry. "What's in an hour?"

"Dinner," Lissa said. "I'm buying."

"What's the occasion?"

"Just thought everyone could use a good meal," Lissa said.

"Ah," Kozlowski said knowingly. "Someone looked in Finn's refrigerator."

"It wasn't pretty," Sally said.

"I think I liked you better when you were less grateful and more sullen," Finn said to her.

"An hour," Lissa said again. Finn looked at her and nodded. Then he went to his desk and started digging out from the messages and mail that had piled up during his daylong absence from the office.

Liam sat in a rented van parked on the square a half block down from Finn's office. There was a newspaper in front of him, opened to the sports section. Liam didn't follow any American sports, but he wasn't looking at the paper. He was watching the door to the lawyer's office. He'd been there for more than an hour, waiting. He'd passed by the place once, determining that it was empty. He'd scouted the area, getting an idea for the layout. There was a back door to the little office, but it didn't look as if it saw much use. He assumed they would be entering from the front. The square was the best spot from which to observe. It was close enough to get a good look at the building, but far enough away that he wouldn't draw too much attention. It was near a small row of stores; in the rain and cold, he didn't look too far out of place. The van was a nondescript white delivery vehicle, dappled with patches of rust and textured with dents from hard use. The interior was stripped to the metal, rippled and grungy, with pockets of moisture bordering on small puddles that seemed never to dry no matter what the weather. He could have been waiting to pick up or deliver just about anything.

The woman showed up with the girl about a half hour after he'd settled in with the paper and a cup of coffee. When he saw them enter the brownstone, he double-checked the address. They looked like a mother and daughter, but that didn't fit with his information.

The two men arrived twenty minutes later. It was clear which one was the lawyer. The younger one was thin and tall, and dressed in an expensive suit. He carried a leather case with him, and he had a serious look on his narrow face. The man with him looked nothing like a lawyer. He was solid and older, and his thin overcoat flapped around the calves of his cheap slacks. He moved deliberately, and his head swung from side to side, taking in everything around him. He reminded Liam of many survivors of the troubles on both sides. They were quiet, serious men. They were the men he worried about coming up against.

He'd done enough background to identify the adults. Finn, Kozlowski, Krantz. He knew their names and ages and roles in the tiny little firm that was representing Devon Malley. They all had solid reputations, but they were in over their heads.

The girl was a surprise. Liam didn't like surprises. Her presence at the office might mean nothing. She might be a niece or the daughter of a friend who had errands to run. And yet he had this feeling—an intuition—that there was more to it than that. A lifetime had taught him never to ignore his intuitions. Very often they came from that deep spot in the brain that noticed something the conscious mind had missed. He'd learned that paying attention to his intuition could save his life.

He leaned back into the car seat to mull things over. Information was the most valuable commodity in any profession; more so in Liam's than others. It was clear that he needed more of it now.

The restaurant was a huge family-style place in Charlestown. Only a glass partition separated the diners from an open kitchen with wood-burning stoves. The patrons could watch their meals being prepared, and it gave the place a sense of intimacy. It was the kind of restaurant that required connections or a three-month wait for a reservation on a weekend night. Midweek, though, it was merely bustling, and determination was all that was required to get a table on a walk-in basis.

The four of them were sitting at a table near the middle of the restaurant. It was a big, round, heavy oak slab, finished unevenly to maintain the rustic feel of the place. It could have seated eight, and with just the four of them, they had to keep their voices up to hear each other over the din.

Not that it mattered through much of the evening; the conversation was spotty. Finn, Kozlowski, and Lissa usually talked about their work when they ate; it was a time when they could fret over their most pressing cases. That night, however, their most pressing case concerned the father of the girl who was sitting directly across from Finn. He couldn't discuss the case openly, but he couldn't get it out of his head, either.

"How was school?" he asked at one point, trying to break the awkward silence that had settled over the table.

Sally looked up, surprised. "It sucked," she said after a moment.

"Why?" Finn asked.

"It's school. School sucks."

"What sucks about it?" Finn continued.

She twirled some pasta onto her fork and stuffed the mess into her mouth. "You really wanna know?" she asked as she chewed.

"Yeah," Finn said. "What grade are you in?"

"Eighth," she said.

"Okay, eighth grade," Finn said. "What sucks about eighth grade? Do you have any friends?"

"Not really," she said.

"Why not?"

"Because the kids are assholes. Why would I want more assholes in my life? I got all I can handle."

Finn winced. He'd grown up on the street, but the disparity between the girl's age and her demeanor was still unsettling. Most people didn't master cynicism until at least their late teens. "How about the schoolwork?" Finn asked. "Do you like that at all?"

Sally laughed. "It's an inner-city school; there is no real schoolwork. If you're not stabbing someone, you're an honor student as far as the teachers are concerned."

"Do you learn anything?"

She shrugged. "I learn what I want to learn."

"What's that?"

She pushed the food around on her plate. "I like reading," she said at last. "English class is okay. The teacher is a joke, but I like the books."

"What are you reading?"

"Right now? *The Adventures of Huckleberry Finn*," she said grudgingly.

"Good book. You like that one?"

"Yeah."

"Why?"

She looked him in the eye. "Because he's a kid and he takes care of himself. He doesn't need other people to survive and he doesn't take any shit."

The table went silent for a moment. She put her fork down on her plate, and it made a sharp, definitive noise—like an exclamation point. Finn reached out and plucked a roll from the basket on the table, tore off a piece, and dipped it in the olive oil on the table. After a moment, he said again, "Good book."

Lissa cleared her throat. "You could make friends," she said. "It wouldn't be hard for someone as smart as you."

"What the fuck is this?" Sally said loudly. A few people at other tables turned to look, then glanced away quickly. "I'm fine. I don't need your pity, y'know. I need a place to sleep, that's all. I'll be gone soon enough."

Lissa looked embarrassed. It wasn't a look that came naturally to her. "We're just trying to help a little, that's all. It might be nice to get to know you a little better."

"How about if I get to know you a little better, then?" Sally said.

"We'd be fine with that," Lissa replied.

Sally looked at each of them in turn, a prizefighter sizing up opponents. "How old are you?" she asked Finn.

"Forty-four," Finn replied.

"And you're a lawyer who lives alone in a nice apartment in Charlestown?"

"Yeah." Finn took a sip of his wine. He was more of a beer drinker, but as long as Lissa was paying, he didn't mind having a glass of a nice cabernet. It relaxed him.

"So you're gay."

Finn almost spat out a ten-dollar sip of the wine. Whatever relaxation he'd achieved vanished. "What?" he choked out.

"I've seen your apartment," she said. "No curtains, no pictures, no pillows on the couch. The refrigerator's empty and there's one toothbrush in the bathroom. There's nothing that looks like a girl's ever been there ever. You're not ugly, so I assume you're a fag."

"I'm not gay," Finn replied. He tried to keep the defensiveness out of his voice.

"Gay," Sally said, nodding her head.

"I am not gay!"

"Hey," she said, "I got no problem with it. Probably make me sleep better at night."

"I don't have a problem with it either," Finn said. "I'm just not gay."

"Are you dating anyone?"

"No," Finn admitted.

"Gay."

Finn looked over at Lissa. She looked amused. "What's so funny?"

"This is," Lissa said. "In fact, it pretty much defines funny."

Finn turned to Sally. "I was dating someone. We lived together and it didn't work out. That was a while ago, and I just haven't found anyone else since then, okay?"

"Who was she? Did she have a penis, or was she like, an imaginary girlfriend?"

"No," Finn said. "She was Koz's partner when he was on the police force."

Sally looked over at Kozlowski, who nodded. "Huh," she said, clearly shocked that she was wrong. "So if you're not gay, then why don't you have a new girlfriend?"

Lissa laughed. "She's got you nailed, Finn. That's a question I've asked over and over," Lissa said. "I'd kinda like to hear the answer."

She wasn't going to hear the answer, though, because before Finn could even begin to formulate a response, Sally turned on Lissa. "You two are dating, right?" she asked, nodding at Kozlowski. He'd been silent for most of the dinner, and now he squirmed at the notion of being drawn into the conversation. Lissa took the bait, though.

"We are," she said, nodding. Kozlowski shot her a look, but she waved him off. She clearly wasn't about to back down.

"For how long?"

"A year or so," Lissa replied. "Maybe a little longer."

"Why aren't you married?"

Finn had to admire the girl; she played rough. Lissa was now squirming as much as Kozlowski was.

"It's complicated," she said.

"Why?" Sally asked. "You don't love him?"

"No, I love him."

"He doesn't love you?"

Everyone at the table looked at Kozlowski. He looked at the cutlery. Finn had the impression he was contemplating picking up the steak knife and gouging his own eyes out.

"No, I'm sure he loves me, too," Lissa said, answering for him. Sally kept looking at Kozlowski for a moment, though, until he gave a slight nod.

"Okay, you love him and he loves you," Sally said. "You both seem normal, so what's the deal?"

"We've talked about it," Lissa said hesitantly.

Finn, who had been enjoying the show, was shocked by the pronouncement. "Really?" he said.

Lissa looked back and forth between Finn and Kozlowski. Kozlowski shook his head and raised his hand, signaling that she was on her own. Then Lissa settled her gaze on Finn. "This isn't how we wanted to tell you this," she began.

Finn felt his eyes widen. "You're kidding, right? You two? Married?" The expression on Lissa's face turned like the sky during a sudden, violent summer storm. "I don't mean that the way it sounds," Finn stammered. "I mean why not you two, right?" Lissa's eyes darkened further. "I mean, that's great. I really do, it's great. What brought this on?"

"Are you pregnant?" Sally asked. She wasn't letting up on the attack.

"No!" Lissa said. Her voice was loud and sharp, and cut through the clamor of the restaurant. She shook her head and took a deep breath and said in a more reasonable voice, "No."

Finn looked at the two of them, not sure what to say. "Holy crap, can you imagine that? The two of you as parents?"

"Let's not get ahead of ourselves," Lissa replied.

"Why not?" Sally asked. "You're not getting any younger."

Kozlowski leaned in toward Sally and said quietly, "You know, Huckleberry Finn nearly got himself killed a whole bunch of times traveling down the river. The story could've gone another way."

"No sweat," Sally said. "I feel like I know you guys a lot better already. How about you guys? Can we put the twenty questions game on hold for a little while?"

Finn took another sip of his wine. Then he raised his glass. "To getting to know each other—a little more slowly," he said. Everyone around the table raised their glasses.

It took a moment before anyone said anything else. Finally Sally spoke. "So," she said. "What's the deal with my father? Is he getting out anytime soon, or am I going to have to play Trivial Pursuit with you guys for the rest of my childhood?"

Finn took a deep breath. "It's complicated."

"Didn't we just have this conversation?"

"No, this is genuinely complicated. I'll get your father a new bail hearing. It may take a little time."

"Why did he freak out today?"

"I don't know," Finn replied. He didn't like lying, but he could think of no better option.

"Maybe he wanted to get away from me."

"You're smarter than that," Lissa said.

"Am I? What would you do if you found out you had a kid you never wanted? Would you run?"

Lissa considered the question. "No," she said. "I wouldn't."

"Maybe you're a better person than my parents."

Finn said nothing. There was nothing to say. He could have tried to persuade her that he knew how she felt. After all, his own parents had abandoned him. He'd had to grow up quickly and learn to fend for himself, just as she had. There was a difference, though, and he knew it. He'd never known his parents. To him, they were specters in the mist. On his good days, growing up, he'd convinced himself that there was a reason beyond selfishness for their absence. He'd invent myths—romantic tales of intrigue that had forced his parents to leave him. The story of Moses in the bulrushes, told to the children in the orphanages by stern nuns, had always appealed to him. Perhaps, like some biblical king, he'd been set adrift for a purpose, and his mother and father lived their lives watching over him until the day when they could reveal themselves to him.

They were childish dreams, but he'd clung to them. Deep down, he still did. And that was what set Sally apart. She could hold no such illusions. She knew who her parents were, and they knew her. Her abandonment was personal. He could never convince her otherwise, because he didn't believe it.

————◇————

It took a few moments for them to finish their coffee and for Lissa to pick up the tab. They left quietly; there was a melancholy feeling they all shared in their silence. Outside, the weather matched their mood. The rain had let up enough to allow them to walk without getting drenched, but a light sprinkling continued. The air was warm and humid again. Finn could feel the barometric pressure in his ears, and it made it seem as though something in the atmosphere was getting ready to explode.

As the door closed behind them, they didn't look back. If they had, they might have noticed the man settling his check at the table near the window, two over from their table. He was of average height and build, and the only things that stuck out about him were his black hair and eyes against his fair skin. He'd arrived just after them, and sat at the table by himself, casually listening in on every word of their conversation.

Chapter Twenty-Three

Thursday morning was a total loss for Finn. It was as though he were swimming in a pool filled with mud. It would be easier if he could go to the police and enlist their help. That wasn't an option for him, though. His client wouldn't allow it, and he was bound to obey Devon's wishes. Sometimes it seemed as though the canons of legal ethics were drawn with an eye toward creating as many dilemmas as possible for lawyers, blind to the difficult realities faced by those who paced the courthouse halls.

He started the day by dropping Sally off for school in the morning. She seemed in mildly better spirits after a decent night's sleep. She was still quiet, but regarded him without animosity. Perhaps, he thought, she was coming around.

He let her out in front of the school. "One of us will be here to pick you up when school ends," he said. "Probably me or Lissa."

She nodded and said, "Thanks." Then she slammed the door and headed up the stairs to the main entrance and Finn pulled away.

Thanks. It was such a simple little word, said millions upon millions of times every day without thought or reflection. To the woman at the Dunkin' Donuts counter who poured your coffee. To the man who held the elevator door for just a second longer to let you on. To the kid who bagged your groceries at the store for a summer job. It was said over and over and over, to the point where it almost lost meaning and became a part of the blur of modern reality. Said but never felt; heard but never acknowledged.

That was not the case with Sally. For her, common courtesy was a luxury—one that she clearly had rarely been afforded, and was hesitant to bestow on others. And so when she said the word to Finn— *thanks*—it made him feel as though, just perhaps, he was doing a good thing.

That feeling of accomplishment lasted only a moment, however, and as he swung the car around and headed for the office, he confronted reality. He would spend part of the morning putting together a motion for a new bail hearing. It made sense: he couldn't get Devon out of jail until a new hearing was set. He would file the motion and then convince Devon that he was better off out of jail. Accomplishing that seemed a long shot. The man's fear had been evident at their last meeting, when Devon explained the situation to him. He seemed determined to remain in jail, where he believed he was safe. Even if Finn could convince his client, though, there were no guarantees that bail would be set after Devon's behavior at the last hearing.

In the meantime, Finn felt helpless. It seemed as though there was nothing he could do to move the matter along, and he was stuck playing inadequate surrogate father to Devon's daughter.

By the time he pulled up to the office he'd worked himself into a sweat, just wrestling with his options. That, in turn, made him angry with himself. Lissa was right after all. Devon was his client, not his family, and this wasn't, in the end, Finn's problem. There was no rational reason he should treat it as though it were.

He opened the car door and stood up. Arching his back to stretch out, he looked around him. The weather was warming, little by little, and the buds were beginning to appear on the trees along the street in Charlestown. It was a beautiful place in so many ways; it retained much of the charm of the Old World. He'd built a good life for himself, he thought. Or, if not a life, at least a good professional reputation. He was far better off than he would have been if he'd stayed on the path of his youth. Few others were so fortunate. If he could, he was determined to give Sally the best chance she could have at a normal life. Right now, that meant working to get her father out of jail.

———

Liam Kilbranish was no longer watching the lawyer. He would return to that soon enough; for the moment he had other things to do.

He took his time. He was careful. He made sure that he knew the layout of the neighborhood well. One of the things that made planning difficult in this city was the layout. It had grown in fits and starts, without any semblance of the urban planning that one might find in a more modern city. Streets followed the original cow paths of premodern times, and neighborhoods had sprouted up, grown, died, and sprouted up again in a whimsical manner. As a result, the streets had few patterns and twisted and turned in an illogical stitching of one-way lanes and dead ends. Knowing the streets was paramount. The likelihood that a chase would ensue was low, but he had to account for the possibility. If it happened and he was unprepared, it would be over in moments.

Once he was sure that he had memorized the area, he went back to the safe house in Quincy. He had to make preparations there, too, if his plan was going to work. The place had a basement, which made things easier. It was a shallow space, with a low ceiling and walls that blended cement with the natural bedrock that had been blasted away to hollow out the ground underneath the little house. There was a furnace that looked as if it had been replaced within the past decade, and a water heater that was smaller than he would have chosen. There were no windows, which was a blessing, and the only way in or out was a staircase leading up to a kitchen. With a little work it would be perfect for his purposes.

Broadark was sitting on the couch, and he watched as Liam went up and down through the doorway in the kitchen, getting the place ready. The television was off; the man had given up his channel-surfing habit. Instead, he was watching Liam intently, and Liam could tell that he wanted to say something, though he held his tongue for a while.

It took less than an hour, and then he was ready. He sat at the table at the kitchen, checking over his weapons.

"Are you sure?" Broadark asked at last.

"I am," Liam replied.

"This was never part of the plan."

"Plans change."

"They do," Broadark agreed. "It's not always a good thing when they do. If this goes badly, there will be questions. No one wants us to put the organization in this kind of light."

"It won't go badly."

Broadark had nothing to say to that. To question any further would have brought the two men into a confrontation from which there was no backing down, and both of them knew it. He stood and walked over to the window, looking out into the cement yard. "When?" he asked.

Liam was strapping the knife to his ankle. He checked his pistol and slipped a fully loaded clip into the handle. He wouldn't need the automatic. Not for this task. "Soon," he said.

———◆———

Finn worked through the morning. He drafted the motion for a new bail hearing in Devon's case, taking extra care to make it a work of his finest advocacy. Once he finished with the motion, he moved on to get some work done on other cases. He could feel Lissa looking up at him on occasion, studying his demeanor. Normally they would talk to each other periodically, and he generally showed her his work so that she could look it over. Not that day, however. He was too wrapped up in his own thoughts, and he didn't feel like sharing them at the moment.

At one point Lissa got up and walked over to him. "You all right, boss?"

"Fine."

"You sure?"

He looked up at her. "There's nothing more I can do," he said. "I can write the briefs, I can make the arguments, but that's it."

She nodded. "That's true."

"It pisses me off," he said. "I should be able to do more."

She flashed him an understanding smile. "That's bullshit," she said. "But at least it's nice bullshit. It's what makes you who you are."

"My bullshit makes me who I am?"

"Yeah," she said. "It does. True of everybody else, too, so don't feel bad. Your bullshit is better than most." She leaned in close to him. "But that doesn't mean it isn't bullshit all the same," she said softly.

He took in a deep breath and exhaled; returned her smile weakly. "Is that all you wanted to say to me? You had to walk across the room to tell me that? I'm full of shit?"

"No," she said. "That's not all."

"What else, then?"

"It's almost one-thirty."

"So?"

"So, Sally gets out of school at one-thirty. You're already going to be late."

He looked at his watch and sighed again. "Damn, I almost forgot."

"Almost?"

"Fine, I forgot." He looked at the papers strewn across his desk. "I have no idea when I'm gonna get the rest of this work done."

She looked at him for a long moment. He could sense a change in her recently. Something he was having trouble putting his finger on. She had always been one of the harder people he'd known. She didn't let people in easily, and life seemed to roll around her without making a dent. But she seemed softer now, somehow. Perhaps it was just his imagination.

She walked back to her desk and picked up her car keys. "I'll get her," she said.

"You don't have to," Finn replied. He stood up and pulled his jacket off the back of his chair, feeling in the pockets for his own keys.

"I don't mind," Lissa said.

"I appreciate it, but she's my responsibility." He was moving toward the door, but she stepped in front of him.

"Finn," she said, "she's not your responsibility. You do understand that, right?"

"We can't just leave her at the school."

"I don't mean right now. She's not your responsibility long-term."

"I know," he said.

She looked at him. "Do you?"

"I do. I just want to do what I can to try and keep her father out of jail."

"A lot of it's out of your control, though. Even if you get Devon out on bail, you know he's gonna go back in after the trial. You're a good lawyer, but you can't change the fact that you have a guilty client. Not just guilty; dead to rights."

"I know," Finn said. "But I've got to try. Maybe with a little time on the outside, Devon can figure out someplace for her to be. Someplace better than where she would otherwise end up."

"There are lots of kids in the system who do just fine," Lissa said. "Sally's tough. She may be fine."

He nodded. "Maybe. But maybe not." He tried to step past her, but she moved to block him.

"You wanna tell me what this is really about?"

"What do you mean?"

"Don't bullshit me."

He put his head down and took a deep breath. "There are moments in life you'd like to have back. Times you wish you could go back and change the things you did—change the things you didn't do." He looked up. "The system's overwhelmed. It'll put kids anyplace they're out of the way. The last foster home I was in, I was fifteen. No one in their right mind takes in a fifteen-year-old. But this family ran sort of a group home. They got fifty bucks a week from the state for each kid they took in, so they'd take in anybody. They had about eleven of us when I was there. They had a bunkhouse out in the back where we all slept; one side for the boys and one side for the girls."

"Sounds cozy."

"Not the word I would have chosen. There wasn't a lot of love in the place. And the kids . . . well, let's just say the kids had their issues. Three of the older boys, in particular. They were into drugs. Into the gang scene."

"So were you, right?"

"Fair enough," Finn said. "But these three were different. Vicious. There was this one little girl, probably around thirteen, who was like a lost soul. See, most of us had been in the system our whole lives. We were used to it. We knew what to expect. But this one girl had grown up with a family. I'm not sure what happened to them; the girl didn't talk about it. Something bad enough for her to end up in this god-awful place.

"Anyway, she kept to herself mostly. She had a diary and she spent a lot of time writing in that. Like her own form of therapy. One day one of the three boys stole it. He brought it into the boys' bunkroom and started reading from it. It was sad and pathetic and everyone started laughing. Then this girl walked in and realized what was happening. She went berserk. She attacked the kid who had the book, kicking and screaming at him. He and the two others got a hold of her and just started whaling on her. Beat the hell out of her. She kept fighting, though, as long as she could. Finally, when the fight was gone from her, the three of them picked her up and carried her into the girls' bunkroom. They kicked everyone out; threatened to kill anyone who ran to the main house—not that I think anyone there would have cared. They locked the door. I can still hear the girl crying."

Lissa pursed her lips. "That's not your fault," she said. "You were a kid, and there were three of them. There was nothing you could have done."

"Maybe not. But I didn't even bother trying. You know what I did? I pulled out a bag and threw my shit in it and left. Never went back. Figured I was better off on the street. Still, I like to think that if I had it to do over, I'd do it differently."

"And this is your chance to prove that?"

Finn shrugged. "I don't know. Maybe."

Lissa shook her head. "It won't change what happened. It won't do anything for that little girl in the bunkhouse, and I'm guessing in the end it won't do anything for your conscience either."

"Probably not," Finn admitted. "Worth a shot, though."

"If you say so." Lissa walked over to her desk and picked up her keys. "I'm going to pick Sally up."

Chapter Twenty-Four

Sally was waiting outside the school. It was nearing two o'clock and the place was deserted. It wasn't the sort of place where students hung around after the bell sounded. She wondered whether anyone was actually coming to pick her up. They'd probably forgotten. Who could blame them? She wasn't their kid.

She moved around to the side of the building, to the alley by the church, and pulled out a cigarette. She could see the street from where she was if someone pulled up. Lighting the cigarette, she let her bag hang to the ground. If no one came within a few minutes, she'd start walking. Charlestown wasn't close, but she wouldn't have any problem covering the distance in an hour or so. If that was what it took, it was fine. She could take care of herself.

She was taking her third drag when she heard them. They were coming from behind the school, walking up the same route they'd followed the day before. All she heard was the laughing, but she knew instantly it was them. That was just the way her life went.

They saw her as soon as she turned. The older boy's eyes narrowed, like those of a hunter picking up the quarry. They stopped for just a moment. He raised his bandaged hand and pointed to her. "It's that bitch!" he yelled. Then they were running toward her.

She was on the move even before he yelled. Her adrenaline was pumping as she took off toward Dorchester Avenue, footsteps behind her pounding in her ears. She had a head start of twenty-five yards or so, and she was fast, but she knew they would catch up to her eventually. Her mind worked methodically. She first thought of heading back into the school, but the doors were locked and bolted after classes ended. The church was just to her right, but there was no guarantee that there would be anyone inside, and her encounter with the priest the other day had been less than cordial. Served her right, in some ways, she thought. She should learn to control her mouth better.

She hit Dorchester Avenue in full stride and headed back toward the city. There was a gas station and convenience store a couple of blocks up, and with luck she could make it to that area before she was caught. It wouldn't guarantee her safety—this was the sort of neighborhood where people minded their own business, and there was every possibility that people would merely watch as she was dragged away, but getting to a well-populated area was her best chance. She might take a beating, but being out in the open in front of people would possibly limit its duration.

She was halfway there when the van pulled in front of her.

It was a nondescript delivery van, and it screeched to a stop, its front wheels hopping the low curb, cutting off her path. At first she was relieved. She hoped it might be a cop, or maybe some Good Samaritan witnessing her plight and coming to assist her. The man who got out of the driver's side wasn't wearing a uniform, though, and he didn't move like a cop. Cops moved slowly, with a confidence born from the knowledge that, in most situations, no one was willing to question their authority. The man from the van moved with confidence as well, but it was a different brand of confidence. It was the confidence of someone who lived on the other side of the law. Someone accustomed to danger; accustomed to moving quickly and deliberately; accustomed to dealing with problems with split-second decisiveness. He was of average height and build, but he was wiry. He had jet-black hair and dark eyes that were focused on her.

He came around the front of the van and stepped in front of Sally as she tried to squeeze past the hood. She tried to duck him, but he was too fast, and he swung his arm out and grabbed her around the neck. She struggled, but he tightened the muscles in his arm, closing her neck in the crook of his elbow, cutting off her air.

She tried to scream, but nothing came out, and she started to panic, thrashing her body from side to side.

"Stop," he said simply.

She craned her head around to look at him. He wasn't even breathing hard.

Just then she heard the pounding of the boys' footsteps slowing down behind her. "Fuck you doin'!" the boy with the bandage yelled.

"Back away," the man said. She could hear the Irish in his voice. He still had her tucked off balance, but he was holding her with only one hand. She wondered whether she might be able to break free with one strong twist. His hold on her seemed like an iron vise.

"Fuck you!" the boy shot back. His voice sounded angry but indecisive. "She fucked with me, now I'm gonna fuck with her!" He and his posse weren't moving forward, but they weren't retreating, either; they were milling around within a few yards of them, their feet shuffling back and forth on the pavement.

"Back away," the man said again. This time he put his free hand into his jacket and withdrew a gun to punctuate his imperative. He pointed it at the boy, his arm extended fully, his eye looking expertly down the barrel of the pistol. "Now."

The boys stumbled back a few steps, their hands raised. Then they turned and sprinted back in the direction from which they'd come. If they'd had tails, they'd have been tucked between their hind legs, Sally thought. She wouldn't miss them, but she wasn't thrilled to trade for the guy with the gun.

He pressed the pistol to her forehead, right between her eyes. As the gun came toward her, she could see straight down into the round hole of the barrel, into the abyss. "You're getting in the car," he said. "Any trouble and you'll be dead."

"Why?" she asked. It came out without thought. He pressed the gun harder into her face, and Sally felt the metal digging painfully into her skin. "Okay," she said. "I'll get in the car."

If there were people around, Sally couldn't see them. In all likelihood there were people looking out their windows, watching. Maybe someone had even called the police, but they wouldn't arrive in time. And when they went from door to door, asking for information, no one would tell them anything. That was the code. Lie or die. Talking to the police was a sure way to get killed; everybody understood.

The man with the gun eased the pressure on Sally's neck and pulled her up so she could regain her balance. He kept enough of a grip on her, though, that she couldn't break free. Even if she could have, she had little doubt that he wouldn't hesitate to shoot her. Something in the man's eyes made that clear; he was for real.

He led her around to the driver's seat and pushed her in, making her crawl across the front seat. As she was getting in, another car pulled up. It was the sleek BMW sedan Lissa Krantz drove. The lawyer pulled up behind the van and got out. "Sally?" she called. Her voice was full of strain. "I was afraid I missed you."

She was walking around the front of her car, toward them. Sally was still only halfway into the front seat, the man standing over her. She looked up at Lissa, and flashed a pleading look. Just at that moment, the man turned toward Lissa and pointed his gun at her. "Get back in your car," he said.

Sally could see Lissa stop, shocked by the gun. "What the fuck is going on?" she asked. She wasn't moving back to her car.

"Get back in your car, now!" the man yelled. It was the first time he had raised his voice or showed any emotion. At that volume, he sounded like pure evil, and Sally was sure that Lissa would back away and get into her car. She was wrong.

Lissa reacted without hesitation. She rushed the man with the gun, ducking her head low and leading with her shoulder. She looked like a mini-linebacker taking a run at a quarterback. She must have surprised him, because he failed to react in time. One shot rang out, but it was after Lissa had driven her shoulder into his chest and it went high and wide. He was thrown back into the door, which rocked unsteadily on its hinges. Lissa continued her attack, throwing her small fists into the man with determination, though little effect. "Run, Sally!" she yelled.

Sally hesitated for just a moment, and then struggled to get past the man. It was no use, though. He had regained his balance, and he pushed her down, wedging her in the door. Then he turned to Lissa. His first blow struck her on the side of the head, and it stunned her. She didn't fall, but the expression in her eyes changed, glassing over as she stood up straighter. He hit her again, this time in the stomach, doubling her over as she cried out. The third blow was to the top of her head, with the butt of the gun, and it put her down. She crumpled to the curb, lifeless.

Sally screamed, "No!" and reached out to her, but he grabbed her arm and hoisted her up. He was remarkably strong, and she thought for a moment he'd broken her arm. If he had any such thought, it gave him no concern, and he shoved her into the van.

His gun was pointed at her; his finger was on the trigger. "Over," he ordered her. "Now." His voice had regained its equanimity, and he slid into the front seat, almost on top of her. She slid over and sat in the passenger seat. The car was still running and he dropped the transmission into reverse, hit the gas, and backed into the street. Sally gasped as they bounced over the curb, thinking that they might have run over Lissa's unconscious body lying next to the car. As he put the van in drive and pulled away, though, she could see her lying there, apparently still in one piece.

He pulled out and sped up, his gun still pointed at her head. He drove fast, and turned down two side streets with confidence before slowing to a pace that wouldn't attract attention.

Twice she glanced back behind them, hoping to see someone following them. There was no one there, though, and as they pulled farther and farther away from the neighborhood, the adrenaline began to wear off.

Only then did she begin to fathom how much trouble she was in.

Chapter Twenty-Five

"Where's Lissa?"

Kozlowski was standing in the doorway to the back office where he spent most of his time holed up. He was leaning against the doorjamb, his polyester slacks straining against the muscles in his leg, his secondhand-store jacket flapped open, revealing his shoulder holster and gun. A caricature of himself.

"She went to pick up the girl," Finn said. "Why?"

Kozlowski shook his head. "No reason."

"You guys got a date to register for china patterns this afternoon or something?"

Kozlowski looked confused. "What?"

"China patterns. That's what people do when they decide to get married, right?" Finn said. "They go out and they pick out china patterns? Silverware, too. New towels, sheets, crockery, the whole shootin' match."

"Fuck you."

"How about hot plates? Either of you guys got a hot plate?" Finn waved his hand, dismissing the concern. "Don't worry, I'm sure you'll get three or four once you register."

"We're not doing that," Kozlowski said. He sounded definitive.

"You have to. A marriage isn't legal without a china pattern." Finn shook his head. "I didn't see it coming."

"Really? Someone with your sensitive feminine instincts? I'd have thought you knew before we did."

"That's good; I like that." He looked at the older man; Kozlowski shifted uncomfortably. "Marriage," Finn said.

"Marriage," Kozlowski repeated. He shrugged. "We've been together for over a year," he said.

"I know, that's what I don't get. Seemed like you guys had it all figured out; like you guys had what everybody else is looking for. You really want to risk screwing it up?"

"I love her," Kozlowski said.

"Of course you do. So why do you want to risk losing her?"

"I risk losing her by marrying her?"

Finn nodded. "Lissa? Yeah, you risk losing her by marrying her. She's not the marrying type. Neither are you. You might've been once, when you were younger. If you'd gone a different way, you could've settled down with some strong, silent Polish girl and had a dozen kids. Not now, though."

"Maybe you don't know us as well as you think you do."

Finn laughed. "I know you better than that. I know you both better than you know yourselves."

"This gonna be a problem?"

"Not for me. Not unless you guys screw it up. I need both of you here. I don't want either of you thinking you can get out of your commitments to me by getting married to each other."

Kozlowski shook his head. "We won't screw it up."

"No?"

"No."

"Promise?"

"Fuck you."

Finn smiled. "I suppose that's the best I'm gonna get, huh?"

"More than you deserve."

"You're gonna tell me what *I* deserve?"

"I said I love her, not that I deserve her," Kozlowski said. "I'll take it."

"Fair enough," Finn said. "Just don't screw it up."

"You said that already."

The phone rang, and Finn leaned over to pick it up. "This is Finn," he said. He could hear the noises in the background, and he sat up straight. They were unmistakable sounds: children crying in the background; adults hollering, their voices full of stress; a public announcement in an automaton's voice echoing off a linoleum floor; sirens in the distance. They were hospital sounds.

"Is this a law office?" the woman's voice said.

"It is," Finn replied. "Who is this?"

"This is City Hospital. Does a woman named Lissa Krantz work there?"

"Yes. Why, is there something wrong?" Finn glanced up at Kozlowski, who was returning his look, an edge of concern reflecting Finn's own tension.

"She's okay," the woman said. "At least she should be. She was involved in an altercation."

"What kind of an altercation?" Finn asked. "What are you talking about?" He looked at Kozlowski and shook his head in an attempt to look reassuring. From the look on Kozlowski's face, it was clearly not working.

"I don't really know, sir. That's all the information I have. Is she married?"

"Sort of."

"The doctor told me that we should get her husband here if possible, for when she wakes up."

"Wakes up? She's unconscious? What's going on?"

"I'm sorry, I only have the notes they gave me. The doctor's in with another patient, and it's a little crazy around here. You'll have to come down to the hospital to get the full information."

"Okay, we'll be right down," Finn said. He was about to hang up the phone, but he paused. "Wait," he said. "What about the girl?"

There was a pause on the other end of the line before the woman spoke. "What girl?" she asked.

———❖———

"They said she was okay?" Kozlowski said.

"Yeah." They were moving as soon as Finn hung up the phone. Finn forwarded his office phone to his cell and locked the door to the office. Kozlowski was already in the car when Finn got there.

"Did they say what happened?" Kozlowski asked. His voice seemed calm, but Finn could hear the man's teeth grinding together, and the muscles in his jaw and shoulders were flexing in a disjointed, spasmodic rhythm.

Finn shook his head. He was worried about Lissa, but the nurse who had called said she was going to be okay. His primary concern was locating Sally. "She'd probably head to the office," Finn said. "Either that or my apartment."

"Who?" Kozlowski's full consciousness was devoted to Lissa at the moment.

"Sally," Finn said. "If Lissa never got to the school to pick her up, she must've set off for Charlestown on foot."

Kozlowski shrugged. "Maybe."

"Can you think of anyplace else she would go?" Finn cast a quick look at Kozlowski as he drove.

"I have trouble thinking of anyplace she wouldn't go." He looked at Finn. "What? You've seen her. She's been on her own for a while, I'm sure she's got lots of places she can go—none of them good."

Finn turned his attention back to the road. "She's my responsibility," he said.

"I'm sure she'll be fine," Kozlowski said.

Finn's cell phone rang in his pocket. He pulled it out and took a quick look at the readout. The call was being forwarded from the office; the number was blocked. It could be the hospital, Finn thought.

He pressed the button to accept the call and put the phone up to his ear. "This is Finn," he said. He heard nothing but static; he was traveling through a weak signal, and the noise from his car made it difficult to hear. "Hello?"

"I have the girl," the voice said.

"Who is this?" From the accent Finn had a pretty good idea, but he could think of nothing else to say.

"Devon will know who I am," the voice said. "Tell him I have her. Tell him I want the paintings. If I get the paintings, I'll let her go. If not, I'll kill her."

"I don't understand; what paintings?" Finn bluffed.

"Devon will know." The man's voice made Finn shiver.

"What if Devon doesn't know what you're talking about? What if he doesn't have any paintings?"

"That would be too bad. Particularly for the girl. His daughter, as I understand it? Either he gives me the paintings, or he trades himself for his daughter. If I have time with him, I'll find out for myself whether or not he knows anything. Otherwise, she dies. Tell him."

"I'll tell him."

"One more thing," the man said. "Don't go to the police. If I think they are involved, I'll kill her. Then I'll come after Devon. Then I'll finish off the woman from today and her old man. Then I'll come after you. Are we clear?"

"Crystal," Finn said.

"Good."

"I need time to get him out of jail," Finn said.

"I'll give you a day, then I'll call back."

"I don't know that it'll happen that fast."

"One day, Mr. Finn," the voice said. "Then I'll kill the girl."

"I'll see what I can do."

"You'll do better than that. I'll call tomorrow at the end of the day. Six o'clock. Have Malley out, and be ready with an answer. Otherwise, I'll be coming." The line went dead.

Finn clicked his phone off and slipped it into his pocket. Kozlowski was still looking at him, saying nothing. "Not good," Finn said.

"Devon's Irishman?" Kozlowski asked.

Finn nodded. "He's got Sally. He says he'll kill her if he doesn't get the paintings. Either that or Devon trades himself for her."

"That's not good," Kozlowski agreed. "I take it he's the one who put Lissa in the hospital?"

"Probably. He says that if we go to the police, he'll kill us all."

Finn could see Kozlowski's jaw muscles grow tighter. "Can't you make this goddamned car go any faster?"

Chapter Twenty-Six

Boston City Hospital was on Massachusetts Avenue, just across the Roxbury border from the South End. The area had traditionally been one of the more dangerous in Boston. Gentrification had edged its way in uneasily during the explosion of real estate costs in the city in the 1990s and early 2000s, but it remained a high-crime neighborhood. Boston was the home to many of the world's greatest hospitals; due largely to its location, BCH was not considered one of them. It served an urban community without the money or the connections to get into Mass General or Brigham and Women's. Nevertheless, it was a place with a solid reputation, and a wealth of experience in treating trauma victims.

Finn and Kozlowski gave their names at the desk and were directed to a nurse in an office off to the side of the emergency room. She, in turn, took their information again and made a call to page another nurse. That nurse came down and led them through the emergency room waiting area to an elevator and up to the second floor. No one would answer any of their questions. It wasn't clear to Finn whether the silence was a result of lack of knowledge or adherence to procedure.

On the second floor, Finn and Kozlowski were introduced to a doctor who at least seemed familiar with Lissa's status. He was young enough that Finn considered asking for someone older. He was wearing a stethoscope, though, and the nametag on his white coat read "Dr. Jeffson." Finn suspected that questioning his competence wasn't going to get them information any quicker.

"She was found on Dorchester," Dr. Jeffson said. Even his voice sounded young. "She was lying unconscious by the side of the road; her car was parked a few yards away. At first the suspicion was that she'd been in some sort of an accident, but there was no damage to the car, and her injuries are more consistent with an assault. She was hit over the head with something solid. The police are interviewing people, trying to determine exactly what happened, but I wouldn't hold your breath. It's not the sort of neighborhood where people see anything."

"Is she okay?" Kozlowski asked. The concern in his voice was plain, but he was keeping it under control at least.

The doctor blinked at them. "Oh, I thought someone already talked to you about her condition."

"Not really," Finn said. "The woman who called said she thought Lissa would be okay, but that's it."

"Ah," the doctor said. He took Finn by the elbow and led him discreetly over to the side of the corridor, as though it would give them some privacy. "I take it that you're the boyfriend?" he said to Finn.

"No," Finn said. He nodded to Kozlowski. "He is."

The young doctor looked over at Kozlowski. His eyes showed his surprise, but to his credit he didn't miss a beat. "Sorry," he said. "Mr. . . . ?"

"Kozlowski."

"Yes, Mr. Kozlowski, Lissa is going to be fine. We still don't know about the baby, however."

"What baby?" Finn asked.

Jeffson glanced at him, then said to Kozlowski. "I'm sorry. I didn't mean to . . ."

Finn almost fell over. He looked at Kozlowski, wondering whether the news of the pregnancy would come as a surprise to him. It clearly didn't, though he rocked backward at the mention. "What happened?" he asked.

"It appears that she was also hit in the abdomen. We don't know whether it has caused any damage yet. It looks as though she's around ten weeks; we're going to run an ultrasound as soon as the equipment frees up. Then we'll know more."

"Okay." Kozlowski looked stunned. "Is she conscious?"

"Yes, she woke up about twenty minutes ago. She hasn't said much. The police wanted to interview her, but she said she was too tired; I got the impression she wanted to talk to you first, and she's clearly worried about the pregnancy."

"Can I see her?"

The doctor nodded toward a door down the hallway. "She's in room 217. I'll be in as soon as an ultrasound frees up."

Lissa lay on the bed, both hands resting on her belly. She couldn't believe what was happening. Any of it. Her head was killing her, and the fact that her thoughts were being pulled in multiple directions didn't help any. She couldn't stop thinking about Sally, and the worry was devastating. She had avoided the policeman's eyes when he first tried to question her. She put her arm over her face and told him that she couldn't concentrate. That was true. She also said she didn't remember what happened. That was a lie. She had to lie, though. She needed more information before she involved the police. The Boston Police Department was a blunt instrument, and it wasn't clear that that was what was needed at the moment.

She was so worried about her pregnancy that she felt sick. It was odd; she hadn't wanted to get pregnant in the first place. When her doctor informed her that she was, she'd had mixed feelings. Now that it looked as though she might lose the baby, she couldn't imagine not carrying to term—not having Kozlowski's child. It made her feel paralyzed.

Kozlowski walked into the room. He came straight to her and took her hand. She worked to choke back tears.

"What happened?" he asked.

She rubbed the back of her free hand across her nose and sniffled. "It was him," she said. "Devon's Irish guy. Had to be. He took Sally." A tear ran down her cheek.

Kozlowski nodded. "We heard from him. He said he's going to kill her if he doesn't get the paintings."

"I figured. I was late picking her up. We were late. We fucked up. Maybe if I'd been there earlier . . ." Her voice trailed off.

"He still would have gotten to her," Kozlowski said. "Think about what he did to Murphy and Ballick. This isn't a guy who's going to be stopped. Not yet."

"I don't want to think about what he's done."

Kozlowski said nothing for another moment. "How about you? You okay?"

"That's what they say." She looked down at her stomach. "They don't know about the baby."

"I talked to the doctor," Kozlowski said. "The ultrasound will be freed up in a little bit. We won't worry about it until then."

"Right," she said. "No point in worrying." She looked up at him. He had the type of face that was difficult to read. Right now, though, his tension was plain. She squeezed his hand. "Maybe we were never meant to be parents," she said.

"Maybe." He looked out the window. The room faced to the south, out onto Route 93, which wound its way through Dorchester down toward the South Shore, toward the suburbs with their houses and their lawns and their picket fences. It was a world of domestic tranquillity neither of them knew or particularly wanted to know. And yet at the moment it was a world she envied with all her heart. "We're still getting married, though," he said after a moment.

"If the baby's dead we don't need to."

He looked back at her. He wasn't crying; she gave thanks for that. It wasn't who he was. It wasn't who she wanted him to be. "It's not about need," he said. "I want to."

She took a deep breath, then nodded. The door opened, and Dr. Jeffson walked in with a nurse. He looked at them with the curiosity Lissa had seen on so many faces before; that wonder at the two of them together as a couple. She didn't care. She knew what they were doing together; that was all that mattered. "The ultrasound is available," he said. "Are you ready?"

Lissa looked up at Kozlowski and gave his hand another squeeze. "We are," she said. "We're ready."

Finn was waiting downstairs in the lobby. He wondered whether he should have gone in to see Lissa. Normally there would have been no way to keep him out. There were few people more important in his life.

Nothing seemed normal anymore, though. He'd never felt like a third wheel with Lissa and Kozlowski until a few days before. They were a couple; he understood that. And yet they didn't act like a couple. They didn't cling to each other the way so many other couples did. Their relationship seemed built on stronger stuff than mutual dependence. As a result, his presence in the middle had never seemed to weaken it.

Things had changed. He had to give them a little more space now. When the doctor had pointed to her room and said that she could have visitors, Finn merely nodded to Kozlowski. "I'll wait downstairs," he'd said.

Kozlowski didn't argue. Finn half expected Kozlowski to tell him to come in with him, just to make sure that she was all right. He hadn't, though. "I'll meet you down there in a little while," he'd said. With that, he'd turned and walked down the hallway toward her room. Finn stood there for a moment, then headed toward the elevator.

He was sitting on a bench, trying to focus on Sally's kidnapping, working through all the various ugly possibilities, when Kozlowski walked off the elevator forty-five minutes later.

Finn could tell nothing from Kozlowski's face. The older man walked over to him, looked down. "We've got work to do," he said.

Finn got up. "How is she?"

"She's fine. They're keeping her for a night, just to make sure."

"The baby?"

Kozlowski nodded. "Still alive. Let's go." He turned and walked toward the lobby exit. Finn had to walk quickly to keep up. "We've got to get to this guy," Kozlowski said. "He'll kill the girl. He's not just fucking around."

Finn agreed. It was the only conclusion he'd come to about which he was sure. "Should we bring in the police?" he asked. "Maybe the FBI? It's a kidnapping, so they'd have jurisdiction."

Kozlowski shook his head. "I thought about it. This guy's desperate. It's not just about the money, there's something else driving him. That means he's unpredictable. The cops and the FBI work from a standard playbook that depends on predictability. We call them in, he'll know, and he'll kill her without even thinking twice. We need to get to this guy ourselves."

"How?" Finn asked. "I've been sitting here, racking my brain, trying to come up with some way to find him, and I've got nothing."

"We won't find him," Kozlowski said. "There's not enough time, and he's smart enough to be holed up in a place we'd never locate."

"So? What do we do?"

They were out at the car, and Kozlowski was opening the passenger-side door. He looked over the roof of the car at Finn. "We find the paintings."

"What?"

"He wants them," Kozlowski said. "Why not give them to him?"

Finn blinked back at him. "Well, yeah. That sounds good in theory; in practice it seems a little unrealistic, doesn't it?"

"Why?"

"I don't know. Maybe because every relevant law-enforcement agency in the world has been looking for those paintings for twenty years and hasn't come up with anything. That doesn't even include all the journalists, private investigators, art houses, and every profiteer with any knowledge of art."

"We've never looked for them," Kozlowski pointed out.

"You sure you're not being a little bit overconfident?"

"Probably," Kozlowski said. "You got any better ideas? Maybe this will give us back some control. Besides, we have a better reason than anyone else to find them."

"How do we even know that they're still in Boston? In all likelihood they were sold a long time ago and moved out of the goddamned country."

Kozlowski shook his head. "They're here. This asshole helped steal these things almost twenty years ago, and he's *here, now*. Not only that, but he seems pretty fuckin' *sure* that someone here knows something. He's smart, we know that much; and he's careful. Careful enough to torture and kill a bunch of people and not leave behind anything that's got him caught by the cops. A guy like that doesn't make the kinds of moves he's making after twenty years unless there's been some reason—unless he's learned something concrete."

Finn considered this. "Okay, that seems logical," he said. "There's only one problem with it. It assumes that a guy who's running around torturing and killing people is rational. That may be a stretch."

"It may be, but if we want to have any hope of getting the girl back, we have to make that assumption. If it's wrong, then we're fucked and he's going to kill her no matter what we do."

Finn started the car, let the engine run for a moment. "Fine," he said. "I'll buy all that for the moment. But I need to know one thing."

"What is it?"

"Is this personal? Because of what he did to Lissa?"

Kozlowski took a deep breath. "He took the girl. The daughter of our client—a girl we were taking care of. He assaulted Lissa, and he could have killed my child before it was even born. It doesn't get any more personal than this."

Finn stared back at him. "Good," he said. "That's what I wanted to hear. So where do we begin?"

"Where every investigation starts," Kozlowski replied. "At the scene of the crime."

Chapter Twenty-Seven

Finn made the call from the car. Sometimes being a lawyer seemed like a life strung together in a series of unpleasant phone conversations. *Your parole was denied; the judge ruled against you; there's a problem with the contract.* Nothing in his experience, though, had prepared him for a call as difficult as this one.

"Devon," Finn said. He stopped. He couldn't figure out how to say it.

"What's wrong?" his client asked.

Finn took a deep breath. "Sally's been kidnapped." Three words. The worst three words Finn had ever uttered.

"What the fuck are you talking about?" Devon said after a minute. "How? When?"

"A couple of hours ago. From her school." Finn could hear Devon suck in air like a drowning man pulled from the ocean.

"Was it him?"

"Yeah," Finn said. "We got a call from him within the last hour. He said she's okay, but he's only gonna let her go if he either gets the paintings or he gets you."

"Did you tell the cops?"

"No. He told us that if we did, he'd kill her. She's your daughter, though. If you think we should get the cops involved, we will. It's your call."

"No cops," Devon said. "He's not the kinda guy who bluffs. He'll kill her. I gotta deal with this myself. Can you get me outta here?"

"Probably," Finn said. "I've got a motion for a new bail hearing ready, and I can get it filed today. After the last hearing, it's not gonna be cheap, but they'll set bail."

"I don't care what it costs. Just get me out. It's me he wants. That's her only chance. When do you think the judge will hear it?"

"He's got a motions session tomorrow. I'll try to get it scheduled for then."

"Get it done. I gotta get outta this place." Devon sounded deep in despair.

"It's the best I can do," Finn said. "It's not gonna be an easy hearing."

"Okay," Devon said. "Finn, I'm worried."

"I know," Finn said. The guilt ripped at him. "I'm sorry, Devon. I didn't know. I didn't even think that this could happen."

"It's not your fault. It's mine. All this is my fault."

"We'll get her back," Finn said with false confidence.

"We will." Devon sounded even less sure than Finn felt. "I'm gonna make sure we get her back."

<hr>

The Isabella Stewart Gardner Museum wasn't far from the hospital. It covered half a block on Fenway Drive, next to Simmons College, just around the corner from the Museum of Fine Arts and Northeastern University. Across the street to the east was a patch of garden that was the last natural remnant of the swampy fens that had once covered much of the area west of downtown Boston.

Finn had never been to the Gardner before, and he was surprised by its exterior. He was familiar with the larger Museum of Fine Arts, with its towering Ionic columns and broad marble staircase leading up from the sidewalk to the main entrance. He'd been to the Boston Public Library, with its imposing neoclassical facade, rising from the center of Copley like some great mausoleum. It seemed to Finn that such pomp was a necessary hallmark of cultural landmarks. The Gardner had none of it. From the outside, the museum begged for little attention. It had gray-brown stucco sides, set flush to the sidewalk, with a stubby steel door for an entrance that for its lack of pretension could have been admitting them to a college dorm.

Finn and Kozlowski walked through the dark entryway, paid their admission fee, and walked into the main section of the museum. Upon entering, Finn felt transported. Before him was an enormous three-story indoor courtyard garden, roofed by a great glass ceiling allowing in all the sunlight of the day. Rustles of clover and ivy covered the ground surrounding an intricate mosaic that was centered under the transparent ceiling. Across the courtyard from the entrance, a large fountain with inverted Chinese fish-dragons was framed by an elaborate two-way staircase. About the courtyard were strewn various works—headless statues, urns, and obelisks—looking almost haphazard in their placement. And yet there was an order to it all, as though the informality of their selection and display was central to their purpose. Above, balconies set against huge arched marble windows observed the scene.

"Nice," Kozlowski said.

"Yeah," Finn agreed.

The entire building was centered on the courtyard, with galleries and halls ringing the place on every floor.

"I guess we should find out who's in charge," Kozlowski said. He walked over to an information desk, off to one corner of the ground floor. The woman there blended well into the place. She appeared to be in her fifties; her dark hair was streaked with gray. Her clothes were respectable, demure, and prim. They were neither expensive nor shabby. She was looking down at the desk, motionless. Finn wondered for a moment whether she might be part of an exhibit. Kozlowski walked over and stood in front of the desk. She must have seen him; he was too imposing a presence to go unnoticed. But she didn't look up. "Excuse me," he said in a polite tone after a moment.

"Yes?" she said. She still didn't raise her eyes, giving the impression that whatever she was studying was far too important for her to be pulled away at the first effort.

"Can we talk to the manager?"

With the question, her gaze was drawn upward, and she looked directly at Kozlowski for the first time. Her head remained at a downward angle, as if she was still deciding whether he merited a shift in her actual body position. "Manager?" she said. "No. We don't have a manager. We have a director."

"He's the person who's in charge?"

"He is."

"Is there any chance we could talk to him for a moment?"

This time she seemed to latch on to the *we*, and she craned her neck at an angle to get a line of vision around Kozlowski, examining Finn. She took only a quick look, and didn't seem impressed. "Can I ask why?"

"We have a couple of questions about the art theft."

With the mention of the robbery, her posture straightened. Her brow knit itself tightly and her eyes narrowed angrily. "We don't answer questions about the theft," she said. "Not ever."

"Never?"

"Not ever."

Kozlowski's voice became serious. "My name is Kozlowski," he said. He took out the leather billfold in which he kept his private detective's license and held it up. It had his picture and looked official. He kept his eyes on the woman's and she took only a glance at the identification. "We're chasing down a lead in a more recent crime that may be related. It would be helpful if we could talk to him just for a moment."

The look on the woman's face soured even further. "What additional information could you people need beyond what we've provided over and over again? It's been twenty years, do you really think there's anything more that anyone here has to say to the police?"

"Please, ma'am," Kozlowski said. "It will just take a moment of his time."

She shook her head in frustration, but picked up the phone and punched in three digits. She turned away from the two of them as she spoke, and her voice was swallowed up in the enormity of the marble lobby. Then she turned around and hung up the phone. "It will be a few minutes," she said. "He's very busy."

"I'm sure, ma'am."

"He said you can wait for him up in the Dutch Room, if you wish."

"The Dutch Room," Kozlowski repeated. He turned and looked at Finn. "The Dutch Room."

Finn gave him a blank stare.

The woman let out a condescending sigh. "Up the stairs to the right," she said. "It's where the Rembrandts and the Flinck used to hang before they were stolen."

"Ah, the Dutch Room," Kozlowski said.

Finn nodded. "Of course, the Dutch Room."

"Thanks very much."

She was still shaking her head as the two of them walked up the stairs. She probably would have been muttering as well, if it wouldn't have struck her as an unpardonable breach of etiquette.

The second floor was just as breathtaking as the first. It, too, was built around the huge courtyard, and it consisted of a series of gallery rooms lined up one after another, each looking out through ornate balconies down to the garden below.

They turned right at the top of the stairs and walked along the hallway to a large arched doorway that led into a huge room paneled in dark wood. It had towering ceilings and antique chairs upholstered in heavy fabric. The walls were covered in green silk and lined with large dark oil paintings, many of them portraits. The faces of the long-dead peered out from their places on the walls. For some reason, Finn felt as though they were judging him; it made him feel depressed.

In a few spots there were empty frames hanging on the walls. The frames were, admittedly, works of art in and of themselves. They were heavy, ornately carved works painted in gold leaf. And yet, left alone, without the canvas and paint, they seemed sad and out of place.

Finn was about to ask Kozlowski about the empty frames when he noticed a man sitting in the corner of the room. He was propped up in a wooden chair, his head leaning against the wall, his eyes closed. Finn looked at Kozlowski and motioned toward the man. He wondered whether the man was dead, and walked over quietly to take a look.

He was old—Finn was guessing in his seventies—and his clothes were battered. His jacket was heavy wool, a half season too late, and the threads were fraying at the lapels. The elbows looked shot through. The man's face was gray and his eyes were sunken back into their sockets, surrounded by dark skin. It took a moment for Finn to see the man's chest moving ever so slightly, giving at least the suggestion of life. Finn waved his hand a few feet in front of the man's face.

"He's fine," a voice said behind Finn. He turned to see a tall, trim man in his late fifties. He was wearing a tailored suit of charcoal-gray, a bright white shirt, and an azure tie with a matching pocket square. "Detective Kozlowski?" he asked, looking back and forth between the two visitors.

"I'm Kozlowski." He extended his hand.

The man shook it, though there was a look of reluctance on his face. "I'm Paul Baxter. I am the director of the museum, as well as the chief curator." Finn thought he detected a hint of the Old World in the accent. It could have been an affectation of the Boston Brahmin many well-heeled New Englanders took to, but Finn thought there was hint of Irish to it as well.

"Thank you for talking to us, Mr. Baxter," Kozlowski said. He motioned to Finn. "This is Scott Finn, my partner."

Baxter nodded to Finn, but didn't walk over to shake his hand. "Is there news? We haven't heard anything for days."

Kozlowski and Finn exchanged a look. "What was the last update you received?" Kozlowski asked.

"Nothing. No update. The only information we've had was from the call I got from the FBI last week."

Kozlowski frowned. "You've heard nothing since then?"

Baxter shook his head. "Nothing."

"Who did you speak with the first time?"

"Special Agent Porter."

"How much information did he give you?" Finn noted the care with which Kozlowski crafted his questions.

"Not much," Baxter scoffed. "Just that Interpol had received word that someone was trying to fence the paintings. That was it. No further information; just the request that we give them any information that *we* came into possession of to *them*. Honestly, I don't know how you law-enforcement types keep your jobs. Twenty years, and I'm supposed to run this place effectively without basic information? I haven't even told the board about this because there have been so many disappointments in the past. If they find out that I'm keeping this from them, I can't even imagine the fallout."

Finn looked at Kozlowski with admiration. He'd been a great police officer, but his talents would also have made him formidable on the other side of the law. Without lying, he'd pulled an enormous amount of confidential information from Baxter.

"I understand your frustration," Kozlowski said. He looked at the man sleeping in the corner. "Would you prefer to discuss this some-place else?"

Baxter glanced briefly at the zombie, then shook his head. "No, that's fine. That's Sam. Sam Bass. He was an assistant here forever. The museum gave him a pension two years ago, but he has no place else to go during the day, so we let him have the run of the place. He wouldn't mention anything to anyone, even if he was awake; he knows that if he causes any trouble I won't let him back in the place." He raised his voice slightly. "Isn't that right, Sam?"

The old man snorted and shifted his head; then he settled back into his slumber.

Baxter ignored him. "What else can you tell me?"

Kozlowski shook his head. "Not much. This is ultimately the FBI's jurisdiction. Did they mention anything to you about a possible Irish connection?"

Baxter looked unnerved. "No," he said. "Why? Do they think there is some connection to Ireland?"

"I'm sorry," Kozlowski said. "If they didn't talk with you about their information, I certainly can't. As I told the woman downstairs at the desk, we are technically only investigating a different crime—the assault of a woman in South Boston. There is some suspicion that the assailant may be connected in some way with those who committed the theft here. Is there anything you can tell us that might help?"

Baxter looked offended. "No. Of course not. If there was anything I could do to help, don't you think I would have done it already? I had only been here at the museum for a few weeks when the theft oc-curred. It remains the only stain on my reputation."

The man's tone was defensive, and Kozlowski's eyes narrowed on Baxter. "You'd tell us if you had any additional information, wouldn't you, Mr. Baxter?"

The director looked as if he might swallow his tongue. His face nearly turned purple. "Don't think I'm unaware of the speculation,

Detective Kozlowski. Your colleagues on the police force and in the FBI have never been subtle in hinting that they believe that I might somehow be involved. I consider these speculations slander." He took a deep breath and composed himself. Looking at both Kozlowski and Finn, he did his best to affect an air of dignity. "Now, Detectives, unless you have any additional information you can share with me, I have a great deal of work to do."

Kozlowski looked at him for a long moment. "Of course," he said at last. "We'll be in touch if there is anything else we can share with you."

"I look forward to it." Baxter turned on his heels and left the room.

Chapter Twenty-Eight

"Do you think he was telling the truth?"

Kozlowski asked the question once Baxter had left the room. He and Finn were left standing there, taking in their surroundings. The empty frames hung before them like skeletons—sad reminders of the beauty stolen from the world.

"About what?" Finn asked. "That he's looking forward to hearing from us again? I don't think so."

"No, about whether or not he was involved in the theft. He seemed awfully defensive. Did you notice the accent? Sounded Irish to me."

Finn chuckled. "Well, if an Irish accent is enough to convict someone of art theft, then half of Boston's population needs to be in jail."

"Half of Boston's population isn't in a position to know everything about the security of a museum that houses billions of dollars of art. Half of Boston's population doesn't walk around in three-thousand-dollar suits."

"It was a nice suit," Finn admitted. "I'm not sure it'd be enough to get a conviction, though." He walked over to one of the empty frames. The walls were covered in a jacquard silk in a lush forest-green pattern, and the fabric showed through the neatly hung frame. If you didn't know that a painting had been stolen from the spot, you might think that the frame was hung there in jest, or as some great cosmic riddle. "I wish he hadn't left," Finn said. "I had a few questions about the theft."

"Like what?"

"Like why haven't they replaced these empty frames with pictures? They must have some extra artwork lying around here somewhere. If not, I'm sure they could buy some. Having these empty frames where the stolen art used to be seems macabre."

Kozlowski shrugged. "Who knows why? When you're dealing with art—and rich people—logic doesn't have to apply."

"They can't replace the paintings," someone behind them said. The voice came like an echo from the dead, crackling sharply from the back of the room and reverberating off the walls and high ceiling. Finn and Kozlowski turned.

The corpse was awake now. Sitting up in the hard wooden chair at the back of the room, with the head no longer slumped to the side, but held aloft by a slender twig of a neck. The eyes were open, though still hidden deep beneath the shadow of a prominent ocular ridge. The skin, while still gray and dark under the eyes, was no longer slack. The eyes traveled slowly from Finn to Kozlowski and back again. "They aren't allowed to replace the frames," the corpse said.

"Why not?" Finn asked, after a moment.

"It was in Mrs. Gardner's will." The accent was unusual. It was Bostonian in origin, but muddled. Finn could hear the hard consonants of Southie or Charlestown or Dorchester, but there was also a mix of the extended vowels of upper-class Boston. It was as though a former accent had been painted over, but remained underneath.

Finn looked at Kozlowski. "It was in Mrs. Gardner's will," he repeated. He looked back at the corpse. "Why?"

The man rose from the chair, and Finn felt as though he were witnessing a resurrection. "Do you not know the story of this place?" he asked.

237

"No," Finn said. "I don't."

"Well, you should," the corpse responded. "If you plan on finding the paintings, you really should." He looked at them carefully. "That is why you're here, no? To try to find the paintings?"

"You're treasure hunters," the man said. "I've seen hundreds like you in here in the past."

"No," Finn replied. "We're not."

"Well, you're not the police, that much is clear. The police always show their badges the first time they meet someone. My name is Sam Bass," he said. "As Mr. Baxter already told you."

Finn looked carefully at him. "You were awake," he said. "The whole time, you were eavesdropping."

Bass dismissed the accusation with the wave of a hand. "At my age, it's hard for me to tell for sure when I'm asleep and when I'm awake. You'll learn that someday, if you're lucky." He looked around the great room. "I spend most of my time here, in the museum, and it all blends together—the time I'm awake, the time I'm asleep; the time I'm alone, the time I'm not. It's like being trapped in an Impressionist painting, where all the lines are smudged and run into one another. Sometimes I can almost feel myself slipping into this place; becoming a part of it. It would be a nice way to go."

"You like it that much here?" Finn asked.

Bass gave an amused smile, and for a moment his face took on a sparkle of life infused with charm. "'Like' is too weak a word, Mr. Finn. This place saved my life." He shuffled toward them. "Come, I want to show you something."

He led them toward the door and back out to the staircase. His pace was slow and his steps unsteady. Finn had to fight the urge to reach out to take hold of the strange old man's elbow as he brought them down the long hallway. "I grew up poor," Bass said. "In the 1930s and

'40s, a lot of us grew up poor. Not like today's poor. Today, you're poor if you don't have a forty-inch flat-screen TV. Back then you weren't poor until you were starving. It was a bad time. As a child, I watched people fight and claw for food. That was how people survived back then. It seemed the only way. Only I was no good at it. I was small and frail and hungry a lot."

He walked through the arched doorway at the far end of the hall and turned right, into a smaller room. He paused for a moment, as though walking and talking at the same time was wearing him out. Then he continued, heading toward the far end of the room. "The only time I managed to work up the courage to take anything larger than a scrap from a rat was when I was nine. It was from a large town house not far from here. Some lazy housekeeper left the door open to the kitchen, and a whole loaf of bread just sitting out. I was so hungry, and it was right there." An odd look of guilt was still evident on his face. "I took it," he said. "I took it and I ran." He shook his head at the memory.

"It was a loaf of bread," Finn said.

Bass looked at him. "It was my honor. And I gave it up for a loaf of bread. It's the sort of thing you don't appreciate until you're older."

"Were you caught?" Kozlowski asked.

The old man shook his head. "Not by the police. I ran in fear. Fear of getting caught. Fear of stumbling on someone bigger and hungrier than me. I had no place to go that was safe. But as I passed this place, I saw there was a door open. It was dark and seemed empty, so I ducked inside. I only intended to stay here for a moment. Long enough to eat the bread, nothing more. I had no idea what this place was." He was at the far end of the room, and he walked through the doorway into the next gallery.

"What happened?" Finn asked, following the strange old man into the next room.

"I saw her," Bass said. He pointed up at a painting on the wall.

Finn looked up. It was a portrait of a woman, looming over the gallery. Finn sensed she was beautiful, though it was hard to tell. She was painted from a distance, lingering in a darkened doorway, her white dress flowing about her like a loose shroud. She might have been smiling, but if so it was an enigmatic smile; like the Mona Lisa with a dose of sensuality. "Isabella Stewart Gardner. Mrs. Jack, as she was called. This one was painted by Zorn."

Finn moved closer to inspect the painting. He could feel Kozlowski at his side.

"Beautiful, isn't she?" Bass remarked.

"Maybe. I can't tell," Kozlowski replied.

"No, I suppose not," Bass conceded. "I believe that was intentional. It's said that Mrs. Jack wasn't conventionally pretty. Her features were slightly out of proportion, and portraitists—even Sargent—fudged when it came to her face. But her figure was magnificent."

Finn turned and looked at Bass, and the old man gave him a mischievous wink. "She was remarkable in many ways, they say," he continued. "She died in the twenties, before I ever saw this place, before I was born. She built this place. Brick by brick, stone by stone, painting by painting. They say that it is the only museum of its kind in the world—a museum that represents the vision of a single person; a woman at that. Think of how remarkable that is given that the place was opened in 1903. Fifteen years before women could even vote. And yet she did this." He waved his arm around, indicating the entire place. "The building was designed, according to her specifications, to resemble one of the great Italian palazzos of Venice, turned inside out. The beauty is on the inside. She scoured Europe for the greatest works she could find over the course of three decades. Then she arranged all of it in the galleries herself. That's why they can't replace the empty frames—her will is very specific; nothing is to be changed. It is her own personal vision that survives."

"Seems a little crazy," Finn said.

Bass smiled. "Maybe. That's what a lot of people said about her back when she was alive. She didn't completely fit in here in Boston. She had a more cosmopolitan view of the world, and she didn't conform to the more proper Victorian mores. They say she used to take the lions from the zoo for a walk on a leash. She threw lavish parties for artists and philosophers and authors. She liked doing things her own way. She was a feminist in the truest sense of the word, before it became fashionable."

"And she must have been rich," Kozlowski pointed out.

"Yes, she was rich. Her parents had money; her husband had money. Still, money doesn't make a person great. What she did here was great. She overcame the death of her son, the death of her husband, and a number of great sadnesses in her life. She never gave up, and she poured her soul into this place. That's why the robbery was so much more than a mere crime."

Finn looked at the old man. His eyes were focused on the painting of the woman, almost as if in a trance. "You know an awful lot about her," Finn said.

He smiled and pulled his eyes from the painting to look at Finn. "I should. I've been here for over sixty years. The night watchman found me that night, curled up on the floor in this room, the bread still under my shirt. The curator was working late. The guard wanted to call the police. He probably should have, but the curator stopped him. He asked me what I was doing, and I told him. I told him everything—about the bread; about the street; about being alone. No one had ever asked me anything like that before. My entire childhood came pouring out. Then he asked me why I was still there—why I hadn't eaten the bread and left. Without thinking about it, I looked up at this painting. 'I'm here because of her,' I told him."

Bass looked back up at the painting. "I think he understood. I'm lucky; few others would have. He just nodded, and asked me if I was willing to work for her. I told him I was, and I've been here ever since.

I've done just about every job there is to do here. I started out as a janitor, keeping the place clean. I learned a little about electrical work and plumbing and painting, and made myself useful in any way I could. I've always regarded her as my savior, and I've tried hard to repay her. When I got older, I learned about the paintings themselves—their history and how to care for them. My only hope was to always make sure they were safe. I failed at that, clearly."

"It must have bothered you when the place was robbed," Kozlowski said. It sounded to Finn like he was prodding the old man.

Bass looked at them both, tears of anger in his eyes. "That wasn't a robbery, it was an abomination. It was a betrayal."

"Baxter was the director at the time?" Kozlowski asked.

Bass looked at him and chuckled. "Baxter thought you were the police because you sound like the police."

"I used to be on the force," Kozlowski said. "He assumed. I didn't correct the assumption. I never misrepresented myself."

"Ah," Bass said. "So you're lawyers."

"I am," Finn said.

Bass looked at him, then pointed to Kozlowski. "He's been around you for too long. Only a lawyer would draw his kind of distinction. Why are you here?"

"You already know—you said it earlier," Finn said. "To find the paintings."

"But why?" Bass asked. "Why are you looking for the paintings? You said you're not treasure hunters; so what then? What's your interest?"

Finn said, "We need to find the paintings because a little girl's life depends on it. I can't explain it any more than that, but I'm telling you the truth."

The old man looked at him. "I believe you," he said. "If you find the paintings, will you protect them? Will you return them to the museum?"

"If we can," Finn said. "We'll do everything we can."

Bass seemed to consider this for a long time. "All right," he said wearily. "What do you want to know?"

"Anything you can tell us that might help. Anything you know."

"But I don't know anything," Bass said. "I've talked to the police a dozen times over the decades; given them every scrap of information I had; nothing's done any good."

"What do you know about Baxter?" Kozlowski asked. "Is there any chance that he was involved?"

Bass shrugged. "I don't know him well enough to tell. He's a bit of a tyrant at times. He and I have never really gotten along. He only tolerates me because I've been here so long the trustees view me as a part of the institution. But his betrayals are on a smaller scale. I'm not sure he even has the imagination to have conceived of something like the robbery. Besides, the police checked him out. They checked us all out."

"He was wearing some very nice clothes," Kozlowski noted. "Expensive clothes. Where does he get his money?"

Bass looked down at the fraying lapels of his own jacket, and Finn instantly wished Kozlowski had been more tactful. "As you might suspect, I don't know much about fashion or the cost of nice clothing," he said. "I never made much more than minimum wage, so from my perspective, I've always thought of Baxter as rich. I don't know if he has money beyond what he makes here. I never thought to wonder."

"Did that ever bother you?" Kozlowski asked. "Did you ever feel like you deserved more respect around here? More money, maybe?"

For a moment, Finn thought perhaps Bass would be offended or angry. But he just looked at Kozlowski with a contented smile. "You may not understand this, but no. Without this place, I would have been dead before I turned twenty. Because of this place, I spent my life surrounded by beauty and comfort. No matter who was in charge, nothing about this place has ever made me feel disrespected."

"Is there anything else you can tell us that might be helpful?" Finn asked.

Bass looked pensive for a moment. "Nothing specific. My impression, though, was that the FBI was very concerned about the offer to sell the paintings that was apparently put out recently."

"You heard the call?" Finn asked.

Bass shook his head. "Not exactly. But I saw Mr. Baxter's reaction, and I heard his conversations with a number of others at the museum after the call. You may have noticed, I'm treated as if I'm invisible. It has its advantages at times."

"What was his reaction?"

"He was excited. Or perhaps agitated would be a better word. He seemed to truly believe that something was happening that might bring the paintings back to this place."

"Is that particularly unusual?" Kozlowski asked. "I would think a guy in his position would be thrilled at the prospect."

"Of course," Bass replied. "If there was really a chance. But we here at the museum have lived through dozens of false leads and rumors regarding these paintings. It has gotten so that we are skeptical about anything we hear. Baxter didn't seem skeptical after talking to the FBI the day they called."

"Why do you think that was?" Finn asked.

Bass shrugged. "I don't know. As I said, I didn't hear the conversation. Maybe they had more specific information this time."

"Maybe," Kozlowski said. He didn't sound convinced. "Or maybe Mr. Baxter knew something himself this time."

"I wouldn't know," Bass said. "I suppose that unless Baxter wants to talk with you, only the FBI can tell you more."

Kozlowski nodded. "That's exactly what I was thinking."

Chapter Twenty-Nine

Finn and Kozlowski emptied their pockets into bins as they passed through the entrance to the Kennedy Federal Building and walked through the metal detector. It occurred to Finn as he gathered his belongings on the far side of the X-ray machine that, should the trends continue, he could soon expect to be frisked vigorously walking into the neighborhood grocery store.

They headed to the elevator and crowded in with a dozen others, many of them wearing bright plastic badges identifying them as federal employees. Most wore the long, bored expressions of civil servants enduring their own version of purgatory, forced to deal with forms filled out in triplicate by an angry, impatient citizenry all too eager to roll eyeballs and issue heavy sighs at the government's inefficiencies. The only solace they found was in the occasional opportunity to really screw with the most obnoxious. It was cold comfort to them, Finn was sure, but he supposed it beat none at all.

The trip to the Gardner Museum had been helpful in orienting them, but it wasn't enough. It gave them no leads. If they were going to have any hope of finding the paintings, they needed some inside information from the authorities, and there was only one way to get that.

"You're sure your guy's here?" Finn asked Kozlowski as the elevator door opened on the seventh floor and they stepped off into a fluorescent elevator lobby with stained, battleship-gray industrial carpeting.

"He said he would be," Kozlowski said. "If he said he would be, he will be."

Finn accepted it with a nod. Kozlowski had burned his share of bridges in his law-enforcement career, Finn knew. That was just a part of who he was—he didn't suffer fools, and he had no political savvy. The pencil pushers and ass-coverers who often seemed to thrive in the world of bureaucratic law enforcement had hated him and ultimately succeeded in ending his career. But many of the others—the real cops—never lost respect for the man, and the respect of people like that was priceless. It provided contacts that made Kozlowski one of the most valuable assets to Finn's practice.

Kozlowski had reached out to an FBI agent he had worked with in the late nineties trying to clean up the fallout from John Connolly's relationship with Whitey Bulger. He and his contact had forged a friendship over long hours and heavy stress, and the friendship had stuck even after it was all over.

The sting of the Connolly affair was still felt by the Bureau, even down in Washington. But in Boston it was defining, and many speculated that the damage was enough to neutralize any effectiveness the feds could have in the city. John Connolly was an agent from South Boston who had risen through the ranks in the eighties and nineties, winning commendations and promotions from his campaign to shut down the Angiulo branch of La Cosa Nostra, which operated out of Boston's Italian North End, and ran the mob for the Patriarca family in Providence. With bust after bust over a ten-year period, Connolly brought the Italian-American mob to its knees with amazing proficiency, culminating with the 1986 RICO indictment of crime underboss Gennaro Angiulo and others.

Unfortunately for the FBI, Connolly had obtained much of his information from Whitey Bulger, who was acting as a high-level snitch, turning over information in dribs and drabs as suited his purpose. In exchange for the information, Connolly provided Bulger with protection, warning him of any ongoing investigations and tipping him off whenever the local or state authorities were closing in on him. He also provided information about state informants that allowed Bulger to protect himself by murdering those helping the cops to build a case. When the whole scam was revealed in 1994, it went nuclear. Connolly was arrested, tried, and convicted. In 2000 he was sentenced to twelve years in prison for his role in several of Bulger's murder sprees. Before he was arrested, though, Connolly managed to get word to Bulger that everything was collapsing, and Bulger skipped town, one step ahead of the law, as always. Since then, Bulger had remained one of the most wanted men in America—second only to Osama bin Laden after 2001. Reports had circulated through the years that he had been spotted in London and Ireland, as well as in other parts of Europe, but he remained at large.

The Connolly affair did enormous damage to the FBI's reputation in the Boston law-enforcement community. The state and local cops had been trying to make a case against Bulger for years, with various wiretaps and investigations. They had come close so many times, only to have Bulger seemingly outsmart them at the last instant. When it was revealed that the FBI was responsible for Bulger's elusiveness, the normal festering interagency rivalries that are inevitable in law enforcement broke into open warfare.

In the wake of the scandal, Kozlowski had been assigned to work with the feds to wrap up certain aspects of the Bulger case, rounding up some of those within Bulger's gang against whom cases could be made. The brass and politicians figured that if the local cops and the FBI could work together in closing those cases, it might help to repair some of the damage. They were partially right. Kozlowski had worked well with his FBI counterpart, and they had earned each other's respect. Any additional benefit to the relationship between the enforcement organizations themselves had been minimal and short-lived. At an organizational level, there was no trust between the cops and the feds in Boston. Many suspected that there never would be again.

Finn and Kozlowski walked to the end of the elevator lobby and opened the door into a long hallway. The walls were white with long scuffmarks along them; it had been some time since they had last been painted. Kozlowski motioned to the right and headed down the hallway to a glass door at one end with the FBI seal stenciled on the window. He walked into a small waiting area; Finn followed. There was a desk with a receptionist in front of a door at the far end. She was young and pretty and wholesome, with a telephone headset perched smartly on perfectly combed light brown hair. She looked to Finn like Judy-the-Time-Life-Operator from late-night infomercials. Kozlowski walked over to her. "Tom Kozlowski," he said. "I'm expected."

She looked up at him with a neutral gaze; Finn wondered whether an FBI receptionist received any special training. She pressed a series of buttons and spoke into her headset. At least Finn assumed she was speaking. Her lips moved, but even standing in front of her he couldn't hear a word she was saying. Perhaps that was the special training, he hypothesized. It was a neat trick in any case. She pressed a button again and looked up at Kozlowski. "He'll be right out."

"Thanks."

Kozlowski walked away from the receptionist's desk. Finn was tempted to loiter in front of her, perhaps catch her eye—he'd always had a thing for Judy-the-Time-Life-Operator—but Kozlowski beckoned him over. "I don't want you to talk," he said.

"Ever?"

"In there," he said. "I'm tempted to leave you out here. This guy trusts me, but this is delicate. He's gonna be a little hesitant to say anything in front of you as it is."

"I'm not staying out here," Finn said.

Kozlowski nodded. "I figured you'd feel that way. So you come in. But don't speak. The more you say, the less we'll get out of this. You understand?"

"Yeah," Finn said.

Kozlowski frowned at him. "I'm serious."

"I got it. No talking."

Kozlowski looked at him for another moment or two before letting his gaze drop. If he'd had time to think about it, Finn might have been annoyed, but the door behind the receptionist's desk opened and Kozlowski's contact walked into the waiting area. He was a tall black man. Much taller than Finn had anticipated. Six-four, at least, and lean in an athletic way. He was a dominating presence. He looked around the room once before saying anything. Finn followed the man's eyes with curiosity; Finn and Kozlowski were the only ones in the place other than the receptionist.

"Kozlowski," he said. It seemed an acknowledgment and little more, but Finn had been around cops for long enough to recognize the code.

Kozlowski nodded but said nothing. It was like some strange Kabuki dance. Neither one had extended his hand. They just stood there looking at each other.

Then the agent looked at Finn. "Who's this?"

"He's Finn," Kozlowski said. "Scott Finn, this is Special Agent Rob Hewitt."

———

"Finn's my partner," Kozlowski said. Then, as an apology, "He's a lawyer." They passed through the reception area and walked into the back offices.

"So was I once," Hewitt said.

"It's curable?" Finn asked. He could feel Kozlowski's glare, and he reminded himself not to speak.

Hewitt led them through a large open area overrun with cubicle dividers covered with gray industrial fabric. It resembled so many corporate offices Finn had been in over the years. There was a hush to the place, and men and women in business attire were hunched diligently over their computer screens. Missing was any of the clattering and mayhem that often broke out in local police stations. The FBI didn't deal with anything so mundane; their targets were higher profile. The only obvious indication that he wasn't in a bank's back office was the fact that many of the men in their cubicles had their jackets off, and their shoulder holsters and guns were visible.

Hewitt brought them through the maze, around toward a long hallway, and into an interior conference room. They went in ahead of Hewitt and he closed the door behind them. They sat around the conference table. It was a cheap piece of furniture. "Okay, Koz," Hewitt said. "You said you needed to talk to me. I'm here."

"Yeah," Kozlowski said. "Thanks for seeing me on such short notice."

Hewitt shook his head. "No thanks needed. Ask what you need to ask."

"It's about the robbery at the Gardner Museum that happened back in '90. You familiar with it?"

Hewitt was silent for a moment. "Sure," he said slowly. "It's the biggest art theft in modern history. Still unsolved. I'd have to be dead not to be familiar with it."

"What's the status of the investigation?"

Hewitt's eyes narrowed. "Why do you ask?"

Kozlowski shook his head. "Can't really get into that."

"Can't get into it?" Hewitt leaned back in his chair. He looked back and forth between Finn and Kozlowski. "That puts me in a little bit of an awkward position."

Kozlowski nodded. "I understand that. I wouldn't ask if it wasn't important."

Hewitt looked at the former cop for a moment before answering. Then he shrugged his enormous shoulders. "Truth is, I don't really know. I hear bits and pieces from time to time, but it's nothing more than rumor. You know how it is, Koz—it's not my case, so I don't have a whole lot of real information."

"Whose case is it?" Kozlowski asked.

"Art Theft Program. It's a relatively new division at the Bureau; they started it up in 2002. There are only ten agents or so. Scattered around the country, but they're based out of the home office in DC. The division's headed up by a guy named Angus Porter. He was a field agent up here in Boston back in the eighties and nineties. He used to dabble in a lot of the local stuff—organized crime, drug trafficking, the usual crap we all work on in satellite offices. But he got bit by the art bug. Boston was a major player in the stolen-art world, even before the Gardner got taken. A couple of years before, a guy actually plucked a twenty-million-dollar painting off the wall at the Museum of Fine Arts and ran out the door with it. There wasn't any security at all. True story."

"The guy got away with it?"

"For a while. The painting was eventually returned to reduce his sentence on another heist that didn't go quite as well for him. But there were lots of stories like that back in the day. Angus started the process of pulling together information on the thefts and the movement of the paintings. Studied the fences, the transactions, took art classes—became a real expert. After the Gardner job he started lobbying the brass to start up a special division. It took him a dozen years, but they finally gave in and assigned him a half dozen agents and a budget. I'm sure he wanted more, but I gotta give him credit. After 9/11 we were so focused on the antiterrorism issues that I'm shocked he got anybody's attention."

"I'm surprised, too," Kozlowski said. "Diverting any resources from antiterrorism to find lost paintings seems like a waste of manpower."

"In principle, I don't disagree," Hewitt said. "But I've helped out on a couple cases, and you'd be surprised how big a business it is—and how tied in it all is to some other very bad things. Drugs. Terrorism. Extortion. It's all related."

"How so?"

Hewitt gave an ironic grimace. Finn figured it was the closest he ever came to a smile. "I could give you the basics," he said. "But from the look on your face, you don't want the basics. If you're looking for the best information, the guy to talk to is Porter."

"Do you feel comfortable calling him?" Kozlowski asked.

Hewitt thought about it for a moment. Then he stood and walked to the door. "I'll do better," he said.

Chapter Thirty

Finn shifted his feet as he and Kozlowski sat alone in the conference room at the heart of the FBI's offices in Boston. Talking to Kozlowski's trusted FBI contact made Finn nervous. Talking to an FBI agent neither of them had ever met made him nauseous. He and Kozlowski knew about a kidnapping and they hadn't reported it to the police or to the FBI. They were already arguably guilty of obstruction of justice. In addition, his client had participated in the robbery at the Gardner Museum—the very crime about which they were asking questions. Just having the conversation with the FBI agents was putting them all at risk, and Finn didn't like it.

He was still fretting when Hewitt walked back in, another man behind him. It would have been difficult to imagine two more physically different people. Hewitt was huge, with a massive upper body and giant hands. Porter was tiny, with shoulders pinched at the top and a neck that looked too thin to support his head. His hands were wiry and small. Finn guessed his age in the mid-fifties, and he had a disdainful look that made him resemble a British filing clerk.

"Gentlemen," the second man said. "I'm Special Agent Porter, in charge of the FBI's Art Theft Program. Special Agent Hewitt tells me you are looking for information about art theft. Specifically the Gardner Museum theft."

"Yes," Kozlowski said. "I'm Tom Kozlowski. This is Scott Finn, he's an attorney."

Porter remained standing. "May I ask what your interest in the Gardner theft is?"

"We can't answer that right now," Kozlowski said.

Porter looked at Hewitt and Hewitt shrugged. "Special Agent Hewitt speaks very highly of you, Detective. That carries some weight in my book. Perhaps we can talk for a little while? There is always the chance that you'll develop the same trust in me that you have in him." Porter spoke like a college professor. His diction was perfect, and there was a hint of an upper-class accent. He spoke slowly and chose his words carefully. "So what is it you want to know about the theft?"

"You were in the Boston office when the Gardner was hit?" Kozlowski asked. "You were one of the agents originally assigned to the case?"

"Yes. I have been involved in the investigation from the beginning."

"At the time, were you also working with the organized crime unit in Boston?"

"Yes."

"Did you work with John Connolly at all?" It was a pointed question, the implications of which could not be overlooked.

"That's out of line, Koz!" Hewitt protested.

"No, no, Robert," Porter said. "It's a fair question." He smiled. "I did work on cases involving organized crime in the eighties and nineties, Mr. Kozlowski. But I had no involvement with the tainted informant program. I was involved in the prosecution of the Angiulo offshoot of the Patriarca family that resulted from the information disclosed by Mr. Bulger and others, but I never ran any of my own informants. And I never had any idea where we were getting our information.

Agent Connolly kept that information to himself. As a result, I never had the opportunity to become involved in anything untoward. Believe me, it was an issue that was seriously weighed by the Bureau before it approved the funding for the Art Theft Program."

"I'm sure it was."

"And, as you can see, they still saw fit to put me in charge of the new division. That should give you some comfort."

"Should it?"

Porter smiled. "You don't strike me as the kind of a man who likes to waste time, Detective," he said. "Assuming that to be the case, you must have a very good reason to come all the way up here to ask questions about the Gardner Museum, yes?"

Kozlowski leaned forward in his chair. "We understand that there was recently an offer made to sell the paintings," he said, turning back to Porter. "Is that right?"

Porter shifted uncomfortably in his seat. "I compliment you on not beating around the bush, Detective. Where did you come by that information?"

"From the director at the museum. Baxter. Is it true?"

Porter looked as though he were sucking on a lemon. Finn guessed he was either angry or constipated. "Under what circumstances did Mr. Baxter tell you this?" he asked.

"No circumstances," Kozlowski said. "We had some questions about the theft."

Porter wasn't done with the lemon yet. He folded his hands together and looked down at them. "In any conversation I had with Mr. Baxter, I indicated that he was to keep any information to himself," he said. "It is crucial to the case. You understand my surprise at the notion that he would have just blurted this out to you, Mr. Kozlowski."

"Maybe you should have been clearer with him," Kozlowski said.

"Perhaps. You didn't, by any chance, represent yourselves as law-enforcement officers, or give Mr. Baxter reason to think you were officially connected in some way to the investigation, did you?"

"We never represented ourselves as anything we weren't," Kozlowski said. "I showed my private investigator's license to the woman at the desk. You'll have to ask Baxter what he believed. It's true, though?" Kozlowski pushed. "There has been an offer to sell the paintings?"

Porter cleared his throat. "These paintings have been missing for nearly twenty years. They are the most valuable pieces of stolen art in the world—worth an estimated five hundred million dollars. I'm going to need more information from you if I'm going to continue this conversation."

"What do you need?" Kozlowski asked.

"First and foremost, I need a reason to believe you two have something to offer me. I need a reason to believe you aren't full of bullshit."

Kozlowski turned to Finn. "Your call."

Finn thought about it for a moment. "A client of mine who may have information that would be helpful to the investigation," he said at last. "He's got a problem you may be helpful in solving. If we could work a trade, would you be interested?"

"I might be," Porter said. "What can he offer?"

"Under the right circumstances, he might be able to offer a lot."

"Is he directly connected to the theft?"

"I can't go there yet. Not without knowing what you can offer in return."

Porter closed his eyes in thought for a moment. "Let's handle it this way: I'll talk to you generally about the theft and the things that are well known. I won't discuss the specifics of the investigation, though. Not without more information from you."

"Fair enough," Kozlowski said.

Porter cleared his throat. "I assume you know the basics about how the thieves tricked the guards to gain access?" Finn and Kozlowski nodded. "Once inside, it was an easy job. The museum had virtually no security systems in place, and the thieves were able to spend close to an hour and a half in the place. In many ways, it was the perfect robbery. In other ways, it was a mess."

"How was it a mess?" Kozlowski asked.

"Well, first, the mixture of art that was stolen was very odd. Several of the paintings stolen were exceptionally valuable. Vermeer's *The Concert*, for example, is one of the most valuable paintings ever stolen. Similarly, Rembrandt's *Storm on the Sea of Galilee* is an exceptional work, worth nearly as much as the Vermeer. It was the only seascape known to be painted by the Dutch master. Other paintings by Flinck and Degas were worth less, but still justified the effort. Some of the other works taken were comparatively worthless, though. It doesn't really make sense. It is as though the thieves had some good information, and some bad information."

"Are there any theories as to where the paintings are now?" Finn asked.

Porter looked at him. "Hundreds. We have chased over ten thousand tips, to no avail. There are more theories about who did this and why than there are police officers in Boston. No one has gotten it right yet, and the paintings have still not been found."

"Do you have a favorite theory?" Kozlowski asked.

Porter considered the question. "I do. And I might share it with you if I had reason to believe you had legitimate information to give to me." No one said anything. "I need more, gentlemen. Otherwise I can't continue."

"There were two men involved," Finn said after a moment. "One had a list of the valuable paintings. The other didn't know anything about art; he was just the entry man. He took advantage of the opportunity. That's why some of what was stolen seemed worthless."

"Your client?" Finn said nothing, and Porter smiled. "Of course.

That would explain a lot. And it fits with some of the information we have."

Finn felt as though he'd been taken. "So? Where do you think the paintings are now?" Finn demanded.

"I think the paintings are still here in Boston," Porter said.

"Why?"

"You see," Porter said, "first you have to try to get into the head of the person who planned this. To do that, you have to understand both the nature of the art theft industry and the psychology of the art thief."

"Industry?" Finn said. "Can it really be called an industry?"

"Depends on what you consider an industry, Mr. Finn. We estimate stolen art to run in the range of six billion dollars a year." Kozlowski let out an astonished whistle. "That's according to the United Nations. It's probably more. In terms of economics and volume, the illicit trade in art and cultural property ranks second only to the drug trade."

"How do they move it all?"

"That's the rub," Porter said. "It's become very difficult to move paintings and artwork in recent years. Art isn't like most other commodities. It is, by its very nature, identifiable. Twenty or even ten years ago, that wasn't much of a problem. A painting could be stolen in one country, held for a number of years and then sold in another country. Often the buyer would have no idea that the work was stolen at all. Many countries have laws that allow such an 'innocent' buyer to keep the painting even if it is later discovered to be a stolen work. However, using the Internet, law-enforcement agencies now cooperate with most of the world's major art galleries and auction houses, and we have developed a catalogue of stolen art that is so comprehensive that it's become difficult for any buyer to 'accidentally' buy a work that's been stolen. Plus, the laws in most countries either have been or are in the process of being changed such that the purchaser must prove a reasonable provenance—a chain of authenticity and legal custody—in order to retain ownership. There has also been such an onslaught of lawsuits from people to recover stolen works going back even to World War II and the Holocaust, that the cost of buying or selling stolen art has become very often too high."

"So why would anyone steal art?" Kozlowski asked. "Seems like it's a lot of work for relatively little gain."

"One would think so," Porter said. "But the relative risk for thieves is still often well worth it. First of all, the dangers involved are low compared with other illegal activities. Much of the art in the world is held in private collections—in houses and estates—which have little or no real security. Even many of the museums in the world are minimally protected. The criminal penalties for art theft also tend to be significantly more lenient than those for other lucrative illegal activities—like trading in drugs or weapons. Finally, even if the paintings are difficult to fence, there are other ways to collect. Some are ransomed back to the museums. Even at a fraction of their value, the transaction can net the thieves millions. They hit museums or private residences and then offer to return the paintings for the insurance money."

"Why didn't that happen in this case?"

"The Gardner Museum was uninsured. It's a private institution with one of the largest collections in the United States. At the time, they viewed the cost of insurance premiums as prohibitively expensive."

"They had no insurance?" Finn was incredulous.

"None," Porter replied. "That's probably why no demand was made. Insurance is usually necessary for any institution to pay a ransom. In theory, there are other ways the thieves can profit. The theft could have been commissioned by some wealthy client with a fetish for these particular works. Or the works may have been collateralized in connection with other criminal activities."

"I don't understand," Finn said.

"Stolen artwork has become a second currency among criminals.

It's traded as collateral for purchases of weapons or drugs. Art is often easier to transport than huge sums of cash, and makes transfers easier. In addition, drug and arms dealers are looking for ways to invest their enormous illegal profits. Stolen art is one place where they can plow huge sums of money."

"But you don't think that happened with the artwork stolen from the Gardner?"

Porter shook his head. "I don't think so. It is possible, of course. Perhaps they are hanging right now on the wall of some grand mansion of one of the world's great crime figures—sort of a real-life version of James Bond's *Dr. No.* I think it's too romantic a notion, though."

"What makes you believe the paintings are still here, in Boston?"

Porter laughed bitterly. "Perhaps I'm just an optimist. I still have hope."

"Why?"

"Because this is Boston," Porter said. "In 1990, most crime in Boston was run by Whitey Bulger. He was at the height of his power. Nothing like this happened in Boston without his involvement. So I start with the assumption that Bulger was tied in. But it's equally clear to me that Bulger didn't plan this job himself."

"Too complicated for him?" Kozlowski asked.

"It's not the complication factor," Porter responded. "It's the subject matter. Bulger was a smart man, smart enough to recognize that this was outside of his area of expertise. Plus, it's not clear that he would have had a good idea of how to move these effectively unless he already had a buyer."

"So the question is, who was the buyer," Kozlowski commented.

"Well, yes and no. In fact, it's fairly obvious who the buyer would have been."

"Who?"

"The IRA," Porter said. "At the time, the Republican movement was the most active group in art theft. They were linked to dozens

of high-profile thefts in the late eighties and early nineties throughout the United Kingdom and Europe. It was how the movement sup-
ported much of its paramilitary activities."

"Terrorism," Kozlowski corrected him.

"Yes," Porter agreed. "Terrorism. There are those—particularly in
Boston—who would take issue with that characterization, but I certainly don't disagree. They funded a large portion of their operations
with money made from the theft of precious art."

Finn shook his head. "Art buying bullets. Ironic."

"Ironic, perhaps," Porter said, "but hardly surprising or unusual.
Artwork has often played a significant role in funding terrorist activity—still does today. Consider Iraq. According to intelligence esti-
mates, the artwork looted from the Iraqi museums after the American
invasion is still providing a significant percentage of the revenue used
by the terrorists there to fund their campaigns. Hitler made the capi-
talization of plundered art a centerpiece of his plans. Even as far back
as the Greeks and Romans stolen art was used to fund insurrections
and massive armies on both sides of virtually every dispute in history."

"And you think the IRA sold the Gardner Museum paintings?"

Porter crossed his arms. "It feels like I've been doing most of the
talking. That doesn't seem quite fair. It's clear that you have a client
who claims to have been one of the men who pulled the robbery off."

"I can't officially confirm that for the purposes of this meeting,"
Finn said.

Porter rolled his eyes. "How quaint. We're going to go through
the absurd charade of using hypotheticals? Fine. Hypothetically,
why would your client come forward at this point? What's happened
now? Is he afraid that someone is selling the paintings out from under
him?"

Finn shook his head. "I don't think he even knew that someone was trying to sell the paintings. But the other man involved in the robbery must have found out, and he's come back."

"Come back? Come back from where?" Porter asked. Then he smiled again and answered his own question. "Ireland."

Finn just stared at him.

"Don't worry, Mr. Finn, I'm not looking for an admission to use in court. It makes sense, though. The IRA was successful in the art theft business, but they got too greedy in this case. This was the greatest art theft in history. There was no insurance to provide a ransom, and within hours, it was international news. It would have been virtually impossible for them to sell the paintings on the open market. They would have had to sit on them for a long time. Like twenty years. Even if those in the IRA had wanted to get the paintings, it would have been problematic with their organization crumbling and Bulger on the run. It would also have been difficult to move the paintings, so they most likely remained here in Boston."

"But now someone is trying to sell them," Kozlowski said. "That would probably get those who were once in the IRA pretty pissed off."

"So it appears," Porter said. "I assume you gentlemen have heard about the untimely demise of Vincent Murphy and Eddie Ballick? Of course you have. And if your hypothetical client is tied in with all this, he can't be feeling too comfortable right now, can he?"

Finn and Kozlowski looked at each other, and Kozlowski raised his eyebrows.

Porter reached into a file he had brought with him into the room and pulled out a picture. It was the face of a man Finn had never seen before, but it fit the description Lissa had given them of the man who'd attacked her and kidnapped Sally. He had dark hair and black eyes that stared into the camera with an evil, lifeless gaze. "Have you seen this man before?"

Finn shook his head. No," he said honestly. "Who is he?"

"His name is Liam Kilbranish," Porter said. "He is a former IRA operative. Our terrorism task force picked up information from their British counterparts recently that he fled Ireland, headed to the US."

"I thought the IRA was dead," Finn said.

"It is," Porter said. "The ceasefire was reached under the Good Friday Agreement in 1998. There were years of negotiations that followed, with the major sticking point being the process of disarming all paramilitary organizations in Northern Ireland, including the IRA. In 2005, the IRA finally capitulated, and international weapons inspectors verified the decommissioning of the IRA's arsenal. By late 2006 the independent monitoring commission ruled that the IRA was no longer a threat."

"But that's not the whole story?" Finn asked.

"It never is, is it?" Porter said. "This is a struggle that went on for more than three quarters of a century. Most of those involved in the fight have been willing to put down their arms and work to maintain the peace. That's a significant achievement."

"But not all?" Finn said. He pointed to the picture. "Not him?"

"As with any cause, there will always be those few who refuse to accept anything but total victory. There is a small cadre of former IRA operatives who are still looking to ruin the peace and begin the fighting all over again. Kilbranish is one of them. His family was killed when he was a boy."

"Why was he headed to the United States?" Finn asked.

"I think you can figure that out," Porter said. "Kilbranish is known for two things: his brutality, and his skill as an art thief. If he thought there was a way to recover the Gardner paintings, he wouldn't hesitate. The IRA has no weapons and no money. If the troubles are to start fresh, they would need an enormous influx of cash. Our informants tell us that once the offer to sell the paintings was made, this group of IRA leftovers paid a hundred thousand dollars for confirmation that the offer was genuine. They received that confirmation."

"How?"

"Paint chips and dated photographs. The photographs could be doctored, but the paint chips can be tested to provide a reasonable degree of certainty. It looks as though the offer was genuine."

"So these people are going to buy the art back?" Finn asked.

Porter laughed. "Hardly. They have no more to pay. Besides, if our theories are right, Kilbranish was involved in the original theft. He would view the paintings as rightfully his. He's here to bring the paintings back his own way."

There was silence for a moment. Finn wished there were windows in the conference room; he felt as though the walls were closing in on him.

"Let me be very clear, Mr. Finn: if your client helped Kilbranish rob the Gardner, and Kilbranish doesn't have the paintings now, your client is a dead man. You know what he did to Murphy and Ballick. He'll do the same to your client. Of course, you already know that, don't you? Otherwise you wouldn't be here. He needs to come in. We can help him."

Finn thought about Sally in the hands of the man Porter was describing. It made him feel sick. "He can't come in."

"Why not?"

"Because," Finn said.

"If he's worried about being prosecuted for the robbery, I'm sure we can work something out on that. Particularly if the paintings are recovered." Porter was practically drooling, and Finn saw Hewitt shoot a questioning look toward him.

"It's not that," Finn said. "Although some sort of an agreement that he wouldn't be prosecuted would be needed. There are other considerations, though."

"Like what?" Porter demanded. "If he doesn't come in, he'll be dead in a matter of days. It's that simple."

"I wish it was that simple." Finn took out a card and handed it to him. "Let me think about it and we may be back in touch."

Porter reached into his jacket and pulled out two cards of his own. He handed Finn and Kozlowski each one. "I hope you will be." He walked over to the door and opened it for them. Just as they got to the door, though, he closed it slightly, blocking their path. "There is one thing you should explain to your hypothetical client, Mr. Finn," he said. "If he does not come forward, and we find him . . . all bets are off. I have no doubt in those circumstances that the Justice Department will bring its full weight to bear on him and anyone else involved."

Finn looked at Porter. When they stood next to each other the size difference was striking, and yet the FBI agent no longer seemed small. There was an intensity to him that was intimidating. "I understand, Agent Porter. I'll keep that in mind."

Chapter Thirty-One

She had known fear before. It had been a constant companion of hers; like a shadow that faded from time to time, but was always present. She had never known fear like this, though.

The basement was dark. She could feel the mold and mildew surrounding her. On her skin; in her hair; in her nose; growing all around her, choking off her air. It gave her panic a physical presence, and she tried unsuccessfully to put it out of her consciousness.

She had to focus. The one thing that had kept her alive through her short and difficult life was her ability to keep her head, even as everything around her was falling apart. She needed that strength now, but every time she tried to take a deep breath to settle herself, the stench of decay invaded her lungs, carrying with it a new wave of terror.

She looked around the basement. It was difficult; her arms were strapped together with duct tape and she was lying on her side on the stone floor carved from the bedrock. Every time she turned, the tape ripped at her skin, sending flashes of pain up her arms. She was secured to a pipe in the corner of the basement, prevented from repositioning herself. But with some effort and pain she was able to turn enough on her back so that she could see the place in its macabre entirety.

It was little more than a glorified crawl space, perhaps five feet high.

Above her the floor joists were visible, with ancient, fraying strips of insulation tucked into the gaps. In many places the moisture had eaten its way through the strips, and yellow-brown strands of matted fiberglass hung in frozen drips, like toxic stalactites. There was a furnace in the corner, covered in rust and oil residue, with its piping reaching up toward the rest of the house, like tentacles grasping for freedom.

She heard the door open and the footsteps on the stairs, and strained even further to get a better look. The man descended slowly, the rotted wooden planks on the ancient stairs creaking painfully with each step. He'd said little to her in the car, making clear only that if she shouted or tried to get away he would kill her.

When they'd arrived at the little house, he'd reiterated his threat and told her to walk in front of him to the door. He pushed her into the house and forced her quickly into the basement, which he'd prepared for her arrival. Other than telling her to lie down, he said nothing while he tied her down. He used a last strip of duct tape to seal her mouth.

Now he reached the bottom of the staircase and bent slightly to avoid bumping his head on the flooring above. Moving toward her, he picked up a small crate and brought it over, putting it down next to her head and sitting down. He looked at her for what seemed like a long time, saying nothing. She looked back, searching his face for some sign of pity or compassion. She saw none.

The gun he'd held from the moment he'd grabbed her was still in his hand, and he placed it on the ground next to him, the barrel pointing at the back of her head. He reached out and pried loose a corner of the tape that covered her mouth. He gave a hard and fast pull, ripping it from her face. She gave a short, involuntary cry, and he picked up the gun again, holding it over her. She choked back tears.

There was an air of expectation to his demeanor, as if he was waiting for her to say something. If so, she was determined that he be disappointed. In spite of her fear, she didn't want to give him the satisfaction of showing weakness. After a moment he reached into his jacket pocket and pulled out a bottle of water. He twisted the cap off and moved the bottle at an angle toward her, holding it up to her lips. "Open," he said.

She opened her mouth and he tipped the bottle up, letting the water run down toward her. It was awkward, and most of the water ran down over her cheek, splattering on the floor. It was cold, though, and her mouth was thick with fear. The water tasted good, and she lapped at it, swallowing hard to get as much as she could.

He took the bottle away and reached into his pocket again, this time pulling out a cereal bar. He unwrapped it and dangled it in front of her mouth, lowering it so that she could take a bite. "Eat," he said.

She did. When she had finished the cereal bar, he put the water bottle and the wrapper from the cereal bar into his pocket. "Do you have to use the bathroom?"

She hadn't even thought of it until that moment; she'd been too scared. "Yes," she replied.

He pulled a long knife out of a sheath hanging from his belt and cut the tape that was wrapped around her wrists and the pipe to which she was attached. It left her arms taped together, but she was free from the ground, at least. She sat up awkwardly. "Where?" she asked.

He pointed to a corner of the basement. A blanket was draped over a rope tied to the ceiling. It provided little privacy. "There's a can behind there," he said.

"Can I use the bathroom upstairs?"

He shook his head.

She could feel the tears running down her cheeks as she moved over to the corner, but she brushed them away. Once she was done, she stepped from behind the blanket. He hadn't moved.

"Lie back down," he said.

He wrapped the duct tape around her wrists, securing them again to the pipe coming up from the floor. Then he tore off another strip just long enough to cover her mouth.

"You don't have to," she said. "I'll be quiet."

He shook his head. "Close your mouth."

"Why are you doing this?"

"Close your mouth."

"What do you want?"

He reached forward and pasted the tape hard to her face. "Nothing you can give me," he said. Then he stood and walked to the staircase, stooped over to avoid the ceiling. The steps groaned as he walked up toward the light from the floor above. It seemed to Sally that the noise was even louder than when he had come down. Then the door closed, and the basement was dark again. She pulled at the tape, just to make sure that there wasn't any chance that he'd been sloppy and left enough give for her to pull free. He hadn't, though, and the tape pulled painfully at her skin again.

She put her head down, resting it on the dirty concrete in the puddle that had formed from the water that had spilled from her lips. The tears came freely at last, dripping off the side of her face and mixing with the water on the floor. She wasn't much for self-pity, and yet there was a point at which even she couldn't bear any more. She wondered whether she had reached that point.

<hr>

Sean Broadark was sitting on a stool in the kitchen when Kilbranish came up. It was the first time Liam could remember the man coming off the sofa in the living room.

"What the fuck do you think you're doing?" Broadark asked him. Liam had never heard the man express anger before. Anger wasn't a soldier's emotion. It clouded a soldier's thinking. It was a bad sign.

"I'm getting the paintings back," Liam replied. He moved past the man and into the living room.

"This was never part of the deal," Broadark said, following him. "I never agreed to this."

Liam stopped and turned, facing Broadark. He squinted at the other man, so close to him that the pits on his face looked like lunar craters. Liam wondered which of them had lost the greater degree of sanity. He supposed it didn't really matter. "You didn't agree to what, Sean?"

"Kidnapping," Broadark replied. "The taking of innocents."

"Innocents?" Liam laughed. "Those are high-minded principles for you to be expressing, friend. Have you never killed children?"

Broadark's face twitched with rage. "Only when necessary, and never on purpose."

"Not exactly an altar boy's motto, is it?"

"I am serious, mate," Broadark said. "No one approved this. I won't be a part of it. I was sent to help you, but not in this."

"I didn't ask for your help. Just don't get in my way."

"That decision isn't mine. I'm calling this in."

"Fine," Liam said. "Do you really think that anyone is going to give up a chance at this kind of money for one girl? If that was the case, the cause never would have carried on for this long. Don't you understand? These paintings are our lifeblood. They're our last chance." Liam moved back into the kitchen.

Broadark stood there for a moment. Then he pulled out his cell phone. "The decision's not mine to make," he said. He started walking toward the front door.

Liam moved after him. "Okay," he said in an even voice. "Make the call." Even as he spoke, though, he was pulling his knife out of its sheath. He came up on Broadark from behind quickly. At the last moment, Broadark realized his mistake, and he began to turn. It was too late, though. Liam swung his arm over Broadark's shoulder and drove the knife hard through the rib cage. Broadark stumbled and fell forward. Liam could see the man's hand searching for his gun, and he dropped to one knee behind him, grabbing him by the forehead and pulling his head back, exposing his neck. "I warned you," he said. Then he pulled the knife across Broadark's throat. The cut was deep and effective, and whatever life was left in Broadark's body deserted it instantly. He fell heavily on his face, his arms splayed out to the side. Liam quickly rolled him on his back and stabbed him once more in the chest to make sure that the heart was stopped. With the body in that position and no further heartbeat, it would limit the amount of blood that he would have to clean.

Liam stood up and took a deep breath. He walked over to the sink and ran some cold water, sliding the knife under the flow, watching as it turned from deep red to pink as the blood was washed down. Then he turned and looked at Broadark's body. There was nothing to be done about it, he told himself. He was committed. His only option now was success.

Chapter Thirty-Two

"Do you think he'll come in?"

Porter was standing in the doorway to Hewitt's office. Hewitt looked up from his work. "Finn's client? Maybe. He's making a mistake if he doesn't. I've been reading up on our friend Mr. Kilbranish. I wouldn't want this man after me."

"No," Porter agreed. "Nor would I. I don't understand why they didn't jump at the idea."

"Particularly with you offering pardons you didn't have any authority to offer."

Porter shrugged. "I just said we could work something out. I didn't make any firm offer of immunity."

"You came close. And that was certainly the impression you gave them."

"Maybe. Like the detective said, I didn't misrepresent anything. If they misunderstood, that's their issue. They know the rules of this game."

"Fair enough," Hewitt said. "I still don't know whether their client is coming in. The question is: what do we do with him if he does?"

"That's easy," Porter said. "We use him as bait. We lure in Kilbranish, and we put together whatever information we get so that we can recover the paintings."

"Bait sometimes gets eaten. Have you thought about that?"

"That's not my concern."

"It is if you run an operation with the man. His safety becomes your responsibility."

"Technically, that's true. But it's hardly my main worry. There's half a billion dollars out there in rare art. Art that has been missing for twenty years, kept from the public's view. Art that could be used to fund all measure of criminal and terrorist activities. These are my main concerns. If the only collateral damage we suffer is the loss of the men who stole the paintings in the first place, I consider that a success."

Porter was looking off into space, and he seemed almost serene. At that moment, it occurred to Hewitt how little he actually knew about the head of the Art Theft Program. "Kozlowski and Finn would probably disagree. I know their client would disagree."

"That's not my problem," Porter responded. "My focus is on the artwork."

"I don't like this," Sanchez said.

Stone was sitting behind the wheel of the unmarked police car. Sanchez was next to him, and they were parked outside Nashua Street Jail. They had tailed Finn from the hospital to the Gardner Museum to the Federal Building to Nashua Street. All that activity in just a few hours.

"Something's happening."

Sanchez nodded.

"At least we know we were right about the paintings. They wouldn't have gone to the Gardner if it didn't have something to do with the artwork."

"So it seems," Sanchez said. She cursed herself; there was so much information right in front of her, and yet she couldn't put the pieces together. "Being right doesn't mean much if it doesn't lead to an arrest. We're still two steps behind, and if we don't catch up soon, something's gonna go down and we're not gonna be ready for it."

"So, what do we do?" Stone asked. "You want to pick up Finn and Kozlowski?"

She shook her head. "Wouldn't do any good." She took an exasperated breath. "What do we know?"

"I checked with the hospital," Stone replied. "They said the Krantz woman was brought in early in the afternoon. It looks like she was the victim of an attack, but she wouldn't give the doctors any information about what happened."

"And Finn and Kozlowski went straight from there to the museum." Sanchez's head spun.

"Right. I talked to the director there briefly. He wasn't at all happy to see me, by the way. He said they were asking questions about the robbery twenty years ago. Wouldn't tell me much more."

"And from there, they went to the feds."

"Right. Looks like they went up to the eighth floor. Unless we want to make an official inquiry, we're not gonna know who they met with, but I can take a guess."

"Hewitt."

"That's my bet. I heard he and Kozlowski worked together back in the day."

"Were they close?" Sanchez asked.

"It's Kozlowski," Stone said. "I don't think he's the type to really bond, but word is they worked well together and they got along."

"And now they're back here at the jail." She tried to do the math, but none of it added up. "What the hell," she said. "Could they be working with Hewitt?"

"Anything's possible."

"But why? Unless they're all in on something together." She closed her eyes for a moment and tried to relax. "Hewitt worked organized crime back when Whitey ran things and Connolly was giving him information. That was the same time when the museum was hit. Koz was a cop back then. Great reputation, great connections, but a pain in the ass to everyone. Now Finn represents Malley—a thief who worked for Bulger back then. And all this started with the murders of two of Bulger's men who themselves may have been involved in the theft." She opened her eyes. "It can't be, can it?"

"Whatever it is, it's moving," Stone said. He nodded toward the front steps of the jail. "Here they come."

Sanchez looked over and saw Finn and Kozlowski hurrying down the steps. They weren't talking, and other than glancing quickly at the traffic as they crossed the street, their eyes were focused forward. Whatever was happening, it looked as if it was going to happen fast. They reached the other side of the street and climbed into the convertible they had parked across the street at the rehabilitations hospital.

"What now, boss?" Stone asked as the convertible pulled out of the parking lot.

"Follow them," she replied. "They're our only solid lead right now."

"How is Devon doing?" Lissa asked. She looked better, but only marginally. She was sitting up in the hospital bed, and she had fresh bandages on her head. The cuts on her face were still pronounced. Kozlowski was standing against the wall; Finn was sitting on the chair next to Lissa's bed. The door was closed.

"Not good," Finn said. "He's worried about his daughter, mainly. I think he also knows what giving himself up to Kilbranish means, though." He looked out the window. The sun was nearly down, and the suburbs to the west glowed with the last of the sun's efforts. It made for quite a contrast, as they sat in the grimy hospital room with its stink of disinfectant, death, and disease.

"Do you think he'll go through with it?" Lissa asked. Her hands worried the blanket on her lap absentmindedly.

"I think so," Finn said. "She's his daughter."

"He's only known she existed for a year or so," Kozlowski pointed out skeptically. "He may try to skip."

"I don't think so," Finn said. "Devon was never a great liar; he's not smart enough. He talks about her like she's his last hope in the world. I think he'll do whatever he can to protect her. I think he genuinely cares about her."

"There's caring, and then there's *caring*," Kozlowski said. "I don't know that a year is enough time for him to lay down his life for her, daughter or not."

"Your child hasn't been born," Finn said. "What would you do to protect it?"

Kozlowski shifted on the wall, and Finn could see the muscles tense underneath his jacket. "Don't compare me to Devon," he said quietly.

"Fair enough, I'm just saying I think I can read him on this. In any case, we're not going to let him out of our sight once he's out of jail tomorrow. Where he goes, we go. Period. If he tries to run, I'll tie him up and deliver him to Kilbranish myself."

"We should have protected her," Lissa said. "*I* should have protected her." She pulled so hard at the blanket, Finn thought it might rip.

"It's not your fault," Finn said. "We didn't know."

"We knew enough," she replied.

He nodded. "Maybe we did. But then it's all our faults. We'll get her back."

"You have a plan?" she asked.

Finn laughed bitterly. "Not really. I called in a favor at the clerk's office and got Devon's new bail hearing put on the calendar for tomorrow. That's the best I could do. First we have to get him out—and after his little charade the other day there's no guarantee that's going to happen. Once we get him out, we wait for Kilbranish to call."

"Then what?"

"I don't know."

"We're not really going to give Devon up to this psychopath, are we?" Lissa asked. "There has to be another way."

Finn looked up at Kozlowski. "Maybe there is," he said. Kozlowski nodded. "Are you thinking what I'm thinking?"

"Probably," Kozlowski said. "It's the only thing that makes sense."

"There's only one way to know for sure," Finn said.

"What?" Lissa demanded.

"We give him the paintings," Kozlowski said.

She looked back and forth between them. "We don't know where the paintings are. Do we?"

"No," Finn said. "We don't. But I think we may know who does."

Chapter Thirty-Three

Devon's second bail hearing was scheduled for two-thirty on Friday afternoon. Finn arrived at one o'clock to talk to the clerk to make sure Devon would be called first. He didn't want to take any chance that an earlier case would get bogged down and Devon would be returned to jail without the issue even being heard. It was a little tricky; he was calling in a serious favor from the clerk to set the schedule. Still, he had made it a practice of treating all the clerks at the courthouse well—a trick he'd learned when he first started out as a public defender—and they appreciated it. Judge Platt's clerk had been predisposed in Finn's favor ever since he'd given him his Red Sox tickets on the first-base line so he could take his son to a game on his birthday. It wasn't a bribe, strictly speaking; there was no *quid pro quo*, and Finn would never ask for preferential treatment on the substance of a case. It did allow him to cut some corners on procedural issues, however. There was no question that what he was asking now would burn the last of any goodwill the tickets had earned him.

Kristin Kelley, the assistant district attorney who had argued at the arraignment, was not in the courtroom that morning, which was a blessing. Instead, the young man who had been with her was there, along with a woman who appeared even younger than he. Just looking at her made Finn feel old, but he banished the thought and focused on the argument at hand.

Judge Platt entered the courtroom at nine twenty-five, looking as bored with his existence as ever. "Call the first case," he grumbled after everyone was seated.

"Case number 08-CR-2677, Commonwealth versus Devon Malley! Come forward and be heard!" the bailiff shouted.

Devon was brought in. He was wearing his prison fatigues, and he was chained at the wrists and ankles. Platt had his head down and was looking through case files as Devon entered, and it took a moment for him to look up. When he did, though, his forehead wrinkled in disgust. He called his clerk over to the bench, and they engaged in an animated discussion for a moment before the judge waved him away.

Platt turned his attention to Finn. "Mr. Finn, so nice to have you back in my courtroom," he said. "Are we going for two out of three falls today?"

"No, Your Honor," Finn said. "Before we begin, my client would appreciate the opportunity to address the court briefly, if possible?"

Platt glared at Devon. "That so, Mr. Malley?"

Finn nudged Devon. "Yes, Your Honor," Devon said.

Platt crinkled his nose, as if he smelled something offensive. "If you must, go ahead," he said.

Devon cleared his throat. Finn had rehearsed the speech with his client the night before, but still his palms were sweating as Devon began. "First," Devon said, "I want to say I'm sorry to Mr. Finn, my lawyer. He and I have known each other for a long time, and I got mad at him the other day. I shouldn't have hit him, and I'm very sorry about that." Devon paused, looking at the judge. Finn searched for any change in the man's demeanor, but could sense none.

"Second," Devon continued, "I want to say I'm sorry to the bailiffs and the others who were in the courtroom the other day. I know what I did put them in danger, and I don't have any excuse for that."

"Is that it?" Platt asked.

"No, Judge. I want to say I'm sorry to you. This is your courtroom, and I disrupted it."

"You disrespected it," Platt interjected.

Devon nodded reluctantly. "I didn't mean it to have anything to do with you, Judge. I didn't mean to show disrespect, but I understand that that was how it looked. I'm very sorry. It won't happen again."

"You're goddamned right it won't," Platt grumbled. His voice had no conviction, though, and Finn could sense that he was slipping back into his habitual disinterest. "Mr. Finn, I believe we were discussing bail when your client interrupted us, is that right?"

"That's correct," Finn said.

The young assistant district attorney stood. "If I may address this issue, Your Honor?" he said.

Platt peered over his glasses down at the man. "Mr. Hendricks, do you have anything to add that Ms. Kelley did not address the other day?"

"Only that in light of Mr. Malley's outburst the other day—"

"I was here, Mr. Hendricks. If you are about to instruct me on the weight I should give that in determining bail, then zip it. You don't need to remind me of Mr. Malley's behavior. Do you have anything else—anything new—to add?"

Hendricks's mouth moved silently for a moment, as if he was willing the words to come. "No, Your Honor," he said finally. "I don't."

"Didn't think so," Platt said. He looked at Finn. "Counselor, I assume you've been wandering these halls for long enough to know when to keep your mouth shut?"

"I have, Your Honor. Thank you."

Platt looked at Devon. "Mr. Malley, at the time when you assaulted your attorney the other day, I was about to set a very low bail. Hell, I was even thinking about granting your release on your own recognizance. Now, because of your outburst, I am considering not setting bail at all." The speech seemed rehearsed, but as the words came out of his mouth, Finn could feel the last of Platt's anger slip out with them. His indignation was gone, and now he just seemed tired. He took a deep, weary breath. "Never mind; what's the point," he said. "Bail is set at fifty thousand dollars. Bailiff, call the next case."

The courtroom broke into motion. The bailiff shouted out the case number of the next matter, and another defense attorney stepped up to the bar, putting his briefcase down on defense counsel's table. Another bailiff moved over and took Devon by the elbow, and Finn stepped back from the table. Devon looked at him.

"Don't worry," Finn said. "I have a bondsman lined up. It'll cost five grand to post. I've got the money ready, and I'll cover it."

"Thanks, Finn. I'll pay you back."

"Goddamned right you will," Finn said. "I'll have you posted in ten minutes. It'll take another hour to process you out, but I'll meet you out front."

"Okay," Devon said.

Then he was gone, and Finn was standing alone in a room full of people. The hearing had been the easy part, he knew. From here on, it was going to get a lot harder.

The man who had abducted Sally repeated the same ritual over and over. Every few hours he would come down the stairs to give her a sip of water and a bite to eat. There was no kindness; he showed no more feeling toward her than he might toward a plant he was watering. If anything, the longer she was there, the less humanity he seemed to have.

Sally had changed, too. She was now at the point where she might have preferred dehydration to the periodic maintenance. At first, her situation had seemed unreal. That changed when the man brought the body downstairs.

She'd seen that there was someone else in the house when he hurried her through toward the basement, but the man with the dark hair had pushed her downstairs too quickly for her to get a good look at the other man. Now she'd had more of a look than she'd ever wanted, and she knew that if she lived through the ordeal, the man's face would haunt every minute of sleep she might manage to have.

She couldn't tell what was happening when she heard her captor open the door the night before, grunting his exertion. She could hear him dragging something down the stairs, and it sounded as if the planks would snap as the weight slammed down, step by step. She knew it was a dead body by the time it reached the bottom of the stairs.

Now he lay there, not more than ten feet from her. The man with the black hair hadn't even bothered to turn the body over on its stomach or close the eyes; he lay on his side, frozen in death, staring at her. The tongue dangled from the lips, dark and synthetic, like a rubber toy hanging stiff and thick. She could see a deep wound on the chest, and the slice through the neck caused the head to tilt back, revealing what looked like a huge second mouth.

It was starting to smell.

The body chased away any doubt of the danger she was in. She understood fully now that if she was to survive this, it was going to take all of her focus and concentration. She thought briefly about giving up; hoping for death. She'd led a life thick with disappointment and despair, and it wouldn't be unreasonable for her to call it quits now. After all, hadn't she suffered enough?

The thought was fleeting, though. If anything, the reminder of what death was—brutal, and lonely, and final—sharpened her desire for life. As she lay there, plastered to the cold, unforgiving cellar floor, she made a vow to herself that she would never again let anyone determine the course of her life. She was done with grown-ups; done with parents; done with relying on others. From now on, she would rely only on herself. That thought gave her hope for the future. That thought strengthened her will to live.

———

Finn went straight to the clerk's office at the courthouse once the bail hearing was over. As he walked, he placed a call on his cell phone to a bail bondsman and confirmed the amount needed to secure Devon's release. The bondsman was one with whom Finn dealt regularly—a colorful character named Shifty LaRue, whose interests extended to nightclubs and parking lots—and he sent over a messenger with all the forms needed. Finn paid the messenger with a check written on the firm's account, and within a half hour Devon was brought down in street clothes. He was sweating despite the fact that it was in the fifties outside and there was a chill in the courthouse.

"What now?" Devon asked.

"First, we need to deal with finances," Finn said.

"What do you mean?"

"You know what I mean, Devon," Finn said. "I just laid out five thousand dollars to get you free. That's on top of nearly twenty thousand we've got sunk into this case in fees so far. Plus, it's going to get more expensive as the case proceeds."

"Jesus, you're fuckin' kidding, right?" Devon said. "My daughter's been kidnapped; we've got to get her back."

"And we will. I've been on the outside, and my people and I have been dealing with this shit for a week—shit that you knew about and didn't share with us. For Christ's sake, Devon, you put me and my people in harm's way. My associate ended up in the hospital because of you, and this psychopath almost fucked up her pregnancy."

"I thought you didn't care about the money. That's what you said."

"That was before. I changed my mind; now I want to get paid."

"I told you, you're gonna get paid," Devon said. "But first we get Sally back."

Finn shook his head. "Bullshit. We get paid now, or you're on your own. Period. That's not negotiable, Devon. Hell, I don't know where you're gonna be tomorrow. I'm not gonna get stiffed. You say you can pay? Prove it."

Devon put his hands in his pockets and looked away. "Fine," he said. "You want your fuckin' money, I'll get you your fuckin' money."

"Good."

"But then you're in this. To the end."

"As long as we get paid, we're in this to the end," Finn agreed.

Devon hesitated a moment. Then he said, "We gotta go to my apartment."

Finn put his hand out toward the courthouse exit. "You lead the way," he said.

Kozlowski was waiting for them outside. He'd spent the morning and the first part of the afternoon getting Lissa released from the hospital and set up in her apartment.

"How's she doing?" Finn asked.

"She'll be okay," Kozlowski replied. "I told her to keep the door locked and not let anyone in unless it was you or me. I also told her to keep the phone in her hand and 911 on speed dial."

"Kilbranish isn't going after her," Finn said. "He wants Devon." He looked at his client and saw the man shiver.

"Where to?" Kozlowski asked.

"Devon's apartment," Finn replied. "We're gonna get paid. Then we can deal with getting Sally back."

Kozlowski nodded. "My car's in the lot around the corner," he said.

"You don't think the three of us can fit in the MG?"

"Fuck you."

"Right."

Finn left his car parked, and the three of them headed to the public lot on State Street where Kozlowski had left his car. It was a giant gas-guzzling Chevy Caprice that was at least ten years old. It had enough room in it for a tennis match, though, and even Finn had to admit it was better suited to their needs that day.

No one spoke on the ride to Devon's apartment. Finn hadn't been there since the day he'd picked up Sally. It was hard to believe that was only four days ago. Since then, it seemed as though his entire world had changed, and not for the better.

Kozlowski parked his car in front of the apartment, and they all climbed out. The apartment hadn't changed. It was still a rathole. Maybe he could take some solace in the fact that the rest of the world went on unaware of the chaos going on all around it. Maybe that provided the only semblance of stability there was in the universe.

Devon pulled out his keys and opened the door. As soon as they stepped in, they all smelled it. It was impossible to miss—the unmistakable stench of rot and decay. "Holy shit, I think I'm gonna throw up," Devon said.

Kozlowski pulled his gun out. "I'll go first," he said quietly.

"Okay," Finn replied. He hung back as Kozlowski moved into the apartment. There wasn't much to search. There was a living room in front; in the 1920s, when the place had been built, it had probably been called a parlor. There was nothing amiss there, though. At the back of the living room there was a door and a hallway.

"Where do those lead?" Kozlowski asked Devon.

"The door goes to the kitchen," he said. "The hallway goes to the bedrooms and a bathroom."

"How many bedrooms?"

"Two."

"Anything else back there?"

"A closet, but that's it."

Kozlowski held his gun at the ready, with two hands, pointed at the ceiling. He moved across the living room to the hallway. For such a large man, it was amazing the way he could travel without any sound, Finn thought. "Stay here," he said.

Finn looked at Devon. "We'll stay here," he said.

Kozlowski disappeared down the hallway. It seemed as if he was gone for a long time, though it was probably only a minute or so. He came back out and shook his head. "Nothing," he said. He motioned toward the kitchen door and gave a signal for Finn and Devon to remain where they were. He slid along the wall, his gun still at the ready. Then he swung around the corner, pointing the pistol in front of him as he went, and disappeared through the door. A moment later he yelled, "Found it!"

Finn glanced at Devon and then the two of them moved toward the kitchen. The stench intensified as they approached the door, until it grew overpowering. Then they stepped into the room.

The kitchen was small, little more than a galley, and Kozlowski was standing in the middle of it, making it difficult to see. Moving to the side, though, Finn could see what was causing the stench.

The refrigerator door was standing open, and there was food on the counter. Flies buzzed around a smorgasbord of hamburger meat and ham that had been left out.

"That fuckin' bitch," Devon said. He moved around Kozlowski to get a better look. "Fuckin' Shelly. She did this on purpose."

"Probably," Finn said.

Kozlowski opened a window. "It can be cleaned."

"I know, but still," Devon said.

"You left her with your mess for a couple of days," Finn pointed out. "She probably figured turnabout was fair play."

"Fuck," Devon said.

"You've got bigger problems than this," Kozlowski pointed out. That brought them all back to reality.

"The money," Finn said to Devon.

Devon pulled some paper towels off a roll on the counter and swept some of the mess into a nearby garbage can. "This is fucked up," he said, holding his head away from the smell.

"I'm serious, Devon," Finn said. "We don't get paid, and we don't move on from here."

Devon threw the paper towel into the garbage can. "You're a bloodless shit," he said. "You wait here. I'll be right back. It's in back."

Finn shook his head. "Do we look stupid?"

"I swear to God, it's in back," Devon said. "I just don't want you to see where."

"That's too bad," Finn said. Devon hesitated. "All we want is what you owe us, but we're not letting you out of our sight until this is settled. I don't give a shit whether you trust us or not. If you want to get your daughter back, we're doing this right now."

"Fine," Devon said at last. "Knock yourself out." He walked out of the kitchen and around into the hallway. As Finn and Kozlowski followed, Finn took a good look at the place for the first time. As bad as it looked from the outside, it got worse the deeper into the apartment he traveled. The living room was tiny, and the furniture was fraying and stained. The back hallway had been carpeted sometime in the 1950s, from the look of it, and there were places where it had worn through entirely. Everywhere the walls were stained and shedding paint. Finn shuddered to think of Sally living there.

Devon walked halfway down the hallway and then turned into the bathroom. Finn and Kozlowski would have followed him in, but there wasn't enough space for two grown men inside. They kept an eye on him from the hallway.

Devon stood on the edge of the tub and reached up to what looked like a vent in the ceiling. He pushed the vent cover up gently, then slid it to the side. Reaching into the opening in the ceiling, he withdrew a sack. He held the sack in front of his body, away from Finn and Kozlowski so that they couldn't see. After a moment, he reached up again and replaced the sack, then slid the vent cover back into place.

He stepped down off the tub and walked back out into the hallway. Holding out his hands, he said, "There's thirty-five thousand there." Finn looked at the stack of cash. It was tightly packed, wrapped in orange bands denoting five-thousand-dollar bundles. There were seven bundles. "That's five thousand for the bond, twenty thousand for the work you've done so far, and another ten to cover the next bit. That gets you all in," Devon said.

Finn slapped the money out of his hands. The bundles fell to the floor, and Devon reached for them instinctively. "What the fuck!" he yelled.

"You stupid, lying motherfucker," Finn said.

"What? Count it, it's real!"

"I don't give a shit about the money, you stupid asshole." Finn reached out and grabbed Devon by the shirt and threw him up against the hallway wall.

"What do you mean?" Devon's voice was cracking, and he looked confused as he tried to wrestle away. Finn held his neck, though. "What the fuck are we here for?"

"Where are the paintings, Devon?"

Devon's confusion morphed to panic. "I don't know what you're talking about!"

Still holding on to Devon's neck, Finn leaned back and punched his client in the face. Devon crumpled to the floor. "Don't give me that shit, Devon. We know."

Devon jackknifed on the hallway floor in front of Finn, his hands covering his head. "Know what?" he choked out. "I don't understand!"

"Cut the shit, Devon, or I'll turn this over to Koz here. He was a cop for twenty-five years; you don't think he's got some experience getting people like you to talk?" He knelt down, putting his face right up next to Devon's. "We know you were the one who offered to sell the paintings. You gave potential buyers photographs and paint chips to prove the offer was real. That means you know where they are. Now you're going to tell us."

"Fuck you!" Devon yelled. "You don't know shit!"

"I know that you live in a shithole roaches wouldn't set foot in for all the fuckin' mess. I know you haven't been doing any steady work for Murphy or Ballick or anyone else for years. I know that you just reached into your ceiling and pulled out thirty-five thousand dollars without batting an eye, and if you'd had that kind of money for any amount of time, you wouldn't be living here. And I know that the IRA paid someone one hundred thousand dollars for confirmation on the paintings. It doesn't take a fuckin' rocket scientist to put all this together, Devon. Are you really this stupid?"

Devon was still lying on the floor. It seemed as though the physical pain had subsided, but he looked utterly defeated.

"I also know that this Kilbranish out there has got your daughter, and he's going to kill her if he doesn't get these paintings. Doesn't that mean anything to you?"

"It means everything to me!" Devon yelled. "It's the only god-damned thing I care about. I'm giving myself up. I'll trade myself for her, and I'll take the pain! Even death!"

Finn shook his head in confusion. "But don't you understand? You don't have to. He doesn't want you, he wants the paintings. If we give those to him, he's not gonna give a shit about you anymore."

"Fuck you," Devon said. "You wouldn't understand."

Finn looked at Kozlowski. He was staring at Devon, his eyes narrowed. It was clear that he had no better insight than Finn about what was going on.

"Where are the paintings, Devon?" Finn asked again at last.

Devon looked up at him. "You wouldn't believe me if I told you," he said.

Chapter Thirty-Four

The last time Devon saw Whitey Bulger was in December of 1994. It was a dangerous time in Southie; a dangerous time for everyone with connections. The tension in the projects and down along the water crackled as the crisp New England winter set in. There had been a crackdown in recent months on bookmakers across Boston, and people—connected people—had been slipping out of sight. There were whispers everywhere that something was coming. No one knew what or when or how, but that didn't stop people from believing. They talked about it as if it were an impending apocalypse; a nameless threat hovered everywhere, making everyone jumpy. There's nothing more dangerous than a community of nervous gangsters.

Devon was at home in his apartment three days before Christmas. Despite the success at the Gardner Museum years earlier, the promise of advancement and opportunity had never materialized. It was as if the whole thing had never happened. The fallout from the robbery in the law-enforcement community was so heavy that the Gardner job wasn't something he could use; if anything the attention paid to the investigation made him radioactive. Those who knew of his involvement had stayed away from him for years. Worse, he had spent the entire time looking over his shoulder, sure that he would be eliminated at any moment by Bulger or one of his men, just to clean up the loose ends.

When the phone rang and he heard Bulger's voice on the other end of the line, his heart stopped. "I got a job for you," Bulger said.

"Okay," Devon said, the perspiration spreading over his body like the winter fog. "What is it?"

"Not over the phone," Bulger said. "Tonight. Meet me at the liquor store. One o'clock."

"Sure thing, Mr. Bulger," Devon said.

When he hung up the phone, Devon's first instinct was to run. He went to his bedroom and opened his drawers, wondering what he would need to take. After a moment, though, his knees gave out and he slumped to the bed. The truth was that nothing he could take would make a difference. A change of clothes and fifty bucks; that was the sum total of his existence. The only thing that kept him alive was the odd job Murphy threw him occasionally. If he left, he'd have nothing. Less than nothing, even.

As he sat there, he thought hard about his situation. If Whitey had wanted him dead, he'd have had it done before now, he figured. It was a rationalization, but he had nothing else. He even convinced himself that maybe this was the start of good things for him—the fulfillment of a promise made years before.

He arrived a few minutes early at the liquor store out of which Whitey ran his business. The lights were off. He went to the front door and pushed. It was locked. He looked around and walked to the back of the building. As he approached he could see that the back door was cracked open ever so slightly. He pulled it open half a foot.

"Mr. Bulger?" he called out softly.

"In here," came a voice.

Devon thought he would throw up. He could see nothing but darkness inside, and he assumed his life was over. He hesitated.

"Get the fuck in here," the voice said.

Devon took a deep breath and stepped into the building. He'd passed up whatever chance he'd had to run. "Where are you?" he asked into the darkness.

"Back here. Storage room."

Devon moved slowly, his hands feeling for danger out in front of him. After a moment he caught the dim shadow cast by a small light toward the back of the storage area. He walked toward the light, feeling slightly more sure-footed as he got closer and the light gave him a better sense of the room. When he got to the door, he pushed it open.

Bulger was there. There was a table in the center of the room, and on the table was a large wooden packing crate. "I need your help movin' this," Bulger said.

Devon looked around, expecting to see someone else from Bulger's crew. It was just the two of them, though. "Sure thing, Mr. Bulger," Devon said. "Where to? The other room?"

Bulger shook his head. "I got a truck outside," he said.

"Oh," Devon said. "Sure. No problem."

The crate was lighter than Devon had expected. It was a two-man job, but not a strenuous one. The truck outside was a custom van. It had thick brown shag carpeting on the inside and little round bubble windows on the back end. It was the kind of a van Devon had always wanted growing up—the kind guys from the neighborhood got laid in.

He and Bulger loaded the crate into the back and closed the rear doors. "Get in," Bulger said. He tossed Devon the keys. "You drive."

Devon climbed into the driver's seat; Whitey sat next to him. He started the engine and let it idle for a moment. "Where're we goin'?"

"Charlestown." Whitey wasn't looking at him; he was looking out the window, scanning the parking lot from every angle, looking in the rearview mirror to see if anything was moving. Devon had never seen him nervous before. It didn't do anything to put Devon at ease. He put the van in gear and pulled out.

Under other circumstances, the drive might have been pleasant. The temperature hovered in the high twenties, and light flurries drifted weightless through the beams cast by the headlights. A thin layer of snow had cleansed the city earlier in the day, and it had remained cold enough for the snow to stick. As Devon crossed through Southie and into Boston, he hesitated. "Which way you wanna go?"

"Charlestown Bridge," Bulger replied.

Devon nodded and took the right onto Atlantic, then followed it around, peeling off onto Surface Road, which followed the shadow of the raised highway that separated downtown Boston from the North End, onto North Washington to the four-lane bridge that crossed into the southeastern part of Charlestown. At the far end of the bridge there was a light. "Take Chelsea Street," Bulger ordered.

Devon turned and headed north, through Charlestown on the eastern part of town. The place glowed with the holiday season, colored lights warming the street scene through brownstone windows. To the right was the Navy Yard, with its virgin luxury condos; to the left was the flat below Monument Square, with its redeveloped brownstones, their roof decks proclaiming the city's recent gentrification. With the snow, it looked as though they might have traveled through time to be cruising through the place fifty years earlier.

Chelsea Street quickly fell into the night shadows of the Mystic River Bridge, which towered over the water, headed to Chelsea, where LNG stations and industrial smokestacks dominated the landscape. To the right, the Navy Yard withered away to shoreline, and to the left, the refurbished town houses gave way to battered housing projects. The contrast as they headed north was striking.

Chelsea Street crossed the Little Mystic Channel and turned into Terminal Street at the water's edge out on Mystic Wharf, a twenty-acre chunk of landfill where Boston's Public Works Department stored *its vehicles. The place was covered in concrete and jutted out from the mainland into the Mystic River. Thousands upon thousands of ghostly vehicles lined up in an endless parking lot. It was a wasteland, with only a few buildings squatting fat and ugly at the edge of the river.*

"I'll tell you when to stop," Bulger said as they approached the western end of the mammoth wharf. "Turn in here, to the right."

Devon turned through a gate. There were two visible buildings, low and long, running perpendicular to the river. A faded sign on one read "Charlestown Self-Storage." "Around back," Bulger said.

They wound around onto a narrow driveway out back that hair-pinned by the edge of the water, following the back of the building to a narrow drive in between the two structures. Halfway down, Bulger said, "Park here."

Devon stopped the van.

"Get out."

Devon did as he was told; Bulger followed. He looked around nervously as he walked to the back of the van and opened it up. The two of them leaned in and grabbed hold of the crate, hoisted it up, and carried it toward the only door Devon could see. Once there, they set it down and Bulger took out a key. He opened the door and held it with his foot while the two of them moved the crate inside. Then he let the door slam, and they were swallowed up in darkness so complete Devon wondered for a moment whether he was dead. He felt around with his hand on the wall and found a switch, flipping it. A jaundiced light flickered on. "Turn the fuckin' light off," Bulger hissed. Devon looked at him, confused, but turned the light off. A moment later, Bulger flipped on a flashlight and slipped it under his arm. It was a weak light, creating little more than gray shadows, but it was enough for them to maneuver down the long, narrow passage. "Down at the end," Bulger said, and the two of them walked jerkily down the hallway.

There was little that Devon could see, but then he was pretty sure he wasn't missing much. Narrow blue sliding doors lined the hallway, each of them lonely and silent. They reminded Devon of prison cells stacked up side by side; a mausoleum of solitary confinement, the screams of the occupants silenced and forgotten.

When they arrived at the end of the hallway they put the crate down and Bulger used his flashlight to locate another key and unlock the door. He reached down and grabbed hold of the handle at the bottom of the door, sliding it open. Motioning to Devon, he picked up one end of the crate again, carried it inside the little storage room, and then pulled the door down behind them.

The room couldn't have been more than six by ten, only slightly bigger than a jail cell, and it had no ventilation, no insulation. Devon could see their breath as they exhaled, caught in the weak light still cast by Bulger's flashlight. In the center of the room stood a narrow wooden box, about five feet tall, eight feet long, and three feet wide. Devon's first thought was that it resembled a coffin.

Bulger opened the door to the box from one end; it had a metal clasp that held a swinging door closed. Devon had never seen anything like it. The interior was lined with a rich, luxurious cloth. It looked like silk, but a deeper silk than he'd ever seen. "What's that?" he asked.

"Mind your fuckin' business," Bulger said. "There's a hammer in the van. Get it, and get the fuckin' crate open."

Devon did as he was told. It took a few minutes for him to pry off the lid to the crate, but once he did, he could hardly believe his eyes. There, inside the crate, were all of the paintings and drawings he and the Irishman had taken from the Gardner Museum years before. "Holy fuck," Devon said.

"You ain't kiddin'," Bulger agreed.

The last time Devon had seen the paintings they were rolled up and piled on a table at the auto body shop. Now they were mounted on wood, and they looked well cared for.

"I thought the Irishman paid you for these," Devon said.

"He did. We've tried twice to move them out of the country, but there's still too much fuckin' heat. I'm holding them for our friends until it's safe. In the meantime, we gotta take care of them. You don't stretch 'em out, and they crack," Bulger said. "This box is like a humidor; it'll keep out the moisture and protect 'em. These things get ruined and they're fuckin' worthless."

"Where'd you get it?"

"I know a guy," Bulger replied. "I had him make it. That's all you need to fuckin' know. Now hand them in to me, one at a time."

It took just a few minutes for them to transfer the paintings to the box. Bulger closed the door and latched it.

Bulger turned to Devon. He had his knife in one hand and a set of the keys to the storage facility in the other. The knife turned menacingly in his hand. "There are three sets of keys to this place," he said. He tossed the key in his hand to Devon. "Now you got one, and I got one."

"What about the third?"

"You don't need to worry about the third," Bulger said. Without warning, he reached out and grabbed Devon by the throat, pushing him into the wall. "You even think about fuckin' me on this, and I'll do things you can't even imagine, you got that?" He held the knife less than an inch away from Devon's right eye. "I'm more serious than you'll ever fuckin' know."

"I don't understand," Devon said. "Why do I need the key?"

"Because if I'm not around, someone's got to get our Irish friends their shit if they show up lookin' for it."

"What about the other guy?"

Bulger laughed. "He's not in a position to help out our friends." He turned serious again. "Three of us," he said. "That's all there is that know about this place. And I know the other guy ain't gonna fuckin' cross me; so if this shit disappears, you're the only guy I'm comin' after."

"I wouldn't fuck you," Devon said.

Bulger kept the knife where it was for another minute. Then he pulled it back and put it away in its sheath. "Good," he said. "Now help me get this fuckin' crate back to the van."

Devon started helping with the crate. "Why me?" Devon asked after a moment.

Bulger laughed. "I don't trust nobody who isn't scared shitless of me," he said. "Some other guys, they might think they could take me. They might think, if things ain't goin' my way, that's their chance. You ain't gonna think that way no matter what happens, are you?"

Devon looked down. "No," he said. "No, I'm not, Mr. Bulger."

Bulger looked at him and smiled. "I told you once before, call me Jimmy," he said.

Bulger dropped Devon off back at his apartment and peeled away. Devon never saw him again. A day later, rumors began to spread that the Justice Department had obtained sealed indictments against Bulger's Winter Hill Gang. Bulger himself was tipped off by his FBI handlers and slipped away before he could be arrested. In the fifteen years since, no one ever called on Devon to get the paintings.

Chapter Thirty-Five

Devon finished telling them everything. They were sitting in the living room. Devon was on the battered, fraying sofa, his shoulders sunken. Finn was sitting on a plain wooden chair, looking at him. Kozlowski was standing against a wall.

"You made the offer to sell the paintings," Finn said.

Devon nodded. "Two weeks ago. I went to the self-storage place. I took the paintings out and took pictures of them, and I scraped a few flecks of paint off two of them so I had the proof. I put them back where they were. Then I put the word out that they could be bought."

"And you were the one who called the cops to tip them off about the job you were doing at Gilberacci's. You wanted to get arrested."

He nodded again. "I didn't know what the fuck to do," he said. "When I started this, I thought Bulger was the only worry, and I figured it was worth the risk, 'cause there's no fuckin' way he was coming back now. But after I put the word out about the paintings, I started hearing talk about some Irish guy coming to town to look for them. I figured it had to be the guy. I knew him nineteen years ago—knew what a sick fuck he was. I panicked. I figured the safest place for me was in jail, and I knew you'd be able to get me out eventually when things calmed down. It seemed like the only thing to do."

"Not only that, but you knew with us working for you, you could find out what was going on. You sent us out to find out whether Murphy and Ballick had been killed, so you'd know whether the rumors you heard were true."

"I did it for Sally," Devon said. "To keep her safe."

"Good thinkin'," Kozlowski said.

"Fuck you!" Devon yelled. "What was I supposed to do? I was sittin' on more money than any of us have ever seen! I wasn't givin' that up without a fuckin' fight!"

"How much are you asking for them?" Kozlowski asked.

"Twenty-five million."

"A bargain for art worth half a billion," Finn said.

"I'm not greedy," Devon said.

"No," Finn said. "Just stupid."

Devon looked down. "Yeah. Just stupid."

Finn rubbed his face. "Why?" he asked. "You kept it quiet for eighteen years. Why risk it all now?"

"I never had a daughter before," Devon said. "She deserves better than what I can do for her. She's so fuckin' smart, y'know? She could be anything if she got the chance. She's the only thing in my life I've done that's any good. I wanted to do right by her."

"Well, now you're gonna have the chance. You're gonna give up the paintings to get her back."

Devon shook his head. "I'll give myself up to get her back. The paintings are hers. She keeps them. At least she can get the reward for them; that's five million. That's more than I could ever give her. It's more than I'm worth."

"Don't be stupid, Devon," Finn said. "She needs a father more than she needs five million dollars."

Devon looked up at him and laughed. "You been watching too

many fuckin' after-school specials, Finn," he said. "I'm a piece of shit. She'd be better off without me. That's not self-fuckin'-pity, I know what I'm talkin' about. With money like that, she can start a life. A real life. Not the gettin'-by shit I can give her."

"You may be right," Kozlowski said. "She may be better off without you. I don't know. I do know that it doesn't matter, though; we're giving him the paintings."

"Why?"

"Because it's the only way to keep her safe."

Devon looked confused. "I don't understand."

"Koz is right," Finn said. "Shit, Devon, you'll end up telling Kilbranish where the paintings are anyways; he'll get it out of you."

Devon shook his head. "I can take the pain. I won't tell him shit."

"Oh, Jesus, Devon, think about it! You couldn't keep from telling us after I blew you a fuckin' kiss. You really think you're gonna stand up to what this psycho will do to you? You'll promise to tell him if he promises not to hurt Sally, and he'll promise. And then, you know what? He'll kill her anyway, just to cut the trail off. Even if you somehow manage to keep you mouth shut as he slices your nuts off—and you won't—you think that'll end this for him? You think he's gonna pack his shit up and head back to Ireland humming a happy fuckin' tune? No, he'll go after Sally just to find out if she knows anything. Then he'll come after me, and he'll come after Koz, and he'll come after Lissa on the chance that you've told us something—which, by the way, you have."

"I've got enough to do in my life," Kozlowski said. "I don't need to spend my time hunting down some whacked-out leprechaun just to protect my people."

The realization spread over Devon's face. "But then Sally has nothing!" he cried, in agony. "She'll have shit!"

"She'll have you," Finn said.

"Same fuckin' thing." He was sobbing now. His head was down and his shoulders were shaking silently.

"Maybe," Kozlowski said. "But it'll have to do. It beats being dead."

No one said a word for a few moments, and Devon's silent outburst died down. Finally, he pulled his hands away from his face. "Okay," he said. "Okay, we'll do it your way. How do we do it?"

Finn and Kozlowski looked at each other. "First," Finn said, "we wait for Kilbranish's call. He said he was calling at six. Then we set up a meeting to trade the paintings for Sally."

———

Special Agent Hewitt was parked on Devon Malley's street, facing east. He'd been tailing the lawyer all day. He followed him to court and ducked down in the back of the courtroom during the bail hearing. He watched as Finn, Malley, and Kozlowski went to pick up the other car, and he followed them to Southie.

He got Devon's name off the courtroom schedule and called it in to Porter, who was back at the office. "I'll run him through the computer," Porter said. Twenty minutes later, Porter called back. "He's a thief," he reported. "Small-time, but he had some connections back in the day with Murphy. The apartment they're in is his."

"He could be our guy," Hewitt said.

"Could be," Porter replied. "Something's going down."

"Feels that way, doesn't it? Word at the courthouse was that the lawyer pulled some strings to get this guy's bail hearing scheduled early. No reason for the hurry unless something's happening."

"Have you got GPS with you?"

"Yeah. I was afraid they might just be stopping off for a second, but from the look of things, they may be here for a while. The car's a little way down the street from the apartment. Could be tricky, but I think I can handle it."

"Good. Get it planted, and keep an eye on them. Let me know if anything happens." Porter hung up without waiting for a reply.

Hewitt looked at his phone. He had the distinct feeling that Porter viewed himself as fully in charge of the investigation now, and thought of Hewitt as nothing more than a glorified gofer. It hadn't been that way at the start. Porter had come to Hewitt and asked a favor. He said he had a solid lead on the Gardner case, but needed to keep the investigation closed. He said there was a chance there was a breach in the Art Theft Program unit, and he wasn't willing to risk losing the Gardner paintings over it. He even offered to share the credit for any success they had. Hewitt was beginning to get the impression that the amount of credit that would actually come his way would be minimal.

He picked up the cardboard cup of coffee he'd bought at noon and took a sip. The coffee was cold and stale, and he almost spat it out. He grimaced; he'd have thought by this time in his career he wouldn't be sweating his balls off on a stakeout. Looking around, he spied a Dunkin' Donuts across the street. He needed to take a leak and get a new cup of coffee. Before he could do either of those things, though, he had a job to do.

He reached into the glove compartment and took out a small black box the size of a cigarette lighter. Turning it over on its side he flipped a switch, and checked to see that it was working. He opened the car door, got out, and walked up the street, toward where the giant Caprice was parked. When he got alongside the rear bumper he pulled a dollar bill out of his pocket and let it slip out of his hand and drop to the curb. As he bent down to pick it up, he quickly slid the little black box under the car's rear fender. He stood up and walked across the street toward the Dunkin' Donuts.

Stone and Sanchez were in their unmarked car a block up the street from Devon's apartment, facing west. "What do you think?" Stone asked.

"I don't know anymore," Sanchez replied. "What the hell are they doing in there?" It was nearing six in the evening, and they'd been at the apartment for close to an hour. Sanchez had one of the guards at the courthouse let him know when the hearing was over. They'd waited outside and followed Finn and Kozlowski from the courthouse.

"Maybe the paintings are in there," Stone said. Sanchez couldn't tell whether he was kidding.

"Stranger things have happened."

"Can you imagine? Half a billion dollars' worth of art in a shithole like that? Chances are the rats would have gotten to the paintings anyway. They'll come out all full of holes. Hopefully it's that shitty modern art and it won't matter."

"If the guy who did Murphy and Ballick finds these guys, everyone in there will come out full of holes," Sanchez said. "Keep your eyes open."

"Oh fuck," Stone said.

"What is it?"

Stone pointed up the street past the apartment. It took a second for Sanchez to see what he was talking about. Then she saw him: a tall black man in a dark suit and sunglasses, heading toward them. "Hewitt," Stone said. He stopped next to Kozlowski's car and bent down to pick up something that had fallen out of his pocket. "GPS?"

"Gotta be." They watched as Hewitt stood and crossed the street, headed into the Dunkin' Donuts. "Shit," she said.

"How the fuck did he get here?"

"He must have followed them too," Sanchez said. "Goddammit."

"What do we do now?" Stone asked.

She thought about it for a moment. "Maybe it isn't such a bad thing," she said. "I don't think he's seen us, and we know he's gonna be tailing them from a distance using the GPS. As long as we follow him, we can keep up our surveillance of Finn and Malley, and at the same time we can get some idea of what the feds are up to."

"You still don't trust them, do you?" Stone asked.

She looked at him. "Never have, never will," she said.

Chapter Thirty-Six

No one in Devon's apartment felt much like talking. Their only discussion concerned the plan to swap the paintings for Sally.

There wasn't much to it, really. Calling it a plan at all might have been generous, but it was the best they could come up with on such short notice. Finn's office was, they decided, the best place to make the exchange. It was the kind of a place where it would be quiet enough at night that people would mind their own business. At the same time, it was close enough to a decent neighborhood that if gunshots were fired, the police would be called quickly. That might make Kilbranish think twice about opening fire.

The call came in to Finn's cell phone at six exactly. The phone was sitting out on an empty wine box that served as a coffee table, and the three of them were staring at it as if it were some supernatural charm. They all jumped when it rang. "He's punctual," Finn said. He picked his phone up and answered on the third ring. "Finn here," he said.

"Mr. Finn, do you have an answer for me?" Kilbranish asked.

"I do," Finn said. "We've got the paintings."

He could hear Kilbranish's breathing get heavier on the other end of the line. "So, Devon was planning on crossing me," he said. "Devon made a mistake."

"He did," Finn said. "We're gonna correct that mistake tonight, though."

"Yes, we are. But if he crossed me once, he'll do it again. How am I supposed to trust you?"

"You don't have a choice," Finn said. "If you want the paintings, you'll trust us, *Mr. Kilbranish.*" He said the name with emphasis.

"Very good, Mr. Finn," Kilbranish said after a moment. "You know who I am."

"I do. I only tell you that because if anything goes wrong, I've written a letter that I'm giving to a colleague of mine. The police and the feds and Interpol will know who and where you are within hours. So things better not go wrong."

"That's all up to you. I want you to put the paintings in a car and send your client to meet me," Kilbranish began.

"No deal," Finn said. "We'll do this our way."

"You don't dictate terms, Mr. Finn. I do. I have the girl."

"And I have half a billion dollars of stolen art. Art that you've traveled across an ocean after two decades to find. You have a girl I met a few days ago. Her father didn't even know her last year." As Finn spoke, Devon's face turned white, and he got up, reaching for the phone. Kozlowski pushed him back down onto the sofa. Devon struggled for a moment, but the detective put a hand on his mouth, pushing the back of his head deep into the cushions. Physically, Devon was no match for Kozlowski. "If you think you have all the leverage," Finn said into the phone, "think again. We'll do this, but only on our terms."

Kilbranish didn't answer immediately, and Finn feared he'd pushed too hard.

"When and where?" Kilbranish said at last.

"Ten o'clock," Finn said. "My office in Charlestown. You know where it is? We'll have the paintings. We make the exchange, then you leave."

The breathing was still heavy. "Just two of you," Kilbranish said. "No one else."

"Just me and Devon," Finn agreed.

"If you cross me," Kilbranish said, "I'll make sure you die. I kill for a living. I'll kill everyone you know. You understand that?"

"I understand," Finn said. "If this goes the way it's supposed to, you won't have to worry. You'll have the paintings, and as long as we're safe, no one will ever know what went down."

"I'll be there," Kilbranish said. Then the line went dead. Finn closed the phone.

Kozlowski let go of Devon's face. "What the fuck!" Devon screamed as he jumped off the sofa. "Don't touch me again!"

"Then don't jeopardize this plan again," Kozlowski said quietly. "You do anything that puts me or Finn or your daughter in danger, and I'll kill you if I have to."

Devon looked at Finn. "Why did you say that? Why would you tell him no one cares what happens to Sally? If he kills her, I swear to God, I'll kill you both!"

"Calm down, Devon," Finn said. "I had to say that. I had to make him think that he has less of an advantage than he really does. It's the only way."

"I didn't fuckin' agree to this!" Devon yelled. "I didn't agree to lose control!"

A police car went by the apartment, its siren blaring and its flashers casting colorful shadows through the windows in the living room. They all looked out nervously, and no one said anything until it had passed.

"None of us are in control anymore," Finn said. "The most we can do is to try and manage this the best we can. And I don't give a shit what you agree to, Devon, this is about one thing now. Getting Sally back. That's it. You do what you're told, and we'll all get out of this alive. Just remember, this guy won't hesitate to put a bullet in your daughter. Keep that in mind."

"What did he say?" Kozlowski asked. "Will he be there?"

"He'll be there," Finn said. "He said if anything goes wrong, he'll kill us all."

Kozlowski stood up and took a deep breath. "Then I guess we'd better make sure that nothing goes wrong."

———

Kilbranish hung up the phone at the house in Quincy and went straight to the door that led down to the basement. He had to move quickly; he wasn't waiting until ten o'clock.

As he moved down the steps, he caught the stench. Broadark's body had been there for more than a day. The basement was cool, but not cool enough to prevent decomposition, and it was clear from the smell that the organic processes had begun in earnest. A few more hours and the smell would make its way upstairs. By the time the next person entered the house, the body would be found in short order. That was fine with him, though. He had the place rented for the rest of the month. By the time anyone else came in, he'd be long gone. With luck, he'd be fighting again.

She no longer turned toward him when he came down the stairs. For the first day she'd jumped every time the stairs creaked. No more. That was normal. He'd had enough experience in kidnapping to recognize the signs of acceptance. It happened to all of them eventually, and it made his job easier—not only in that it made her less likely to try to escape, but in that it made her seem less human. It was easier to kill them once their spirits had been broken.

He moved over toward her and sat on the crate near her. He nudged her in the head with the muzzle of his gun. "It's time," he said.

At that, she turned her head and looked at him. He could see the terror in her face, and he could read her thoughts. She was wondering whether he was going to kill her now. *Good*, he thought. It was right that she remain frightened.

"I'm going to cut the tape on your hands. I'm taking you to your father."

He reached forward and pulled the tape off her mouth. She still winced when it pulled the skin off around her lips, but not nearly as much as she had the first time. He had to give her credit for that, at least; she was no princess.

She worked her mouth in circles, testing its coordination as he cut the tape away from her hands. "Are you letting me go?" she asked.

"That depends on your father," Liam said. "If he and his lawyer do what they were told to do, I'll let you go."

"If not? If they don't do what they were told to do? What happens to me then?"

He said nothing, and continued to work at the tape, cutting it away from her feet now. He didn't have the time to deal with this sort of melodrama. She sat up and rubbed her wrists. The skin around them had been torn completely away now; he figured she'd been testing the strength of the restraints. The same was true of her ankles.

"Tell me," she said. "What happens to me if my father fucks up?"

He pointed his gun at her, holding it inches from her forehead. "Then you die. If you or your father or the lawyer doesn't do exactly what I want, then I'll kill you without even thinking about it. Do you understand that?"

She nodded.

"Your life is in your father's hands."

He watched her as it sank in; watched her digest the information. For a moment there was a flicker of hope in them—just an inkling of the spirit he had seen in the first day or so. Then it vanished, and her eyes went flat again. He wondered why, but in the end it didn't matter. It was no concern of his.

"We've got to get back to the office in Charlestown," Kozlowski said. "If it's just gonna be you and Devon, I need eyes in the place."

"What are you gonna do?" Finn asked.

"Wire the place up with cameras," Kozlowski said. "Every corner, every square foot of the office. Right down to the toilet. If this asshole takes a leak, I want to see what he's got hidden in his pants."

"How long will it take?"

"Half hour. Forty minutes, tops."

"Okay," Finn said. "Let's get it done."

They put Devon's money back in the bag in the bathroom ceiling—they'd figure out what to do with that later—and headed back out to the car. The three of them piled in and Kozlowski pulled out, headed back to Charlestown.

Two minutes later a nondescript American-made sedan with federal plates pulled out, following the electronic tail attached to Kozlowski's car. Another thirty seconds later an unmarked Lincoln spun a U-turn and fell in line, following the FBI.

Chapter Thirty-Seven

Liam sat in the van up the street from the lawyer's office at seven o'clock. Had he been sure the paintings were in the offices already, he'd have considered storming the place, but there was no way to know. Besides, it was still light out, and the area was busy enough that a full frontal assault would likely draw attention. Even if he couldn't go in now, he wanted to make sure he knew exactly what was going on in the hours before the exchange—who was there, who was coming, who was going. And so he waited, and he watched. As he'd noted many times before, information was the most valuable commodity in his line of work; right now, he needed as much of it as he could get.

As near as he could determine, there were only three people inside the offices: the lawyer, his partner, and Devon Malley. At the sight of Malley, Liam felt the bile rise in his throat. All of his feelings of anger and betrayal now centered on this one man. Bulger had fled Boston before he'd been able to deliver the paintings. Murphy and Ballick—the only others who had been involved in the heist—were dead. That left only Malley as the object of Liam's rage. The only logical conclusion was that Malley was selling the paintings for himself. Taking what rightfully belonged to Liam's cause. Were it not for the chance to get the paintings back, and to provide the funds necessary to continue the struggles at home, he would have gotten out of the van and killed the man with his bare hands. It would have been satisfying, but it wouldn't have accomplished the mission. He looked back into the van's cargo hold. There were other ways to make sure his true revenge was taken.

She was in back, bound with tape again by both wrists and ankles, gagged and secured to the side of the van, covered with a swath of heavy canvas. He was being careful with her; she'd done all that he'd ordered, behaved as a pliable bitch, eager to please her master. But underneath, he sensed a deep well of determination that put him on edge. He would not take her cooperation for granted. As much as he hated the offspring of the man who had stolen from his great cause, he had respect for her strength. That respect, however, would not prevent him from making her the instrument of his revenge.

He turned back to watch the lawyer's office again. The blinds were closed, and as the light faded outside, he could see loose shadows betraying movement inside. Something was happening. Perhaps they were moving the paintings into place; perhaps they were setting a trap for him. There was no way to know for sure, but he would find out somehow before he went in. He had more experience in these sorts of dangerous situations than just about anyone in the world. He would prevail.

As he sat there, his mind picked momentarily over a lifetime spent at war. He knew no other way but hate, and if the hate died, he would cease to exist. He'd gone all in when he killed Broadark. If there had been any doubt before, there was none now; if he didn't get the paintings back, he would be killed by his own, and the cause for which he'd given his life—for which the lives of his entire family had been taken—would die as well. Even if he managed to secure the paintings and get them back home, he might be killed. He'd gone that far over the edge. He could accept that, however, as long as the hope remained that the struggle would continue. As long as the battles raged, he felt that he and his family would live on in some small way.

He shook his head, bringing himself out of his ruminations. He needed a clear head to do the job ahead of him. He'd worry about the rest once his task was completed.

He looked back again at the canvas lump in the back. She hadn't moved; hadn't made a sound. That was good. She gave him the leverage he needed.

It took Kozlowski nearly forty-five minutes to get the office set up. He moved quickly, but with deliberation, making sure that all the tiny cameras in his arsenal were placed so that they were fully hidden, but still gave him maximum visibility. As he stalked his way about the office, Finn and Devon sat in the main office, fidgeting.

"What's taking so long?" Devon asked. No one answered. "It's fuckin' pointless. You think he's not gonna kill us all anyways?"

"Think happy thoughts. What makes you say that?" Finn asked.

Devon shrugged. "Just a feeling I have. He doesn't seem like the kind of a guy who lets bygones be bygones. If he feels like somebody's fucked him, he's gonna even up the score."

Kozlowski paused and looked around at Devon. "Thinking that way'll get everyone killed. We go into this with our eyes wide open and one goal—getting your daughter back. You do what you're told, and there's a good chance that everyone's walkin' away from this. I'll be watching it all go down from just out back. If I get the feeling that things are slipping away, I'll be in here faster than you can believe."

"Faster than a bullet? What do we do if he starts shooting?"

Kozlowski walked out of the main office toward the back. He returned carrying a pistol and handed it to Finn.

"I hate guns," Finn said.

"More than being shot?" Kozlowski asked.

Finn put the gun in his pocket. "We shouldn't have to use guns at all," he said.

"We shouldn't be in this position at all," Kozlowski said. "Here we are, though. Just having the gun will probably convince this guy he's better off taking what he came for and letting the rest go."

"Where's my gun?" Devon asked.

"Shut up," Kozlowski said.

"What am I supposed to do when the shooting starts?" Devon asked. "You expect me to fuckin' duck?"

"No," Kozlowski said, "I expect you to throw yourself over your daughter to make sure she's safe."

Devon started to open his mouth, then stopped. He nodded.

Finn looked at his watch. It was nearly eight, and even through the blinds he could see that the sun was nearly down. Twilight glittered through the gaps. In a few minutes it would be dark out. Finn couldn't decide whether that was a good thing or a bad thing. "How much longer you got?" he asked Kozlowski, who had returned to adjusting the tiny cameras placed around the room.

"A few more minutes," Kozlowski said. "I want to test the monitors in the car to make sure everything's working right."

"We should get out of here soon if we're gonna have time to get the paintings and get back here."

"We'll make it," Kozlowski said. "When we get back, everything will be ready."

He said it with ultimate confidence. Somehow, though, Finn felt little comfort.

<hr />

Hewitt and Porter sat in Hewitt's car, parked up the street. They were keeping a loose watch on the law offices; they were close enough to see whether people were going in and out, but too far away to see much else. That was okay, though; they had the GPS device planted, and the lawyer's car was back at the courthouse. If they were going anywhere, it was going to be in Kozlowski's Caprice.

"What do you think?" Hewitt asked Porter.

Porter was sitting in the passenger seat. Hewitt had picked him up from the FBI office in a minor detour when their quarry had left Malley's apartment. Porter looked nervous; he didn't strike Hewitt as much of a field agent. He also had a feeling that Porter's obsession had taken him over. "I don't know," Porter replied. His forefinger rubbed back and forth across the bridge of his nose. "Something's going on, that's for sure."

"Maybe they're just preparing a defense on Malley's theft charges."

"At eight o'clock?"

"He's a lawyer."

Porter shook his head. "It's something bigger than that."

Hewitt shrugged. "If you say so."

Just then Finn, Kozlowski, and Devon emerged from the front door to the law offices. "Here we go," Hewitt said. He started the car.

Porter reached over and turned the engine off. "Give them a good solid head start," he said. "I don't want to attract any attention. We can follow them on GPS; we don't need to have them in sight. If they realize they're being tailed, they'll call off whatever they're planning."

"What if something happens before we catch up to them? They could be in danger."

"If they're in danger, they put themselves there," Porter said. "It's not my problem. I'm not going to risk the recovery of the paintings protecting the people who are mixed up in all this. They had a chance to come in and work with us. They passed."

"You'd let people get killed over this?"

Porter looked at him. "If it's that or letting the paintings slip away again, I wouldn't even hesitate."

Stone and Sanchez were even further away from Finn's offices than the FBI agents. The light filtering out from the lawyer's windows was little more than a distant beacon, but it was enough for them to see the figures coming out the front door. They waited, watching as the Caprice pulled away, staying put as they watched the feds in the car two blocks ahead of them bide their time for several minutes. Staying put ate at Stone. "We're gonna lose them," he said.

"No we won't," Sanchez said. "Hewitt and his friend aren't going to let them get away that easily. They've got them tagged; all we have to do is keep Hewitt's car in sight, and they'll lead us where we need to go."

The traffic on the street was still heavy. Cars passed them, headed to dinner, or home from a late night at work. Cars pulled out from their parking spaces, and others rushed to take their places, excited at the luck of finding a spot in the parking-challenged town. A white cargo van that had been making a delivery pulled out a block ahead of them, and Stone had to crane his neck around to keep his eye on the FBI car. Still they waited as the minutes ticked inexorably by. "This is gonna kill me," Stone said.

"Just another minute."

The lights in Hewitt's car came on. It eased back in its parking space, making room to pull out, then shot forward onto the street, following the Caprice's path.

"Now," said Sanchez.

In one motion Stone turned the engine and threw the car into gear. They were a block behind, and Stone was petrified they might get caught at a light. "Motherfucker," he muttered to himself. "We lose them, and I swear to God I'm gonna shoot you, then turn the gun on myself."

She looked at him. "You questioning my judgment?"

He nodded. "I'll follow your lead, and I'll let you call the shots. But don't expect me not to question you when it's just you and me. When it's just us, I'll question everything we do if I think there's a reason." He was focused on keeping the tail, and his eyes were riveted on the road ahead of them, but he could feel her staring at him. "What?" he said. "Is there a problem with that?"

She turned away and looked out the windshield as they stayed within sight of Hewitt's car. "No," she said after a moment. "There's no problem with that at all."

For the first time since they had been riding together, he felt that they were partners.

Chapter Thirty-Eight

Kozlowski steered the car northeast, through the quaint brownstones and Newport-styled clapboard town houses going for two million a pop, down along Warren to Chelsea Street, the dividing line that separated one Charlestown from another.

As they pulled down Chelsea and out around onto Terminal, Finn looked across the Little Mystic Channel toward the Newtown Projects. The name might have been appropriate in the sixties, but now it seemed like sarcasm.

Near the end of the road, they came to an open gate. "Pull in here," Devon said.

Kozlowski pulled in and headed north, toward the water. Two cement structures sat long and flat, running north-south, set nearly flush against the edge of the river. The sign that read "Charlestown Self-Storage" had been repainted, but otherwise the buildings hadn't changed much in twenty years. "It's around the back," Devon said.

Kozlowski followed the path Devon had traveled with Bulger fifteen years before, out around by the water, onto a narrow strip of driveway, then back up into the darkened, narrow alley between the buildings. "Park here," Devon said, halfway down.

The three of them got out of the car and walked to a door set in the side of the building. A weak bulb protected by a rusted casing screwed into the cement above the steel door threw off barely enough light for them to make their way with confidence.

"You got the keys?" Finn asked.

"Right here," Devon replied. He pulled out two keys and tried one in the lock. It worked on the first try, and he pushed his way in. Once inside, he reached over to the wall and flipped a light switch. Nothing happened. "Bulb must be out," he said. "Anybody think to bring a flashlight?"

"Yeah," Kozlowski said, reaching into his jacket pocket and pulling out a slim black-steel flashlight and flipping it on, pointing it down the long narrow corridor.

Finn looked at him. "You're good."

"I think shit through."

"What's that like?"

"It's the last one on the left," Devon said, following the beam of light down the hallway. Once he got to the last door, he grabbed the padlock. "Gimme some light."

Kozlowski pointed the flashlight at the padlock, and Devon used the second key to pop it open. He removed the lock and leaned down, grabbing the door and sliding it up.

The darkness inside the tiny storage unit was so complete Kozlowski's flashlight had difficulty penetrating it. The beam crawled into the corners first, covering the parameters of the space, as if Kozlowski expected someone to be hiding within. There was nothing. The cement floors and cinderblock walls were cold and uninviting. Then the beam moved to the center of the room.

It was there. A wooden box that looked solidly constructed, sealed at the corners. "That's it," Devon said. No one moved; the three of them stood there looking at it as if it were a treasure that held the secrets of the universe. "You wanna see 'em?"

"We don't have much time," Finn said at last. He looked at his wristwatch, but it was too dark for him to make out the time.

"You checked them recently?" Kozlowski asked.

"Yeah," Devon said. "When I took the pictures and got the paint chips."

Kozlowski nodded. "Let's get moving." He stepped into the storage room and put his hand on the corner of the box. It moved easily, and he looked down at the bottom, his flashlight illuminating the small wheels at the corner of the box. "Handy," he said. He walked around to the back of the box; Finn and Devon stood on either side. The three of them rolled the box out like pallbearers, paused after it was past the threshold while Devon closed the door and replaced the lock, then continued down the hallway.

Walking slowly so that the narrow container wouldn't tip, Finn felt as if the walk back down the narrow passageway took forever. As they passed each of the other storage doors in succession, his heart beat a little faster. It was almost as if he believed that one of them might open and someone might jump out. It was absurd, of course, but something about the place gave him an eerie sense of the supernatural.

They got to the end of the hallway and Devon opened the door, holding it ajar with his foot. They all lifted gently to get the wheels over the lip of the entryway, and then they hit the cement outside the building. Finn checked his watch again, this time in the watery light of the lightbulb over the outside of the door. It was after eight-thirty; they still had time. He nodded and they began rolling the box again.

They loaded the box into the giant trunk of the Caprice. As large as it was, they couldn't close the back fully, and Kozlowski used some rope to tie the lid of the trunk down. It wasn't perfect, but they only had a short drive back to Finn's office.

They climbed into the car and pulled out slowly, following the drive between the buildings back toward the river the way they had come.

When they reached the corner of the building, Kozlowski began to turn, then jammed hard on the brakes.

There in front of them, blocking the narrow egress, was a white van. It was backed up against the corner of the building, and standing by the side of it was a man with jet-black hair. He was next to the driver's-side door and there was barely enough room between the van and the low wall that ran along the river for him to stand. Sally was standing in front of him, bound at the ankles and wrists, a piece of duct tape covering her mouth. He was using her as a shield, and he had a gun to her head. He held the gun up and signaled for them to stop. "That's far enough!" he yelled.

"Slowly," Sanchez said as Stone pulled the car into the self-storage parking lot at the end of Terminal Street. Their lights were off, so they wouldn't be spotted. They could see the FBI agents sitting in their car down toward the end of the first building.

"What now?" Stone asked as he pulled the car into a spot where they could maintain a good view of Hewitt and his partner.

"We wait," she said.

"You serious?"

She looked at him. "You got a better idea?"

Using the GPS to track people had its advantages and disadvantages. On the one hand, modern technology had become so sophisticated that Hewitt and Porter could pinpoint the location of Kozlowski's Chevy on the little driveway in between the two buildings. From the GPS mapping, they could see that there was only one way out, so all they had to do was wait, watching the corner of the building, for them to come back around. On the other hand, because they felt secure with the tracking device, they hadn't felt the need to keep the car in sight. When they showed up at the self-storage on Terminal Street, they were probably three or four minutes behind Finn and Kozlowski, and they had no idea what was happening.

"Should we go around the building?" Hewitt asked. "See what's going on?"

Porter gnawed at a fingernail. "No," he said at last.

"We're blind out here," Hewitt said.

Porter studied the GPS map. "We go around the building, we'll be spotted. We stay here, we can see anyone coming out."

Hewitt looked over at the other agent. "It's a storage unit. I can only think of one thing they'd be picking up," he said.

Porter considered this. "Move closer to the corner of the building," he said. "Be ready to stop anyone coming out."

No one moved in the Caprice for a moment. They just sat there, staring straight ahead at Sally. Staring at the man. Staring at the gun he was holding to her head. There was no way around the van; it was parked diagonally across the drive, its nose near the riverbank. The doors at the rear of the van were open.

"Fuck," Finn said.

"Get out of the car! All of you!" the man yelled.

The three of them did as they were told. They were about twenty feet away from the van. "Sally, are you okay?" Devon shouted.

The tape over her mouth prevented an answer. "She's fine," Kilbranish said for her. "She won't stay that way, though, if you don't do what you're told."

"We're doing this at my office," Finn said to Kilbranish. His voice sounded petulant, even to him.

"Plans have changed. Take the paintings out and load them in the back of the van." He was careful as he spoke to keep the girl in front of him, blocking any shot. There was nothing she could do; her limbs were bound.

Finn looked over at Kozlowski. He could tell that his partner was deciding whether to pull out his gun and take the man down. Finn didn't think the odds were particularly good. Kilbranish sensed the hesitation and pressed the gun harder into Sally's temple; hard enough to force her head painfully to the side. "Do it now!" he yelled. "Or I swear to Jesus I'll kill her right here!"

Kozlowski nodded at Finn, and the two of them moved to the back of the car. "It's gonna be okay," Devon said to his daughter.

Kilbranish sneered. "Shut up. She wouldn't be in this if it wasn't for you."

"You're getting what you want," Devon said. "Just don't hurt her."

"Hurry up!"

Kozlowski got the rope holding the trunk closed untied, and he and Finn lifted the box out of the back, setting it down gently on the rollers. They pushed it around to the front of the car.

"Put it in the van," Kilbranish said. He took the gun away from the girl's head for a moment and pointed it over her shoulder at Finn and Kozlowski. "Keep your hands where I can see them."

Finn and Kozlowski moved the box to the back of the van and hoisted it up, laying it on its side.

"Close the doors," Kilbranish ordered. He was up toward the front of the van, and as they swung the doors closed, Finn couldn't have been any more than ten feet away—almost close enough to touch him. He looked up and he caught Sally's eyes. They didn't look scared. They looked angry and determined.

"Step back!"

Finn and Kozlowski moved back slowly. Devon hadn't moved; he remained by the side of the car, looking at his daughter. His hands were extended from his body, as if he was reaching out to her. "You've got what you wanted, you let her go now!"

Kilbranish was holding Sally around the neck with his arm, pointing the gun at her head again, holding her up as she leaned precariously with her feet bound together. "Not yet," Kilbranish said. "I haven't got everything I want yet. You crossed me."

"I didn't," Devon said. "I had nothing to do with any of this."

Kilbranish shook his head. "You crossed me. If we'd had the paintings, if we'd had the money, the movement would never have died. You killed it. You and yours."

"Please," Devon said. "Please give me my daughter back."

"You want her back?" Kilbranish said. "Then you take her back!" He pushed her hard in the back, not toward Devon, but toward the slurry wall that ran along the edge of the river, falling off on the other side to a deepwater slip at the edge of the pier. With her feet bound, Sally had no way to stop the descent. Her hands shot out in front of her to brace her fall, but it was useless. Her shins hit the wall and her momentum carried her forward, over the edge and into the water.

"No!" Devon screamed. He rushed forward to the spot where Sally had gone in. As he did, Kilbranish was in retreat, headed to the van's open driver's-side door. He turned and let loose a volley of gunshots. Finn hit the ground, looking up just in time to see Devon dive into the water.

Kilbranish fired twice more in Finn's and Kozlowski's direction, but they were wild efforts, intended more to buy time than to actually hit anything. He jumped into the van; the engine was running, and he hit the gas, kicking up rocks and dust as he peeled out.

Kozlowski took a few running steps after the van, drawing his own gun. "Koz!" Finn shouted. The ex-cop turned around. "Forget him, he's not our problem! We've got to get to Sally and Devon!"

Finn ran to the edge of the river, looking down into the black water. He could see nothing. The wind off the shore churned the river, and he couldn't even tell for sure where Sally and Devon had gone in. He looked behind him and saw Kozlowski hesitating. "Koz, I need your help!"

"I can't swim!" Kozlowski yelled back.

"You don't have to; you need to help us out when I find them!"

Kozlowski took one last look at the back of the van as it sped away. Finn could see that the cop in him wanted to give chase. He'd been a police officer for too long for the instinct to die. After a moment, though, he pulled himself away and ran to the river wall where Finn was standing.

"You better be here when I come up!" Finn told him. Then he jumped into the frigid river without waiting for a response.

Chapter Thirty-Nine

It all went so fast, Sally didn't know what was happening. One moment she was looking at her father; the next she was airborne—twisting the way people fall in dreams, waiting for an impact that seemed never to come. Her hands were wrapped in tape, and paddled the air as she turned over and over in the fall. If it truly had been a dream, she would have woken with a start, heart racing, hands shaking as she breathed deeply to calm herself to a point where she might be able to get back to sleep.

She wasn't dreaming, though.

When she hit the water, she experienced a pain greater than she'd known in her life. She went in headfirst, and as her forehead made contact, she thought she'd hit cement. Her neck snapped back, and it felt as if she'd been hit with a baseball bat. Next she felt the water. It spread out from her head down to her shoulders, and then engulfed her. She thought for a moment it was blood, spilling from a gash on her head, burning her with an icy-hot fire as it ran like a waterfall from what she could only assume was a mortal wound. It wasn't until her lungs expanded that she realized what had happened, and then the panic truly set in. Her mouth was gagged, and as she breathed in reflexively the water flooded into her nostrils, through her sinus passages, and down her windpipe into her lungs. The sensation sent her body into spasms, her inability to breathe intensifying her body's desperation. She involuntary gasped for more air. It was a vicious, self-reinforcing cycle.

In that moment she went under she knew she was going to die. She felt her life ripped away with complete certainty, and she experienced a torrent of memories and emotions. They assaulted her, violent and unbearable. She fought against them, thrashing back and forth as they closed in on her. Finally she gave in, and her body went still. She'd fought her entire life, but at that moment the fight was too much for her; at last she let herself drift with the current of the river.

Stone and Sanchez heard the shooting. "We gotta get in there," Stone said. He started the car, but left the lights off.

Sanchez looked over toward the car where Hewitt and the other FBI agent sat. They were closer to the building, closer to the drive that wound around toward the back, in the direction from which the gunshots had come. Sanchez was hoping they would be moving in that direction, so she and Stone could maintain their surveillance—not only of Finn and his crew, but of the FBI as well. Hewitt and the other agent gave no sign of moving, though.

"What are they doing?" Sanchez asked no one in particular.

"They're not doing a goddamned thing," Stone said. "We've got to move."

Sanchez still hesitated.

"C'mon, boss. We've got to get in there."

Finally she nodded. "Okay, let's go."

Stone hit the gas. As he pulled out from the parking space he flipped the switch on the portable flashing light and reached out to put it on the roof of the car. Then he grabbed the wheel with both hands and pushed the gas pedal to the floor. They sped down along the side of the building, accelerating as they approached the corner near the river's edge. As they neared the end of the drive, they passed the two FBI agents, still parked. Sanchez looked over at them, saw their faces illuminated in blue by the flashing light on top of the car, stretched in shock.

She turned her attention back to the assault. They were just about at the corner of the building when she pulled out her gun and readied herself for the confrontation.

———

When Liam's foot hit the gas pedal, he breathed a sigh of relief. It was done: Malley and his people would be busy trying to save the girl, and Liam had the paintings. His mission was complete. He had succeeded.

He was still unsure how he would get the paintings out of the country; he didn't even know where he would spend the night. He couldn't return to the house in Quincy; the girl was probably dead, but he couldn't take that chance—if she survived, the place was compromised. These were problems he could deal with, however. There were enough people in Boston still loyal to the cause. As for getting the paintings out of the country, it had been twenty years; the investigative pressure that had prevented Bulger from getting them out of the country two decades earlier was surely gone. Once his superiors learned that the mission had been successful, they would make sure that the paintings made it to Ireland.

He was thinking through his plans and gathering speed as he came around the corner of the building. He could do nothing when the car appeared in front of him.

He saw the flashing blue light first, and he instinctively hit the brakes with both feet. There was no way to avoid the collision, though; the police car was coming around the corner at full speed. He let out a scream of rage as he saw the front of the onrushing car disappear underneath his bumper. He could feel the van ride up onto the hood as it crumpled in toward the two silhouettes in the front seat. He saw them for only a split second before the air bags deployed in the van, and he was thrown back into the seat. It felt as though his nose was broken, but he ignored it. He was too angry to feel pain.

He flailed at the air bag with his arms, buying enough space to get out of the van. The door was bent, and he had to throw his shoulder against it before it gave way.

His mind was churning, assessing his situation. He had to deal with one issue at a time, and the first priority was making sure the police officers in the car were dead. If they survived, he would lose whatever head start he had, and law enforcement would be on him before he could move the paintings. Once they were dispatched, he could figure out his transportation problem—his van was totaled.

He staggered out of the van, looking back briefly to make sure the box with the paintings was still intact. That it was gave him a renewed sense of hope and urgency.

His head was throbbing as he walked around the front of the van and looked into the front seat of the unmarked police car. There were two of them, and they were shaken, but alive. The woman in the passenger's seat looked a little older than Liam. She was shaking her head, trying to regain her bearings. She looked up at him, confusion on her face. A younger man was in the driver's seat next to her, already struggling to free himself from the air bag. The steering wheel was bent forward and looked as though it had been pushed back toward him, though it didn't appear that it had gone far enough to cause any bodily damage. Instead, it just hindered his efforts to get out of the car.

Liam raised his gun and pointed it at the woman. She looked at him through the cracked window, comprehension coming to her slowly through the fog of the crash. Then she shouted, "No!"

A gunshot rang out, and the woman jumped. She didn't struggle against the pain, though, and now it was Liam who was confused. He looked down at his gun and saw that he hadn't pulled the trigger. The gun was still held aloft, and it seemed to have tripled in weight. He looked at the woman in the car with consternation, and raised his gun slightly with great effort.

A second gunshot rang out, and this time the force of impact spun Liam on his axis. He was knocked back onto the hood of the unmarked police car, facing the rear of the car. He could see a large black man twenty feet from him, pointing a gun at his head. "Don't move!" the man said.

Liam looked down and saw two dark stains on his shirt: one on his left shoulder, one on his chest. Only then did he realize that he'd been shot. "You bastard," he said. His breath was weak, and it came out as a whisper. He struggled to get more air in his lungs. He looked up at the man. He was advancing, his gun still leveled. Liam realized he still had his gun in his hand and he raised it, pointing it at the man with the gun. "You bastard!" He shouted it this time as he went to pull the trigger.

He never felt the third shot. It hit him just above the right eye socket, shattering his ocular ridge and traveling through his brain before blowing out the back of his skull. His body slumped back onto what was left of the hood of the police car, and then slid to the ground, leaving a deep red stain in its wake.

The FBI agent who had shot him moved forward and nudged him with a toe, just to make sure he was dead. There could be no doubt.

His mission was over.

Finn wasn't expecting the cold. He jumped before he had time to think, and when he hit the water all the muscles in his body seemed to contract at once. His head popped out of the water and he took a second to orient himself. He took a deep breath and pushed himself under, swimming down with all his strength.

His eyes were open underneath the water, but they were useless. He could see nothing. So, instead of using his eyes, he used every other part of his body, flailing about with his arms and legs, hoping to knock into Devon or Sally. It seemed like a pointless strategy, but he had nothing else, so he kept it up. After a moment he surfaced again to take another breath, then went under again.

It didn't take long for him to lose hope. He felt tiny and impotent in the water, and the odds of his finding either Sally or Devon seemed astronomical. Still, no matter how long the odds, he owed them every last chance.

As he rose to surface for the second time, his hand grazed something off to his left. He reached out in that direction, but as he did, he lost his wind, and accidentally sucked in a lungful of water. He swam up, breaking the surface, coughing and spitting. Somewhere in the distance he heard gunshots. He took another deep breath and dived in the direction of the object he'd felt.

It took only a few strokes under the water before he felt it again. He reached out and grabbed for it. A shoulder, he thought. He used both hands to inch along the limb until he could grab on to the arm. He pulled the body over, wrapped an arm around the neck, and then kicked with all his strength for the surface.

He knew it was Devon before he broke the surface—the body was too big to be Sally's—and the realization was devastating. It had been several minutes since Sally had gone into the river. The chances of finding her now were gone. She was lost.

Finn paddled over toward the wall at the edge of the river. He could hear Devon spitting up water. "Koz!"

Kozlowski was nowhere to be seen.

"Koz!" he yelled again. "Where the hell are you?"

Kozlowski's head appeared over the edge of the wall. "Here!" he yelled.

Finn worked his way over. "Pull him out," Finn said. "I'm going back for Sally." Finn grabbed on to the wall and pulled Devon over. Kozlowski reached over the wall and took hold of his arm. Devon's eyes were closed, and he was still choking on water. His face looked ghostly white.

"No," he spat out. "Sally!"

"I'm going back for her," Finn said.

"Please!"

"I'll do everything I can to find her," Finn said. "I swear."

Kozlowski started pulling on Devon's arm, lifting him from the water.

"No!" Devon said one more time. His eyes opened, and he looked at Finn. "Get her out first."

Finn looked at him, not comprehending. Then his eyes followed the path down Devon's other arm—the one still dangling in the water—and saw that his hand was grasping a wrist just under the water. A small hand extended from his grasp, and the arm disappeared into the black water.

Finn reached out and grabbed hold just below Devon's hand and pulled. He could feel the body moving fluidly. "Take her!" Finn shouted to Kozlowski.

Kozlowski let go of Devon and reached over the wall, grabbing hold of Sally's arm. He hoisted her up as if she were a toy. Devon slipped under the water briefly when Kozlowski let him go, but Finn grabbed him and held him afloat. A moment later Kozlowski appeared again and reached down to pull Devon over the wall.

Finn was left alone, and he clung to the stone wall that kept the river in its place. He was breathing hard, shivering against the cold. After what seemed like an eternity, Kozlowski grabbed hold of his arm, and he felt himself lifted up out of the water.

Chapter Forty

Finn was last out of the water, and as he flipped over the river wall he looked frantically for Sally. She was lying a few feet away on her back, her face bluish-white and bloated. Duct tape still held her mouth shut. She wasn't breathing.

Devon was lying a few feet away, gasping for breath. "I'm okay," Devon said. "Help her."

Kozlowski was already at work, pulling the tape off her mouth and rolling her on her side. As the tape was released, water spouted from her mouth. Kozlowski put his huge hand on her abdomen and thrust it in and up, releasing another wave.

"Do you know what you're doing?" Finn asked.

"Sort of."

He rolled her on her back and put his head to her chest to listen for a heartbeat. "Nothing." He put his hands together and started a round of CPR, pressing heavily on her sternum several times, then tipping her head back and breathing into her mouth.

"What's happening?" Devon asked, his view blocked. "Is she all right?"

"Not yet," Finn said.

"Oh God, please do something!"

"We're doing everything we can," Finn said. "She was in the water for a long time." He watched as Kozlowski continued the process for several minutes, working back and forth between pumping her chest and breathing into her mouth. At one point Kozlowski looked back at him and shook his head. Finn dug into his pocket for his phone, but the water had ruined it. He looked up and was surprised to see Detectives Sanchez and Stone watching from nearby. Behind them he could see the wreckage of the white van. Hewitt and Porter were looking it over, trying to get the back doors opened. Finn's first instinct was to ask them what had happened—how they got there, and what had happened to Kilbranish—but instead he said simply, "Call an ambulance."

"They're on their way," Sanchez responded. Looking down at Kozlowski she asked, "Will she be all right?"

"I don't know," Finn replied.

As he spoke, he heard Sally cough, and her body convulsed, rolling to the side, spitting up what seemed like gallons of water. Kozlowski sat up and looked at her. She went still again, then spasmed once more, retching as her body tried to expel more of the river. After another moment she took a breath, and the flow of air caused a horrid coughing fit. Finn put his hands on his knees and nearly collapsed.

"Is she okay?" Devon demanded.

Finn looked at Kozlowski, who nodded. Devon looked relieved, but his face remained ashen. He was leaning over on his side, supporting himself on one elbow. He looked strangely frail. "Are you okay?" Finn asked.

"I'm fine. Just a little out of breath is all."

"Me too," Finn said. Devon looked more than winded, though, and Finn moved over toward him. Devon's arm was draped across his chest. As Finn drew near he could see a dark stain spreading over his shirt. "Shit, Devon," he said. "You're shot."

Devon looked down at his shirt; there was no surprise on his face.

"I'll be fine," he said. "I just need to catch my breath." He smiled as he spoke, but his eyelids were fluttering unsteadily.

Finn turned to Stone. "Where the hell is the fucking ambulance!" he shouted.

Hewitt could hear the commotion over by the water. He was tempted to walk over to see what was happening, maybe even offer to help, but couldn't; he needed to keep an eye on Porter. He seemed to have lost his grip on reality. He was tugging at the back doors to the van, yelling, "They're in here! I know it, they're in here!" The door wouldn't open for him, though.

Hewitt put his hand on Porter's shoulder. "It's jammed," he said. "Accident crew'll be here in a minute; they'll get it opened."

Porter spun on him and slapped his hand away. His eyes were wide. "A minute? Don't you understand? The paintings are here! We've found them. Help me get these goddamned doors opened!"

Hewitt hesitated.

"Come on, goddammit!" Porter shouted at him. "Help me!"

Hewitt stepped forward and gave a pull on the doors. They didn't open, but they creaked and groaned angrily; he weighed at least twice as much as Porter. He gave another tug, this time throwing his back into the effort.

The doors swung open, nearly knocking Porter to the ground. He dodged them and scrambled up to look inside, and saw a large wooden box. "They must be inside," Porter said. "Help me get this down."

Hewitt reached forward and the two of them unloaded it. Porter circled the container as if he were trying to seduce it. "We're about to make history," he said. Porter found the brass clasp on the front end of the box and flipped the latch. He paused for a moment, the door still closed, breathing heavily. Then he threw the door open.

"No," he said.

Hewitt couldn't see into the box; Porter was blocking the way. "What?"

"No!" He yelled it this time; screamed it.

"What is it?" Hewitt said.

Porter turned around. Any hint of sanity was gone. He looked desperate and shattered. "It's empty!" he screamed. "It's fucking empty!"

—◦—

Finn could hear the sirens whining in the distance. They sounded too far away. Sally was still unconscious, but she was breathing steadily on her own now. Kozlowski had bundled his jacket into a pillow and put it under her head, and he'd pulled a blanket out of his car and spread it over her.

There seemed to be less they could do for Devon. Finn had started to put pressure on the wound in the chest, but after a moment he realized that the bullet had gone through the body, and Devon was bleeding out of his back as well. The black-red stain underneath him grew endlessly, and Finn could see him slipping away. "Hold on," he said. "You're gonna be okay." Finn couldn't imagine words less convincing, but he said them anyway.

Devon nodded. "I'll be okay." His voice was little more than a whisper. He turned his head so he could see his daughter, lying a few yards away. "She's fine," Finn said. "She's gonna be fine."

Devon gave a weak smile. "She's a piece of fuckin' business," he said. "I wish I coulda done better for her."

"You're doing fine," Finn said. "You can do more when this is over."

"From Walpole, or the fuckin' grave? I'm goin' away any way you look at it. We both know it."

"Shut up," Finn said. "You hired a miracle worker, remember?"

"I did that," Devon said. "Thanks. I got one more favor." He coughed, and a thin sliver of blood ran down his chin from the corner of his mouth.

"Sure," Finn said. "Whatever you need."

"Make sure Sally's taken care of. Make sure they put her someplace good. Maybe look in on her every once in a while. She gets the right chances, I swear to fuckin' God, she could do something with her life. She could be good at something."

"Don't worry about it," Finn said. "I'll make sure she's okay."

"I got your word?"

"You've got my word."

Devon looked back at his daughter. He seemed to relax. "It's not that bad," he said. "It doesn't even hurt." For just a moment, he looked at peace. Then the peace was shattered.

"Where are they!"

Finn looked over and he could see Porter running toward them, Hewitt following closely behind. "Where the hell are they!" Porter yelled again. He seemed dislodged. His eyes were wheeling, darting from Stone and Sanchez to Kozlowski to Finn. Finally his gaze settled on Devon. "You're the guy? You're Malley?"

Devon said nothing.

"Where are they?" Porter screamed. "Where are the goddamned paintings?"

Devon looked confused. "They're in the box," he said.

"They're not! The box is empty!" Porter went to Devon and pushed Finn aside. He reached down and grabbed Devon's shirt. "Where are they? Tell me!"

Finn stood and grabbed Porter's hands, pulling them away. "What the fuck are you doing?" he yelled. "He's been shot." He was ready to throw a punch, but Hewitt stepped in, pushing him back.

"Let it go," Hewitt said to Porter.

"He knows!" Porter screamed. "He knows where they are!" He started toward Devon again, but Hewitt held him back.

"Not now," Hewitt said. "Let it go."

Finn bent down again. Devon's breathing was shallower. "Take it easy, Devon."

"They were there," Devon said. Finn had to lean in to hear him. "I pulled them out less than two weeks ago; I put them back. I didn't move them."

"It's all right," Finn said. "It's gonna be all right."

"I swear to God, Finn," Devon said. He could do little more than mouth the words. He looked over at his daughter again. "I swear."

"Just hold on." The sirens had grown louder, and Finn looked up to see the red lights flashing just beyond the corner of the self-storage building. "They're here," he said. "You're gonna be fine." He looked back down at Devon. His head was turned to the side, and he was still staring at Sally. His eyes, though, had changed. There was no hint of recognition in them; they looked emotionless and cold. "Devon?" Finn said. He took hold of Devon's face and turned it toward him. It was heavy and it flopped over at an awkward angle; there was no tone to the muscles in the neck. "Devon?" Finn said, louder this time. He slapped the man's face; the eyes didn't blink.

Suddenly the area was swarming with people. Gurneys rolled over, and a man in a paramedic's uniform pulled on Finn's shoulder, telling him to move away. He moved back and watched as they poked and prodded and pumped, trying to yank Devon back to life. Finn could tell it was pointless, and their efforts lost urgency after a few moments. They started checking their watches as they worked to get the body on a stretcher, making sure to document the attempted revival process for the hospital records. They wheeled the body away, pretending that all wasn't lost, as though something more might be done at the hospital with better equipment. Finn knew better.

Porter was still screaming about the paintings. Hewitt was trying to calm him down. At one point Finn had the sense that the FBI agents and the BPD detectives were in a heated argument, but he couldn't follow it. Their voices warbled unsteadily and he had trouble making out the words through the fog in his head.

He walked over to where two other paramedics were working on Sally and stood next to Kozlowski. The effort was going better there: they seemed satisfied that she was out of danger, and they were spending their energies making her comfortable as they clipped a pulse monitor to her finger and strapped an oxygen mask to her face to make her breathing easier. As they loaded her into the ambulance, she opened her eyes. It looked as if she was trying to talk.

"It's okay," Finn said. "You're going to be okay." The words felt hollow. He'd said them too many times already that night.

She tried to talk again, and Finn could hear the heart monitor ping faster. "Just relax," said one of the paramedics, but that only sped the ping pace. He looked at Finn. "You know her?"

"Yeah."

"You wanna come in the ambulance? We need to keep her calm right now; she's in shock."

She was looking at him, and her heart rate was settling slightly. "I'm not her family," Finn said.

The paramedic looked back and forth between him and Sally. "Maybe not," he said, "but you seem to be calming her down. We could use your help."

Finn thought about the promise he'd made to Devon. He looked at Kozlowski, who nodded. "Yeah," he said. "If you think it'll help."

The paramedics lifted the gurney into the ambulance, and Finn climbed in behind them. One of them slid up front into the driver's seat; the other stayed in the back, making sure the monitors were working. Finn lowered himself into a seat across from the gurney, up by Sally's head.

"You can hold her hand," the remaining paramedic said.

Finn hesitated, then reached out and took her hand. He could feel her squeezing his hand tightly, hanging on for dear life. He squeezed back, and that seemed to calm her. She tried to talk again, but Finn couldn't make out the words. He thought maybe she was asking about Devon, but there was no way to tell. "You're all right," he said. "Just relax." She looked at him and nodded.

A moment later, she closed her eyes and drifted off to sleep.

Chapter Forty-One

Devon's funeral was at eleven on the Wednesday of the following week. There was no service, just a rectangular hole in the ground on a brown plot of grass off a dead-end street in Dorchester. The casket was suspended above the pit, ready to be lowered hydraulically into the ground. The cherrywood was polished to a shine that reflected the bright sun from above; it was the top of the line. Finn figured there was no reason to skimp; he used the cash that Devon had stashed in his apartment to pay for the plot, the service, the short obituary in the paper, and the coffin. The rest he put into a fund for Sally. He couldn't bring himself to take the fees the firm had been promised. It didn't seem right; he'd failed Devon, after all.

It was a Catholic cemetery, so a priest was present, though when he asked Finn what he wanted him to say at the burial Finn told him nothing. It didn't seem there was much to say. Two grave-diggers stood nearby, ready to fill in the hole once the casket was lowered. Other than that, it was just the four of them: Finn, Kozlowski, Lissa, and Sally. No one else showed up. The priest went through the ceremony quickly and quietly enough that Finn could hardly hear the words. That, too, was fitting, he thought.

Sally was quiet throughout the service; she'd said little since she'd been released from the hospital a few days before. She stood there, staring at the casket as if she was trying to unravel a riddle. Finn understood: the fact that there would never be answers wouldn't keep her from asking the questions.

When the service was over, a switch was flipped, and the casket descended into the ground. The four of them stayed until the process was over, but turned before the first shovelfuls of dirt were thrown on top. They didn't need to see that.

They walked away silently, Kozlowski and Lissa holding hands, their heads down. Finn had his hands in his pockets, walking close to Sally. As they came up the hill, back toward the car parked in the narrow lane that wound around through the cemetery, Finn saw a figure standing under a tree, watching the grave-diggers work from a distance. Sally saw it, too. She stopped. "It's her," she said.

"Who?" Finn asked.

"My mother."

Finn squinted into the sun, trying to make out something more than the silhouette. "You sure?"

"Yeah, I'm sure."

"What do you want to do?"

"I don't know." Sally stood there for a long moment, just staring at the woman under the tree. "I should go over, I guess," she said at last.

"If you want to."

"Will you come with?"

"Yeah." Finn called over to Kozlowski and Lissa, "We'll catch up."

He and Sally climbed the short hill toward the tree where the woman stood. As they approached, Finn could see she did not look well. Her hair was short and disheveled, and she wore loose-fitting clothes over emaciated limbs. She must have been in her late thirties, but she looked much older. She looked at Sally as they approached.

"Sally!" she called. Her voice was shrill with forced surprise, as though a father's funeral were the last place she would have expected

342

to find a grieving daughter. She opened her arms as if she was expecting a big hug. Sally stayed next to Finn.

"What are you doing here?"

"I read about your father in the paper," she said. "I'm sorry. I thought you were better off with him than me. It's over now, though; you can come home with me." She was smiling, but tears were streaming down her face, and it had been long enough since she had bathed that they made tracks on her cheeks. Her eyes were glassy, and it seemed she was having trouble focusing.

"Where?" Sally asked.

The woman waved her arm. "Oh, I got a place, don't worry."

"Where?"

"I'm gonna get a new one." She was no longer looking at her daughter. "We'll be happy now."

It took a long time for Sally to answer. "I think I'm gonna figure something else out," she said at last.

"You sure?" The woman's voice sounded sad. Relieved, too, though.

"Yeah, I'm sure. I'll be fine. Don't worry."

"Okay, then," the woman said. "You take good care of yourself, and I'll come visit, okay?"

"How will you know where to find me?" Sally asked.

The woman waved her hand again. "Don't be silly, a mother always knows."

They stood there in silence for another moment, with Sally looking at her mother and her mother avoiding her daughter's eyes. Finn looked at the ground. Finally Sally said, "Okay, Mom, I gotta go." She turned and walked away before her mother could say anything more.

Finn caught up to her and walked beside her. "You okay?"

"Fine." She was walking quickly, back to Lissa and Kozlowski, who were standing by the side of the car, looking back at them.

"You sure?"

343

"Fuck her," Sally said. "I'm better off alone."

Finn put a hand on her shoulder as he walked. "You're not gonna be alone," he said. He wasn't looking at her as he said it. As they walked, he saw her arm come up and wipe something away from her eye.

———

Kozlowski bought the drinks at the pub back in Charlestown: a scotch for himself, a beer for Finn, and a Coke for Sally. Lissa ordered a glass of merlot, which brought a look of surprise from Finn.

"Doc said a glass of wine every once in a while wouldn't hurt the baby," she said. "Feels like a day when a glass of wine wouldn't hurt anybody."

"This doctor any good?"

"Yeah, he is. You got a problem?"

Finn shook his head. "No."

"My mom smoked crack when she was pregnant with me," Sally said. Everyone at the table looked at her, unsure what to say. "Of course, it's not like I'm a poster child for reproduction." She stood up. "Where's the bathroom?"

"Back around down the hall to the left," Lissa said.

Once she was gone, Kozlowski asked, "We gonna talk about it?"

"Not today," Finn replied.

"We gotta talk about it at some point," Kozlowski said. "We need to find a place for her to live."

"I'm not putting her in the system," Finn said. "Not right now. She can stay with me for a little while."

"She's not a puppy," Kozlowski said. "You can't just keep her for a little while and then take her back to the pound when she shits on the rugs."

"That's not what I'm doing."

"What are you doing?"

"I'm trying to help."

"Trying to help?" Kozlowski looked at Lissa. "You believe this?"

She looked down at her belly. "Yeah, I do. Let's leave it for another day."

"You too?" Kozlowski shook his head.

"Another day," she repeated.

"Fine," Kozlowski said. "What about the other thing that no one wants to talk about? We gonna keep ignoring that, as well?"

"Works for me," Lissa said. "Devon's dead. Kilbranish is dead. Half of Bulger's old crew is dead. Doesn't seem like anything good's gonna come from talking about it."

"Something good could come from it for Sally," Kozlowski said. "Reward's five million. We find the paintings, and that's a lot of good."

"You're not gonna find the paintings."

"How do you know? Devon had them two weeks ago. Maybe he moved them."

"I don't see how Devon could have moved them," Finn said. "He was with us from the minute he got out of jail."

"He could have moved them before he went in," Kozlowski said. "Then he led us to the self-storage knowing they weren't there."

"But why?" Finn asked.

"Because they were worth half a billion dollars," Kozlowski said. "Maybe he still wanted them for himself. Maybe he still wanted them for the girl."

Finn shook his head. "He knew what was at stake, and he cared too much about his daughter to take that risk. For Christ's sake, he went into that river after her with a bullet in him. Besides, he knew he was dying. If he'd moved them he would've told me where when he had the chance."

"What other possibilities are there?"

"We know what other possibilities there are. Devon said Bulger told him there was one other person who knew where the paintings were."

"Porter?" Kozlowski offered.

"No," Finn said. "Did you see him with Devon down at the river? He was having a breakdown when he realized the paintings weren't there, and I don't think he's a good enough actor to pull off that kind of performance if he was the one who moved them himself. I think he's genuinely obsessed with finding the goddamned things."

"Who, then?"

"Hewitt."

"No," Kozlowski said. "I know him; he's not behind this."

"Come on, Koz," Finn said. "I know you're friends with the guy, but he was working on the organized crime task force back in the eighties and nineties. He would have had plenty of opportunity to get to know Bulger. He had contacts that he could have used to orchestrate the whole thing."

"I don't buy it." Kozlowski wasn't budging. "There were plenty of others who would have had just as much motive, just as much opportunity."

"How many of those others were involved in this investigation? How many of them were there when Devon was killed? How many of them shot Kilbranish?"

"Fuck you, you're wrong."

"How can you say that?"

"Enough!" Lissa interjected. Her voice was loud enough that the bartender turned and looked at them. She lowered the volume. "Who cares?" she demanded. "These are just paintings we're talking about. Who the fuck cares where they are now?"

"They're not just paintings," Finn objected.

"Yes, they are," she said. "They're just paintings. They're expensive paintings. They're nice paintings. But they're just fucking paintings. And they're paintings that have gotten people killed. Whoever has them now will kill whoever they have to to keep them, and I'm not letting either of you be next on the list. It isn't our problem anymore. Do you two understand me?"

The two men looked at the table, not answering.

"I'm serious about this," she said. "I want both of you to just fucking drop it. We have a law firm to run, we have a little girl to deal with, and we have a baby on the way. This ends now."

Kozlowski looked at her and took her hand. "Okay," he said. "I'll drop it."

She looked at Finn. "You?"

He didn't look up at her, but he nodded. "Fine," he said. "I'll leave it alone."

"Do I have your word?"

"Yeah," he said. "You have my word."

Chapter Forty-Two

Lissa and Kozlowski got married a month later. The ceremony, such as it was, took place in City Hall, that great monument to Brutalism in the center of nine acres of cold brick and cement. Finn wondered whether Lissa and Koz had considered the symbolism. Probably not. Their minds weren't drawn to such mischief in the way his was.

It was just the four of them. Finn served as best man and Sally as maid of honor. The officiant, a young woman who worked as an assistant clerk for the city, was a justice of the peace. She held a laminated card in front of her eyes and chopped through sterile questions with all the emotion of a telephone operator. As she ticked through the ceremony intended to bind the lives of the people before her, Finn couldn't help hearing her voice as he had thousands of times before: "For English, press 'one' now; *para espanol, apreiete 'dos' ahora.*"

That was okay with Finn. In reality the Commonwealth had no power to tie Lissa and Koz together. That decision was theirs alone. Whether the union was blessed or consecrated or legally binding was bunting and little more. If they were solid together, the rest would take care of itself. If not, no piece of paper—not even one signed by an assistant clerk of the City of Boston—would do them any good.

When the questions had been read and the answers given, the woman said, "That's it. If you got fifty dollars, you're married."

Kozlowski and Lissa looked at each other. Finn couldn't tell whether they seemed different. "Do I kiss the bride?" Kozlowski asked.

The assistant clerk shrugged. "I guess. Long as you got the fifty dollars."

Finn dug into his pocket and pulled out three twenties and handed them to her. "I got it," he said. "You can keep the rest."

The woman took the money and stamped two forms in triplicate. "You want the receipt?" she asked Finn.

He shook his head.

"Now?" Kozlowski asked.

"Yeah, now," the woman replied.

Finn watched as Kozlowski and Lissa leaned into each other. They seemed awkward about the kiss, even after living together for nearly a year. Finn wondered whether everything had changed, and worried briefly that they might not make it. As soon as their lips touched, though, he could see both of them relax and they melded into each other, all tension gone.

The assistant clerk left before the kiss was over. "Congratulations," Finn said.

"Thanks," Lissa replied. They took the escalator up from the basement. The building's interior made its facade look cozy. When they got to the main floor Lissa said, "Shit." Looking at Sally, she corrected herself. "Shoot. I left the marriage license on the counter." She looked at Finn. "Come back with me?"

"Sure," Finn said. He looked at Sally. "I'll be back."

"I'll be here."

On the escalator down, Lissa said, "She seems to be doing okay."

Finn nodded. "I think she is. She's got her good days and her bad days. The good outweigh the bad at this point."

"I'm glad," Lissa said. "How are you doing?"

Kozlowski stood in City Hall's cavernous lobby, waiting for Finn to return with his wife. *My wife*, he thought. The reality staggered him. He'd given up on the notion of marriage years ago. He'd figured he was past the point where anyone could fall in love for the first time. He'd been wrong.

The girl was there with him, standing a few feet away, looking at him. He tried to avoid her gaze, but found it difficult. He couldn't figure out why she was staring. It took a minute before he realized he was smiling. "What?" he demanded.

"Nothing," she said. "I didn't know you smiled."

"I don't."

"Me neither. You should do it more. The scar doesn't look so bad."

He grunted. After a moment, he said, "So, how are you doing?"

"Fine."

"Finn treating you okay? Making sure you get enough to eat?"

"He's okay," she said. "He doesn't seem like a perv."

"High praise."

"I don't mean it that way. I mean it's good. It's just weird."

"What is?" he asked.

She thought about it. "I never had a normal life before. I'm not used to it."

He looked her up and down. She was wearing a dress. Her feet were still covered in her heavy black boots, but it was the first time he'd seen her in anything other than sweats. "You're gonna be okay," he said.

"You think?"

He nodded. "I can usually tell. You keep the right people around you, you'll do fine."

She seemed to accept it. "You're gonna be okay, too," she said.

"You think?"

She nodded. "Just put the toilet seat down. Devon never caught on; I almost fell in a couple times. He said he was too old to change. Don't be like that. Don't be too old to change. You leave the seat up, you'll lose her."

"Thanks, I'll keep that in mind."

She looked toward the escalator, and Kozlowski had the impression she was looking over to see whether Finn was coming back. He'd disagreed with Finn about taking her in while they figured out what to do. Now, though, he thought it had been good for her.

———◦———

"I'm fine," Finn said. Looking at Lissa, he could tell she was skeptical. "I'm serious." No decisions had been made regarding Sally, but she was still staying with Finn. They both knew that the time was approaching when they would have to figure out something permanent.

She frowned. "It can't go on like this, boss. You know that, right?"

"I know. Did I mention that you look great?" She did, too. As promised, she hadn't worn white. She was a realist, not a romantic.

"That's nice of you. I feel like shit."

"Morning sickness ends after the first trimester, right?" he asked. "You must be there almost."

"Almost. They say it's different for everyone, though. And you're changing the subject."

"I am."

"You can't do it," she said. "Not anymore. A kid isn't like a girlfriend. You can't string them along forever while you make up your mind. Kids can't defend themselves the way we can."

"Have you met Sally?"

"Oh, please, Finn. Can you even see the way she looks at you? You're like her hero. She looks at you like a lucky kid looks at their father. She looks at you like maybe she's gonna have someone in her life who's gonna look after her. Take care of her. The way her parents should have. You need to recognize that. You need to see it and deal with it. Because if you let it go any further—if you let her get comfortable—and then you cut her loose . . . God help you."

"I know," Finn said. "I'm still trying to figure it out. I thought having her around would be a pain in the ass. I thought I'd hate it. Truth is, I don't."

"Great. Just realize what you'd be getting yourself into. Once you're really in, there's no going back."

Finn nodded. "I'll get it figured out."

"Soon," Lissa said. She looked at him for another moment as they headed back to Kozlowski and Sally. "Is there anything else bothering you?" she asked.

"No," he said. "What else could be bothering me?" He wondered whether she would ask about the paintings. He wasn't sure what he would say. She didn't ask, though; she simply stepped up on tiptoe, pulled down on his shoulders, and kissed him on the forehead. He was grateful; he wouldn't have enjoyed lying to her.

Chapter Forty-Three

He'd kept his word to her for a couple of weeks: he'd given up on the investigation into the stolen artwork. He tried to keep the promise longer, but the questions swirled in his mind. What he knew and what he suspected danced together seductively until he was obsessed. And so, on his own, at night, he would surf the Internet for every scrap of additional information he could get—about the Gardner robbery and anyone who might have had anything to do with it. When that wasn't enough, he tapped some of the other private investigators he sometimes used for jobs not worth Kozlowski's time. He kept his obsession hidden from Lissa and Kozlowski.

On the Friday afternoon before the Fourth of July, a week after Lissa and Kozlowski got married, he pulled his notes together and went over them one final time. There was no way for him to avoid it anymore. With a heavy sigh, he placed the call. Then he walked outside, climbed into his car, and drove to the museum.

As he walked through the front door, he half expected alarms to go off and security guards to rush at him accusingly, as if he were the reason the paintings had been lost again. It didn't happen, of course. The woman at the front desk didn't even notice him as she took the twelve-dollar admission fee. There was a security guard walking by, and he glanced at Finn, nodded politely, and moved on.

Finn climbed the staircase slowly. The place didn't feel the same as it had when he and Kozlowski first went there. The theft had been theoretical to him then. A myth. The events of twenty years earlier hadn't affected his life yet. Now the robbery felt personal to him; it seemed an affront in the most intimate sense.

He turned the corner at the top of the stairs and headed down the hallway to the Dutch Room. There was no one there; the place was dead. The paintings on the wall seemed to mourn the empty frames that hung alongside them.

He walked over and stood in front of the spot where Vermeer's *The Concert* had once hung. He'd never seen it for himself; he'd only seen photographs, but he'd watched documentaries where people wept in remembrance of its beauty. He wondered whether he would have felt the same way, or whether he would have passed by it without notice; perhaps even uttered some crass joke at the absurdity of the homage others paid it.

He stood there for a long while, losing all sense of time.

"It is difficult to let go, isn't it?"

He hadn't heard anyone enter the room, but recognized the voice. "It is," he said.

"I understand. Perhaps better than anyone."

Finn turned around. Sam Bass was sitting in the same chair where Finn and Kozlowski had first seen him, sleeping like the dead. He looked worse now. He'd lost more weight, and the sides of his tattered jacket hung from his shoulders like curtains from a rod. His skin was graying, and his eyes had receded even further into their sockets. "I read about you in the papers," he said. "I'm sorry this didn't turn out better."

"Me too," Finn said.

"I'd give almost anything to have the paintings back here, where they belong. Where people could enjoy them, marvel at them."

"A little girl lost her father. She'd give anything to have him back, too."

Bass nodded. "I read about her. She was the one you were trying to save, when you came here? I'm very sorry for her."

"Her name is Sally," Finn said. "She's remarkable."

"I'm sure she is." The old man scratched at the thick layer of patchy gray stubble covering his chin. "Did you see them? The paintings? The papers said that they had disappeared again, but they said they were there in Charlestown all along. Did you see them before they vanished?"

Finn shook his head.

"Pity. You would have liked them. I can see you would have liked them." He sighed. "I don't suppose the police learned anything that might lead to their recovery."

"Not really. Not that anyone is willing to discuss. I have my own theories."

"Of course you do," Bass said. "We all have our own theories."

"If you wouldn't mind, I'd like to discuss mine with you," Finn said. The man hesitated. Finn looked at his watch and saw that it was approaching five o'clock. "The museum closes soon. We could go someplace to sit and talk. I'll buy you a drink."

The old man studied Finn's face. He nodded. "Yes," he said. "I think I'd like that."

They walked north, along the Fenway, and found a café a few blocks away on Brookline Street. The weather was fine, and they took a table outside. The waiter brought them a plate of bread and glasses of water. "Would you like a cocktail?" he asked.

"I'll have a beer," Finn said. "Anything on tap would be fine." He looked at Bass. "You?"

"I have some health issues," he said. "My doctor says I can no longer drink."

"I'm sorry," Finn said.

Bass looked up at the young waiter. "I'll have a glass of chardonnay if you have one." As the waiter left, Bass closed his eyes and turned his face toward the sun. He looked even closer to death outside than he had in the darkened gallery of the museum, and Finn wondered how long it had been since the man had been out in the daylight. "Are you enjoying your youth, Mr. Finn?" he asked, his eyes still closed.

"I have my days."

"Well, if I could offer you one piece of paltry advice, it would be to enjoy your youth. It passes quickly. Whatever it is you love, dedicate yourself to that. If you can do that faithfully, that is the key to happiness."

Finn thought about it for a moment. "I'm still trying to figure out what I love."

Bass laughed as though Finn had told one of the funniest jokes he'd ever heard. When his laughter died down, he said, "Give it some thought. I'm sure it will come to you." He opened his eyes and leaned forward. "You said you wanted to discuss your theories about the paintings?"

"I did," Finn said. "I . . ." The waiter brought their drinks. Finn sat back and let him put them down. Once he'd walked away, Finn began again, his voice lowered. "I wanted to ask you some questions about Paul Baxter."

"Our illustrious director," Bass said. He picked up his wine and held it under his nose, swirling it around as he inhaled deeply. "I can't drink it anymore," he said, "but I still enjoy the aroma of a decent chardonnay. What would you like to know about Baxter?"

"He started at the museum a month or so before the robbery?"

"That's right."

"What were his responsibilities at the time?"

Bass folded his hands in his lap. "He's the director. He was in charge of the museum," he said. "He had responsibility for the entire operation."

"Yes, I know, but what does that encompass, exactly?"

Bass thought for a moment. "That encompasses everything. He had responsibility for the preservation of the place. He was in charge of maintaining the building, making sure the place ran smoothly, making sure everything was taken care of."

"How about maintaining the art itself?"

"Of course," Bass said. "He had people helping him, obviously, and there is a curator, but ultimately he was responsible for the preservation of all of the pieces in the museum."

"And security?"

Bass nodded. "Security, too. After the theft, he oversaw a total overhaul of the security procedures and systems. He had new alarms installed and implemented new protocols for the security guards. In every way, he made sure that what happened that night could never happen again."

"What about the finances? Was he in charge of those, as well?"

Bass shrugged. "The museum has a director of finances, but that person reports to the director. The financial health and sustenance of the place was ultimately Baxter's responsibility."

"That's what I was guessing," Finn said as Bass lifted his wine to his nose again.

"These are all pointed questions, Mr. Finn. Do you mind if I ask what they are all about? You don't really think that Paul Baxter had anything to do with the robbery, do you?"

Finn shrugged. "It's possible. The way I figure it, there are only a few people who could possibly have been involved—who could have helped to plan the robbery, and who could have also known where the paintings were hidden. Baxter's one of the people at the top of that list."

"Do you mind if I ask who the others are?"

Finn shook his head. "Not at all." He took a long drink from his beer. "Two of them were associates of Whitey Bulger's. Mob guys. Vinny Murphy and Eddie Ballick. They were definitely involved in the robbery—they brought in Devon Malley to do the job. They partnered him up with a man named Liam Kilbranish."

"The newspapers talked about the two of them," Bass said. "They were killed, right?"

"That's right," Finn said. "Kilbranish was IRA. A hard-core case, and he came back to find the paintings. Speculation is that he wanted to start the troubles back up, but he needed money to do it. According to Devon, after the robbery, Bulger kept the paintings. He was supposed to get them to the IRA somehow, but he took off before that happened. Devon said Bulger told him that there were only three people who knew where the paintings were hidden. Bulger, Devon, and one other. The question is: who was the third? Because both Murphy and Ballick were in on the job from the start, it's possible it could have been one of them."

"But you don't think so," Bass observed.

"No, I don't," Finn said. "It's pretty clear in the end that Bulger didn't trust anyone in his organization. These two guys were fairly high up, and they had lots of other guys loyal to them. I don't think Bulger would have risked giving them the chance to cross him. More importantly, Kilbranish killed them himself—tortured them—and if they'd known where the paintings were, he probably would have gotten it out of them."

"You think?"

"He would have been very persuasive."

"Who else, then?" Bass asked.

"There are two FBI agents who could possibly have been involved.

They were both here in Boston at the time of the robbery, and they were both working on different aspects of the investigations into the Boston mob. So they could have developed the ties necessary. One of them, though, clearly didn't know where the paintings were. I saw him the night everything went down, and he was out of his mind."

"How about the other one?"

Finn sat back in his chair and took another swallow from his beer. "Rob Hewitt. For a few weeks after Devon was killed, I thought he was probably involved. I was sure he'd moved the paintings. But the more I thought about it, the less sense it made."

"How so?"

"The way Devon described the robbery, it's pretty clear that they had some help from someone who was familiar with just about every aspect of the museum. They had a complete understanding of the security systems; they knew how many guards would be on duty; they were given detailed maps of the entire place. Hewitt was in the FBI, so it's possible that he could have gotten a lot of this information just by snooping. But there are other things that don't fit. For example, Bulger also gave Devon and Kilbranish a list of which paintings to steal. I don't think Hewitt would have known enough about the art in the museum to give them that kind of information. Plus, whoever helped Bulger hide the paintings knew a lot about how to preserve the art. When they were stolen, the paintings were ripped out of their frames and rolled up; but when Devon saw them again, they had been professionally stretched and remounted. And the box they were kept in was specially designed to keep the paintings from suffering any more damage. Hewitt didn't have that kind of expertise. I suppose it's possible he could have learned about those sorts of things, but it seems unlikely."

"Which brings you back to Baxter."

Finn nodded. "It does. He would have had all the necessary knowledge to help pull off the robbery, plus he would have been able to help Bulger take care of the paintings afterward."

"Have you shared your theory with the police?" Bass asked.

"Not yet," Finn said, shaking his head. "I may, if I get more comfortable with my theory, but right now it's all speculation, all circumstantial. Besides, even with Baxter there are things that don't quite fit."

"Like what?"

"Like how would he have gotten hooked up with Bulger in the first place? I suppose Whitey could have sought him out and put a gun to his head, but that would have been awfully risky, and Bulger wasn't known for taking chances like that. There's also the insurance issue."

"The insurance issue?"

Finn nodded. "Bulger arranged all of this with the IRA, which had a history of art theft. That's one of the ways they funded their part in the troubles. But the IRA had a fairly standard method of operation. They would steal paintings and then ransom them back to the owners for the insurance money. Only in this case, the Gardner Museum didn't have any insurance. That's why they had such a hard time disposing of them. From what you're telling me, Baxter would have known there was no insurance, and that knowledge probably would have put an end to the entire plan before it started."

"Maybe," Bass said. "But you never know; they might have taken their chances and gone ahead with it anyway."

"It's possible," Finn admitted. "As I said, it's all really just speculation."

"As far as it goes, though, it still seems that Baxter is the most logical suspect."

"One of them," Finn said. "There's one other."

"Who?"

Finn looked at his beer. It was almost finished, and he took the last sip. "You." He raised his hand to get the waiter's attention to order another beer.

"Me?"

The waiter came over. "I'll have another," Finn said. He looked at Bass's glass and noted it was still full. "You all set?"

Bass looked bewildered. "Yes, thank you."

The waiter sauntered away toward the bar. "Yes, you," Finn said. "In a lot of ways, you fit better than anyone else. You'd been working there for, what, forty years when the robbery took place? You would have known as much about the security system as anybody. You also would have known which paintings were most valuable. You told us yourself that you had worked at nearly every job at the place, and had even worked for a while helping to preserve the paintings, so you could easily have designed the box they were kept in. One of the few things that you probably wouldn't have known was that the museum had no insurance. I'd be surprised if you ever worked in the business end of the operation. Am I right?"

Bass stared at Finn, his lower jaw dangling. "I never worked in the business office," he said.

"I figured," Finn said. "Plus, I did some checking. You told us you grew up poor. You stayed poor even after you started working at the museum. Poor enough to qualify for a little apartment in the Old Harbor projects in Southie, which is where you've lived for almost fifty years. Less than six blocks from where Whitey Bulger grew up. You must have tried hard to lose the accent, but a little bit of it comes through every now and then."

The waiter arrived and set Finn's drink down on the table. "Anything else?" he asked.

"No, we're good, thanks," Finn responded. He took a sip of the beer. "There's really only one thing that doesn't fit," Finn said after a moment.

"Which is?"

"Motive. I still can't figure it out. If you were involved, you clearly didn't make any money off the robbery, and that knocks out the motive that usually drives people in situations like this—greed. From what I can tell, the museum has treated you pretty well. Maybe not perfectly, but I've seen the way you talk about the place; it's pretty clear that there's no revenge at issue here. So, I can't figure out what your angle would have been." He took another drink.

"I'm not sure how you expect me to respond to all this," Bass said.

"I expect you to tell me the truth," Finn said.

"The truth is I don't know what you're talking about."

"I think you do. When we first talked to you in the museum, you described the robbery as a 'betrayal.' It seemed like an odd choice of words to me at the time, and it stuck. You can only betray something you love; something you have some loyalty to. It seemed like you knew what you were talking about. Like it was personal."

A light shade of crimson shone through the gray of Bass's face. He stood up. "I don't appreciate your insinuation, Mr. Finn."

"Sit down."

"Why would I?"

"Because I'm meeting the police at the museum in twenty minutes, and I still haven't decided whether I'm going to tell them my theory about you."

Bass stood by the side of the table, tottering slightly, hanging over Finn like some half-dead apparition. "You wouldn't. You don't have any proof."

"Proof?" Finn laughed. "Who cares about proof? I've got a viable theory about the greatest art theft in history. I'm guessing it's a theory that hasn't been checked out very carefully before. The cops would have looked at you, sure." Finn looked up at Bass and held his fingers up in a square, as though examining him through a camera. "But I'm guessing they passed by you pretty quickly and got on to people they thought were more likely suspects. Now they could take their time. Check you out thoroughly. Go through your records, search your apartment, check if you've rented any self-storage recently. Even if I'm wrong, it would be a serious hassle. I'm guessing someone your age might not even be able to survive it. Stress is a real killer, they say."

"Why would you do this?"

"Because my client is dead. A girl lost her father. I want to know why." He pointed to the chair beside him. "Now sit."

Bass sunk into the seat. He closed his eyes and turned toward the sun again. "What would you do?" he asked. "If I said you were right, would you tell the police?"

"Depends," Finn said.

"On what?"

"On whether you give me a good enough reason not to."

Bass sat very still for a long time. "I'm dying," he said at last.

"We're all dying," Finn replied.

"The doctors say a year at the outside."

"I'm sorry. But that's not a reason."

Bass opened his eyes and picked up his glass. He didn't even bother to sniff the wine this time; he took a long drink. "I love the museum," he said. "I love what it stands for. Can you imagine, building something that beautiful? One person. One vision. And then leaving all that beauty to the world forever? It is, perhaps, one of the greatest accomplishments I can think of." He was looking off at some distant point, and his eyes had lost their focus. Then he looked sharply at Finn. "That place saved my life," he said. "It fed me. It clothed me. It took me in. But more than that, it gave me a reason to live. In some ways, it gave me life itself. That sounds delusional to you, I'm sure."

Finn shook his head. "No," he said. "It doesn't. But it doesn't explain why you would steal from a place like that."

"To save it."

"I don't understand."

"You see, Mr. Finn, I didn't have much of a choice," Bass said. "Jimmy Bulger could be—how did you put it before?—very persuasive."

"He threatened to kill you?" Finn guessed.

"No, no, he knew me too well for that. He knew that I would never hurt the museum to save myself."

"What then?"

"He threatened to take it all away from me. To take it away from the world." Finn stared blankly back at the old man as he continued. "I lived in that neighborhood for a long time. I knew Bulger's mother, and I was nice to her. He never bothered me until that one time, when he came to me and he told me that a friend of his wanted to rob the museum. I was outraged. I told him I would call the police, right then and there, and I would have, too. He knew it. So he used the only thing I ever loved against me. He told me that if I didn't help them, they would burn the museum to the ground. It wasn't an idle threat, either. I knew he had the people who could do it. That was always the greatest fear at the museum—a fire. Even if it gets put out, the damage to the building, and the destruction of the artwork from the fire and smoke and water, would be catastrophic. He told me all this; told me what they would do. And then he grabbed me by the shoulders and said, 'Sam, only you can save the museum.'" Bass's hands shook at the memory, and he took another sip of his wine. "It was a rationalization, I know, but I accepted it. We struck a deal; it would be a one-time thing, and then they would leave the museum alone forever."

"You chose the paintings," Finn said.

"I did. They wanted the most valuable, and only a few. I gave them almost all that they wanted."

"Except *The Rape of Europa*, by Titian."

"That's true. I didn't give them the Titian. Bulger was angry when he read the papers the next day and learned that I hadn't told them to take the most valuable painting in the place, but I didn't care. There are stories of how proud Mrs. Jack was when she acquired that painting. She had parties just to celebrate, and she called her museum complete with it. The depths of my betrayal wouldn't go so far as to sacrifice that painting. In the end, Bulger got over it. I think he ultimately thought it was a good thing, because the choice of artwork confused investigators—particularly with the knickknacks that Devon Malley apparently decided to pilfer while he was there."

"What did you get out of it?" Finn asked.

"Nothing," Bass replied. "I wouldn't have taken any money even if they'd offered—and they did. All I got out of it was a promise that Bulger would leave the museum alone after that, and that he would put the word out to other thieves that the museum was under his protection, so that no one else would ever attempt a robbery again. Other than that, I thought it was ended for me."

"But it wasn't," Finn said. "Not quite."

"No, not quite. Bulger came to me some time later and told me that he hadn't been able to get rid of the paintings. He said he needed to hide them, and he wanted my help to make sure it was done in a way so that they wouldn't lose their value."

"And you helped him."

"Of course," Bass said, his eyes wide. "The only thing worse than the paintings being stolen would have been for them to be destroyed. As long as they were protected, there was always a chance that they would find their way home. So I stretched the canvases for him, and remounted them. Then I helped him build the storage box and I made sure that it would keep the paintings safe in the self-storage room."

"What happened next?"

"Nothing. Not for fifteen years. I managed to put the whole thing behind me; managed to tell myself that I had done the right thing to protect my museum; managed to tell myself that Mrs. Jack would appreciate what I'd done for her, even. Only the empty frames on the walls served as a reminder, but I managed, even, to live with them. Then two months ago I heard that the paintings were being offered for sale. There have been rumors before, but not like this. Baxter made clear that this seemed to be genuine. When I had been diagnosed six months before, I wrote out a note that told where the paintings were so they would be found after I died. I thought that I might fix this all, in the end. With the offer to sell the paintings, though, all that was slipping away, and it looked like they would be lost again. I couldn't let that happen."

"So you took them?"

Bass nodded. "I took them. I watched the self-storage for two nights. Once I was convinced it could be done, I used the key Bulger had left with me so I could get in and check on the paintings to make sure they were being preserved, and I took them. It took me almost an entire night, and the exertion nearly killed me, but I did it."

"And more people died."

Bass looked down at his wine, and his face grew sad. "Rest assured, Mr. Finn, I will be judged by higher powers than you shortly, and I don't believe I will be judged well."

Finn sat there for another few moments, with neither of them talking. He raised his hand to the waiter and pantomimed a signature in the air to indicate that they were ready for the check. "One last question," Finn said. "Why not return the paintings now? You'd be a hero."

Bass shook his head. "I'd be a Judas. I am an old man, with little life left in me. The only solace I have is Mrs. Jack's museum. It is the only thing in this world that ever truly gave me joy. If it was revealed that I had participated in the robbery—that I had kept quiet all these years . . . ? No, Mr. Finn, I would certainly not be a hero, and I have little doubt that I would no longer be welcome in the museum. In my home. It's selfish of me, I know, but I still believe I had the best intentions, and I am not yet willing to give up the one thing that I love. Given how little time I have, it will be enough that the paintings are returned upon my death, don't you think?"

"That's a question for your own conscience," Finn said.

"It is." Bass leaned forward. "The question for your conscience, Mr. Finn, is what will you tell the police?"

Finn took a twenty out of his wallet and put it down on the table to cover the drinks. "Do you have a will?" Finn asked.

Bass shook his head. "I have nothing of value."

"Come by my office tomorrow," Finn said. "I'll have a will ready for you to sign."

"You're thinking about the paintings? The reward, maybe?" Finn nodded, and Bass nodded back. "Very well. I suppose you're entitled to the reward for ensuring the paintings find their way back to the museum."

"I'm not entitled to anything, and I wouldn't take it if I was. You're going to leave the paintings to the girl, so she can return them. She lost her father. If anyone is going to get a reward, it's going to be her."

Bass seemed to consider this. "Do you think it would work? I was involved in the robbery. If I leave them to her, can she still collect the reward?"

"I don't know, but if there's a way I'll find it."

"Five million dollars for a young girl." Bass let out a low whistle. "A lot of money."

"It is," Finn conceded. "I don't even know whether she'll want it. Those paintings killed her father. She may want no part of the reward. But the decision's gonna be hers if I've got anything to say about it."

Bass nodded. "That seems reasonable to me," he said. "What time do you want me at your office?"

Finn stood up. "Early. Seven. Before anyone else is in the office. I don't want anyone else to know about this."

"I will be at your office at seven," Bass said. "What will you tell the police?"

"Nothing. I'm your lawyer now. Anything you tell me is protected by the attorney-client privilege. Not only am I not obligated to tell the police anything, I could be disbarred if I did."

"Thank you, Mr. Finn," Bass said.

"Don't thank me. I'm doing this for Sally. It's what her father wanted and he was my client. I'm just doing what he wanted me to. If it wasn't for that, I'd be telling the police everything." He turned and walked away without looking back.

Finn walked back to the museum along the Fenway. Summer was in full bloom and the garden park was full of joggers and strollers and weary city souls seeking a respite as they trudged home from work. His car was parked just in front of the museum. A familiar dark Lincoln was parked askew behind him, the ass end of the thing jutting out into the road. Detective Stone was sitting on the hood, watching Finn approach.

He looked at his watch as Finn got within speaking distance. "You said five-thirty," he said. "You're late."

"Sorry," Finn said. "I got tied up."

"So, what is it that you needed to talk about?"

Finn chose his words carefully. "I thought I would have some information I could give you that might be helpful."

"What is it?" Stone asked. He was still leaning on the car, his head down, watching Finn carefully.

Finn shook his head. "I was wrong. There's nothing useful I can tell you."

Stone just continued to stare at him. "That's why you asked to meet me? To tell me there's nothing you can tell me?"

"I'm sorry."

"You're sorry," Stone repeated. He looked away, watching a fit young woman as she ran along the dirt park path across the street. "There's more to it than that, isn't there? Something you know. Something you're not going to tell me."

Finn shrugged. "What is it that you care about, Stone? What is it that you really love?"

Stone's eyes continued to follow the young woman from behind. "I love catching criminals," he said. "I love seeing the bad guys go away."

"What if there are no bad guys?" Finn asked. "What if there are just fucked-up people doing the best with what they've been dealt?"

"Doesn't matter what the hand is. If they play it crooked, they're the bad guys." The jogger rounded the corner and disappeared from sight. Stone turned to Finn. "What is it you love, Counselor? What is it you really care about?"

Finn thought about it for a moment. "I care about my clients," he said after a while.

"All of them?"

"Some more than others, but yeah, all of them."

"What about the bad guys?"

"That's not for me to judge."

Stone stood up. He reached into his jacket pocket, pulled out his wallet and slipped a business card out of the folds. He handed it to Finn. "You change your mind, you decide you have something to tell me that might be useful, gimme a call."

"I will."

Stone got into his car and pulled away into traffic. Finn was left standing there, alone in front of Mrs. Jack's museum. The gate had been closed, the door pulled shut. The modern security system that hadn't been in place twenty years before protected it now. The guards inside were well trained and armed.

Looking at his watch, he saw that it was almost six. He got into the car and started it up, pulling out in a hurry. He was making dinner for Sally and Lissa and Koz at his place tonight, and he was late. He smiled to himself; it would be a simple evening, but he couldn't remember looking forward to anything quite so much.

Acknowledgments

This novel is, of course, a work of fiction. Many of the details regarding the robbery at the Isabella Stewart Gardner Museum, however, are based in fact. Some of the specifics regarding the events of that night were obtained from police reports. Others were gleaned from numerous news articles and scholarly work regarding the robbery. The rest is fictional dramatization. The crime remains (as of the writing of this novel) unsolved, and this book is not intended to suggest the guilt of any individual. While some news articles and books that have speculated regarding the possibility of cooperation in the robbery by someone connected with the museum, I am aware of no proof that the robbery was an "inside job." Further, while many have hypothesized that James "Whitey" Bulger was likely involved in the robbery either directly or indirectly based on his stranglehold on organized crime in Boston in the early 1990s, I am aware of no proof that this is the case. His inclusion in this novel is for dramatic purposes only.

I was aided in my research by innumerable third-party sources, including articles by Stephen Kurkjian in the *Boston Globe*, and by Tom Mashberg and Laura Crimaldi in the *Boston Herald*. The 2004 documentary *Stolen*, directed by Rebecca Dreyfus, is an excellent film and a very helpful resource, and the nonfiction book *The Gardner Heist:*

ACKNOWLEDGMENTS

The True Story of the World's Largest Unsolved Art Theft by Ulrich Boser provided additional detail based on the notes of the renowned art theft investigator Harold Smith. I recommend both to anyone interested in learning more about the robbery.

For those seeking additional information regarding the Gardner museum itself, or the fascinating life of Isabella Stewart Gardner, I recommend *The Isabella Stewart Gardner Museum: A Companion Guide and History* by Hilliard T. Goldfarb and *Mrs. Jack: A Biography of Isabella Stewart Gardner* by Louise Hall Tharp. For additional information regarding art theft in general, and art theft investigation, the books *Museum of the Missing: The High Stakes of Art Crime* by Simon Houpt and *Stolen Masterpiece Tracker* by Thomas McShane and Dary Matera are very informative. I am also indebted to a number of individuals familiar with the specifics of the Gardner investigation and the general workings of the various groups of organized criminals in Boston over the years.

I owe an enormous debt to Mitch Hoffman, a wonderful editor who brought out the best in me and the manuscript: your suggestions and guidance were invaluable, and the book would not be nearly the work that it is without your help.

Thanks to David Young, Jamie Raab, Elly Weisenberg, Kim Hoffman, and all the wonderful folks at Grand Central Publishing who worked on the production end of the book, including Mari, S. B., Allene, George, and Anne. Your support and assistance are greatly appreciated.

My thanks also to the great people at Macmillan, including Maria Rejt and Trisha Jackson, as well as to Arabella Stein at the Abner Stein Agency in London. You have been a pleasure to work with.

For the gang at the Aaron Priest Agency—Lucy Childs, Frances Jalet-Miller, Nicole Kenealy, John Richmond, and Arlene Priest—and in particular for Aaron Priest and Lisa Erbach Vance: I thank the fates every day for bringing me into contact with you. Without your help and support none of this would have been possible.

Thanks to my wonderful family: my parents, Richard and Martha; my brother, Ted, and his wife, Betsy, and their family; and an extended family and cadre of loyal friends for keeping me grounded and focusing (when I take a deep breath) on the things that are most important in life.

For Reid and Samantha, protect your dreams as you get older. I love you more than you will ever understand.

For my wife and my love, Joanie: I couldn't do any of this without you. You are a wonderful partner, the best mother any children could have, and my greatest source of support.

Finally, I would like to thank all of the teachers I have had over the years who nurtured my love of language, my appreciation for drama, my fascination in the law, and my curiosity in the world around me. There are too many to name them all, but I would like to mention James Godrey, Carey Fuller, Dick Pike, Bill Moore, Jim and Susan Wright, and Roger Schecter.